CW01497630

Charlotte Le Page

THE PUNISHMENT CUPBOARD

AUSTIN MACAULEY
PUBLISHERS LTD.

A CIP catalogue record for this title is available from the British Library.

ISBN 978 1 78455 404 0 (Paperback)
ISBN 978 1 78455 406 4 (Hardback)

www.austinmacauley.com
First Published (2015)
Austin Macauley Publishers Ltd.
25 Canada Square Canary Wharf
London
E14 5LB

Printed and bound in Great Britain

NEMESIS

"Damn the bloody moon," the young woman murmured to herself as she unclipped her skis and propped them against the trunk of a Norwegian pine.

Timing was of the essence, but with or without the moon, the job had to be done tonight. She studied her watch. Half an hour was all the time she had.

Dressed in a white ski suit and a white woollen hat pulled down over her forehead, she would normally blend in with the terrain. But the bright moonlight illuminated the scene, creating iridescent glimmers of light upon the snow-covered landscape. Lowering her dark glasses from the top of her head, she shielded her eyes against the glare and then cautiously approached the railway lines. The only sounds in the isolated spot were the gentle whispers coming from the tips of the tall spruces in the forest behind her, and the pounding in her ears as her heart thumped in her chest. Ever since the age of nineteen the young woman had undertaken many dangerous assignments, but even after four years of countless acts of retaliation against the enemy, her heart had not learned to steady its frantic beating. She relished the exhilaration that came with danger, but above all, she savoured the taste of sweet revenge.

Her code name was Nemesis.

Kneeling beside the track, she hardly noticed the sharp gravel. Experience had taught her to tape padding to her knees to stop the painful shards digging into her flesh. She unbuckled her shabby rucksack and slowly looked around.

Nothing moved, not even the bushes that were silhouetted in the moonlight on top of the embankment. The awesome white stillness wrapped itself around her, much like a shroud covering a corpse. Peeling off her gloves, the young woman delved into the bag and removed a ten inch stick of dynamite. Holding the cylinder horizontally, she wafted the tube gently from side to side under her nose as if smelling a priceless Havana cigar. It was part of the ritual. What she held in her hands called for respect. It had the capacity to cause havoc and death to those whom she despised. Groping in the bag again she found the blasting cap.

It was then that something made her shiver, causing her to hesitate before plunging the fuse into the tube. She felt it – like an aura of evil. Turning her head slowly sideways she looked to her left. Nothing stirred, not even the bushes on the embankment. She turned her head to the right. Nothing! Just whispers coming from the tall spruces in the forest behind her. The woman turned her attention to the job in hand.

"You're losing your grip, girl," she loudly admonished herself.

But it came again, the feeling that something or someone was walking over her grave. Her primal instinct immediately activated her senses. She leapt up like a young gazelle, aware of impending danger.

The first bullet cracked loudly onto the railway line shooting firework sparks into the air. Her heart leapt into her throat as the noise ricocheted through the silence. She recognised the guttural language barking the order for her to stand still. From behind the bushes, silhouetted in the moonlight on the embankment, four uniformed men emerged and stood triumphantly with feet apart and rifles pointing down on her. The radiance of the moon beamed like a spotlight, stripping her of any cover. Fear paralysed her as a short stocky man with a large round face, slowly and victoriously advanced towards his prey. His thick lipped open mouth sneered at her, evoking a picture of a gargoyle hanging over the guttering of a church. He raised his black leather gloved hand and roughly pulled the hat from her head, allowing her long blonde hair to cascade onto her shoulders. The dark glasses fell into the snow and a large brown shoe deliberately crunched them to fragments. In his other hand he carried a 9 millimetre automatic Luger pistol. She recognised it as the weapon carried by the worst bastards of all. The skull emblem in the lapel of his long black leather coat confirmed that he was part of the dreaded Geheime Straatpolizei.

"Is this the woman, Nemesis?" he bellowed.

"Yes, her real name is Inger Svenerson. She's part of an Oslo Group," came the reply from the embankment.

Inger's fury raged at the shock of hearing the voice of one of her own countrymen.

"You filthy Quisling bastard!" she screamed in the direction of her betrayer. "You fu...,"

The butt end of the pistol struck her across the jaw sending her reeling sideways. The taste of iron and blood filled her mouth as a back tooth was wrenched from its socket. With disdainful arrogance she spat the tooth and blood into the snow at her enemy's feet leaving a crimson scar against the whiteness. Her eyes watered from the agonising pain shooting up the side of her face.

"So you thought you could blow up the train, you stupid bitch," he barked.

He grabbed hold of her long hair and pulled her head to within an inch of his face.

"Who's with you?" he snarled.

"I'm alone, I'm alone. There's no one with me," Inger spluttered, her injured jaw making it difficult to speak.

The gargoyle face sneered again. Inger spat in his face. He wiped the bloodied spittle from his cheek with her hair, before letting go.

"You'll be talking soon. You all do. We have some convincing ways of making you talk. You'll be begging us to let you die, little Inger," he laughed.

Her worst nightmare had become a reality. She had fallen into the hands of the Gestapo, and they would show her no mercy. Too many members of her Group had suffered a fate far worse than death and the prospect of what they would do to her filled her with dread. She had envisaged the scene she was now facing, many times, and knew exactly what she had to do. She would rather die than surrender to the scum that had polluted her beautiful country for the past four years. 'You will not take me alive,' her brain screamed. 'For God's sake girl, run!' But her petrified legs remained rooted to the spot in suede ski boots that had filled with lead. She pressed her hand into the side of her jacket and felt the cold hard steel of the small calibre, point 32 revolver that was her constant companion. She had killed nineteen Germans at close range, but had lost count of the number she had killed with the Sten gun when out ambushing their road convoys with her Group. Inger had no regrets about shooting Germans. The more she killed, the better. She didn't look upon them as human beings. They were the enemy. It was easier to kill that way. She had had many close calls, fleeing through the forests with the enemy close on her heels and with her lungs on fire as they screamed for air. But now there was nowhere to run.

From the corner of her eye she glimpsed the four uniformed soldiers slithering down the embankment towards her. Her brain no longer registered the agony in her jaw. Sheer terror had over-ridden her pain as she felt her stomach sink to the pit of her belly. 'For Christ's sake run you stupid woman. Run!' The man before her turned his head towards the descending soldiers and in an instant she seized her chance and took flight, running wildly alongside the railway track.

The second bullet hit her before she had gone ten yards. It skimmed the top of her right shoulder taking with it a chunk of flesh and a piece of material from her jacket. But she kept running. Booted feet crunched loudly on the gravel behind her.

It was then that she heard it - the train she had set out to derail - the 9.15pm out of Oslo - carrying the enemy on leave to the neighbouring neutral country.

The third bullet struck her in the left shoulder sending her crashing to the ground. They were only winging her. They wanted her alive. They wanted to tortuously wring information out of her. Terrifying thoughts raced through her head. 'Oh God, don't let them take me alive. Get up. Run girl, run.' Levering herself upwards, she screamed in pain as her injuries rendered her arms too weak to hold her weight.

Desperation forced her to her feet. A cacophony of alien voices bellowed their orders for her to halt. She mouthed the words, 'like shit, you fucking bastards!', and willed herself to stumble on.

The roar of the train drew nearer, forcing the air in front of it into a funnel of wind. She began to weaken through loss of blood and pain and her legs lost the will to move.

The hunters had driven their quarry to a standstill.

She slipped her right hand into the jacket pocket and felt the cold power of the small revolver.

A hand grabbed her left shoulder. The steel fingers pressed excruciatingly into her wounded flesh. Yelping in pain, the woman quickly turned her head towards the hand. A silver ring bearing a malevolent Nazi swastika circled a finger. In a flash, she sank her teeth into the back of the hand and bit as hard as she could, hardly noticing the searing agony from her damaged jaw. The hand loosened its grip.

It was just behind her - the unstoppable monster that carried the enemy she had set out to destroy. In a flash she pulled the gun from her pocket. With a shaking hand she fired at point blank range into the face of her pursuer. Then, with the speed and grace of a gazelle, and with her face splattered by enemy blood, the beautiful young woman leapt sideways into the path of the train.

Inger's close range kills now numbered a score, but the train roared on, carrying the enemy on leave to the neighbouring neutral country.

THE RADIO MESSAGE

Standing on the bridge of his ship, the captain raised his binoculars to his eyes and slowly swung them, almost full circle, to survey the forty Merchant Ships and the escort vessels that made up the Atlantic Convoy. The occasional lone U-boat still posed a threat, but in 1943 the Allied Fleets had successfully defeated the German submarines that had been the scourge of the North Atlantic.

The handsome sailor was the youngest captain in the Norwegian Merchant Fleet. He spoke fluent English and stood five feet eleven inches tall with striking dark good looks and gentle brown eyes that belied the steel core running through him. His thick black hair was cut short, almost military style, and his long dark lashes and dark arched eyebrows were the envy of many women who knew him.

His Merchant Ship had been in the mid-Atlantic when his country had capitulated to the Germans in April, 1940. But his vessel had avoided seizure by the enemy when he and every Norwegian Captain deliberately defied the Nazi order, sent out from Oslo Radio, for all Norwegian vessels to put into neutral ports. They scornfully cocked two fingers and joined the Allied Fleet. His ship had found safe haven in England, in the Port of Liverpool.

As he continued to scan the Merchant Fleet and her escorts his mind pondered on the thousands of sunk merchant ships and drowned sailors. Almost one hundred and seventy five corvettes, destroyers and frigates had been lost, but along with the bodies of brave mariners lay thousands of tons of precious cargo littering the sea bed. The outcome of the war depended on getting millions of tons of essential war materials and food, safely to a British Port. The Battle of the Atlantic was one conflict that had to be won for the survival of the nation.

How the hell had he survived the carnage, he wondered? He let the binoculars dangle round his neck and shut his eyes. He could still see them, those ships of over three thousand tons, on fire. His mind conjured up the exploding tankers spewing their precious black fuel over the surface of the ocean like a thick suffocating blanket. With broken backs they slowly and majestically sank before his eyes, leaving nothing but a pall of smoke as a remembrance of brave mariners. He re-heard the barrage of ungodly sounds that so often echoed in his nightmares as he recalled the desperate cries of men, burning alive and screaming for help. The captain believed the heat of battle bore a resemblance to Dante's Inferno - the fire, the chaos and the almost inhuman sounds of souls crying out to be saved. "Abandon all hope, you who enter here." Those words revolved around his head as he witnessed man's capacity to create his own hell on earth. But his orders were to keep his Merchant Ship moving, no matter the cost, leaving the escort vessels to protect the convoy and its cargoes. Picking up survivors was not the priority. He had no choice but to obey his orders, but leaving fellow seamen in peril did not sit well with the captain.

He opened his eyes and concentrated his gaze on the agitated surface of the ocean. Nothing advanced towards his ship. No torpedo, just below the surface, moving with the velocity of a rocket, on a trajectory that lined it up with the bow, amidships or stern. He owed so much to his engineer, who, through the telegraph to the engine room had followed his captain's orders quickly and accordingly to go full ahead or hard astern. The evasive action had saved his ship in a split second of decision making. The captain had nothing but respect and admiration for his crew who, on every voyage, unquestionably put their lives on the line.

11

Without saying a word to the Officer of the Watch, he left the bridge and took a tour of inspection of his beloved ship. He knew every part of her, every wound that had been tenderly patched. He heard every groan as her structure contorted against the elements and he felt her pain. She proudly sailed under the swallow tailed Nortraship house flag with the gold anchor set in the top left hand corner. He looked towards the stern where the flag of the Norwegian Shipping and Trade Mission enthusiastically flew from the flag pole. He gave a casual, but fond salute.

The captain returned to the bridge where the entrance stood open, just as he had left it. The atmosphere within was relaxed and convivial, yet when on the bridge and under attack, he commanded with the confidence of a man with salt water running through his veins.

"Tea, two sugars," he said, to the Officer of the Watch.

"Tea, two sugars for the captain," the Officer of the Watch relayed to a Junior Seaman.

The captain smiled as he approached his day cabin. The need for him to be on the bridge at all times when in action, meant he spent weeks on end in the confined space, snatching some sleep. It was a lonely existence. He kissed his index finger and traced it round the faces of his two beloved girls who smiled from the photograph pinned to the cabin's bulkhead. The very presence of their images had, he believed, given him something to fight for and a will to survive. He could never abandon all hope when he had so much reason to live. Pinned on the opposite bulkhead, a garish poster, he picked up in America, claimed 'Loose Lips Sink Ships.' It depicted a vessel nose diving to the bottom of the ocean.

The tea arrived, strong, sweet and piping hot, the way he liked it. He lit a cigarette, confident that his ship, her cargo of munitions and her crew would return safely to port.

"God willing, we should be back in Liverpool by this time tomorrow," he cheerfully announced to his Officer of the Watch. The Officer ignored the comment as he walked to the bridge entrance.

"Yes?" he queried of the young Radio Officer who stood waiting outside.

"A radio message has just come through for Captain Svenerson from the Red Cross in Geneva, Sir," the Radio Officer replied.

THE ASSIGNMENT

The captain's ship safely docked in her home port of Liverpool. He sat grief stricken and numb on the quayside watching the cranes discharging the cargo from the holds, but seeing nothing.

His beautiful Inger was dead at the age of twenty three. He had met her on a frozen Scandinavian mountainside skiing her way to Oslo with a shabby rucksack of small firearms and dynamite strapped to her back that she had picked up in Sweden. Their paths crossed as he skied to Sweden to catch a fishing boat back to England after secretly returning to Trondheim to sort out his family affairs. His parents had been shot with ten other Norwegians as a reprisal for the disruption caused by the Resistance Movement to the railway system. There were no affairs to sort out when he got there. His parents were already buried and the Nazis had confiscated his father's fishing fleet. It had broken his heart, when told by those people who had been made to watch the shooting that his gentle mother had clung to his father only to have rough hands tear them apart before the firing began. His hatred of the Germans occupied his thoughts as he skied the snow covered slopes, until the beautiful young woman arrived on the scene to engage his mind with romantic notions.

The young couple were married in Sweden on their third meeting. They knew it was futile having protracted engagements during a war. With the uncertainty of the future one grabbed every opportunity of happiness. And they had been so deliriously happy. Never again would he hold her fabulous body in his arms as they passionately loved one another. Never again would he twirl her long blonde hair round his finger or stare into her beautiful wide-set green eyes. Her skin had been like porcelain with a flush of red to highlight her cheekbones. He would never hear her voice again or laugh when in frustration she would shout, "Dritt! Dritt! Dritt!"

"Shit! Shit! Shit to you too," he would laugh back at her.

Inger had been a headstrong young woman with a zealous determination to right the wrongs inflicted on her nation. But beneath her tough exterior was a gentle, petite woman with unquestionable courage.

The captain's dark pit of despair left him too deadened to feel the bitter weather or respond to the presence of a young man in army battle dress standing beside him.

"Captain Svenerson. May I speak with you?" the man asked. The captain stared into space. "Excuse me, Captain, did you hear me? I am an Officer of the Special Operations Executive and I need to speak with you."

"I'm so sorry, I was miles away," the Captain apologetically replied. "What is it you want to speak to me about?"

He knew of the SOE - that secret body of men and woman. The Norwegian Section of the SOE had seriously disrupted Hitler's atomic bomb programme in 1943 when blowing up Norway's Vemork heavy water plant.

The captain listened attentively to the proposal put to him by the officer. His knowledge of the North Sea and the Norwegian fjords was fundamental to the plan, but, without hesitation he agreed to voluntarily skipper a fishing boat and sail with her crew of five to Norway, with an essential and desperately needed cargo of arms and Intelligence Personnel for the Norwegian Resistance Movement.

But the captain had his own agenda. His co-operation carried one condition. He needed the help of the Resistance to safely bring to him the one and only precious thing he had left in the world. His terms were agreed. But he was about to make the biggest mistake of his life.

One week later, under cover of darkness and without navigation lights, the dangerous assignment took the fishing boat out of Scapa Flow into the North Sea. The bitter cold wind slapped Captain Svenerson across the face with an icy hand and the wet deck froze his feet. His shouted orders were lost in the bedlam that came from the crashing waves and the howling of the wind. Once in open waters and at full ahead the powerful engines struggled to make headway against the oncoming gale. He thrashed the engines, getting as much out of them as he could, determined to get the job done in less than two days. A wall of sea rose up in front of the boat drawing more and more water into the belly of the wave until it towered above the vessel.

"Jesus Christ!" the captain yelled. "Come on girl you can do it, you can do it."

With bow on, and gripping the wheel tightly, he ploughed the vessel upwards to the pinnacle of the wave. He breathed a sigh of relief as he hit the crest and glided back down the other side before the wave broke behind him. Occasionally a rogue wave forced the fishing boat into a trough, pitching her dangerously from port to starboard. Waves lashed the deck making visibility almost impossible.

"Cap'n, will ye fucking slow down?" a loud voice bellowed from the deck. "We's a sliding all over the fucking place."

"Fasten yourselves to the fucking stanchions then," he bellowed back. "And send the boy down to the galley to make a strong brew. And put some rum in it."

The captain had cut his nautical teeth crewing on his father's fishing fleet until entering Naval College and rapidly rising to become an officer and then a captain. He loved the sea yet never lost his respect for her power and treachery.

The turbulent water and the wind battled ferociously for supremacy, making for difficult progress as the captain struggled with the wheel to keep the vessel on the pre-determined course he had set. Eventually the fishing boat's ice-breaker bow slowly crunched its way through the frozen sea as he neared his homeland.

After many warming mugs of hot tea, laced with rum, the familiar coastline of the South West Region of Norway came into his view. He slowly sailed up the Lysefjord into his occupied country.

A flashing light told him he was expected. He signalled an acknowledgement.

In the dead of night and in silence, a host of Resistance Workers swarmed like bats from the cliffs of the fjord. Boxes of Mark 4 Enfield rifles, Bren guns, Sten guns, grenades, ammunition and explosives, climbed up the slope at the hands of a continuous chain of faceless and nameless men and women. Five Norwegian SOE Agents, who had received commando training in Scotland, disembarked and evaporated into the night. The Captain watched in awe as his countrymen took possession of the arsenal intended to help liberate his country from the plague of Fascism.

A young man approached and carefully handed a well wrapped bundle to the captain.

"Thank you, thank you, captain," he said. "We were all devastated by the loss of your wife. She was a very brave young woman."

"Yes she was," the captain replied. "My Inger was fearless, but tell me how did she die? I know she was caught, but the Red Cross gave me no details. I have nightmares thinking about what they did to her."

"She wasn't captured," he explained. "She purposely threw herself under the train. They knew she was going to be there. Inger was betrayed."

The captain gripped the stanchion on the side of the boat as if searching for strength. His voice wavered as he spoke.

"Oh God no! Who was it? Do you know who the Quisling was?"

"Yes, we have dealt with him. He will betray no more. Our people are starving, Captain. Inger was betrayed for a loaf of bread and a box of dried fish. The Germans are trying to starve us into submission, but we will never yield. They take anything up to eighteen or more innocent hostages and shoot them every time the Resistance sabotages the railway or blows up their road convoys. But we will fight on, just as Inger would have wanted. She always said she would never allow herself to fall into the hands of the Gestapo. She couldn't guarantee her silence under torture. Inger said it made her a coward, but that can never be. We owe her our lives. She will never be forgotten."

The captain, unable to speak, simply nodded his head.

"You must go now," the young man said. "May God be with you on your return journey. And when you get back to England, thank them for their support and tell them that Norway will fight on, until we drive the Nazis from our shores and into hell."

The speed of the coordinated operation enabled the fishing vessel to sail away, once again, under cover of darkness, out of the fjord and back into the North Sea.

The captain had always been a man of action. A man, by the very nature of his command, that made split second decisions with unwavering conviction. He had never questioned his own abilities or his judgement, but as he neared his destination doubts surfaced as to whether or not he was doing the right thing. But what choice did he have, he wondered?

After docking the boat he made a train journey from Scotland back to the City of Liverpool. His resolve began to falter as he carried his precious cargo to the Office of the Welfare Department.

"My daughter's name is Lori Svenerson. She is ten months old. Her Mother is dead," he brusquely said to the mystified elderly woman who carefully took the child from him.

"She's lovely," the Welfare Officer sentimentally replied. "Is she for adoption?"

"No definitely not! I will return for her when this bloody war is over. Just care for her please, until I get back." His voice broke as he spoke.

The captain kissed his sleeping child and marched quickly from the room before the amazed woman could respond. He stared despondently at the hard unyielding pavement beneath his feet as he strode towards the docks. It was all too harrowing as he fought back his tears. The captain loved his little girl. She was all he had left in the world. He had met her for the first time when she was six months old. His joy had been overwhelming. And now on their second meeting he was handing her over to an old woman who was a stranger. He comforted himself in the knowledge that the war was gradually coming to an end, so it wouldn't be for too long. He shook his head, looked up, straightened his back and then walked on with purpose. He had a ship to command and it was due to sail on the next tide.

The astonished woman re-adjusted her glasses that had perched on the end of her nose and stared into the face of the sleeping child.

"Well then, where are we going to put you, little Lowry?" she muttered to herself as she picked up her fountain pen and opened a thin pink file.

Christian Name... LOWRY
Surname.............. STEPHENSON.

She slowly wrote in capital letters then hesitated and frowned.

"Is that Stephenson with a ph or Stephenson with a V?" she asked the baby.

The sleeping child made no comment. Since she had already written the name with a ph, she decided to leave it that way.

Sex.......FEMALE

The woman hesitated again, realising she had no date of birth for the child. The man had said she was ten months old. It was now December. She counted back to February.

"Well, little Lowry, everybody has a birthday and a day to celebrate, so I'm going to make yours the third of February because that was my mother's birthday. What do think of that?" The sleeping child, once again, made no comment.

Date of Birth...3rd FEBRUARY 1944
Mother ....DECEASED
Father............MR STEPHENSON (no Christian name known)
Nationality..... BRITISH

Lori Svenerson vanished.

THE BIG QUESTION

A subdued five year old girl sat on the wooden floor in the corner of the playroom and counted the small bruises on the top of her skinny little arm. She counted six. There were many more than that, but she could only count to six. Some were old yellow bruises. Others were purple and blue. The new bruises were bright red and very sore.

The woman, whose name was Miss, always hurt the child's arm when she dragged her to the punishment cupboard. Perhaps if the little girl hadn't struggled, Miss might not have squeezed the top of the small arm so tightly. But the punishment cupboard was the home of the bogeyman and none of the children wanted to go in there with him. She studied the backs of her smarting legs that had been slapped very hard because she had wet her knickers. But the small girl always wet herself when she was in the punishment cupboard. It was so frightening in there, she couldn't help it.

Slowly rolling her sleeve back down her arm, she puckered her brow into a very serious frown and thought hard.

'Where's my mum and dad? Why don't they come and fetch me out of here?'

She had known nothing of mums and dads until a new boy called Tommy told her that everybody had a mum and a dad of their own. His dad's name was Henry and he was killed in something called 'the war' and his mum was named Doris. But she got funny in the head so that's why he was in the orphanage. But how did she get here and why was she here? And did her mum and dad have names like Henry and Doris?

The playroom door opened, putting a sudden stop to her troubled thinking. She ran the back of her hand across her brow and smoothed away the serious frown.

"Toilet, you lot, so get in line," the Miss bellowed from the door.

The children followed the Miss to the toilet and then shuffled two by two into the dining room for lunch. The serious frown re-appeared on her brow. The little girl knew it would be horrible lumpy stew again. She could smell it. Yuk!

THE DORMANT CASE

Captain Leif Svenerson's War may have ended just over five years earlier, but his battle to find the daughter he had lost, continued. He and a Welfare Officer visited almost every orphanage in Liverpool to search through the registers, but no Norwegian child called Lori Svenerson, born on 21st February 1944, existed. He had desperately tried to conjure up the memory of the last time he had seen his daughter, but his recollection had been blurred by the emotion and pain of the events surrounding him at the time. But the captain would never give up, until he held his child in his arms again. She was a part of him and the woman he loved.

On returning from sea the captain was instinctively drawn to the Welfare Department. Perhaps some miracle had happened whilst he had been away. But no! Here he was, once again, sitting in front of a Welfare Officer who looked young enough to still be at school, if her acne and teeth braces was anything to go by. Her mousey brown hair was severely drawn back from her face. Her white blouse and navy blue cardigan gave her an air of prim purity.

"My name is Miss Gardner," the woman said. "And I see from your file that you believe your child has gone missing."

The captain stared at the young woman. She seemed to be a younger version of the useless middle aged, middle class spinsters he had come across in his previous meetings. 'God help us,' he thought. But he was determined not to lose his temper.

"Miss Gardner, a child in your care should not go missing," he calmly said. "I keep running into dead ends and brick walls. You lot may have given up, but I will continue to search for my child until hell freezes over."

"That is your right, Sir," she casually answered.

His patience snapped.

"What d'you mean 'my right,' you patronizing woman? I don't think you bloody lot take me seriously anymore. I have Lori's Birth Certificate," he said, waving the document in the air, "and you repeatedly tell me you have no record of my child. It's as if she never existed. Jesus Christ!" he eventually exploded. "Every time I return from sea I'm passed from pillar to post. My little girl will be six years old next birthday. Don't you bloody understand what it's like to lose her? I'm sick to death of explaining myself to numerous idiots like yourself. One supercilious cow thinks I need to see a psychiatrist. Isn't there anyone in this damn place who fucking cares?"

The Welfare Officer sat, red faced, behind her desk.

"Please Mr Svenerson, I'd rather you didn't swear."

"It's Captain Svenerson," he bellowed. "And I'll swear as much as I bloody like. I don't need some slip of a girl to teach me how to behave."

"I'm sorry, Captain Svenerson," she timidly responded, "I know you're angry. We have left no stone unturned to find your daughter and we definitely have no Norwegian child on our registers, I assure you."

The captain glared at the welfare officer. He took a packet of Senior Service cigarettes from his pocket, shook one out and placed it between his lips. From his other pocket he produced a Ronson lighter and lit the cigarette. His eyes remained fixed on the young woman throughout the silent exercise. He knew he was intimidating her, but didn't care.

"Captain Svenerson," she nervously said. "Maybe your child has been sent to Australia along with...,"

The captain leapt to his feet, causing the woman to shrink back into her chair.

"Are you telling me my daughter...?"

"Please Captain Svenerson, it's just one possibility," she pleaded. "I understand many of our Liverpool orphans were sent to Australia as part of the 1947 shipment. Perhaps Lori was one of them. I don't know. I'm just trying to help."

The captain sat down, almost resignedly.

"Lori is not one of your Liverpool Orphans," he bitterly stated. "She is not a British child. She is Norwegian. Neither is she an orphan. She has a father. I'm sick to death of the lame excuses you all churn out. And now you tell me you send orphan children as cargo to Australia. Isn't that where you used to send your criminals? Well I tell you, young lady, what your department is doing, is criminal. What do you get back in return for all these poor kids?" he asked. "A consignment of sheep carcasses in exchange." He angrily stood up. "I will not rest until I find my daughter and if I find she has been transported to Australia like a child criminal, I'll sue this damned department's ass off. Tell that to your bosses."

The Welfare Officer inwardly sighed, relieved that the irate man appeared to be leaving.

"I'm so sorry. Everything is…."

"Kyss meg i raeva," he swore, in his native language. "I'll be back," he threateningly announced. He swore again. "Dra til helvete," he muttered and slammed the door as he stormed out of the room, sending a picture of the Town Hall in Castle Street, crashing from the wall onto the floor.

He needed to get to the bar of the Exchange. Whisky was the only cure for the way he was feeling.

The Welfare Officer stared at the shattered remains of a picture frame. Relief swept over her. She would happily have kissed the irate man's ass or gone to hell, as he had suggested, if it meant she could be free of the blame for something that was not her fault. She could see from the file that almost every orphanage register had been scrutinised. But no Norwegian female child, with the name Lori Svenerson, existed.

She scratched her head, deep in thought. If what the man claimed was true, then Lori Svenerson had disappeared, but a report in the file, written by a Senior Child Welfare Officer, caught her attention.

20th January 1949

'I interviewed the client on three separate occasions and discussed the case at length with a Senior Mental Welfare Officer, Miss Valerie Rumbald.

I assessed the client to be an intelligent well-spoken man, who, on first acquaintance appeared quite rational. He has, however, undergone considerable emotional trauma throughout the War and has not yet come to terms with the violent deaths of his parents and his wife. Miss Rumbald and I concurred that the client is in denial. We concluded that he is suffering from a form of delayed shock and is obsessed by the memory of his child who also perished in the War.

During our last and final interview I recommended to the client that the case be transferred to the Mental Welfare Team for referral to a psychiatrist. The client became irrational and incapable of listening to reason. His verbal response is unprintable.

However Miss Rumbald and myself have agreed that due to the client's fragile mental state he be allowed to complete his search of the registers of the three Homes not yet visited. Maybe then he will agree to psychiatric help. He is to be accompanied by a Mental Welfare Officer at all times. Meanwhile the case will remain DORMANT.

Miss Rosemary Spensor- Boosey
Senior Child Welfare Officer.

The young inexperienced woman shut the dormant file. As a new recruit she realised why she had been sent to deal with 'that man.' It had been her initiation into the Welfare Department. And she had to agree with the Senior Child Welfare Officer.

Lori Svenerson was dead.

THE LOST CHILD

The small girl, Lowry Stephenson, presented as angry, hostile and rebellious. She had learnt to fight, using her teeth, nails, feet and fists as implements of learning. She was tough. She had to be. Conversely, she could be kind and gentle, vulnerable and lonely, but these were not attributes best suited to her harsh environment. Bullies received a bite, a scratch, a kick or a punch if they threatened her.

The child knew wicked things had happened beyond the high walls that surrounded her. It had something to do with the War when Tommy's dad, Henry, was killed and his mum, Doris, got funny in the head.

Lowry often wondered whether the high walls were to keep the orphans in, or the wickedness out. She lived, trapped in ignorance, oblivious to everything but her own survival. And she was a natural survivor, for she had the capacity to slip in and out of her stark existence by journeying into the safety of her imaginary world.

The orphanage comprised two long rows of large Victorian houses that stared rudely at each other from across a quiet empty road. Twenty children lived in each house, moving up from house to house as they grew older. The small girl lived in the second house down from the big gates, next door to the nursery. A large church, surrounded by a red brick wall, sealed off the street at one end and wide wrought iron gates closed off the street at the other end. The vicar kept guard by the church, but an army of sharp pointed spikes stood threateningly from the top of the gates, daring anyone to leave or enter without permission.

There were many rooms in Lowry's house, all with large doors forever shut against the inquisitive eyes of small people. She, along with the rest of the children, remained confined to the familiar safety of the four rooms allocated to the small orphan boys and girls.

The playroom window drew her to it like a little iron filing to a magnet. The children had no toys in the playroom. They were all in the secret room she visited regularly in the night when everyone was asleep. Lowry often stood for many bored hours pensively staring through the window at the world outside wondering what lay beyond the big spiked gates. She knew her mum and dad were out there somewhere. Perhaps her mum's name was Doris, just like Tommy's mum. Perhaps all mums were called Doris.

"I'm sure today is bin-man day," she said to herself as she haared on the window and drew squiggles in her breath with her finger.

The bin-men always arrived with their horse drawn cart the day after the Vicar had been and he had come to say prayers with the children the day before. Suddenly to her delight the big iron gates swung wide to let the horse drawn cart enter. The gates squealed as they opened and clanged as they shut. The bin-men smiled and waved at the children, who raced to the window, jostling and pushing to get a view. The excited orphans shrieked with delight and were still waving to the bin men when the playroom door burst open.

"Get in line, you lot," the Miss with red hair yelled. "Follow me to the toilet and if any of you have wet your drawers then you'll be getting slapped legs."

Lowry breathed a sigh of relief. She was dry, but she knew snotty nosed little Tommy was in for slapped legs. It was obvious from the damp patch on his trousers. Two lines of children shuffled in their black slip-on plimsolls to the large ground floor bathroom. Six small white toilets, with no seats, lined one wall. It was best not to sit on the cold porcelain bowl after the boys had been. They always splashed everywhere which meant not only a wet bowl, but also a wet floor. Six small white hand basins, with big lumps of carbolic soap resting near the taps, stood opposite the toilets. In the centre of the room three bulging white baths, with huge clawed feet, sat fatly in a line. Lowry hated the twice weekly bath nights on Wednesday and Sunday. The naked children huddled together waiting their turn to climb into the bath. It was like a hurdle race as two dirty bodies clambered in one side and two clean ones clambered out the other. They all used the same water, so it was best to elbow to the front of the naked queue in order to have a clean bath. The steel nit comb made her eyes water as it scraped through her scalp to grab the nits. Sometimes a real live louse appeared, only to be drowned in a bowl of strong smelling liquid. New children, more often than not, arrived with a head full of lice and shared them with everyone, even the grown-ups. And the scratching would start again.

"Hurry up, you lot," the Miss demanded. "Which of you needs dry drawers?"

Seven arms raised and seven legs were slapped. Tommy cried. Miss slapped him again for crying. Stupid really, Lowry thought, because it only made him cry all the more. It was called, 'a something to cry for slap,' just in case the children were crying for nothing.

Lowry liked Tommy. She was used to him smelling of pee. He was a sad, gentle little boy with big round brown eyes, who liked to sit in the corner rocking backwards and forwards. Sometimes, if Lowry was in the mood, she would sit next to him and they would rock together and talk about mums and dads. His dad used to make him little aeroplanes out of wood. Lowry learned that an aeroplane was a thing that could fly. Oh, how she wished she could fly away.

The young girl joined the relieved queue. She stood silently and studied the grown up. She puckered her brow into a serious frown. The child's eyes were hostile. Miss, they were all called Miss, towered above her charges. Her red curly hair framed a long white face speckled with small brown dots. Two beady eyes, with no eyebrows or lashes to frame them, sat either side of a pointed nose. Her chin jutted out so far it lined up with the long nose. The vicious red mouth often exploded with words of fury as it spat out each angry word with showers of saliva. Her bony hands reinforced her wrath with slaps to the face, thighs or bottom. Lowry hated her, and knowing only one naughty word, secretly called her 'Miss Bum.'

The toileted crocodile twisted its way into the smelly dining-room. It was yuk stew again. Five bench tables stood on a noisy wooden floor. Bare cream walls, grimy with tacky little finger-prints, sealed in the smell of stale food that hung in the air. A picture of a serious faced man hung over the fireplace. The children knew he wasn't quite as important as God, but very nearly. The grown-ups called him 'The King.' The cook's name was Grace and Lowry jubilantly stood with the rest of the kids on Empire Day to sing in praise of her cooking. 'God save our Grace is King.'

Tea- times were always good when thick doorstep chunks of bread and dripping were fought over. The objective was to find the slices with juicy brown streaks running through the solidified fat. Rhubarb jam and the Vicar always arrived together on a Sunday. Lowry didn't like Sundays or rhubarb jam or the scary vicar who wore a long black dress. The bin men wore trousers. The vicar's breath smelled strongly of what she believed was cough medicine. His fat hand always sought out her head to ruffle her hair. He grunted as he squatted down to Lowry's level. His fat hand would go up her skirt and rub her bottom and up and down her thigh. Sometimes his fingers would go up her knicker leg, making her jump.

"Has Loory been a good girl today?" he asked

"Me name's Lowry, not Loory," she adamantly told the vicar. "Lowry is me name. Lowry Stephenson."

But unbeknown to the girl the name did not belong to her.

Even the clothes she wore had been worn by someone else and they were much too big. Sleeves dangled over her hands. Baggy black knickers, with elasticated legs, drooped to her knees. 'Hitch your drawers up, Lowry Stephenson.' How many times a day was that barked at her? Obediently, she complied, but a few minutes later they would be hanging round her knees again.

Bedtime came as the happiest time for the girl. She loved the silence. No loud, angry grown-up voices, no children crying, just a big hush and her secret escape into her wonderland.

The girl's dormitory, just like the boy's, housed ten bulky metal framed cots with heavy moveable sides and thick red rubber mattresses. Hanging from a twisted black flex above the hearth of an old tiled fireplace, a dim naked light bulb illuminated a chamber pot that stood on a rubber sheet and often overflowed. The polished wooden floor gave a cold response to warm feet, but through the bare meshed bay window, Lowry could see her favourite tree that waved to her on a windy day when she stared out of the playroom window. The moon occasionally poised like a ball on the top of her tree. It lit up the branches and seemed so close she could trace the circle with her finger. She started at the top and followed the circle round and round.

The young girl waited in her cot for the silence, but doors were still banging closed and muffled voices of grown- ups floated up the stairs. Too soon yet! She would have to wait before she could venture from the dormitory. In the big cot next to her, she could hear her best friend quietly crying. Beth arrived one day from nowhere. She cried when grown-ups shouted at her and when some of the kids called her nigger. Lowry had never heard the word before and thought it a silly name, but she knew how to deal with the bullies of her world, so would kick, scratch, bite and punch anyone on Beth's behalf and enjoy it. Their cots were close enough for small hands to touch through the bars. Beth often sobbed herself to sleep at night and seemed to like holding hands. She wanted to go back home, but they said she was a bad girl for doing naughty things with her granddad. Lowry couldn't imagine what naughty things Beth did with her granddad, because it seems her granddad liked it.

The girl desperately wished for the silence to tell her it was safe to climb over the side of her cot, but the annoying grown-ups were still moving about downstairs. The dormitory door quietly opened. The light from the landing silhouetted a Miss framed in the doorway. Lowry recognised the long thin nose that seemed longer than ever in the shadowy light. It was Miss Bum. Shutting her eyes tightly, Lowry feigned sleep and waited for the gentle click that told her the red haired woman had gone. Her eye lids were already beginning to feel heavy and she stifled a yawn. Tonight she would stay awake. She knew when her finger could circle the moon that a happy time lay ahead. Silence at last.

Climbing quietly over the side of the cot, Lowry felt the cold floor beneath her feet. Her blue striped pyjamas were too big and the legs tripped her up. She bent forward and yanked the abundance of material from around her knees, which enabled her to see her feet. She clutched it upwards towards her tummy with her right hand. The child had tip-toed many times down the dimly lit landing, but she always felt afraid that the bogeyman might hear her when she passed the punishment cupboard under the stairs. All the doors leading off the hall were shut, but she knew exactly which one to open. The room was in darkness. It usually took Lowry three or more jumps to reach the light switch and the effort often caused her to let go of her pyjama pants and they would concertina round her ankles again. Suddenly her hand hit the switch and the room splashed with light. Lowry's friends were waiting, just as they always waited. She greeted them excitedly. The horse, she had named Go-Go, stood patiently waiting for her to mount the saddle. His brown eyes were big round pools of sadness. She stroked his mane.

"Hello my friend. Where shall we go tonight? Will you take me to my tree?" The horse's head nodded gently. She climbed into the saddle, leaned forward and wrapped her arms around his neck. Lowry felt his mane brushing against her face. She closed her eyes and faded away into her fantasy world. The horse slowly rocked forward.

"Jump Go-Go! Jump!" she urged.

The child felt the horse fly upwards and she found herself sitting on a stout branch.

"Where are you? I'm waiting for you."

A flutter of noise drew her attention to the branch opposite. It was the friend who wakened her every morning calling 'Coo Coo. Coo Coo'. Lowry knew the big bird's name was Bloody Dove. She had overheard a Miss say, 'that bloody dove's cooing gives me a headache.'

"Hello, Bloody Dove," she sweetly said. "I wish you'd tell me what you see and where you go when you fly over the wall. If I could fly I'd go away from here and never come back. I'd go and find my mum and dad. Tommy's got a mum, but she got funny in the head so that's why he's here. He says everybody's got a mother called Mum. Do you think my mum's got funny in the head and that's why she hasn't fetched me away from here, Bloody Dove?"

The dove slowly nodded her head.

"When her head's not funny anymore will she fetch me?"

The dove nodded again.

"That's good. I said she would come for me, but Raymond Gubbins said I was a fibber. I know what my mum looks like. She's very pretty and got long black hair and she wears a long white dress. Are there lots of children living in a place like me who's waiting for their mums and dads to fetch them? You can fly to see them when you want to. Oh, I wish I could fly."

Lowry suddenly realised she was talking to herself. Bloody Dove had gone and flown back to her bed. She opened her eyes to find the horse's neck wrapped in her arms.

"I must get back to the dormitory, Go-Go. I'll see you again soon, but I've got to talk to my other friends next time."

The horse's head nodded gently as his small rider dismounted. It usually took just two jumps to turn off the light. The darkness in the hall seemed blacker than ever. The tired girl returned to the dormitory and buried herself under the covers of her cot. She smiled contentedly.

"I'm going to learn me to fly so I can go over the wall and find my mum and dad," she whispered with determination. And she was a determined child.

The rain had been falling since Lowry wakened. She stood at the playroom window watching the rain drops run down the glass to the bottom of the frame. They were racing each other to see who would be first. Large drops splashed from her tree. She felt sad and bored. There would be no playing in the back yard today, the place where she found and collected the little wings that flew from the branches of her tree. They were all hidden behind a pipe in the dormitory next to her cot.

Beth sat alone in the corner of the room. Lowry turned and watched her friend playing with the ring she had given her. Beth tried it on each of her fingers until she decided it looked best on her big toe. Lowry had found the ring amongst the bones in her stew bowl. She had sucked off the meat until it was clean and hidden the bone up her long sleeve. Beth had been so pleased. She didn't smile very often, but when she did it was the biggest and nicest smile Lowry had ever seen, with the whitest teeth.

"This is my bestest ring," she said.

Lowry hated the big boy, Raymond Gubbins who liked to charge round the playroom and purposely collide with smaller children knocking them down like little skittles. He stopped suddenly and approached Beth.

"What's that thing on yer toe?" he asked her.

Beth remained silent. He frightened her.

"Give it 'ere, it's only a neck bone from the stew."

He bent down and snatched it from Beth's big toe. Raymond Gubbins ran off, throwing Beth's 'bestest' ring in the air and trying to catch it.

Lowry's mood had not been a good one and now it was worse. She rushed at him clinging to his back and tugging at his carrot coloured hair. He tried to shrug her off but she hung on.

"You give that back to Beth," she breathlessly shouted.

Raymond Gubbin's knees buckled and they both rolled onto the floor. She tried to punch him, but he wriggled away kicking out at her with his foot. She stood up quickly and kicked him back. An audience of children gathered round, all of them excited on-lookers who shouted and clapped at the fun. Raymond Gubbins was about to stand up when Lowry threw herself on top of him with a thud. He raised his arm to hit her and in a flash she sank her teeth into the white flesh. He screamed and she let go. A little trickle of blood ran from the wound. It was his turn to cry.

The noise alerted the grown-ups and the door burst open. Biting was a serious offence and no amount of struggling released Lowry from Miss Bum's vice-like grip on the child's upper arm.

"Nobody could ever love you, that's why you're here, you horrid little creature!" the woman spat out. "The bogeyman is waiting for you in the cupboard and he'll pull all your teeth out. Let's see if that stops you biting, Lowry Stephenson."

"Please Miss. Please Miss," Lowry begged, as she struggled to be free. "Don't put..."

The small girl's body hurtled into the dark. The door slammed shut and she found herself swallowed up by the blackness. She stood shivering, but not from the cold. She knew the bogeyman was waiting in the corner. She slowly and cautiously looked around, not knowing from which corner the bogeyman might come. It was so pitch black, Lowry didn't know where the corners were.

A sickening smell of badness filled her nose and choked her throat because she knew the bogeyman was very close. She heard the sound of the big twisted things slithering across the floor towards her. They wrapped their cold bodies around her legs and clung tightly. She screamed but the shrill noise echoed through the darkness and petrified her all the more. The din brought the bogeyman from the corner. But from which corner did he come? He was behind her. She could smell his bad breath. Lowry hunched her shoulders to hide the back of her neck, but his icicle fingers always found the spot and she whimpered in fear. Her hair tingled and her skin crawled with little bumps. She raised her arms and instinctively covered her head and squeezed her ears with her elbows.

Lowry wet her knickers. She couldn't help it. Stamping her feet in the puddle sent the slithering monsters away, but the splashing made her socks and plimsolls wet.

Slowly sinking to the floor, she sat in her pool of wetness, oblivious to the cold dampness. She attempted to make herself as small as possible by burying her face into her knees. Her hands tightly covered her mouth to stop the bogeymen pulling out her teeth. The small body rocked to and fro. She didn't cry tears. Lowry had trained herself to stop the tears by clenching her fists so tightly the palms of her hands hurt. It was better than getting 'a something to cry for slap.'

The terrified girl was unaware of the whimpering that involuntarily escaped from her.

"My Mum does love me. She's coming to fetch me. Bloody Dove said she was. Where's the door? Where's the door? My Mum will fetch me out of here. Please Miss, let me out. Please Miss, let me out," she bleated. "I won't bite Raymond Gubbins ever again, but I don't like him. He didn't ought to have taken Beth's ring. Please Miss."

Fear removed all sense of time, only her lurid and colourful imagination, cruelly sustained her punishment. The child felt so much gratitude to the Miss whose hand reached into the blackness and roughly pulled her out. And Lowry didn't mind when her legs were slapped for wetting her knickers. She was safe again.

The little girl sat on the wooden floor in the corner of the playroom and rolled up her sleeve. She counted the bruises on the top of her sore arm. She counted six, but there were now many more new red ones to add to the pale yellow, blue and purple ones.

Not even the moon greeted the subdued girl in her cot that night. The rain caused a blanket that the moon was unable to shine through. She fell asleep quickly. Her friends would wait for her.

Beth's 'bestest' ring disappeared. Lowry continued to search through the yuk stews with their flabby lumps of fat and bones, for a replacement, but never found one. Instead, she found a handle from a broken big white jug in the bin by the back door. The bin was a treasure chest of exciting things – most of them hidden behind the pipe next to her cot. The handle was shaped like a circle. It was big enough for Beth to wear on her small wrist. She had a bracelet instead of a ring.

It was Beth's 'bestest bangle.'

THE MAN WITH GOLD
BUTTONS

The lonely child stood with one foot on top of the other with her elbows pressed against the bars covering the glass and her chin cupped in her hands. Lowry was brooding and staring through the playroom window at the world outside her front door. She wanted to be out there, running, jumping, skipping and flying, but most of all she wanted to find her mum.

In the house opposite, another older girl sometimes stared out from the downstairs window. Was she also wishing she could be out there, running, jumping, skipping and flying and looking for her mum? Occasionally she would shyly wave at the older girl who would shyly wave back. But sometimes they didn't bother. It depended on whether it was a sad day or a happy day for Lowry. Today was a sad one because she was bored and Miss Bum had slapped Beth for wetting her cot again and Lowry didn't like to hear Beth crying.

Lowry's attention was suddenly drawn to the big gates that squealed as they opened. A man and women entered. The gates clanged as they shut. The woman looked like any old woman. She was short and fat and wore a brown coat, a brown hat, brown shoes and carried a brown handbag.

The man was tall. He wore black trousers, a black jacket, a black cap and a dazzling white shirt. But it was all the gold on his clothes that appealed to Lowry. Even the buttons on his jacket were gold. She could see he had four rings of gold on the end of each sleeve. He had more gold round his cap. She had never seen anything so wonderful.

"Beth," she excitedly shouted. "Come and see. It's Mister King who's come to see us with Misses Queen."

Beth ran to the window pursued by the other children.

The man and woman crossed the road onto the pavement outside the nursery. They walked past the babies' house. They were getting closer.

"They're coming to see us," Beth excitedly said.

But they were walking on. They were going to go past the gate.

"No, don't go away," Lowry shouted. "You can't go away. Come back."

She pushed her small hand through the bars and banged loudly on the window. The noise caused the man and woman to stop and turn. The woman nodded her head and walked on. But the man stopped and smiled. He took off the hat with the beautiful gold and waved it at the excited children. He had dark hair and looked kind. The children waved back. He waved again, put on his cap and quickly walked away and caught up with the woman.

"What's all the noise about?" Miss Bum bellowed, as she burst into the playroom. "We could hear you in the kitchen."

She walked to the window to see for herself the cause of such excitement.

"It were the King and Queen," Tommy told her.

The woman laughed.

"That's not the King and Queen, you silly lot," she said. "They're going to see the Home Superintendant. That man's looking for his kid. Now to the toilet you lot, so get in line."

She stared at Tommy's damp patch.

"Are you wet again, Tommy Ollerenshawe?"

THE WOBBLY PENCIL

Lowry's school life was not much better than her home life. The complexities of learning disillusioned her. Her pencil never did as it was told. The letters it wrote were back to front. It wobbled all over the place and fell out of her fingers. She shared her problem with Tommy who still had a runny nose and wet pants. Sometimes he would wipe his sleeve across his face and leave a silvery smear across his cheek, but mostly he'd sniff very hard and make the snot disappear back up his nostril. The same piece of snot spent all day shooting up and down his nose. It made the teacher cross. Both Tommy and Lowry put their pencils in the left hand - it was easier that way - only to be shouted at and told to put it in the proper hand. Lowry's frustration caused her to snap many pencils.

"Did you snap that pencil on purpose, Lowry Stephenson?" teacher shouted.

"No Miss, it just broke in me 'and," she glibly lied.

Sharpening the pencil created a satisfying diversion from writing with it. Putting it into the hole of the sharpener and turning the handle produced points so long, the minute they touched the paper they would break and so would the teacher. Eventually, and in frustration, the teacher tied Lowry's left hand to the leg of the chair with a piece of red braid. Tommy and Lowry took turns to sit in the dunce's chair in the corner during story time on a Friday afternoon. He always cried when the black pointed hat, with a big white D on the front, was put on his head, but Lowry didn't care when she wore it. She flew away into her imaginary world and was wearing a crown.

School kept Lowry busy and she found it difficult to stay awake at night, but tonight her finger circled the moon and she was determined to see her friends again. She had so much to tell them. Passing through the hall she noticed the door to one of the grown-up rooms stood slightly open. She had never been in a grown-up's room before and it took boldness to enter their world, but she triumphed as she opened the door wider and stepped inside. She jumped twice and clicked the light on. She wriggled her bare toes into a soft woolly floor and wandered to a fat chair and climbed onto the yielding seat. Holding the back firmly she bounced up and down. The fat chair groaned. Suddenly, from the corner of her eye she saw something move. Lowry froze. The movement froze. She moved again, carefully this time, whilst keeping a sidelong watch on the spot where something lurked. Her chest began to thump with fright and she gingerly turned to investigate the cause of her fear. The girl discovered she was looking at herself. She bounced again and the girl in the mirror bounced in unison. She smiled, the girl smiled back at her. On a few occasions she had seen her reflection in a window but never before had she viewed herself so clearly and in such detail in a shiny glass.

"That's me. That's Lowry Stephenson," she excitedly whispered.

Dark straight hair covered Lowry's forehead to her eyebrows. Longer hair stopped short, just below her ears. The staring eyes were green and seemed too big for her face. They had long black lashes. She was surprised to see that her nose was smaller than her finger believed. Nose picking was a fun activity for the children, especially when showing everyone what had been found up there. Lowry felt so happy bouncing up and down on the groaning chair. Her eyes remained riveted on the image in the mirror. She pulled tongues, the image returned the insult. She giggled. Through the mirror, she could see a big round table behind her in the centre of the room. On the table, a large sunshine moon glowed at her from a basket in the middle. It seemed to be saying 'grab me,' so she grabbed it.

Clutching her prize, the happy child bolted to the safety of the dormitory. The tiny light shining over the chamber pot gave sufficient glow for her to study the ball. Was it something to eat, she wondered? Her teeth sank into the rough skin. She shuddered at the bitter taste. No, it wasn't something to eat, she decided. Lowry hid the orange behind the pipe in the dormitory along with the wings from her tree and her treasures from the bin.

"Come on you lot, out of bed," the voice shouted, next morning. "Who's got wet sheets?"

Beth timidly raised her hand.

"I might have guessed it would be you again, you disgusting creature," the Miss grumbled as she slapped Beth's thigh. "And you, Lowry Stephenson, won't be going to school this morning because you've got a visitor."

She had never had a visitor before.

"Is it me mum, Miss?" she excitedly asked.

"Don't be silly," Miss answered, as she angrily pulled the wet sheets from Beth's cot.

Lowry stirred her breakfast porridge. A serious thoughtful frown puckered her brow. Why did a visitor need to see her? Had she done something wrong? Was it because she wasn't very clever at school? Had the visitor found out about her sitting in the tree with Bloody Dove and her visits to Go-Go and her other friends? The child found it worrying.

The house seemed unusually quiet when the children left for school. A thin woman came into her view, then turned into the pathway that led to Lowry's front door. She studied the woman who didn't look old. Her pale brown hair was pulled back from her face.

Sitting on the bench in the dining room, Lowry's unfriendly eyes stared at the visitor who had strange wires across her teeth and spots on her forehead.

"Hello Lowry," the woman said. "My name is Miss Gardner and I am from the Welfare and I've come to tell you that we are going to have you adopted so that you can live with a nice family."

Lowry had no idea what the woman was talking about. Welfare? 'Doptid? What did those words mean? She decided to ignore the silly woman. Her eyes were no longer unfriendly, they were hostile. The girl puckered her brow into an angry frown.

"What do you think about that?" the woman asked, with a stupid smile on her face.

Lowry stared at the visitor. She concentrated hard and gritted her teeth. With all her being, she was determined to make the woman disappear. Narrowing her eyes to small slits, she could just see her through her long eyelashes. 'Go away. Go away,' the voice in her head said. She clenched her fists.

"Haven't you got anything to say, Lowry?" the woman asked. "You must have something to say." The child remained mute. "You haven't got a mother or a father so we'll find you a nice family shall we?"

"No," Lowry adamantly said.

The girl felt cross because she did have a mother called Mum, and a dad, and they were coming to fetch her. At the moment the only Father she knew was, 'the one who art in 'eaven.' She had heard all about him from the horrible vicar. Why didn't the woman leave her alone?

"Go away. Go away," said the voice in Lowry's head, but the words didn't stay in her head, they came out of her mouth.

The woman looked surprised and picked up her handbag from the floor.

"Good bye, Lowry," she said. "We will find you a nice family to live with."

The woman left. The confused girl felt angry. She was sometimes unhappy in her world, but it was the only world she knew. Were they going to send her away? She didn't want to go away yet. What if her Mum came to fetch her and she wasn't here?

She didn't like the shouting or the cupboard, and she had to find another bone ring for Beth so she could wear it on her big toe.

Sitting at her school desk, in the afternoon, a very sad and troubled girl sat with her wobbly pencil and back to front letters. What's that word 'doptid' mean? she wondered. She wrote the word boptib down in her drawing book. It still didn't make sense to her. Lowry angrily snapped her pencil in half.

It was important for her to see her friends that night. She had so much she wanted to share with them and her friends were the only people who listened to her. Halfway down the dark hall corridor a noise alerted her to danger. She held her breath, expecting a rough hand to grab her shoulder, but nothing happened. Her bunched up pyjama trousers were clutched tightly towards her tummy like a safety blanket. The creaking stair crunched with the weight of an adult descending into the hall. Like lightening, Lowry streaked into the children's bathroom and hid behind a fat bath. The hall light flashed on. Quaking with fear, she peered cautiously round the belly of the bath and saw Miss Bum march past. She was heading towards the front door. The noise of a bolt sliding open smashed the eerie silence. Voices drifted down the hall. She recognised the voice of Miss Bum, but the man's voice was not that of the vicar.

"I've got the money for yer," Lowry heard the man say. "What 'ave you got for us?"

"We've got sugar, bananas, clinic orange juice, powdered egg and a couple of pounds of scrag neck of lamb," Miss Bum told him. "Wait there and I'll get the bag."

Lowry heard the woman enter the kitchen. Now was her chance to escape back upstairs, but Miss Bum was quickly back in the hall. The girl crawled from behind the bath and peered through the gap in the open door. She watched Miss Bum's back as she returned to the front door.

"Here you go!" Miss Bum said, to the man who was hidden from view. "You'll have to bring the van if you want the doll's house and the doll's pram. Make it next Saturday when I'm on a sleep in. A quid'll do for them. Some kid's grandmother bought a small cot with a doll in it. I'll throw that in for a tanner or two." Lowry heard the man mumbling a reply. "You better go," Miss Bum urgently said.

The door shut with a click and the bolt slid across. Lowry returned to the protection of the fat bath. The hall light went out and the creaking stair crunched under the weight of Miss Bum as she climbed back up to the 'sleep in' room.

Silence settled on Lowry's home, but her heart panicked. The man was going to take her friends away and their little wooden house. Miss Bum was giving them away for something called a 'quidlldoo'. She had to see Mr and Mrs Wooden People urgently.

The door to the little house stood ajar, just as she had left it when she last visited her friends.

"Can I come in?" she asked.

She didn't wait for an answer. She slipped through the small door to be greeted by two tiny people who were still lying in the beds where she had last put them.

"Hello, sorry I haven't been to see you for a bit, but I've been busy at school and talking to Bloody Dove in the tree. Miss Bum is giving you away for a quidlldoo and a cot with a doll for a tanneratoo. I'm going to miss you. Can you hear me?" The tiny people nodded in understanding. "Nothing is going good, 'cos a lady came today and she going to get me 'doptid and I don't want to get 'doptid. I think it means she's going to take me away to somewhere and I don't want to go. Next time I see Bloody Dove, I'm going to ask her to take me with her over the wall. She can learn me to fly and I'll find my mum." The little round wooden people smiled at Lowry. "You don't want to go away do you?" The wooden man shook his head. "Well I don't either, so you can come with me. I'll hide you behind the pipe in the dormitory. The pipe is sometimes warm. I'll look after you."

She carried the little wooden woman and the little wooden man up the stairs and carefully placed them amongst her treasures behind the pipe, that was now cold. Her young mind was racing, making it difficult for her to fall asleep. Why didn't her Mum come and fetch her? Perhaps her Mum didn't like her. Miss Bum didn't like her. But if her Mum came to fetch her she'd be ever so good and then her mum would like her. She fell asleep wrapped in her troubled mind.

Next day and without explanation, Miss dragged Lowry from the yard to the bathroom.

"Hurry up, child and wash your hands," she urgently told her. "You've got a visitor again."

"Has my mum come to fetch me, Miss?"

"No child! Just hurry up, will you?"

Baffled by the rush of it all, Lowry meekly followed Miss into the hall to the main door and into the front garden. A woman, smiling in welcome, stood on the path near where the gate should have been. It seems the War people took it away and never gave it back.

"Who's that there?" Lowry apprehensively asked.

"Don't ask questions. Just go and see the lady and be a nice polite little girl." Miss disappeared into the house. Lowry stood absolutely still and studied the concrete path.

"Look up, Lowry," the woman coaxed. "I can't see your sweet little face."

The child felt awkward. Who was this woman anyway and why did she want to see her? Lowry allowed her eyes to wander to the woman's legs. She was wearing a pair of dark green shoes.

"Would you like to come to my house and see my dog? He's a very friendly fellow and he loves children. Do you like dogs, Lowry?"

She had never seen a real live dog, only the picture of Rover in her school book.

"No, I hates dogs and I don't want to go to your house and I want to go back inside now," the girl truculently said, directing her reply to the woman's shoes. She stepped back as the woman's feet moved towards her.

"All right Lowry, you go back in now and I'll come and visit you again, shall I?"

"No!" Lowry suddenly remembered that she had to be polite, "Thank you, Miss."

That night Lowry wrapped her arms around Go-Go's neck. She shut her eyes and felt herself lifted into her tree where she sat on a branch and shared her troubled thoughts with Bloody Dove.

"You've got to learn me to fly," she pleaded. "I don't want to go to her house and get 'doptid. Please Bloody Dove show me how to fly and I can fly over the wall and hide from her." The dove ruffled her feathers and nodded her head. "If I stand on the top of the back steps and jump as high as I can and wave my arms like you wave your wings, do you think I can fly?" Bloody Dove nodded her head again. "Thank you! Thank you!

You sit on the roof when I do it and you can watch me."

The sun shone. It was Saturday, a no school day. Tucked safely up her sleeves were Mr and Mrs Wooden People. The five high concrete steps that were to be Lowry's launch pad, led down from the back kitchen door to the large yard. Beneath the kitchen window, three more steps, facing in the opposite direction, led to the cellar where Grace the Cook kept her vegetables. Lowry had once sneaked in and bitten into the round golden balls, but they stung her mouth and made her eyes water. The long pink sticks were so sour they made her shudder and as for the big brown things, they left her mouth full of soil.

Lowry grew impatient. Bloody Dove was nowhere to be seen. She sat on the bottom step and watched the children collect the wings from her tree and throw them into the air to see them fly back down to earth. She was going to be flying soon.

Suddenly she heard the comforting sound of Bloody Dove, cooing. Lowry squinted into the sun, but her friend was nowhere to be seen. Slowly and carefully she climbed the five high steps. Playing on the steps was forbidden, but no Miss was in the yard and by the time they found out about Lowry's disobedience she would have flown away. The girl felt exhilarated standing so high up. Beth and Tommy ran across to the steps.

"What are you doing? You'll get into trouble," Beth shouted.

"Come down, Lowry or they'll put you in the punishment cupboard," Tommy begged.

"No! I'm going to fly like the wood aeroplane your dad made for you. And I'm going to find my mum and dad and see Mr King with the gold buttons. I don't want to get 'doptid, so I'm never coming back."

Trembling with excitement she took a deep breath. Bending her knees as far down as they would go she hunched her small body into a tight ball.

"Watch me Beth, 'cos I'm going to fly."

The child lurched upwards with her arms outstretched. Her feet left the ground.

The three small orphan children were unaware that many years later their lives would come together again under tragic circumstances. And Lowry was right. She never came back.

MARCUS MARRIOT

The Board of Trade, who regulated the British Merchant Navy approved Captain Svenersons application to sail as Chief Officer under the Red Ensign. He joined the liner 'SS New Australia.' The vessel was contracted to the British Government and the Australian Government to carry migratory orphans and passengers who were emigrating from Great Britain to Australia on a ten pound ticket. His home port was Tilbury docks in Essex, but when on shore leave the Captain travelled from Essex to London Euston and then on to Liverpool Lime Street Station. The Adelphi Hotel close to the station became his home base.

The Captain hardly noticed the bitterly cold weather. He intended to dump his luggage in his room and get to the bar of the Exchange to meet up with his friend Marcus. The Captain needed a whisky. The two men instantly liked each other when they first met in the bar. Marcus Marriot had previously been a Liverpool Police Officer. He later served, during the war in the desert with Montgomery's Army, winning the Military Medal for bravery. He couldn't remember much about his heroic deed, apart from single- handedly taking on a German tank with alcohol coursing through his veins rather than courage. He had never been happy taking orders and had no ambition to plod his way up the police career ladder. There was no point. He knew he had too many black marks against his name to bother trying. The Police Officer had metered out his own form of justice to those he called 'scumbags.' His belief was, that 'a bit of rough stuff' brought forth the truth far quicker than a cosy chat with arrogant, lying, thieves, rapists and murderers. His beefy granite face glowed with rosy cheeks either side of a strawberry nose and his unruly blonde hair sat like a thatched roof on top of his head. His birth certificate gave his name as Gerald Norman Pickles, but no one was going to take him seriously with that name, so he came up with Marcus Marriott. It had the ring of super sleuth about it. The Captain may have had salt water running through his veins, but Marcus Marriot usually had gin sloshing through his.

Marcus Marriot listened without interruption as the Captain poured out his heart during a long drinking session in the public bar. The drink made the Captain maudlin and his voice broke as he spoke of the terrible loss of, not only his wife, but also his baby daughter. He had always believed his child was somewhere in Liverpool, he told his friend, but there was a possibility that she could be in Australia. One day he would find her. He had to believe that or there was no point carrying on.

"Sometimes I wonder if I should come to terms with the fact that she has disappeared and accept it as another tragedy of the war," the Captain explained. "But I can't. It's the guilt that eats me up. What responsible Father hands his child to a bunch of incompetent strangers and walks away? The bloody Welfare think I'm sick in the head. They don't believe me. They think I'm deranged. I've shown them her photograph, I've shown them her Birth Certificate and still they don't believe me. You believe me, don't you, Marcus? Somebody has to believe me or I will go mad."

The Captain lit another cigarette and knocked back his whisky.

"Leif," Marcus Marriot said, as he delved into his inside jacket pocket. "I do believe you and I would like to help. Take my card and come to my office and we can talk about this again. There has to be an explanation for your daughter's disappearance. I can't promise anything, but short of being dead, which is highly unlikely, your child has to be somewhere and I'm bloody determined to find out where." He pushed his empty glass towards the Captain. "Now come on man, snap out of the self-pity and let's have another drink. It's your round."

The captain studied the card. Marcus Marriot, Private Investigator, it read.

OVER THE WALL

Lowry opened her eyes. The glare from the sun blinded her until a hand appeared and moved the sun away.

"Hello Lowry," a kindly voice said. "You are in hospital, can you hear me?"

She nodded her head.

"Did I fly to here?" she asked.

The man in the white coat smiled.

"No you came in an ambulance. Do you remember falling down the steps?"

Lowry may have been very confused about where she was or what an ambulance was, but she knew she hadn't fallen down the steps.

"I never fell down the steps," she argued. "I was flying like Bloody Dove."

The man looked perplexed.

"Well, Lowry, in your attempts to fly you have broken your arm rather badly and banged your head. So I think you should leave flying to the creatures with wings."

Hospital was a heavenly place. A nurse gave the enchanted child Mr and Mrs Wooden People, explaining that they had been found up her sleeves. Poor Mr Wooden Man had broken his neck in the fall, but a pink plaster was now holding his head back onto his shoulders.

Pictures of Mickey Mouse and Donald Duck were painted on the walls. Lowry even had drawings on her plaster cast. The grown-ups didn't shout and the visitors who came to see the other young patients would bring colouring books and crayons for her. The Doctor gave her a rag doll with a little label saying, 'call me Bunty.' She didn't want to fly away from this place. She wanted to stay forever.

Lowry's experience in the hospital was the source of her determination to be a nurse when she grew up. It was a decision that would set in motion some unexpected events.

Discharge day arrived and the woman in green shoes waited outside the ward doors to meet her.

"Hello again, little Lowry," said the woman whose shoes were now brown. "Come on, off we go!" She took the child's hand as she spoke. "We are going to my house."

Pulling her hand from the woman's grasp Lowry peered up at her face for the first time. She wore glasses and looked old, very old.

"Can't I hold your hand, my dear?" the woman asked.

"No!" came the adamant reply. "Go away."

The woman squatted in front of the bewildered child, putting her arm around the small shoulders. Lowry shrugged it off.

"I'm taking you away from the Home," she gently said. "We are going to live together and see how much fun we can have."

"I don't want go to your house. I want to stay in the hospital," the child wailed.

"Lowry, I want you to be a brave little girl. You will not be going back to the Home and you can't stay in the hospital. You are a special little person, so special things are going to happen to you."

The enormity of her words knocked any resistance from Lowry. She meekly followed the woman out of the main entrance of the hospital with Bunty hanging limply from her hand and Mr and Mrs Wooden People up her sleeve.

The bus journey should have been exciting because the child had never been on a bus before. In fact she'd never seen one and it was green and huge, but feeling unsafe and defenceless spoilt the new experience. People seemed to get on and get off all the time, then more would get on then get off again. A man wandered up and down the passage and up and down the stairs. He rang a bell on a machine and shouted, 'burst peas.'

Through the window she could see huge buildings and busy people with bad tempered faces and scurrying feet. Large windows were brilliantly lit and filled with grown up dolls in fancy clothes. They all looked bored.

"Are you still feeling upset, Lowry?" the woman gently asked.

The girl ignored her. She didn't know how she was feeling.

The bus stopped. Lowry stared in amazement at a man who went past on a long thin thing with a big circle in the front and one at the back. He was sitting down, but his legs were going up and down and round and round. Curiosity got the better of her.

"What's that man doing?" she asked the woman.

The woman leaned across to look out of the window.

"That is a cyclist and he's riding a bicycle," she explained. "Would you like to have a bicycle?"

"No."

The child didn't want anything from this woman. She wanted to go home.

Eventually they came to the woman's 'bus stop,' as she called it, and walked a short distance to a house with a big blue wooden gate that led up a long path to a blue front door. Standing framed in the doorway stood a grumpy faced even older, old lady.

"Where have you been Louise and who's that child?" the old lady shouted.

"Please Mother, just go inside and I'll make us a nice cup of tea," the woman patiently said.

The old lady remained blocking the entrance.

"I don't want your tea, Louise, and you've no right to take another woman's child and bring it here." She turned her gaze on Lowry who shivered. "You go back to your mother now, girl. She must be wondering where you are."

The woman, called Louise, grabbed Lowry's hand firmly and pushed past the old lady. They hurried upstairs to a pretty bedroom.

"I'm sorry you've had such a difficult day," she said, as they sat on a proper bed with no sides. "Let me explain why you are here with me."

Her arm went round the child's waist. Lowry moved away. She didn't like being touched. But the woman continued talking.

"I haven't got a little girl of my own and when I first saw you I thought, there's a lovely little girl, I'd like to look after her. And because you had nobody of your own I've brought you to my house to live with me."

Lowry didn't want to live with this woman and didn't want to hear what she said, either. She held her hands over her ears.

"The old lady downstairs is my mother. She gets very muddled and forgetful, but you must understand she would never hurt you, though she will do things that seem very strange and say funny things, but don't let her worry you."

"I want to go back to the hospital," Lowry bleated, clenching her fists very tightly.

The woman rose from the bed and knelt before the distressed child.

"I'm going to be very honest with you, my dear. I can't promise you will ever go back to the hospital or the Home. This is going to be your home and I am the person who is responsible for you. I will continue to care for you as long as your childhood lasts."

The brutal honesty of her words temporarily impeded any attempt Lowry could make to challenge what was happening. She felt helpless.

"You can call me Lou or Mum. You choose for yourself," the woman said.

"You isn't my mum so go away," Lowry yelled, "and I don't want to stay here. I want to find my mum. I know she's going to fetch me. Bloody Dove said she was."

"Lowry, just listen to me please. The reason you are with me is because you don't have a mother and it's important for all little children to have a mother."

Lowry frowned angrily and clenched her fists even harder.

"I have got a mother called Mum. She's got long black hair and a long white dress and she's not old like you with glasses."

"I'm sure your Mum was very young and beautiful, Lowry. But something must have happened to her because she would have fetched her lovely little daughter a long time ago if she had been able to. Anyway, sweetheart, you don't have to call me Mum if you don't want to."

"I'll call you Miss, then."

"Don't call me Miss, Lowry. I am a teacher and the children in my class call me Miss."

The confused child burst with temper and uncontrollable rage.

"I hates school," she screamed at her, "and I'll call you Miss Bum 'cos I hates you and the old lady downstairs. I don't want to stay here."

Lowry grabbed her chance and raced for the door. Half way down the stairs she felt a hand clutch her shoulder and pull her backward until her bottom flopped onto a stair. The woman hung on, sitting behind the angry child, wrapping her legs around the small hips and her arms tightly around her shoulders. Lowry violently kicked the step with her two feet. The commotion brought forth the old lady.

"Leave the girl alone, Louise. Leave her be. Let her go back to her Mother. I'll have the police onto you. You can't just kidnap another woman's child."

"Go away, Mother," the woman breathlessly said, as Lowry struggled against her. "I told you this morning I would be bringing a little girl back home with me."

"You've taken leave of your senses, you stupid woman," the old lady retorted. "Take her back where you got her from or I'm going to ring the police right now."

She moved towards the hall table.

"Mother, if you pick up that 'phone, I shall give your dinner to the dog. Mark my words. Now go away."

The old lady left and stomped into the kitchen.

The woman rocked back and forth. Slowly and gradually the girl calmed down, exhausted by a day of confusing happenings.

Lowry picked at her evening meal and ate a strange thing called a sausage. She poked at a floppy thing called an egg and some horrid yellow stuff leaked out. Yuk! But the things called chips were good.

"If you don't want that egg, child, then I'll have it," the old lady excitedly said.

"Leave that egg where it is, Mother. It's Lowry's," the woman told her.

Lowry looked across to the old lady and then to the woman and then stared at her egg. These people were very funny. They seemed to be managing to use the things the woman called a knife and fork, but Lowry had only ever used a spoon. She wanted her bread and dripping, with brown streaks in her hands. Lowry picked up the sausage in her fingers and bit it. It wasn't too bad really. She greedily devoured the chips, aggressively stabbing at them with the thing called a fork. She pushed her plate with the leaky egg towards the old lady.

"You can have that yuk thing it's 'orrible," she said.

"Thank you Brigit," the old lady eagerly replied.

"Me name's not Brigit. Lowry is me name."

"Flowery! What sort of a name is that?" the bad tempered old woman retorted. "Why didn't they just call you Rose and be done with it?"

The old lady picked up the steaming cup of hot tea and poured it into the saucer which she then lifted to her mouth. The slurping liquid noisily went down her throat.

Lowry decided these people were very funny.

The woman, Lowry now called Miss Lou, behaved in a manner most unlike any grown-up she had known. Lou never left her side, never stopped talking and laughing and spent the early part of the evening with the curious child exploring every room and cupboard in the fairly large house. No doors were shut except for a door in the hall that was under the stairs. Lowry pointed to the door.

"Miss Lou, is that your punishment cupboard in there?" she asked.

Lou frowned as she opened the door.

"No, my love," she gently said. "It's the cloakroom where we put our coats and shoes. Have a look inside and you'll see."

The child tentatively peered inside.

"Where's the punishment cupboard then?" she asked.

"Lowry, we have no punishment cupboard here. In fact we don't have any punishment at all, only rewards. And we have lots of them, because little children need lots of rewards because they have a lot to learn. Did you have a punishment cupboard in your other home?"

"Yes, it was horrible and black in there where monsters and the bogeyman lived."

"Dear God!" Lou said. "I'll do something about that."

Apart from discovering the magic of a gas cooker, a wireless and the telephone, Lowry discovered that a box in the corner called a television could show black and white magic pictures that moved.

The child yawned, feeling very tired. It had all been too much and too sudden for her young mind to digest. The new bedroom was a colourful place with flowered walls and a bright eiderdown on the bed. New clothes had been tidied away into a cupboard called a wardrobe and folded into a box called a chest of drawers. A teddy bear sat appealingly on a soft lump called a pillow. One of her secret friends had looked just like him. From her pocket, Lowry took Mr and Mrs Wooden People and put them under the pillow with Bunty. The woman attempted to kiss her goodnight. The child pushed her away.

"I'm sorry, my dear," Lou said.

The child had never been kissed before and it didn't feel right.

Lowry woke in the dark hugging her new teddy. The light from the landing reflected into the room illuminating the figure of the old lady bending over her bed. Bony fingers gripped her shoulder. Lowry screamed and bolted upright. The semi-darkness cast hideous shadows of the old lady against the walls as she tugged at Lowry's pyjama jacket sleeve.

"Get up Brigit and go home," she rasped. "You don't live here! Get back to your Mother now child while my daughter is asleep. The stupid woman has gone mad."

The terrified child froze to the pillow as the silhouetted figure struggled to pull her from the bed. She instinctively bit the old lady's hand. The furious old lady picked up the teddy bear and whacked it across Lowry's head. Grabbing Bunty's leg, Lowry whacked the old lady back across the face with the rag doll. Then brilliant light unexpectedly flooded the room.

"Dear God, Mother! What the hell are you doing to that child? Leave her alone and get out of here this minute," Lou yelled.

The old lady shouted angrily.

"That girl is like a wild animal. She's just bitten me and hit me with that doll thing. You've no right to steal another woman's child, Louise, especially a little savage," she bellowed. "Just because you haven't got one of your own doesn't give you the right to steal this one. I'll get the police onto you. That girl's Mother must be half out of her mind with worry." The angry old lady turned her gaze on Lowry. "Get up, Brigit and get back to your own Mother, she's the one who should be feeding you, not us."

Lou eventually jostled the old lady out of the room.

"You poor little mite," she said, on returning to the room. "I am going to get a book and stay here with you and we can read a story together."

"I can't read," Lowry miserably told her. "And I don't want to stay here with that old lady."

"Don't worry, my dear, the old lady won't hurt you, I'll make sure of that and I'll teach you to read."

"I can fight, you know," Lowry proudly announced. "Can you fight?"

"No, I can't fight," the woman chuckled. "And I think I'm too old to learn."

"I'll learn yer," Lowry said, thrilled at the idea that she could 'learn' this woman something.

Lou chuckled again.

"We've got a lot to learn from each other," she said. "And you will be staying here, my dear."

"Miss Lou, I'll stay with you if you want, but only for a little bit and can Beth and Tommy come and stay for a little bit as well?"

"Were they your friends?" Lowry nodded. "Shall we wait and see what happens first?" Lowry nodded again. "And just call me, Lou, sweetheart. You don't have to call me Miss."

Lou left the room and returned with a little blue book. Propping herself against the pillow she opened it at page one and introduced the captivated child to the wonderful world of a little black mole. He was fed up with his spring cleaning and left his dark tunnel to face a new and exciting life with his new friends. It was called, The Wind in the Willows by Kenneth Grahame.

Lowry's heart sank when she woke next morning. Her bed was wet and she hadn't done that for ages. Suddenly a familiar sound made her heart jump for joy. Bloody Dove had found her. The coo, coo came from the trees that lined the avenue where Lou lived. She leapt from her bed and raced to the window. She opened it wide and searched the trees.

"Bloody Dove, I flied over the wall just like you said. Thank you for finding me," she loudly yelled.

And best of all she didn't get her legs slapped for wetting the bed. And her brand new knickers were just right. They didn't droop to her knees.

ARCHIE AND HIS PARROT

Summer holidays were over. Lowry's new school was walking distance away, the same school where Lou taught the top class infants. Whilst Lou was away, Irish Mrs Murphy arrived early to clean the house and give the old lady her lunch. Her short, dumpy, elderly body was covered in a large green overall and her grey curls were hidden by a blue head scarf, tied in a turban. The old lady followed her everywhere, making sure she didn't steal anything. 'That silly Irish woman only comes here to pilfer our food,' she frequently grumbled within earshot of Mrs Murphy who would chuckle delightfully.

School was a lonely place. Lowry had no friends except for Bloody Dove who seemed to follow her everywhere. Her limited knowledge of everyday life and commonplace events caused amusement and derision. But somehow her belligerent attitude sustained her through her early months at school, alleviating the desperate inadequacy she felt when confronted with books, blackboards and her own ignorance. Just like the orphanage, her new school celebrated Empire Day, but with much pageantry. The boys paraded their bicycles round the playground and the girls pushed their doll's prams, all decorated in red, white and blue ribbons. The best decorated bicycle and pram won a prize. Lowry didn't have a pram. She wasn't into dolls and since it was only the boys who were allowed to take bicycles she and Lou spent the evening decorating the rusty garden wheelbarrow in patriotic flags and ribbons. Lowry proudly pushed her wheelbarrow to school. The laughter from the other children made her cross. She wanted to bite, scratch, punch and kick every one of them. But she won a prize! It was a picture of Queen Victoria as the Empress of India. Lowry wasn't impressed. She thought the woman looked fat and bad tempered.

The seven and a half year old officially became Lowry Stuart, Lou's new daughter, almost a year after she had first walked up the path to the blue front door. She was happy living with Lou. Memories of the orphanage gradually faded with time. She often wondered if Beth had been allowed to go back home to her granddad so that she could do those naughty things that he liked and whether Tommy's mum had got right in the head again so he could go home to her. As for her real mum, Lowry was too busy to think about her any more. But there was one important thing missing from her life. She desperately wanted a dad. Why didn't she have a dad to run in the father's race on sports day? Lou was very understanding, but she didn't seem to be making much effort to find one. Lowry decided if Lou couldn't be bothered finding a dad she would find one herself. She gave the dilemma much thought and finally came up with an imaginative solution.

Mr Archibald Cuthbertson lived with a large grey parrot, five doors down. Lou had always said he was a real gentleman. He was a little round man and known as Archie. His thick grey hair stuck out in all directions on top of his head and his thick grey eyebrows curled upwards like two little horns. Lowry liked him even though he was old, but she particularly liked the parrot whose name was Captain Bligh. No matter how often she had heard the parrot recite his party piece she never got bored with it. 'One! Two! Four! Damn it, I forgot three again! One! Two! Four! Damn it, I forgot three again!' Lowry knocked gently on Mr Archibald Cuthbertson's front door. She had an apple in her hand, which was her excuse for calling.

"Good afternoon, young lady," he said, upon seeing Lowry on his door step.

Mr Cuthbertson was once a Commodore Engineer with the Cunard Shipping Line. His wife had been dead ten years, so it was time he had a bit of company. And he once wore a uniform with gold buttons that Lowry loved which made him very suitable to be her dad.

"I've brought an apple for Captain Bligh," she told him. "And I was wondering if you would like to come to our house for your tea today because Lou is looking for a man and she says you are a real gentleman. I know you're very old, but I like you and Captain Bligh."

The gentleman smiled as Lowry handed him the apple.

"Thank you for the apple and thank you for your kind invitation, my dear. Thank your mother for asking me, but..."

Lowry waved her arm to silence him.

"She doesn't know yet, Mr Cuthbertson. I thought I'd ask you first," Lowry quickly interrupted.

The gentleman leaned forward and ruffled Lowry's hair, smiling as he did so. But the girl didn't mind. Archie wasn't at all like the horrible vicar.

"You have made an old man very happy, young Lowry," he chuckled. "I shall always be your friend and so will Captain Bligh, so you call and see us anytime you like."

Lowry played hop-scotch on the paving flags as she went back home. It was worth a try and anyway he was a bit old, she reflected. But she wasn't going to give up looking yet. And Lou was such a nice person she deserved to have a big surprise when Lowry found her a man.

THE REBELLIOUS CHILD

From the moment Lowry opened her eyes until closing them for sleep, Lou relentlessly pursued the child's education, determined that her daughter should 'catch up,' speak correctly and grammatically and have nice manners. The child never understood why grass became grarss, if fat didn't become fart. If a bath became a barth, why didn't next doors cat become a cart? And why change 'jawanna' into the mouthful, 'do you want to'?

Starting Junior School was a natural progression upwards, but Lowry was unhappy with her new teacher, Miss Braithwaite. The class of thirty didn't speak or move, unless given permission. No child dared ask for the toilet during lesson time. If you hadn't gone during break time, and the toilet became a dire necessity, then a ruler across the forearm became more painful than a bursting bladder. The toilet roll hung from a piece of string on the back of the classroom door. According to Lou it was a throwback from the war days when paper was hard to come by. Miss Braithwaite hadn't moved on, she was still rationing her toilet paper so only one sheet was allowed and that was for number twos. Lowry felt sorry for Jimmy Blackett, the milk monitor. He often had a reddened forearm. He seemed to do a number two, twice a day. Sometimes, he waited so long before asking permission to go to the toilet that he tottered to the door with his hand pressed to his bottom in a desperate attempt to hold it in.

Lowry sat at the back of the class as far away as possible from the formidable woman. After two weeks of the teacher's tyranny, she decided she'd had enough. She raised her hand and stood as the teacher nodded, indicating her permission for the child to speak.

"Please Miss, I don't want to be in your class anymore 'cos I don't like you very much."

"Sit down, Lowry Stuart." The class giggled. "Get on with your work," she bellowed. The class went silent. "Do as you're told, you insolent child," she screamed. Lowry remained standing. "Get to the front of the class then or I'll drag you here."

With trembling knees, Lowry walked in fear and stood by the teacher's desk. The woman rolled down the insolent child's socks and slapped the backs of her legs over and over again. Lou had always told Lowry that no-one would ever hit her again. She had lied. The class watched as the bruising continued. Lowry clenched her fists. She wasn't going to cry. Miss was still bending as Lowry punched her. A loud 'ooh' resounded from the onlookers.

"You horrid child," the woman shouted as she threw her onto the bench outside the Headmaster's room. "What is your Mother going to say when she knows you punched me?" The hairs that grew from a large mole on her chin, shook with anger. "I don't want you in my class anymore. Do you hear me?"

She left to go back to her room to terrorise more children.

It pleased Lowry to know that the fat tyrant didn't want her in her class. The best thing for her to do was to walk out of the school. She found the park and sat on her favourite swing wondering what to do next. Her legs smarted painfully. Lowry studied the red weal marks where teacher's podgy fingers had left their patterns in white raised lines against the redness. To her surprise she spotted Lou approaching her. The woman held out her arms in a gesture of welcome. Lowry ran into the safety of the arms and squashed her face into Lou's stomach as she embraced her.

"I thought I'd find you here," she said. "You shouldn't have run away, sweetheart, nor should you have punched your teacher." Lou studied the backs of Lowry's legs. "Good God!"

she murmured. "I'm so sorry. Sometimes we adults lose our temper and do wrong things, just like you do, although we should know better. Shall we go and see your teacher so you can apologise to her?"

"No, no, no!" Lowry shouted, in panic. "She was hitting me first. I never hit her first. She was hurting me and she wouldn't stop. I only punched her once, but she hit me hundreds of times."

The child was expelled.

The only school willing to take Lowry was a fee-paying Convent. Lou and Lowry walked through the great gates and up the tree lined driveway. Looming, and almost half hidden amongst the trees and shrubs, were numerous statues peeping out from the gloom. The large wooden front door, upon which hung a cross, creaked as it slowly opened in response to Lou's knock. Lowry shivered at the thought of what lay behind the enormous door.

"I am Mother Superior," said the grey nun who stood framed in the doorway, "and you must be Lowry." She eyed the girl up and down. "Now say goodbye to your mother, child."

With a quick kiss, Lou had gone.

Suddenly, the girl felt very alone and apprehensive as she followed Mother Superior's big body down the silent corridor. A thick grey blanket covered the nun from head to toe. Even her hands were tucked up her sleeves with her right hand hidden up her left sleeve and her left hand hidden up her right sleeve. Only her face peered out from the grey and white hat. Her wrinkled skin reminded the overawed child of Nana's dried prunes that she soaked every night and ate every morning for her bowels. The girl's new black shoes embarrassingly squealed on the highly polished wooden floor.

"I will show you around, child, before I take you to your classroom, but first things first." Mother Superior dug deep into her pocket and produced two hair grips. "Let me get rid of that fringe and show all of your face. We hide nothing from Our Lady. Do you know who Our Lady is?" she asked.

"Yes," Lowry confidently answered. "It's the Queen."

"Don't be silly, child," Mother Superior huffed. She gathered the girl's fringe into a tuft and clipped it to the top of her head. Lowry touched it to see what it felt like. "Come now, it doesn't matter what it looks like," the big woman scolded. "Do you want to make Our Lady blush with your vanity, Lowry Stuart? Vanity is a sin and we do not have sinners in my convent. Now remove your shoes and put on your house slippers. Come on, hurry up!"

Lowry hastened to do her bidding. They shuffled together along a corridor lined with more statues. The smell in the chapel reminded Lowry of the wonderful smell from Lou's camphor wood chest each time the lid was lifted. A large colourful window acted as a backdrop to a life-size statue of a sad faced man. He seemed to be holding some of his insides in his hands with blood dripping through the gaps in his fingers. Lowry stood in shock, unable to take her eyes from the spectacle.

"What's the matter with him?" she whispered.

"That is Our Saviour, Jesus Christ who died for your sins," Mother Superior said, in hushed tones.

"Why did he do that to himself?" the girl whispered.

"Because he wanted us all to be pure and free from sin," she replied. Her finger pointed towards a big gold cross.

"See, he suffered and died on the cross for all our sins. So remember child to keep a pure mind and a pure heart. Now you are not of the faith, so you won't be using the chapel, but this is where the whole convent assembles on Friday afternoon when the priest arrives to take confession."

The child didn't know what confession was or why the priest came to take it off the whole convent every Friday, but it might be a blessing.

"Does that mean I can go home early on a Friday?" she hopefully asked.

"No!" Mother Superior tartly answered. "You will join the others who are not of the faith and clean the corridors and the staircase. Now follow me."

The woman unexpectedly curtseyed again causing Lowry to blush as she bumped into Mother Superior's bottom as they left the chapel. They shuffled together to the classroom. As they entered each girl rose and stood beside her desk. They all curtseyed in one great tidal wave.

"Good morning, Mother Superior," the room chorused.

"Good morning, ladies," she replied. "You may sit." The tidal wave receded. "This is Lowry Stuart, a new girl who has come to join us," Mother Superior informed the staring girls.

The new girl felt very self-conscious especially since the tuft on the top of head wobbled when her head moved.

"She is C of E," Mother Superior continued, "but I want you to help her with the convent rules and make her first day a good one."

The big grey blanket swept from the room. The teacher, also dressed in a grey blanket, introduced herself.

"I am Sister Michael, your form tutor and here is your desk, Lowry." Piled on the desk were brown, blue, red and green exercise books. "Have you got your fountain pen?" she asked.

"Yes Miss," Lowry replied, wondering why the teacher had a man's name.

The class giggled.

"Ladies, you will not allow yourselves to be amused by Lowry's mistake," she sharply said. She proceeded to explain that she be referred to as Sister and Lowry must stand when spoken to and curtsey before sitting again. "Can you remember all that, my child?"

"Yes thank you, Sister," the new girl sweetly answered.

"No, Lowry, you forgot to stand before you spoke. We shall try again so you can get it right."

The embarrassed girl stood, her face glowing red. She quickly obeyed.

"Yes thank you, Sister."

"That's good! Now a quick curtsey and then you may sit," she said, smiling kindly. Lowry bent her knees. "Just bend one knee, not both. You're not about to jump over a puddle, are you?" The girl at the next desk giggled. "Margaret, you will say five Hail Mary's to atone for your unkindness," she admonished the giggler.

The convent prided itself on turning out well educated young ladies and being ladylike seemed to come naturally to most of the girls. Lowry struggled to make the grade. She could perform sweetly, be demure and polite and even curtsey with one knee, but her performance lacked conviction, because she could never remember to be a lady all the time.

Friday morning, on the dot of eleven o'clock, the girls' dusters and polish flew across the classroom desks, the window sills and floors.

"I don't pay them to educate you and then have you doing all their cleaning as well," Lou grumbled.

She had already written to tell them to leave her daughter's hair alone, so she felt she couldn't complain again.

Every Friday afternoon those 'of the faith' sang, prayed and confessed in the chapel. Those not 'of the faith' cleaned the corridors and spiral staircase. Polishing the floors on hands and knees required pleated skirts to be pinned between the legs when kneeling, to avoid showing navy blue knickers. Lowry spent one afternoon with the Blessed Virgin Mary in the Garden of Repose after a prefect reported her for doing handstands against the convent wall with her skirt tucked into the legs of her knickers. Pulling up the weeds in the rose beds was better than sitting in the classroom. An effigy of Mary, wearing a blue dress, watched her from a niche in the wall. The sinful girl gripped her skirt tightly between her knees to avoid causing any embarrassment to the statue.

During her first six months at the convent Lowry struggled to please her teacher, no matter how hard she tried. Sometimes she raised her hand when a question was asked, but Sister didn't often call upon her, even though she knew the answer. Sister's favourite girls were always good and very holy. Lowry was neither. And it wasn't her fault either, that Lou had taught her silly poetry.

"Does anyone know any poems?" Sister Michael asked, after she had read Longfellow's Hiawatha to the class. Lowry shot her hand into the air. "Good, and do you know the name of the poets who wrote the poems you know?" she asked the proud child.

Lowry stood beside her desk.

"Yes Sister. Ogden Nash wrote one of them and I don't know who wrote the other."

"I've never heard of Ogden Nash," she said. "Would you like to recite the poems to us, Lowry?"

The proud girl cleared her throat and began her recitation.

"Billy in one of his nice new sashes, Fell in the fire and was burnt to ashes. Now, although the room grows chilly, I haven't the heart to poke poor Billy!"

The classroom filled with girlish laughter. The noise died down and Lowry began her second recitation in her best Liverpool accent.

"Mary Mary from the dairy, She'll sell yer goozegogs, Like gear little plums only 'airy."

The giggling erupted again.

"Sit down," Sister said, ignoring Lowry's poems. The perplexed child curtsied and sat down.

Many of Lowry's school moments were spent in Mother Superior's office explaining why she had been seen running hatless and gloveless to the bus stop and why she had been heard whistling in the playground. 'A whistling woman and a crowing hen brought the devil out of his den,' according to Mother Superior. It was the devil that evoked Lowry's disobedience, and the girl would rue the day she found herself in his hellfire. The devil began to haunt her at night. She woke sweating from the heat of his fire. Her behaviour deteriorated as she did battle with the devil and Mother Superior. Lowry hated the convent and hated Mother Superior and hated the silly rules. And she hated the ugly statues that spied on her from their shadowy places.

The end of the school day came as a relief. She didn't mind chanting the prayers before home time. Freedom beckoned. She was going to be running, jumping, skipping and flying with no hat on her head and no gloves on her hands. And who cares if she shows her knickers when doing cartwheels? She was going to cartwheel round the garden with Jolly the dog barking his encouragement. Lowry stood with the rest of the girls, whose heads were bowed in prayer. She stared through the window.

"Who do we love most?" Sister Michael asked.

"Jesus Christ our Beloved Saviour, Sister,' the room loudly chorused.

But Lowry didn't agree. She loved her dog most.

"What was that you said, Lowry Stuart?" Sister bellowed.

"I said I love my dog, Sister, and he loves me, 'cos I don't really know Jesus all that well," she meekly replied.

The face on the normally mild Nun registered fury.

"Stay behind after school and we'll see what Mother Superior has to say about your disgraceful attitude," she shouted.

Mother Superior studied the child standing before her, for a long time, before she spoke.

"You are a disgrace to the uniform and a disgrace to the convent, Lowry Stuart. Your socks are always hanging around your ankles, your tie is never straight and your sleeves are forever dangling over your hands. Look at you, child!"

Lowry couldn't look at herself, because there were no mirrors in the convent. Mirrors made you vain and as for Lowry's sleeves she could blame Lou for that. She hadn't grown into her jumper yet or her black gabardine raincoat. Lowry clenched her fists and dug her nails into the palms of her hands as Mother Superior's voice became more menacing.

"You are heading for eternal damnation. You will remember my words, young lady, when you burn in hellfire, as you surely will. Your hands do the devil's work. He seeks you out because you stray towards him with your disregard for obedience and your lack of humility. You have been born with more than your fair share of original sin, my lady, but you do nothing to rectify the matter." She paused for breath. "I have no alternative but to write to your mother and arrange for her to remove you from my convent. Now leave, and may our Blessed Lord, Jesus Christ, take pity on you." She waved the shocked child away with her hand. The girl curtseyed and left the room.

The statues of Mary and Jesus gazed sadly at the frightened child from their lofty positions either side of Mother Superior's door. Lowry concentrated her gaze on the face of Jesus.

"Please Jesus don't let me burn in hellfire," she beseeched him. "I'll try and love you more than my dog and I'll cut off my fringe for Mary and do all the humility and obedience things Mother Superior says."

He remained stone-faced. Jesus wasn't listening.

"Something is wrong," Lou said, as Lowry pushed her food around her dinner plate. "Can you tell me about it?"

Lowry pushed her plate away from her. Nana made a grab for the lamb chop.

"If she doesn't want it, I'll not see good food go to waste," she said, excitedly holding the chop in her hands. "What about the potatoes, Brigit, do you not want them either? You can keep the peas, they give me terrible wind. I don't know why you keep giving me peas, Louise. They….,"

"Be quiet, Mother, please," Lou retorted. The old lady looked taken aback, but concentrated on shovelling Lowry's potatoes onto her plate. "Lowry, I'm sure I can help. Please tell me what has happened?"

"You can't help. You can't, because I'm going to burn in hellfire forever because of my sins. Mother Superior said I was born with lots of original ones."

Lou placed her hand over Lowry's arm.

"Can you tell me what your sins are?" she asked.

"Yes, it's not being able to do humility and obedience."

"Okay, Lowry, what is humility?"

"I don't know, because I haven't got what it is, Lou. It's one of my sins."

"What sins, sweetheart?" Lou challenged. "No way do young children have sins. They can be naughty, but that's normal. Who on earth is filling your head with such poppycock?"

"It's not poppycock," Lowry shouted back. "Mother Superior said it, and she doesn't want me there anymore because I make Mary blush."

"Mary who?"

"I'm not sure about her last name. She's called Holy Mary Mother of God. She's sometimes called Hail Mary and she prays for us sinners, so we have to bless the fruit she's got in her room."

"Lowry, it is the fruit of her womb that is blessed not the fruit in her room."

"What's a womb?"

"I'll explain some other time," Lou said, "but why is Mother Superior accusing you of making Mary blush?"

Nana banged her spoon on the table.

"How long do I have to wait for my pudding?" she bad temperedly asked. "Are you going to be chattering away to that child all night?"

"Just be patient Mother, please," Lou sighed.

"What have you made for pudding, Louise? I hope it's bananas and custard. My teeth can manage bananas and custard, but why you have to do chops when mince is easier to eat, I just don't know."

"Mother, it's tinned peaches and evap and I'll fetch them soon. Just let me finish talking to Lowry. Please." Lou turned her gaze on Lowry. "Tell me why you…?"

"I don't call opening two tins making a pudding. It's just laziness," the old grump announced.

"Be quiet, Mother! Now Lowry, why are you supposed to make Mary blush?" she asked again.

"Because she doesn't like my fringe and we have to pin our skirts between our legs when we polish the floors in case she sees our knickers."

Lou laughed loudly and Jolly the dog wagged his tail.

"I'm sorry to laugh, sweetheart, but you must admit that if Mary were alive today she would probably be wearing knickers, and as for making her blush because she doesn't like your hair style is just ridiculous."

Nana angrily pushed her chair back and stood up.

"I'll get my own pudding, Louise. How long do you expect me to sit here listening to your stupid conversation about Mary's knickers?"

Nana was ignored so sat down in a huff, but not before pulling tongues at Lou.

"Lou, you've got to believe me about Mary and the devil," Lowry pleaded. "Mother Superior said something about Spotty McDoo, Mrs McDougal's dog, but I don't know what she meant."

Lou looked surprise.

"Do you mean Mrs McDougal, who lives up the road?"

"Yes, her! Mother Superior said I was heading for infernal Dalmatian."

Lou exploded, banging her teacup onto the saucer.

"How dare they fill your head with such cruel nonsense?" she bellowed. "The woman was talking about eternal damnation, Lowry, not a Dalmatian dog. This is preposterous! There is no such person as the devil, believe me. He doesn't exist. He is a figment of people's imaginations, those people who want to control us through fear, and that's exactly what's been going on here. There's no such place as Hell either."

"Yes there is, it's where the bad people go when they're dead. The good people go to Heaven when they're dead," Lowry argued.

Lou sighed heavily.

"No no, Lowry, there is no Heaven and no Hell, only this planet we all live on that we make into our own Heaven or our own Hell. So why don't we stop allowing ourselves to be controlled by fear and make our own paradise now whilst we are able to do so? What's the point of waiting until we're dead before enjoying a bit of Heaven?"

"How d'you make Heaven?"

"By being kind to people and animals, by sharing, by enjoying being alive, by having….,"

"A pure mind and a pure heart" Lowry quickly cut in.

"Something like that, yes," Lou replied. "But Lowry, you will definitely not be going back there. I've been such a stupid woman sending you to the convent, but I thought the nuns would have some compassion for you. What a mess I've made of things. I'm so sorry."

Lowry thought Lou was about to cry. It worried her.

"Don't cry, Lou," she timidly said.

"I'm not crying, Lowry," she explained. "I'm seething with anger. I was paying them to give you a good education, not to brainwash you, or fill your head with rubbish about the devil and Mary blushing. I was never very happy about all the cleaning you did for them either." Lou grinned at her daughter. Her blue eyes twinkled behind her glasses. "Well, little Lowry, that's the end of the convent, the end of the devil and the end of any talk about sins. Now, I will get the pudding and then...."

"About time," Nana interjected.

".......we'll clear the table and wash up the dishes," Lou continued. "Afterwards I'm going to teach you to play chess. I used to play it with my husband, but haven't played it since he died."

Lowry woke early next morning, her body wet with sweat. She felt wretched, her dreams still clear in her head. Why did the devil keep coming to see her at night if he didn't exist? She had to do something to get Jesus to take her sins away. Lou was very clever, but she couldn't do what Jesus did. Mother Superior had told her that he suffered and took away the sins of the world. His hands were bleeding. Perhaps if Lowry made her hands bleed that would stop them doing the devil's work. She wandered into the garden, her clammy pyjamas stuck to her skin in the cold morning air.

"Please Jesus, don't make it hurt too much," she pleaded, as she scrambled over the rockery.

Her eyes searched out a rock big enough for the job in hand. She found one with a jagged protrusion that would serve as a handle. Placing her right hand on a larger stone, Lowry lifted the weapon in her left hand and closed her eyes. Nothing happened. She struggled with the fear of pain and her fear of the devil. The early morning birds stopped their singing and the hush told her they were waiting. She took a deep breath and gritted her teeth. The chunk of rock smashed down onto the small unresisting hand and an excruciating pain shot through the fingers and up the arm causing her to fold over. She didn't know how it happened because she held the rock in the air one moment and the next it had crashed onto her hand. Was it the devil or Jesus who guided that rock? She didn't care anymore.

Blood oozed from under the finger nails and out from the broken skin. She fought to keep the tears in, but they rolled down her cheeks. With so much pain, Lowry knew her sins had been banished. She climbed the stairs to Lou's bedroom and wakened her.

"Lou, my hand hurts so much and it's bleeding," she sobbed. "But all my sins have gone away now."

Lou shot out of bed.

"Heaven forbid, Lowry, what have you done to yourself?" she asked in alarm.

Lou's opinion of Mother Superior must have had the pious nun's ears blistering.

Although her fear of the devil gradually diminished, he still, sometimes, hung around in the darkness.

It was a cold night when loud banging on the front door woke her with a start. An orange glow from the landing radiated into the room like the brilliance of an intense fire. The excited howling from Jolly the dog reverberated through the night, adding fiendish wolf-like sounds to the grizzly scene. Lou appeared. She looked flustered and flushed from sleep.

"Hush, Lowry. It's only someone at the front door," she said, pulling on her dressing gown.

"Don't open it Lou, it's the devil," the hysterical girl screamed.

The banging came again, louder this time. Lowry sprang from bed clutching Lou's dressing gown as they made their way down stairs. Jolly threw himself at the dining room door. He sensed the devilishness of it all.

"Don't let him in. Don't let him in," Lowry screamed, pulling Lou's arm to prevent her from opening the door.

"Hush Lowry, hush," she gently said. "Good heavens! I locked this door, now it's unbolted." She turned the knob and the door opened. The light from the porch lit up two policemen with Nana standing shivering between them.

"Is this old dear from here?" the policeman asked, peering curiously into the hall.

"She's my mother," Lou said, in horrified amazement.

Nana appeared frightened and cold. Her long winceyette nightdress had been no protection against the chilly air. She had put on her thick stockings but without suspenders they had concertinaed around her ankles. Hanging from the end of her red nose a little dewdrop rolled like a tear.

"She was found wandering around the bus depot at Penny Lane," the policeman said, as he escorted Nana into the house. "She's not safe. You want to make sure she can't get out."

"Perhaps she should be in a home," the other policeman helpfully suggested.

Lou bustled about, trying to revive the dying embers of the fire.

"Put the kettle on, Lowry, please," she said, turning to face the officers. "I can't thank you enough for bringing her back. Lowry and I will certainly look after her, but this is her home, she needs no other."

The old lady sat down, exhausted and cold. After putting the kettle on the gas ring Lowry raced upstairs and came down again with Nana's eiderdown and wrapped it around the old lady's shoulders.

"Thank you, child," she appreciatively said. "It's not Sunday is it?"

"No Nana it's Friday."

"Well why are all the shops shut, then?" Nana angrily asked. "I went to get some Everton mints and there wasn't a damn shop open anywhere. Have you got any Everton mints, Brigit?"

"No, Nana, but I've got some liquorice laces you can have."

77

Nana gave out a loud frustrated snort.

"Don't be stupid child. D'you want to give me the runs? Anyway what are these men doing in the house, Louise?" Tell them to go away."

The policemen prepared to leave.

"What was all the screaming we heard?" The officer turned to look at Lowry. "Was that you?"

"Yes," she meekly answered. "I thought you were the devil and you'd lit your hellfire on our landing."

The policemen stared at each other and said nothing.

Lou bolted the door behind them.

"Oh God!" she sighed. "They must think this is a nut house."

THE BRUTAL TRUTH

The sailor's steps were urgent and hurried. Captain Leif Svenerson had just returned from Australia. He had been away for almost eight months. The Australian authorities had been of little help to him. Migratory orphans had been scattered across the vast country and sent to Catholic institutions and Doctor Bernardo's and as workers on the large sheep and cattle stations. The captain had received one glimmer of hope. Lori Svenerson would be too young to have been included in the 1947 shipment. The next consignment of migratory orphans was to be healthy boys, between the ages of fourteen and seventeen, who would be capable of working on the enormous stations.

The letter he carried in his pocket from Marcus Marriot intrigued him. He walked briskly to the private investigator's office in Dale Street that was situated on the top floor of a tobacconist's shop. He climbed the wooden staircase to a half glass, half wooden door, bearing a brass plate. Marcus Marriot Private Investigator, it announced. He tapped lightly on the door and walked straight in. The smoke filled room almost shrouded the man who sat behind a shabby metal desk.

"Leif, you're back!" Marcus Marriot said. His smile was one of genuine welcome.

The investigator bent down and produced a bottle of gin and a bottle of whisky from the bottom drawer of his desk. The captain held up his hand.

"No," he said. "No drink yet. I want you to explain to me what you meant in your letter by, some progress has been made."

"Sit down man, and calm down," Marcus Marriot insisted. "You're like a taut spring. Relax."

The captain took the only other seat in the room, a threadbare winged armchair that had seen better days.

"Leif. There have been amazing further developments since I last wrote you. I believe I have found your daughter, Lori."

The words knocked the captain sideways. He sat ashen faced, feeling his body trembling.

"Say that again," he asked. He needed to hear it twice before he could allow the words to sink in.

The private investigator rummaged in his drawer again and produced two glasses. He poured a large gin for himself and a good stiff shot of whisky for the captain.

"Here, take this, you're going to need it." He pushed the glass across the desk. The captain knocked it back in one gulp. "I have to tell you, Leif, there's good news and bad news. The good news is, Lori is here in Liverpool. She's not in Australia. The bad news is, she was adopted when she was seven years old."

Marcus Marriot allowed a long silence to follow his bombshell. The two men sat silently staring at each other. The captain felt a pressure building in him. It was like a head of steam searching for an outlet before the eventual explosion. He erupted, flinging his empty glass across the room. It shattered against the wall.

"You're telling me my child has been adopted?" he yelled. "How come? It is not possible. I told the woman at the welfare. I said she was not for adoption. There's no way my child could be adopted without my consent. I am her father." He took a deep breath. "God, I feel as if I've been kicked in the teeth. That fucking department must have known where my child was."

Marcus Marriot produced another glass from the bottom drawer and poured a double. He shunted it across the desk.

"Leif, it is not as simple as that. Have a smoke and a drink and let me explain." He lit the captain's cigarette with a lighter he had taken from a German prisoner of war. It was embossed on the front with a large vulgar Nazi swastika. "The reason your daughter could not be traced was because the name Lori Svenerson was never registered. As a private Dick I can usually get access to information, not exactly obtained illegally, but a few bribes here and there often produces results. I tracked down the woman who had been on duty the day you left Lori. She was a part-time receptionist and retired three weeks after you left your child, so no one has ever spoken to her of that day until I called on her. She's getting on a bit, but she did remember the tall good looking sailor who brought his baby to the office. She even remembered he had a slight accent which she thought might have been Irish or Scottish. She also remembered the man was in a great hurry. She couldn't remember his name at first. I asked if the name Svenerson rang a bell, but she said no. I asked her to think back and imagine the day a sailor came to see her holding a small baby in his arms. If he was in a hurry did he hand the baby straight over to her and was it a boy she held or a girl? She still couldn't remember. I asked if the baby cried when the father left and she immediately registered and said it was a girl and she was fast asleep. She couldn't remember the child's first name but her last name was Stephenson. She said she remembered when she was writing up the file that she didn't know whether it was Stephenson with a V or Stephenson with a ph. I asked her which one she used and she said she was pretty sure it was a ph. I knew then I was on the right track. So ergo, there was no point looking for Svenerson. I had to search for a possible link to Ste...." Captain Svenerson opened his mouth to speak again, but Marcus Marriot flapped his hand to silence him. "Let me finish, my friend. In order to discover anything about children in care one has to apply to the court. Confidentiality and all that! Once again, a great deal of palm greasing got me the results. There were four children called Stephenson in care at the time, all roughly the same age as Lori. However the date of birth in the register for the girl I found and who I believe to be your daughter does not correspond with the date of birth of your child, Lori. There is almost a three week difference. But I know why that is. The woman told me, somewhat reluctantly, that the baby's month of birth was February but she had no date and all little children should have a day to celebrate so she made it the same day as her mother's birthday. So I knew I was looking for a girl called Stephenson with a ph whose birthday was recorded as 3rd February 1944. Now, Leif, I ask you, why wasn't Lori's accurate date of birth ever registered?" Marcus Marriot gave the captain a long quizzical look. "Why was that? It would have been a vital starting point when trying to trace her." The captain slowly shook his head. He was feeling numb. He remained silent. "Leif, come on! What happened on that day when you took Lori to the Welfare Office? Speak up man. Surely you must have completed some documentation."

The captain sighed. Silence fell on the room. He lit a cigarette and sat rhythmically flicking the Ronson lighter on and off. It sounded like the ticking of a primed bomb. He came out of his reverie and spoke.

"Marcus, if I had stayed in that office any longer I would have turned and left with Lori in my arms. What I believed I had to do was breaking me. How would you feel to put your child into a stranger's hands and walk away?"

"I understand," Marcus said.

"No you don't, you can't possibly understand, but I had to get Lori out of Norway," Leif impatiently said. "There was nobody to look after her. Inger's friends cared for Lori, but so many of them were being betrayed by Quislings and executed that I had to do something, so I did, I brought her here. Liverpool was my home port. But I had to get back to my ship. We were due to sail on the next tide. I couldn't take her with me, for God's sake! There was a bloody war on. I had to get out of that room fast, before I changed my mind. I handed Lori over to some old woman and fled." He buried his head in his hands. "Oh God! May my child forgive me."

He felt he was about to crack again and quickly took a large gulp of whisky.

Marcus remained pensively silent and stared into the clear liquid in his glass. He looked up.

"D'you know, Leif, in order to get access to files on kids, you've got to jump through hoops and up your own asshole, and due to the sheer weight of numbers of kids in care at the time, I don't think record keeping was a priority. You talk of the Welfare Officer, as if it were her fault, but I must tell you my friend, you and you alone are responsible for Lori being lost in the system. I know it's a brutal thing for me to say, but you have to acknowledge your part in the tragedy."

"Oh Christ! What have I done, Marcus?" he groaned. "When I left Lori, I wept. But I knew the war was reaching an end and thought as soon as it was over I would immediately collect her. It was only supposed to be for a short time. But I know you're right. The anger I have been venting at the Welfare Department all these years, has been unjustified. I quite honestly don't remember much about what happened in that room when I left Lori. I hadn't slept for two days. Having a baby on board a fishing vessel in a rough sea was a nightmare. The train journey was long and I couldn't sleep much because when Lori was awake she demanded my attention. And I had to be back in the thick of it when I returned to my ship. It's no excuse, but I was an emotional and physical wreck. My gorgeous wife had only just died a horrific death."

"I do understand, my old friend," Marcus gently said. "But let me tell you how I found your child. A ten bob note got me the names I wanted. One Stephenson was a boy, so I ruled him out. Another was a girl, but she was a Stephenson with a V not a ph. The next one, a girl, had been discharged from care back to her mother who had served a term in prison for stealing ration books. Finally, I found a Lowry Stephenson. See the similarity? It doesn't take rocket science to work it out, but I believe that is your daughter. Do you know, my dear friend, eighteen days, that's all it was, that made the difference between Lori being found or staying lost in the system. Think about it. Lowry Stephenson – Lori Svenerson. At some stage with the right date of birth those names may have registered with someone as being very close. But there's nothing we can do about it now. However, further investigation revealed she had been adopted."

"Who by? Where is she?" the captain urgently asked.

"I don't know. As I said previously, she was adopted three years ago."

"I must find her." the captain implored. "To think after all these years you have found my daughter and I can't get near her because she has been adopted. I must find her."

"Leif, you must understand that your child's name will have changed again, probably. The only way you can hope to see her again is to seek access through a sympathetic judge in the Family Division of the court. Even then, nothing is assured."

"What's the name of the judge who handled the adoption, Marcus? If I approached him…"

"Leif, Leif," Marcus cut in, "I don't have access to the Court Records of Adoption. I don't know who the judge was. Go and see the Court's Welfare Officer and see if there's a possibility of an audience with a judge in Chambers."

"Jesus, how much longer can this go on, before I can hold my little girl again?" Captain Leif Svenerson sadly groaned. "Christ, what if I never find her, Marcus? How can I live with myself knowing that my stupidity means I may never see my child again?"

"Never say never, my old Viking friend," Marcus Marriot wisely retorted.

THE TREACHEROUS
HUSBAND

Lou gave up trying to find a school that would accept her errant daughter. She settled on two tutors, instead, who would teach English and maths. The rest of the subjects Lou would manage herself. The dining room became a classroom once again with charts, maps and any work that merited a star, on the walls.

A disordered and sometimes chaotic atmosphere prevailed in Lowry's classroom with Nana prowling from locked door to locked door and rattling them in frustration.

"Why has that silly Irish woman locked me in?" she angrily shouted.

Mrs Murphy's hymns filled the house, with the Hoover playing as her backing orchestra. Jolly liked her singing especially when she sang Rock of Ages. Throwing back his head he would howl like a canine soprano when Mrs Murphy reached the words 'Let me hide myself in Thee.'

"I wish that woman and that damn dog would go and hide somewhere," Mr Archer, the English tutor moaned.

Lowry suffered serious bouts of giggling the more he moaned. He was a short man with a greying ginger moustache and gingery strands of hair on an almost bald head. He had retired from teaching at the Liverpool College, an all-boys school, and seemed somewhat uncomfortable in a house full of women. In his youth he had also been a sports teacher which proved to be a blessing when Nana climbed out of the lounge window into the front garden, out of the gate and set off down the road. Mrs Murphy's screeches of terror interrupted the teacher's lesson on socialist reformers such as Charles Dickens and Charles Kingsley. Lowry's précis of The Water Babies had merited a star.

"Jesus, Mary, Joseph! She's gone out of the lounge window," Mrs Murphy breathlessly said, as she burst through the 'classroom' door. "You'll have to fetch her back, Mr Archer. Hurry up will you, before she gets to the main road. Go on, you best be after her. I can't run I'm too old. Anyway she'll only hit me."

Nana hit Mr Archer instead.

He seemed very relieved when it was time for him to leave, yet he, and Miss Roberts, the maths teacher, continued teaching Lowry for two years. She was now a fluent reader and owed so much to Kenneth Grahame's little black mole who had stuck his nose out of a dark tunnel to face the uncertainties of a new life.

Throughout the winter, each Saturday from ten o'clock to two thirty, Lou's seven slow readers arrived for reading practice. Lowry was Lou's trusted helper and she took her responsibilities seriously. The helper kept guard on the 'classroom' door with bribes.

"Nana, if you go back in the lounge I'll bring you a chocolate digestive biscuit and a nice cup of tea."

It was labour intensive. Nana could devour a whole packet of chocolate biscuits in one reading session.

The twelve o'clock march, with Jolly on a lead, led Lowry to the chip shop to buy ten portions of chips to make into chip butties for everyone. On returning home with her bags of chips, Lowry was surprised to see a police car outside the open front door. Two officers stood in the hall looking bemused as Nana sounded off.

"She keeps stealing other women's children," she ranted, pointing angrily at Lou. "We haven't got enough room for all these strays," she moaned. "They'll eat us out of house and home."

"Mother will you go back into the lounge and let me explain to these officers why I have seven of my schoolchildren here," Lou pleaded. Nana refused to move. "Lowry keep the children in the dining room please and give them their chips out of the paper." Lou turned her attention on the officers. "Can you tell me why you are here? I don't understand what......"

"We received a call from this address, Madam, from someone claiming children were being held here," one officer explained.

"Good God, Mother!" Lou exploded. "You rang the police, you interfering old woman. The children's parents will be picking them up at two thirty as well you know. The boys and girls are simply having extra reading coaching and have been doing so for weeks. I will not let them go up into the Junior School unable to read properly. The poor little things won't stand a chance. Don't you ever ring the police again. Do you hear me?"

"Why are we feeding them all, then?" Nana shouted. "You're going senile, Louise. How many more ragamuffins are you going to bring into this house? I've got used to having that one here," the old lady protested, pointing a dagger-like finger at Lowry, "but I'm not putting up with any more of them."

The officers left, suggesting that a phone lock might help.

Lowry had grown very fond of Nutty Nana. She would hold the old lady's hand as she walked her to the local shop for a bag of Everton mints. Sometimes the trips to the shops could be embarrassing when Nana rudely pulled tongues at the people she didn't like the look of.

But the old lady's confusion was worsening as she searched for her husband who had been dead for fifteen years.

"He's got another woman, the rat," she shouted. "I've searched the wardrobe and all his clothes have gone. He's living with some harlot."

Lou repeatedly and patiently explained to the confused old lady that her husband was dead. Occasionally the message registered.

"Why didn't you tell me, he was dead, you silly woman? I would have gone to his funeral," Nana protested angrily.

"You did go to his funeral, Mother. We….."

"No I didn't, you stupid girl," she bellowed at Lou. "Don't you think I would remember going to my own husband's funeral? Wait 'til I get my hands on the philandering rat."

Walks to the park with Nana and Jolly were a nightmare for Lou and a giggle for Lowry. Every male became Nana's treacherous husband.

"So I've caught you with your harlot, you cheating rat," she told an elderly man who strolled with his wife round the rose beds. Nana waved her fist at the astonished woman. "You jezebel!" she shouted.

The elderly couple rushed off as fast as their aging legs would allow.

The park keeper had been targeted so many times he took to hiding behind trees and bushes as soon as he caught sight of Nana, sending Lowry into fits of laughter. Walks to the park came to an end. Nana finally decided 'the silly Irish woman had stolen her husband.' She chased Mrs Murphy round the house with Lou's Slazenger tennis racquet so many times, that the terrified woman spent most of her time locked in the downstairs lavatory until the sound of Nana's snoring from the lounge arm chair enabled her to escape.

Lou's treasure understandably left. She was nearly seventy years old.

With no-one to care for the old lady during school time, she was finally admitted to an old people's home where she died four weeks later. It devastated Lou and consumed her with guilt. Lowry, too, felt the loss of a character that had, in her sweet senility, provided so much harmless entertainment.

Much to Lou's relief the 'powers that be' in the Education Department, decided Lowry could fit back into main stream schooling.

The co-educational school segregated the girls and boys for certain lessons much to Lowry's annoyance. She resented sitting in a class designed to teach her the art of being a dutiful wife when the boys went to woodwork classes. Lowry had pet mice, a hamster, a guinea pig, a terrapin and a large green glass bowl full of stick insects that Lou hated. It seemed to her it would be more appropriate for her to make wooden animal cages. But a girl's education required her to be conditioned to be a subservient woman and learn to darn her husband's socks and wash snot from his handkerchief by first soaking it in cold salt water. Lou and her daughter had no men's handkerchiefs in the house, so two were bought and filled with nasal discharge the night before the 'home making' lesson. There was even a special way of folding the square thing when ironing it making it easy for the husband to flamboyantly pull the handkerchief from his breast pocket and open it with an effeminate flick of the wrist. How pathetic, Lowry grumbled.

She also had to learn to set a tray properly with a starched and ironed tray cloth in case the husband fell ill. With so much starch in her tray cloth the hot iron reduced it to a piece of plasterboard.

"Girls, next week I want you to bring in a nice firm tomato that we will stuff with forcemeat," the teacher instructed.

Lowry, who never paid any attention to the lesson, was astounded. She raised her hand.

"Yes. Lowry, you have a question?" the teacher said.

"Miss, where do you get horse meat from? They don't sell it at our butcher's. Anyway, I don't think it's right to eat horses."

The class giggled.

"Are you trying to be the class clown, Lowry Stuart?" the teacher bellowed. "I said, forcemeat, not horse meat. Now shut up."

Lowry sat down and studied Miss Evans, who, from her title, didn't even have a husband with snotty handkerchiefs and holey socks. The short plump woman with a round red face had come out of retirement to help cover the shortage of teachers. Lowry suppressed a giggle when she realised that the teacher's tubby body, red cardigan and round red face made her look decidedly like a stuffed tomato.

"Are you listening to me girls?" teacher said, surveying the room. "I also want you to bring a nice piece of beef so we can make beef tea as nourishment for an invalid."

Next lesson, Lowry stuffed a tomato and made beef tea. Her stuffed tomato burst in oven and unstuffed itself leaving the skin burnt to the bottom of the baking tray and the tomato's contents flattened into a revolting looking cow pat. The teacher marked her work as two out of ten, but that was for putting the oven on. But Lowry had never known anything so stupid as to boil 'a nice piece of beef,' drink the insipid juice and throw the meat away. She raised her hand to attract the teacher's attention.

"Yes Lowry," the teacher said.

"Miss, d'you think I could take the bits of beef home for my dog? It's a shame to waste it. My nana always said it was a crime for good food go to waste."

"The object of boiling the meat, was to extract all the nutriments so that there is no goodness left in it, or were you not listening, as usual?" the teacher grumbled, "But if you wish to collect the left- overs for your dog, then do it at the end of the lesson."

"Thank-you Miss, that's very kind of you. Jolly will really appreciate it. I'll have to mince it because he's getting old now and his teeth...."

"Yes, yes, just sit down will you," the teacher impatiently said.

"But can I ask one more question please?"

"What is it?" the teacher asked with even more exasperation in her voice.

"Well, I don't understand why the boys can't learn to darn their own socks and wash their own hankies and stuff their own tomatoes. Why just us girls?"

"All I can say, Lowry Stuart, is, I sympathise with any young man you may marry," she shouted. "Now sit down and shut up."

"I'm never getting married, Miss," Lowry continued to argue.

"Well that's a lucky escape for any bachelor, young lady. NOW SIT DOWN," she bellowed.

Despite her grudging approach to the study of domesticity, Lowry remained a happy pupil and stuffed tomatoes and beef tea might come in handy when she was a nurse.

THE JUDGEMENT

The captain and Marcus Marriot sat together on a bench at the Pier Head. They stared in silence at the constantly moving River Mersey that forever made its way to Liverpool Bay then changed its mind and returned. Across the water, the myriad of lights from Birkenhead flickered in the atmosphere like a million candles on God's birthday cake.

"It must have been a terrible blow, Leif," Marcus said, his loud voice breaking into the tranquillity of the night.

"It was, but I think I half expected it. It was a bitter disappointment, nevertheless," the captain answered. "I seem to be thwarted whichever way I turn. I did all the necessary by completing a Notice of Rescission for the adoption to be withdrawn. You see, Marcus, I believed as the natural parent, that my consent was necessary for Lori's adoption. And yes, that is the case, but if more than two years have passed since the adoption the application is no longer valid. I didn't even see a judge. I saw the Clerk of the Court."

The two men continued silently to finish their cigarettes. Marcus flicked his lit stub end into the Mersey. It fizzled out.

"I guess they have to think only of what's best for the child." he said. "I suppose the court believes Lori has had enough disruption in her young life."

"Exactly so," Captain Svenerson said. "She's probably happily settled. She doesn't know me or even know of me. It's too late. I would unsettle her."

"Ah ha," Marcus grunted.

The captain's cigarette end followed Marcus's to a watery extinction. He watched it bob about and then spoke.

"The clerk was very understanding and very sympathetic when I explained the mix up and my part in it. However he made it pointedly clear that the child's welfare was of paramount importance and I was to make no contact or even try to find out her whereabouts while Lori is a minor. I told him it was inhuman of them to prevent me seeing my child and he simply said that if I tried to see her they would serve me with an injunction to stop me. I have to wait until she reaches the age of twenty one before I can do anything. Even then, Marcus, after all that time, she probably won't want to know me."

"You don't know that, my friend," Marcus responded. "Don't start feeling sorry for yourself. At least Lori is not living in an institution?"

"I know, I know," the captain answered. "If she hadn't been adopted, she could have ended up as part of a shipment to Australia. I understand they have also sent these poor kids to New Zealand and Canada as well. It's unbelievable what this country is doing. It borders on criminal. It's child trafficking. It's tragic enough that these kids have no family to call their own, but the poor creatures haven't even got a Country to call their own because they've been booted out of it. It's downright inhuman, Marcus. It doesn't bear thinking of. Lori deserves to be happy. I hope she is, but I long to see her face and see how she's grown. I feel so guilty about abandoning her. I lie awake at night thinking how it could have been if I had only given that welfare woman the details she should have had. My little girl would belong to me again, not have some other man as her father."

"For God's sake, Leif," Marcus impatiently said. "Stop beating yourself up. You didn't abandon her. She had no mother. You were fighting a vicious war. You had no one in Norway to look after her. What bloody choice did you have? But you're right, it would never have happened if you had only given…."

"'I know, I know," the captain impatiently interrupted. "Don't you think I bloody well know? I might just as well have abandoned her. One day I will find my little elskling and I hope to God when I do, she will forgive me."

Marcus placed his arm across his friends shoulder.

"Come on, me old Viking. Let's get to the Exchange before they call last orders. I believe one day soon you will see Lori again. I can feel it in my gin soaked bones."

Were the fates smiling that night on the Pier Head and Marcus Marriot's gin soaked bones the captain wondered?

THE DRAGON

Lowry never lost her determination to be a nurse. At the age of fourteen she entered college to do a four year pre-nursing course. Her time there, with girls of like mind, passed quickly. Textbooks, anatomical diagrams and lectures taught her the rudimentary workings of the human body. Her large circle of friends and she were wild, happy and very loyal. They liked to show off their knowledge of medical terminology on the top deck of a bus.

"How's your epididymis today, darling?" a standard question to any embarrassed young male, who happened to travel the same route.

Learning about the male reproductive system had been one of the most fascinating lectures and the word epididymis the cause of much amusement. The girls even found the term pollux rigidus and hallux rigidus something to giggle about even though it only meant a stiff thumb and a stiff big toe. And a cross section diagram of an erect penis had sent the girls into unbelievable shock. They had been somewhat disappointed that it had only been a diagram and not a picture of the real thing.

Patching holes in linen sheets was a complete waste of time. When were nurses going to get the time to mend hospital sheets? Nevertheless, the sewing teacher was kind enough to write in Lowry's college report, 'good on the whole.'

The girls passed their State Preliminary Nursing Examinations and left college to attend a Residential School for further practical training.

Bed-making, bandaging, bed baths, enemas, pressure points, temperatures, blood pressure, all the possible practical activities to face a new nurse were taught in the mornings. Grapefruits were used to teach how to give an injection. With so much water pumped into them the poor things exploded under the pressure. The afternoons were spent in the lecture rooms with a gormless skeleton and an aging Nursing Tutor.

Lowry had put the bogeyman and the devil behind her, but her first encounter with Matron had her believe she now faced another demon in the form of a dragon.

Matron sat behind her polished desk as the new Student Nurses stood nervously before her.

"Nurses," she began. "You have chosen the most honourable calling any young woman can enter. With diligence and hard work you will bring credit upon yourselves and to the good name of my teaching hospital. Remember, this is a noble profession." She paused to let the information sink in. "I will now collect your birth certificates. They will be returned to you in a few days." The girls rooted in their bags and fumbled for the documents. She studied them briefly until coming across Lowry's. "This is not a birth certificate."

Lowry noted the edge to her voice and bravely stepped forward.

"No Matron, it's an adoption certificate," she told her, "but it has got my birthday on it and I haven't got anything else."

Matron studied the paper, interrupting her reading to look the young student nurse up and down. Lowry stared at the elaborate lacy white hat, rather than into Matron's cold blue eyes that could undoubtedly turn water to stone. Matron's words were clear and brooked no discussion.

"My letter of acceptance to you required that you bring your birth certificate. If I had wanted details of your adoption I would have asked for them." Lowry blushed with embarrassment and humiliation as Matron continued to stare at her with her cold eyes. "Without a birth certificate we cannot arrange for you to receive your salary. If you want to be paid, then I suggest you do something speedily to acquire the necessary document."

"But Matron……."

Her piercing gaze sliced through Lowry like a scalpel.

"Home Sister will escort you to the nurses' home," Matron continued. "Please read the rules that you will find pinned to your bedroom door."

With a wave of her pen the student nurses were dismissed.

Home Sister looked ninety years old. She had a sweet smile and what appeared to be a gentle manner. The group followed her shuffling gait up three flights of stairs to attic bedrooms. Her laboured breathing indicated that she wouldn't be visiting the attic too often, which might be a blessing, Lowry thought.

Helen and Lowry were pleased to see that they had been allocated rooms next door to each other. They had been friends for four years. They treasured each other's friendship. Helen was the only child of late middle-aged parents. After waiting fifteen years her parents were blessed with a daughter. They adored her. Lowry was sometimes a little envious of her friend who had a lovely, chubby, cuddly dad. Helen's laughing brown eyes were set in a round cheerful face with deep dimples either side of her mouth. She had the sweet face of a Mabel Lucy Atwell baby. She hated her naturally curly hair. Every morning she plastered it with hair cream, but by mid-day her curls were back. Nothing bothered Helen. A shrug of her broad shoulders dismissed her cares. Her deep, rumbling infectious laugh came from her wobbly belly. She coped with a great deal of teasing about her size, but her generous nature and ample arms were a wonderful source of strength against the despots who wrote the rules and then applied them with a total disregard for their appropriateness. Helen never broke the rules herself. She secretly cocked a snook and conformed.

Lowry's tiny attic bedroom, just like the others, had brown linoleum on the floor and green and cream walls. It offered much the same welcome as Matron – bleak and uninspiring. Next to the door, upon which hung the 'Rules,' was a standard hospital bed. To Lowry's horror a spare grey army blanket had been folded onto the pillow. No way was she covering herself with something that reminded her of a nun's habit. She slung it in the bottom of the wardrobe where she found her nurse's uniforms all neatly arranged on hangers and previously measured for size - three pale blue dresses, six white bib aprons and six squares of white material to be pleated and made into hats with tiny hat pins. A small chest of drawers and a table and chair completed the austere décor.

"Do not fraternise in one another's bedrooms," Home Sister's voice called from the landing. "The hospital will not take responsibility for theft. I shall leave you to unpack your belongings. No posters on the walls and no wirelesses in your rooms. And nurses, please remember that gentlemen are not allowed in the nurses' home."

Home Sister shuffled away. The group assembled on the landing when the sound of shuffling died away.

"Has everybody else been assigned a prison cell?" Lowry asked. "Or is it just me?"

"Throw some cushions around and put a mat by the bed. They surely can't complain about that," practical Trish suggested.

The girls returned to their rooms to unpack until the sound of jangling keys alerted them to Home Sister's return.

The morning bell rattled the nurses awake at six o'clock next morning. Lowry hurriedly showered in the freezing communal shower room and slipped into her crisp uniform. Breakfast was out of the question. Pandemonium filled the canteen and the queue for food so long she would never have made it onto the ward on time.

At seven o'clock she entered a circular ward to face thirty three sick men on Male Medical. Her morning activities centred round the sluice room with bedpans, urine bottles and sputum mugs for company. One patient's bowel problem required her to extract a sample of his stool with a spatula and poke it into a specimen pot and label it for the laboratory. They were looking for occult blood. She never saw any. She had her eyes closed throughout the exercise. But then she wouldn't have seen it, if it was occult, she realised.

All patients used a bedpan at some stage of the day. No one was allowed out of bed. Fortunately for Lowry, only a handful of patients had bronchial problems. Emptying the metal sputum mugs was a nightmare for her as viscose stalactites of phlegm refused to leave the mug. The stalactites just grew longer and longer. Ward Sister complained that Nurse Stuart was spending too long in the sluice room. She seemed unaware that it wasn't from choice. Mercifully, bowels settled down in the afternoon. This gave Lowry more time with the patients. She quickly learned that many grown men were afraid when illness debilitated them. Embarrassed when they accidently soiled their bed sheets and humiliated when their dentures were removed. Medicines could relieve physical distress, but could not relieve the vulnerable feelings of a patient when confined to a bed and at the mercy of a student nurse just out of training college. The men were happy to discuss their ailments, in fact some of them talked of nothing else. Lowry confessed to being ignorant of most of the conditions they described.

"What's your problem?" she asked a cheerful scouser.

"The quacks call it tabes dorsalis or locomotor ataxia" he knowledgably explained.

"What the heck's that?"

"It's syphilitic myelopathy, you see, me love. Me legs are becoming useless. I have penicillin for it and something for the pain in me back."

Lowry was amazed by his command of medical terminology. She thought she was clever enough knowing what an epididymis was.

"Oh, I am sorry to hear that," Lowry sincerely told him.

He grinned cheekily.

"Don't be sorry, darlin,' I've had me fun. Syphilis is one of the perils of being a sailor."

She approached an old man with thin wispy grey hair.

"Hello," she said. "Why are you in hospital?"

He looked blankly at her and Lowry realised he was deaf. She repeated the question more loudly and he understood, smiling as he comprehended her query. He had three brown teeth in his head, two at the bottom and one at the top that looked like rusty nails.

"It's me heart, Nurse," he explained. "I did have stable vagina, but it's gone unstable."

Lowry giggled and wondered what he was doing on a male ward with an unstable vagina. She walked to the end of his bed and read the clipboard notes. It was the patient's angina that had gone unstable, not his vagina. A voice in the next bed invited Lowry to see his leg ulcers.

"Them's absolute beauts," he proudly told her.

"Please don't touch your dressings," she said, as he struggled to pull the tightly tucked bedding off himself. "I'll see them next time you have them dressed."

"Well, you're in for a rare sight, Nurse," he said, grinning smugly.

Lowry walked off to the kitchen hardly able to contain her pleasure at the thought of a rare sight of suppurating leg ulcers.

Ward gossip acknowledged Sister to be a battle-axe who ruled her empire with bustling efficiency and an obsession for order and neatness. Lowry steered clear of Sister's axe on her first day, mostly doing tasks that required little or no supervision.

Sister was bossy and buxom with most of her weight resting on her stern. Lowry found it difficult to guess her age, but believed she may have done some of her training with Florence in the Crimea. Sister and Lowry came together at five o'clock to 'do beds,' straightening rubber sheets and pulling the draw sheets under the backsides of the patients to give them a fresh piece upon which to sit.

"You have been taught to do hospital corners, I hope," Sister queried.

"Yes Sister."

"Well mine are knife-edged."

"Yes Sister."

They raced round the beds, cornering the counterpanes so tightly as to almost stop the circulation in the patient's feet. A sense of urgency developed. Flowers were whisked off lockers and dumped in the sluice room. Ashtrays were emptied and placed in locker drawers. Books and newspapers were hidden in locker cupboards. Water jugs were filled so that each contained the exact same amount of water. Records on clipboards were tidied into neat bundles. Something momentous was about to happen, Lowry thought. Even the patients who could prop themselves up were sitting to attention. Eventually a third year nurse, who had been running in and out of the ward to peer up the corridor, returned and announced, 'she's coming.' Lowry joined the end of line that had arranged itself in order of seniority.

The ward fell silent. The doors opened. Matron sailed in, accompanied by an entourage of two woman, similarly dressed, but obviously the underlings. Each held open a door to allow her to enter. Ward Sister greeted her warmly before chaperoning her to the patients. Matron and Sister cruised past the beds like Mersey Docks and Harbour Board tug boats. Matron smiled and nodded her head. Each man smiled and nodded back. Matron reached the doors again, stopped, turned and graciously wished the patients 'goodnight.' Lowry had a strong urge to curtsey. The presence had gone and the ward immediately filled with noise again. Hard as Lowry tried, she never felt comfortable with the nightly ritual. There was something almost religious about it and she had no time for anything hallowed.

The young nurse approached the ward with more confidence the next morning. An emergency admission had arrived overnight. He had suffered a stroke leaving him unable to see or speak. His face had twisted into a grimace of torment, but he could hear Lowry and touch her with his one effective hand. Lowry's duties were to attend him. After reading the notes on the end of the bed she approached the patient to feed him his breakfast porridge.

"Hello, I'm Lowry. Can I call you Albert?"

The patient struggled to speak, the noises were garbled and unintelligible. Tucking a towel under his chin, she spooned some gruel into his half paralysed mouth. It dribbled out again. She scraped it from his chin and re-introduced it to his mouth

"I'm so sorry," she told him, regretting the indignity she was putting him through, "but I'm new at this." Porridge fell once again onto the towel. "Bloody hell, you'll starve at this rate."

It dawned on her that Albert couldn't see the spoon as it neared his mouth, consequently he kept opening and closing it like a little fledgling sparrow eager for a maggot.

"Albert when I say spoon approaching, open your mouth as best you can and I'll make sure you don't go hungry."

Albert's hand banged onto the counterpane.

"What does that mean? Are you annoyed with me?"

He banged his hand again. Lowry grabbed it firmly.

"Albert, if I hold your hand, will you squeeze mine, once for yes and twice for no?" He squeezed once. "Brilliant, we're going to work well together," she told him. "Do you mind if I call you Albert?" He squeezed twice.

Nurse Stuart managed to get some nourishment into him as they continued their lopsided conversation.

"Am I going too quickly for you, Albert?" Two squeezes. "Spoon approaching!" The misshapen mouth opened. "When I get a spare moment, would you like me to read to you?" One squeeze. "Albert, I wish you could see your chin. It looks like it's just been pebble-dashed."

His hand fluttered in Lowry's and she knew he was laughing. She wiped his chin before the mixture set like concrete. The Ward Orderly appeared with her trolley.

"Are you going to be there all morning?" she officiously asked Lowry. "There's a stack of dishes to collect."

"I'll be here as long as it takes Albert to finish his breakfast," Lowry sharply retorted.

The voice of Sister interrupted the squabble.

"Nurse Stuart, you will refer to each patient by his title, not his Christian name," she shouted.

"I asked his permission first, Sister. He told me he doesn't mind if I call him Albert."

Her face and voice were contemptuous.

"Go and help with the dishes and don't talk nonsense. The man cannot speak."

She sailed away into her office as Lowry leaned over and whispered to her patient.

"I reckon Sister needs an enema Albert. Constipation is making her grumpy. But it won't be warm soapy water I'll shove up her backside, it'll be a colony of red ants."

Albert enthusiastically banged his hand on the bed.

Filling the daily questionnaire on the patient's chart sheet made Lowry feel very professional as she approached each bed, took temperatures and pulses and asked the routine questions. Passed urine? – tick. BO? Not all the patients admitted to having

BO, but it seemed a strange question to be asking. After completing her task she returned to Staff Nurse for her next job.

"Staff Nurse, what's the significance of asking the patients if they have body odour?" she asked. "Some said yes and some said no."

"What are you on about, honey?" Staff Nurse asked, looking puzzled.

"On the charts" Lowry explained. "There's a column that says, BO."

Staff Nurse opened her mouth and emitted raucous laughter.

"Bowels open, Nurse! Bowels Open! That's what it means." She put her arm around Lowry's shoulder and gave her a friendly hug. "Now come and help me change Mr Pritchard's colostomy bag. He's looking a bit sore."

Poor Mr Pritchard had had a colostomy bag for years, but he had been admitted with bronchitis. His chesty cough, was not only filling the sputum mug, but the effort of coughing was filling his colostomy bag at the same time.

During the next week Lowry spent any spare moment at Albert's bedside. She had never shaved a man in her life, but after three attempts she proudly announced to Albert that his face looked just like a baby's bum. She read The Liverpool Daily Post to him. He particularly liked her to read the deaths column. It seemed to cheer him up to know he was still outliving those who had died. A win for Liverpool Football Club and Shankly's Red Army had his good arm banging on the bed with excitement.

Albert had a great sense of humour. He became Lowry's confidant, clutching her hand tightly as she whispered her opinions of Ward Sister. There were many people in her short life to whom she had never said goodbye. Albert was one of them. He died one night from a massive cerebrovascular accident and his body had gone next morning. She struggled with her sadness for most of the day.

According to Staff Nurse it was best to keep out of Sister's way and always look busy. Lowry trusted and admired 'staff.' Her easy going manner and sense of humour never interfered with her nursing skills, but they made for a cheerful ward when she took over while Sister had a day off.

Each member of the attic gang came off duty with some goodies they had purloined from the ward kitchens. They pooled food and shared the cigarettes the patients gave Lowry as she went round the beds to say goodnight. Almost every brand manufactured was tried and tested by the novitiate smokers. They took turns to play hostess to prevent the smoke permeating the atmosphere too much. Laughter inebriated them. They exchanged gory stories with crude embellishments. Helen was unusually quiet as they sat in Lowry's dingy bedroom.

"What's up, Hel? It's not like you to be miserable," Lowry asked her.

"I've had a bloody awful day and I could kick myself for being so stupid," she replied. Her face took on a pained expression. "Promise not to laugh when I tell you, but Sister told me to prep the woman in bed six because she was scheduled to have her hysterectomy this morning. I miscounted and shaved the pubic hair off the woman in bed seven instead." The delirious laughter caused uproar. It took some time before she could speak again. "It's not funny," she bleated. "The woman in bed seven fumed at the indignity of it all. Sister glowered at me most of the day and the other nurses just giggled every time they saw me."

Lowry tried comforting her miserable friend.

"Come on, Hel, it can't be that serious, they'll grow again. Anyway, why didn't the woman say something?"

"Oh, she did." Helen replied. "But I told her I was only doing what Sister had asked me to do and you don't argue with Sister. Then the woman said she hated hospitals because nobody tells the patients anything." The giggles erupted again. "You lot wouldn't be laughing, if it had been you. It was when the woman said it was stupid because she'd only come in for tests and was going home the next day that I realised my mistake. When I counted the beds again it was obvious I'd shaved the wrong one, but I'd almost finished her by then." Helen stared sadly into space. "Sister spent all day grovelling to the woman and giving me the shitty jobs." A slow smile appeared on Helen's face. "What the heck, girls! You'll never guess what the woman's name is. It's Mrs Bristles." The girls collapsed with laughter again. "Only joking," Helen laughed.

The attic gang's main topic of conversation centred round sex. Most of them were pretty ignorant of the mechanics of sex. They all knew how fish reproduced. Mrs Fish laid her eggs and Mr Fish squirted over the top of them. Not much fun in that, but human sex was a taboo subject on the school curriculum. Pam, who was affectionately known as Ginger Snap because of her orange red hair, boastfully announced that she'd done 'it,' standing up against the bins in the jigger behind her house. She couldn't remember much about the event, apart from the fact that it was a bit of a fumble and over very quickly.

"Didn't the earth move for you, Pam? It's supposed to," Helen asked her.

"No, nothing moved, apart from the bin I was leaning on," Pam replied. "But anyway, guess what I had to do today to a man who'd had his haemorrhoids operated on?"

"What?" the room loudly chorused.

"I had to pass a greasy flatus tube very carefully into his rectum because he was in agony with trapped wind."

"Did you hold your nose and make a quick getaway, Pam?" Tricia laughed.

"No, you daft wazzock," she retorted. "I felt sorry for him. He was dreading his first poo. Mr Fish, his Consultant Surgeon, told him it would be like shitting a hedgehog."

"Did you say Mr Fish was his Consultant Sturgeon?" Lowry chuckled.

The young nurses were not naturally insensitive to the needs of their patients, but off-duty time was a time to share stories and off-load some of the distressing conditions they encountered on the wards.

The girls once again returned to the subject of sex. Lowry had had quite a few boyfriends that she'd met at the local youth club. They were all clumsy gropers, but soon learned when going out with her, that nobody groped her, clumsily or otherwise. She didn't mind holding hands or rock 'n rolling on the dance floor, but inexperienced adolescent French kissing had her running to the nearest tap for a mouth wash.

Ben was different. He was a medical student. Lowry and he met on the ward as the Prof went from bed to bed with his little flock of fledgling doctors. They all wore a status symbol white coat and a stethoscope around their necks like a clinical crucifix. Ben repeatedly winked at Lowry, who initially thought him a cocky upstart. He was, however, more mature than the boys she had been used to, even though he had a cheerful baby face. His thick mop of black hair, was swept across the left side of his forehead, but his eyes were the darkest moody brown. Eventually a mutual attraction developed and they began dating.

Home Sister guarded her newest student nurses like a mother hen, making it difficult to sneak out of the nurse's home. She always hovered by the front door.

"Are you going out again, Nurse Stuart?" she enquired.

"Yes, Sister, I'm dashing home to see my mother. She's not feeling too well."

"Well don't forget to sign out and be back to sign in again by ten thirty."

"Yes Sister."

A couple of seconds later Lowry would jump into Ben's parked car.

Her relationship with Ben became the subject of much interest amongst the attic gang. They were not bothered by the finer points of Ben's and Lowry's conversations, they just wanted to know whether they'd done 'it.'

'It' happened at Ben's birthday bash in his three roomed flat at the top of a house in Sefton Park that was rented to students. Lowry had been invited, but the idea of having to leave the party to sign back in before it had even warmed up, prompted her to ask Helen to cover for her.

"Please Helen, would you sign me in and leave the downstairs lounge window unlocked so that I can climb back in?"

"Good God, Lowry. What if you're caught?" Helen fearfully asked.

"I won't be, 'cos I was sneaking around in the dark when I was about four or five years old," Lowry cockily replied.

The tiny, sparsely furnished flat was home to numerous medical text books, dilapidated furniture and a skeleton. The skeleton stood in the corner dominating the room. Attempts had been made to bestow upon her an appearance of voluptuous sexiness. The bony ribcage looked particularly unsexy dressed in a pink frilly bra. Each double D cup had been stuffed to capacity with hospital cotton wool. A pair of scanty pink frilly knickers modestly covered the pelvic girdle. A pair of sunglasses hid the empty eye sockets and two unopened condoms hung like earrings either side of the gruesome creature's head. Her name was Busty Bonaparte. The lounge overlooked the beautiful park with its big glass palm house. In the corner was a small kitchen with a gas cooker a sink and small cupboard. The bathroom was nothing more than an oversized laundry basket with clothes, towels and socks littering the floor. The bedroom with its single bed was not much bigger than a shoe box.

Lowry surveyed the assembled guests and was surprised to see Staff from her ward drinking a bottle of beer.

"Hi Lowry!" she shouted across the room. "I didn't expect to see you here. How did you manage to escape the clutches of Home Sister?"

"By subterfuge," Lowry shouted back. "But I wasn't here, remember. You didn't see me."

"Course not! I'm as blind as a bat after a few bevies," she said, waving her bottle at Lowry.

Lowry bravely tried a bottle of beer. The smell seemed bad enough, but it tasted like she imagined liquid manure would taste. She finally settled on a gin fizz which seriously affected her inhibitions. She was game for anything as were most of the nurses and medical students who cavorted unashamedly round the room. Her slow smooch and prolonged kisses with Ben left her weak at the knees. She didn't think of a mouth wash - it was all so sweet. Neither of them remembered ending up in his bedroom. They didn't notice the chill in the room or the gossamer canopies a spider had woven across the ceiling.

Lowry may have never done 'it,' and she was quite keen to because something wonderful was about to happen. But how do you do it when you've never done it before? She felt awkward. Should she take off her clothes and lie on the bed? She had never taken off her clothes in front of a man. This was supposed to be a romantic episode but her inexperience left her feeling gauche and stupid.

"Ben," she coyly said. "I've never done this before and it's not as if I don't want to, but I haven't a clue what I'm supposed to do apart from take my drawers off."

"Well that's a good start," he laughed. "If you're absolutely sure, then I promise I will be gentle. But you don't have to take anything off, I can do that."

Ben placed one arm around Lowry's back and the other behind her knees and gently lifted her onto the bed. Slowly and seductively her clothes were removed. It was obvious to Lowry that he'd done this before. She stared in horror at the naked man in front of her. The cross section diagram of an erect penis had been shocking enough, but it was a paltry little gadget compared to the real thing. Lowry gritted her teeth and awaited the onslaught.

They did 'it' in a single bed on a sheet that hadn't been near a laundry for weeks. Lowry, like the rest of humankind, believed that there came a point in the sexual antics of homo sapiens when the earth moved. It obviously moved for Ben, if his grunts were anything to go by, but for Lowry the earth didn't even twitch. She felt sore and wondered what all the bullshit was about.

At two thirty she and Ben sneaked their way to the back of the nurse's home. Slowly and quietly the window eased open. 'Thanks Helen!' Lowry whispered. With a shove from Ben she slid over the sill into the pitch black room.

"God, it's dark in here," she announced. "I hate the dark. God it's so dark."

"Here take my lighter and for Pete's sake don't get caught," Ben said.

They dithered at the window with one kiss after another. Then Ben was gone. Lowry heard his noisy engine disappear into the night. She quietly shut the window and tiptoed to the door. Gingerly turning the doorknob, she pulled. The door refused to budge. She tugged harder, but it remained closed.

"Oh my God, the bloody things locked."

She now knew why Home Sister carried her bunch of jangling keys. They were to lock everybody in and everybody out. Her eyes were beginning to adjust to the dark. She could make out the positioning of the furniture. One course of action remained – stay put till morning. She flicked Ben's lighter. The little flame directed her to the settee that she pushed closer to the wall. Alcohol and frustration had activated her bladder. She carefully watered the rubber plant in the corner and prayed the thing would be alive in the morning. Settling on the floor behind the settee, Lowry slept fitfully for what was left of the night.

The sound of a key in the lock alerted her next morning. She froze. The noise of her breathing seemed to echo through the back of the settee. 'Why do I get myself into these situations?' she wondered. The continuing silence gave her the courage to peer round the end of the settee. The door stood wide open onto an empty room. Without her uniform, she would look conspicuous. She crawled from behind the settee and cautiously peeped round the door - not a soul in sight. "Run girl, run. It's now or never," she told herself, in desperation. Her legs flew up two flights of stairs without stopping. She was about to fly up the third flight when the sound of laboured breathing and the jangle of keys alerted her to danger. Home Sister was on her way down. Lowry sped along the corridor. A second year nurse's bedroom door stood ajar. She bolted inside. The room was empty.

"I'll just fetch my cape and meet you in the canteen," a strong Irish accent shouted.

Thinking on her feet, Lowry dived for the bed and rolled beneath it. Two feet dressed in black Oxford brogues and two ankles dressed in black stockings appeared at her eye level. Eventually the second year nurse finished rummaging in her wardrobe and the feet and ankles disappeared from view. The door shut with a click. It was then that her heart sank. She heard the sound of a key turning. Lowry never bothered to lock her door. She had nothing of any value and anyway she trusted her gang. Looking around the room, she realised that this daft female had nothing of any value either.

"So why lock me in, you stupid cow?" she loudly muttered.

'Why the hell did I go to that effing party?' she angrily wondered. It wasn't as if she had enjoyed the sex, or sleeping behind the settee in the lounge. Now, here she was, locked in somebody else's bedroom with a wooden crucifix on the wall and a statue of Mary on the window sill. Was this Lowry's day of reckoning for her lack of humility and obedience?

She sat on the edge of the bed and surveyed the room. Unlike her room this one was neat and tidy with everything in its rightful place.

"Freud would love this girl," she mumbled. "She's anal retentive. God! She's even got her own polished knife and fork sitting on a white napkin on her table."

A bolt of brilliance flashed through Lowry's head. She walked to the door and studied the lock. Four screws held it in place. As she picked up the knife, she was aware of Mary's eyes following her round the room. She turned the statue around.

"There you go," she casually said. "You can look out of the window for a change."

The first brass screw proved stubborn, but gritted teeth and determination got the screw slowly turning. Within ten minutes, Lowry had the lock in her hand. The door opened. She placed the lock carefully on the floor behind the door in the hope that the occupant would think it had fallen off. Placing the knife back on the neatly folded napkin, she noticed she had buckled the tip of the blade.

"Shit," she murmured.

She walked to the window and turned the statue of Mary so it faced the table and the bent knife.

"See if, by some miracle, you can straighten that knife, please Mary."

She pulled the door behind her so it was almost shut. The corridor was empty. Lowry made it to her room gasping for breath, relieved at the sight of a frantic Helen.

"Where the bloody hell have you been?" Helen scolded. "We all stayed up 'til after midnight."

Lowry removed the pillow from her bed that had served as a sleeping lump.

"So Home Sister didn't come in to give me a good night kiss, then?" she laughed.

"Don't joke," Helen scolded. "I've been worried sick."

"I'm so sorry Hel, but the lounge door was locked," she explained. "I've slept behind the settee, and I think I've killed the rubber plant, and then I got locked in the bedroom of an anal retentive."

"What the hell are you on about?" Helen angrily asked.

Lowry grabbed her clean uniform from the wardrobe.

"Look lovey, I must have a shower. I'll tell you all about it tonight. I'll grab some brekkie from the ward. You go now."

Helen remained.

"Tell me for God's sake. I can't wait all day to find out, but did you do it?"

Lowry grinned.

"I did indeed, and the earth didn't just move Hel, it spun off its axis," she lied.

Upon entering the ward, she first made for the kitchen to grab some toast, only to find Staff spooning porridge into her mouth. She looked like death.

"Jesus, I'm never going to survive this shift," she wailed. "Anyway, how the hell did you manage to get permission to stay out so late? I stayed until one thirty, but you were still there when I left?"

Lowry explained how uncomfortable it had been sleeping on the floor behind the settee. She kept silent about her act of vandalism.

"Good God, kid, you do take risks," Staff said, as she scraped the last of the porridge from the bowl. "And talking of risks, did I see you sloping off with Ben Novak?"

"You did, but I'd never done it before so I didn't know what to expect."

"You little innocent," Staff said, laughing. "Well, young Lowry, you've left maidenhood behind. Welcome to the world of liberated womanhood. And was it what you expected?"

Lowry slowly shook her head.

"Well no, actually. It hurt like hell. When Ben realised that I'd never done it before he was very gentle, but it really was most uncomfortable. He did wear a condom, but I don't think it was a rubber one. I think it was made of sandpaper. If carnal knowledge means having a sore crotch then I'd rather be ignorant of anything carnal."

"The worst is over, honey," Staff said, laughing. "It's fun all the way from now on."

Lowry found herself growing close to the Staff Nurse. The woman was in her mid thirties, with natural blonde hair, blue eyes and an attractive, open and friendly face. She had been offered many opportunities to become a Ward Sister, but had declined promotion on the grounds that as a front line nurse she had more contact with the patients. Staff had done her midwifery course, and had even been a Theatre Sister.

"Well, come on young Nurse, we'd best hit the ward and look busy," she said.

"Yes, I'd best hit the sluice room to empty more bloody sputum mugs," Lowry laughed.

"What d'you mean, empty sputum mugs?" Staff asked, frowning as she spoke.

"Exactly what it says, empty the gunk out in the sink and it takes ages and then..."

"You daft ha'peth," Staff cut in. "You put the sputum mug in the steriliser along with its contents. You don't have to empty them first."

"Why didn't somebody bloody tell me? I've spent ages in that shitty room shaking the stuff out."

Staff roared with laughter. Lowry eventually joined in, with a sense of relief.

"D'you know Staff, if you weren't on this ward, my working day would be miserable," she told her. "Why is Sister so unsympathetic and grumpy all the time?"

"Because she knows she's going to go out the same way she came in," Staff explained. "She's virgo intacta, honey. Sister Mary Jones is a frustrated virgin."

"I wish someone would get her on her back, so she'd get off mine," Lowry bitterly retorted.

Sister's voice boomed from the corridor.

"Nurses, have you forgotten that the patients need attending?"

"Come on, Nurse Stuart," Staff grinned. "The virgin Mary is calling us."

ILLEGITIMI NON CARBORUNDUM

The young nurse could hardly blame the patients for getting her into trouble.

For some reason trouble always seemed to find her.

Most of the lighter moments on the ward came from the men who had been admitted from North Wales. They delighted in teaching her their language and referred to Lowry as 'Cariad Bach'.

"Nurse Stuart is how you refer to her," Sister bellowed at the culprits.

The Welshmen may have thought Lowry was a little darling, obviously Sister did not.

A new arrival on the ward was always a source of interest. It alleviated the boredom for patients who had nothing better to do but sit and stare at each other or get the attention of a nurse by calling for a bedpan. Meal times were eagerly awaited, but disappointingly received once the hospital slops appeared on the plate.

An aging, bespectacled Welsh chapel minister arrived in bed five. He sat upright in his green striped pyjamas with a gentle smiley face and a problem with his prostate.

"Lowry, do us a favour," Mervin lilted, as she held his wrist to take his pulse.

"You've interrupted me and I've lost count now," she chided him.

"It's always races when you take it, Cariad," he grinned. "But you know the patient who's just come in? Well, why

115

don't you make him feel at home by giving him a proper Welsh welcome?"

Stupid Lowry! Approaching the minister's bed she repeated over and over in her head the proper Welsh welcome. His face registered shock as she unknowingly whispered the words that translated into English as, 'may I suggest you stick your finger up your bum.' It turned out to be an unfortunate turn of phrase for the little minister who regularly suffered the indignity of having numerous medical students sticking their fingers up his rectum in order to experience what an enlarged prostate felt like.

Lowry got her own back on Mervin by making him an apple pie bed. It backfired. The man sat uncomfortably with his knees under his chin unable to stretch his legs due to the top sheet being folded in half.

"Have you got cramp, Mr Davis?" Sister asked him, as she past his bed.

"No, Sister, I'm fine. Honest. It's more comfortable like this when there's a touch of wind in the guts."

"Move about a bit, that should shift it," she advised him. "Are you in pain?"

"Not pain exactly, just a bit uncomfortable. I'll be okay, Sister. Don't bother yourself."

Sister approached his bed. Mervin tightly clutched the top of his folded sheet with both hands.

"Where about is the discomfort?" Sister asked, attempting to pull the bed linen down. "Nurse Stuart, close the curtains around Mr Davis' bed," she ordered.

Lowry drew the curtains and watched a struggle ensue as Mervin grimly hung on to his top sheet with both hands as Sister persisted in trying to pull it away from him.

"What's got into you?" she tartly demanded. "Let go of this sheet, this instant."

The more Sister tugged at the sheet the tighter Mervin held on. If Lowry hadn't been anticipating the inevitable discovery and Sister's wrath she'd have found the pantomime very funny. Poor Mervin! He gave Lowry a rueful look and let go of the sheet.

"Is this your handiwork, Nurse?" Sister asked, after discovering the reason for Mervin's 'wind in the guts.' Her face was flushed with anger.

"Yes Sister."

"Make this bed up properly and report to my office in five minutes. You are a disgrace to the uniform."

Now, where had Lowry heard that before?

"That woman would be better off working in the mortuary," Mervin whispered as Lowry straightened out his top sheet. "She's got no sense of humour. I'm sorry Cariad, if I've got you into trouble. I feel it's my fault."

"Mervin stop fretting," Lowry told him. "I'm regularly on her carpet, in fact I've spent most of my life being carpeted for something, so don't blame yourself, or next time I give you your insulin injection I'll use a knitting needle."

Here she was on Sister's carpet again. Sister appeared to have calmed down a little.

"Nurse Stuart, I will not condone any frivolous behaviour on my ward. We nurses must be professional at all times, it's what the patients expect from us. You put Mr Davis in a very difficult position. He may have been entertained by your antics, but we are not here to provide entertainment. Do I make myself clear?"

"Yes Sister," Lowry meekly replied.

The telephone on her desk rang. She ignored it.

"You know, Nurse Stuart, you have the makings of a very good nurse, but until you can learn to obey my orders without arguing, then your ward appraisals, which I send to Matron, will not be good. You must remember that we are the professionals and must maintain a dignified distance from the patients."

She picked up the persistent phone and waved the student nurse away.

"Adolf Hitler's cronies were good at obeying orders," Lowry muttered to herself as she left the room. "And how much dignified distance should I leave between a patient and me when I'm giving him a blanket bath? Stupid cow!"

Two days later Lowry stood on Matron's carpet. She had been summoned to see the 'presence' by Home Sister. One of Matron's underlings coolly ushered her into the room. Lowry was hit by a strong smell of polish and lavender. Matron looked up from her reading and their eyes met. Nothing was said. They stared at each other for a few seconds, like a pair of stags about to lock antlers.

"I have here your appraisals," she said, flicking through some papers. "I had some concerns about you when you first arrived. Your college described you as a rebel, but your work was apparently of a high standard, so I took a risk, which it seems, I am now living to regret. Are you aware of Sister's opinion of you, Nurse Stuart?"

"Yes Matron. I know she doesn't like me," Lowry demurely answered.

"We are not here to be liked, young lady. It is your rebellious attitude, your questioning of the rules and your unprofessional approach towards the patients that Sister deplores. Now what have you to say about that?"

"Matron, I may be everything Sister says, but I have never been unprofessional with the patients. I care about them and if having a bit of light hearted fun with them is seen as being unprofessional, then I'll have to admit to that as well."

Lowry suddenly realised that Matron's thick framed glasses and navy blue dress made her look like a bluebottle.

"Matron, please may I ask if Sister says anything good about me?"

Matron's cold gaze fixed on Lowry who felt much like a lump of shit the bluebottle was about to land upon. The silence was unbearable.

"You leave me speechless, Nurse Stuart," she eventually spluttered. "Your whole attitude is one of defiance. You are not before me to hear what you want to hear. You are here to understand that I shall be watching your progress very closely. Your attitude must change if you wish to remain in my hospital. Is that clear to you?"

"Yes, Matron, but you did ask me if I had anything to say about Sister's...."

"Be quiet!" she yelled. "I don't want to hear another word from you."

Matron puckered her lips so tightly the woman's mouth reminded Lowry of an anus awaiting a suppository. The irate woman banged her hand onto the top of her desk.

"Get out of my office now and take your impertinence with you. I don't ever want to see you in here again," she finally exploded.

Lowry slowly climbed the stairs to the ward, her head spinning. She didn't know what people expected of her. She felt like a piece of plasticine that was being squeezed, twisted and moulded into something that wasn't her. Upon entering the ward the welcoming faces of the patients bucked her spirits. It was also Sister's day off.

"Hi Guys!" she cheerfully shouted. "Who wants to be the first in line for one of my highly polished, solid silver, pre-warmed bedpans with extra sheets of rose scented bog paper?"

The nurse entered the sluice room and stood on a radiator pipe and stuck her head out of the window. She lit a cigarette. It was her defiant way of cocking two fingers. After splashing methylated spirits over her hands, to mask the smell of smoke, she marched onto the ward in step with her rebellious attitude.

Lowry signed out of the nurses' home when she went off duty. She joined Ben sitting in the front of his car.

"How did you get on with Matron today?" he asked.

"How did you know about that? The jungle drums never stop beating in that place."

"Staff told me when I popped to the ward to see you and she told me you were on Matron's carpet having an ear bashing."

"Well, Ben, the old bluebottle thinks I'm unprofessional, insolent, rebellious and any other adjective she could think of to add to my character assassination." Lowry told him. "Next time I come face to face with that bluebottle I shall swat it."

Ben groaned.

"For pity's sake, Lowry, Staff thinks you're a bloody good nurse but rather comical. So why can't you try to obey Sister's orders once in a while and learn to grovel a bit? We all have to grovel sometimes."

"Ben Novak, just you listen to me," she responded heatedly. "Jackboots spring to mind when you talk about obeying orders and as for grovelling, I'd rather empty a dozen sputum mugs. Sister said we were the professionals and we had to keep a dignified distance from the patients. How the bloody hell do you keep your distance from a sick person who needs comforting, Ben? I've held the hand of quite a few patients who have been feeling low, and I've stroked the foreheads of some who have been in pain. Well, if that's unprofessional then there's something wrong with the system. And I don't care if the patients call me by my Christian name. They seem to like me referring to them by their first names, so what the fuck is wrong with that?"

She finished her rant and turned to look at Ben who was grinning.

"What's so funny?" she asked.

"You are," he grinned. "But I happen to agree with you and times are slowly changing. Matron and Sister are of the old school when nurses were as starchy as their hats. Bedbound patients are like captive children who take their medicine, do as they are told and remained confined to bed until given permission to move. Well, my little fire brand, that is about to change. The school of thought is, that patients should move about, get the circulation going to prevent thrombosis, cramp, flatulence and atrophied muscles. I agree that we cannot be over-familiar, but a little compassion and human warmth can make a hell of a difference to a patient. Anyway, my sweet little nurse, under your seat you'll find a bottle of cider and in the glove compartment you'll find a bottle opener."

Lowry felt secure in a car with misted windows. They shared the bottle of cider and smoked three cigarettes. Ben leaned across the passenger seat and on the steamy window, with his index finger, he wrote 'ILLEGITIMI NON CARBORUNDUM.'

"What's that mean?"

"It's Latin," he grinned. "It means, don't let the bastards grind you down."

Lowry suddenly felt cheered. Stuff Matron. Stuff Sister. She was going to snog Ben's face off and do a bit of heavy petting. It was something they both enjoyed.

The nurse's home lacked any magic as Lowry entered the hall.

"Good evening," she politely said to Home Sister who was on her normal nightly prowl.

"Good evening, Nurse. Have you been drinking?"

"No Home Sister. If my breath smells it's because of my new toothpaste. I'm thinking of going back to my old one 'cos I don't like the smell either and the taste is even worse."

She raced up the stairs to the attic.

"Hi my ministering angel sisters," she shouted, upon seeing her friends again.

"May I suggest we have a new slogan to put on our bedroom doors, next to the list of rules? It's illegitimi non carborundum."

"Jesus! Ben's given her a lobotomy," Helen said, to a chorus of laughter.

"He's no doubt given her something. Genital herpes, probably," Trish cynically said.

"It's Latin, you ignoramuses. It means, don't let the bastards grind you down. It's going to be the Stuart family motto from now on," she cockily told them.

The following morning Lowry entered the ward and was immediately summoned to Sister's office.

"Nurse Stuart," Sister said, pleasantly enough. "A new patient arrived early this morning and you are to accompany him by ambulance to the public bath house. He is seventy five years old, confused and filthy dirty. His skin is dark grey and it seems he has body lice and God knows what else. My ward has not got the facilities to deal with such a case. The ambulance will be here in half an hour, so give him a cup of tea and some porridge before you go."

"Yes Sister," Lowry replied. "What's the man's name?"

"Horace Hardcastle," she answered. "Now Nurse, make sure you leave his clothing for the bath attendants to destroy and take with you a blanket and hospital gown for him to return in. I don't want to be reduced to having my ward fumigated so you'll find him in a wheelchair in the corridor by the window."

"Oh, I saw him sitting there as I came on duty. He was singing his head off," Lowry said.

"Unfortunately he's not stopped," Sister moaned, "but remember Nurse Stuart, you are only there to accompany him. Leave everything to the attendants, but remain with him at all times even to the bath."

"Yes, Sister. I'm not expected to accompany him into the bath, am I?" Lowry joked.

"Is that supposed to be funny, Nurse?" Po-face replied. "And get them to fumigate the wheelchair and bring it back. We have a shortage of wheelchairs."

"Yes Sister."

Horace continued his recital all the way to the bath house, although Lowry surmised from his song that he thought he was on his way to Tipperary. The smell emanating from the old soldier reminded the nurse of the fancy French cheese Lou had bought called Brie, which stank out the cold cupboard in the pantry, for weeks.

The austere Victorian bath house was seldom used now that folk with no bathrooms preferred to hang a tin bath on a nail in the back kitchen door awaiting the Friday night ritual family cleansing. Lowry had a friend at secondary school whose family had a tin bath on the back door. Every pan bucket and container heated the water on the gas stove. The bath sat before the coal fire with dad going in first them mum and finally the children – eldest first. The dirty water was baled into buckets and chucked into the jigger at the back of the house. The Corpy were doing their best to provide bathrooms for their tenants, but it was a costly and lengthy process.

A strong smell of disinfectant and chemicals greeted the two ambulance men, the nurse and the singing old soldier. Two beefy male attendants emerged from a back room. It took Lowry a few minutes to realise that one of them was actually a woman, although from a distance it was difficult to tell which was which. Both were dressed in green overalls, green mop caps, wellington boots and thick red rubber gloves.

The ambulance men left to wait in their vehicle, leaving Horace and Lowry to the surreal situation in which they found themselves. The male attendant wheeled Horace into the back room without saying a word to the old man. Lowry followed and the caustic smell nearly bowled her over. The stone floor had recently been sluiced down with disinfectant. Four enormous grey stone baths filled the room with wooden slatted platforms on the floor running along the edge of the baths. One pungent steaming bath was filled almost to the top, awaiting its occupant.

Horace was still on his way to Tipperary. He seemed to have a long way to go.

"Are you okay, Horace?" Lowry asked him. "You are going to have a bath. You'll feel a lot better after that and then I'll take you back with me to a nice warm bed and a hot meal. How does that sound?"

He stared blankly at the nurse, but continued singing.

"Will you move over there, Nurse," the male attendant ordered, pointing to a bentwood chair in the corner. "I'm going to undress him."

Lowry took an instant dislike to the two beefy attendants. Neither one had spoken to the old man or even smiled at him.

"His name is Horace and he's not a bag of dirty washing. He's an old man, who's confused," she angrily said. "And he's my patient."

"He's our responsibility until he leaves these premises, and we're here to clean the old sod up, not engage him in conversation, Nurse," the man said as he pulled Horace's first filthy jumper over the old man's head and deposited it in a large brown paper bag.

Lowry fumed as she watched the beefy bullies take pleasure in the power they had over a helpless old man.

Horace was now saying 'Goodbye to Dolly Gray' and continued to do so until the fourth jumper revealed a vest that had probably been white but was now charcoal. Once the trousers and underpants had been removed it was obvious the old guy had done a lot of scratching. Open sores covered his pubic area and the top of his legs. He wore no socks inside his filthy pumps and his feet and very long toe nails looked like they had been plunged into a bucket of soot.

Lowry felt so sad as she witnessed the sight of a thin, neglected, naked, old man who had obviously done his bit in the First World War.

"Please treat him with dignity," she emotionally said.

"Ignore her," said the attendant whose higher pitched voice indicated she was the female.

"You ignorant pig," Lowry muttered under her breath as she watched them both lift Horace from behind the knees and around his back and splash him into the bath.

A tsunami broke over the sides. Horace gasped, as he said his final farewell to Dolly Gray. But the old man wasn't to be daunted. His recital began again, almost immediately. 'Up to your waist in water, Up to your eyes in slush, Using the kind of
language, That makes the sergeant blush.'

He sang with gusto the song that had kept up the spirits of the boys in the trenches.

The attendants scrubbed the emaciated body until Lowry noticed pink skin emerging from the grime. The singing stopped abruptly as his head was forcibly pushed beneath the surface of the acrid water to eradicate what was living in his grey hair. Another tsunami washed over the side as Horace kicked out with his legs. His head reappeared from beneath the surface but the singing had stopped.

Poor old Horace must have thought he'd fallen into the hands of the Hun, Lowry thought. After dressing the old soldier in the hospital gown and wrapping the blanket around him, she wheeled her patient in the fumigated chair to the ambulance. Lowry saw the old guy smile for the first time as he respectfully saluted the uniformed ambulance men.

Once on the ward, Horace tucked into a hot meal and had a medical examination and was then transferred to Belmont Road Geriatric Hospital.

Lowry hoped he travelled the long route there, by way of Tipperary, in the company of Dolly Gray, whoever she was!

THE SHIP'S CAPTAIN

The young nurse sat beside the bed of a new patient. She held a bowl under his chin as he vomited. The spasm subsided. The man leaned back onto his pillow, then sighed heavily. He was a handsome man, but panda eyed and yellow. His liver was protesting against the amount of alcohol it was having to filter. His notes gave his age as forty three and his occupation as a Ship's Captain.

"Thank you Nurse," he quietly said.

Lowry gently wiped his chin.

"You don't have to thank me," she answered. "All we want is for our patients to get better."

"I think it may be too late for me," he responded.

"No! Don't think like that," she chided him. "It's the patients with a positive attitude who win through. We've had lots of sailors on this ward with either malaria, alcohol problems or syphilis."

"Well fortunately I do not have syphilis," he said, smiling weakly.

"Good, that's one less thing for you to worry about then. Are you okay now? 'Cos I'll have to go and help the orderly sort out morning drinks for the boys. Would you like me to leave the curtains closed around your bed? You look very tired so try and get some sleep. Has the pain in your side gone?"

"It's not as bad as it was," he sighed.

Lowry pulled the bed clothes over her patient's shoulders and stroked his forehead.

"Remember, positive attitude," she whispered.

The daily grind, rubbing the patient's pressure points with soapy water then drying the area with a towel, rubbing gently again with methylated spirits, until the final dusting of talcum powder, was time consuming. Lowry knew that patients with bed sores was a disgraced to any nurse. She enjoyed the banter as she rubbed heels, hips, shoulder blades and elbows. "Now for the final sprinkling of icing sugar to make you smell sweet," she told them as she liberally showered talcum powder over the floor. It was her way of getting back at the bossy Ward Orderly. The disgruntled woman complained at having to sweep Lowry's size four footprints from the fine dusting of white powder.

She heard the new patient vomiting again. He hadn't eaten breakfast and the retching sounded painful. Lowry rushed to his bedside.

"Try and drink some water if you can, it will give you something to throw up." She held the glass to his mouth and the patient drank eagerly. "I'll stay 'til the nausea subsides."

The retching ended. The patient appeared exhausted. The sweat on his face glistened, his dark hair lay plastered to his forehead. Lowry felt sorry for him, even though she knew his problems were self-induced.

"Your diet sheet came up from the kitchen today," she told him. "The dietician has got you on the finest of menus, not even the Queen of England's chef could come up with such culinary delights as these."

"I'm sure it will be delicious," he responded in a 'couldn't care less' manner.

"That's what you think," she retorted. "You're sugar free, sodium free, protein free, dairy free, in fact you might just as well be a vegan."

"What exactly is that?" he asked.

"It's a highly principled person who just eats rabbit food," she quipped. "Anyway are you feeling any better? Hopefully the anti-nausea treatment will kick in soon, but give me a shout if you need anything. I shall have to go and help the orderly with lunches."

"I am feeling a little better and thank you Nurse Stuart," he gratefully said. "May I know your first name?"

"It's Lowry and you're quite welcome to call me Lowry but don't let Sister hear you do it. She's a stickler for formality whereas I'm the opposite. Anyway, how do you pronounce your first name, it's very unusual?"

"Not in Norway. It is said as Layf, but spelt LEIF."

"Okay, I'll call you Leif if that's alright with you."

He nodded and smiled.

What a lovely man, Lowry thought as she approached the kitchen for the lunch trolley.

Visiting time had always been a pantomime to the young nurse. The two ward doors remained shut and stayed that way until dead on three o'clock, not a minute before or a minute after. Faces of anxious relatives repeatedly appeared at the small round windows, each one eager to get a glimpse of their loved one in his pyjamas, sitting in his bed.

"Stand back, nurses," Staff announced as she opened the ward doors.

The stampede in was reminiscent of the January sale at T.J. Hughes's. Lowry groaned. More bloody flowers. It was her responsibility to find vases, keep the water fresh and remove them to the sluice room every night and return them to the patient's lockers in the morning. It was such a waste of her precious time. She could never remember to whom the vases belonged.

"Those aren't mine," one fussy patient had complained. "Mine are chrysanthemum blooms from my own allotment."

Lowry didn't know a blooming chrysanthemum from a withered one. Nevertheless she enjoyed visiting time. It brought a happy hum onto the ward. The patients appeared less vulnerable when a family member sat beside them. Half an hour was nowhere near long enough. But those were the rules made by despots who couldn't give a damn. Grapes and chocolates were shared with Lowry and smuggled under her cape when leaving duty to be distributed between the attic gang. The gifts of black stockings she kept for herself. She was sick of the joke some patients thought hilariously funny. "Can I climb your ladder, Lovey?" As she carried a replenished vase to its rightful locker, she noticed Leif had a visitor. The visitors rosy cheeks indicated he was Leif's drinking partner. She made a mental note to check her patient over in case contraband alcohol had been smuggled in. Visitors had done it before and alcohol was definitely not for Leif. She smiled across at the two men.

"Hello," she said as she approached them both. "How's your diet going down, Leif?"

"It's very bland and uninteresting," he responded. "Fortunately I'm not hungry."

"Well it must be working because you're looking less like a banana than you did when you first came in."

He smiled.

"May I introduce you to my dear friend Marcus Marriot?"

The strawberry nosed gentleman stood up and shook hands with the nurse. He really was quite ugly, until he smiled, and then there was a certain beauty to his ugliness.

"I'm pleased to meet you," he said. "I hear you are a ministering angel, according to my friend here."

She chuckled.

"I doubt Sister would agree with the description, angel, but I must be getting on. Nice to have met you," she said to Marcus Marriot.

Sister's voice boomed like a fog horn across the ward.

"Will relatives leave now and will you please remember, next time, that visitors are not allowed to sit on patients' beds?"

The Mersey Docks and Harbour Board tugboat was chucking her very large anchor about again.

The stampede in became a slow shuffle out with visitors turning to wave and turning to wave again until finally blowing a kiss to a loved one.

Sister visibly relaxed as the last relative left the ward. She hated visiting time. The throng of alien bodies on her ward created disorder.

"Nurse Stuart, go and put the chairs back tidily and remove the rubbish from the locker tops," she demanded. "Also straighten the counterpanes on the beds."

"The odd please wouldn't go amiss," Lowry mumbled to herself.

THE RAMPANT ANARCHIST

"Sister's off for a week, as of tomorrow," Lowry happily told Dai, a cheeky young Welsh patient who had filled Mervin's empty bed. He had been admitted with brachycardia. His heart was beating too slowly causing dizziness. "Now Dai, boyo, it's time for your blanket bath," she told him. "You have two a week and your pressure points done every day, sometimes twice, to make sure you don't get bed sores."

"Sounds good to me," he laughed.

Lowry smiled at him. He didn't know she had the upper hand.

"Okay, Dai, but there's one thing you must understand. If there is any part of your anatomy that misbehaves during your blanket bath, it gets a whack with the pencil I've got in my top pocket."

Dai roared with laughter.

"I can see I'm going to enjoy my stay here," he chuckled. "Would you pour me a glass of Lucozade, please Nurse?" he asked, pointing to the bottle on his locker. "I'm very thirsty."

Lowry handed him the glass of sparkling golden liquid.

"Iechyd da. Twll tin pob Sais," he said, before knocking the drink back in one gulp. "That's what you say in Wales when you have a drink in the pub. It's like you say, cheers."

"I'll be a fluent Welsh speaker before I leave this ward," she said.

There was no need for the pencil in her top pocket. His anatomy behaved itself. She had given him a soapy flannel and told him to do 'that bit' himself, with the towel covering his modesty.

The weekly 'extra special ward clean' always created chaos and also sent Sister into a state of deep mourning. The Ward Orderly and a fellow cohort, cleaned, scrubbed and mopped anything that stood still. All the beds were wheeled into the centre of the room completing a circle whereby the patients could almost hold hands. It amused Lowry to see what looked like a bunch of grown men about to burst into 'ring a ring o' roses.' Her mood was buoyant. She was spending her weekend off with Ben and he had a surprise for her and Sister was going on holiday. Imagine a week's freedom from her tyranny. Lowry wandered into the centre of the circle.

"Gentlemen, it's time for your daily exercises," she announced, surveying her audience with a wide grin on her face. "Please follow my lead and join in the singing. Are you all ready?" The patients grinned and nodded. "You put your right arm in, your right arm out, in out in out shake it all about, you do the hokey kokey and you turn around."

Lowry collapsed into fits of laughter as most of the patients sang and joined in her exhibitionist performance. The Ward Orderly and her cohort stared at the young nurse, shook their heads and tut tutted. 'Miserable old scrubbers,' Lowry muttered.

Staff's voice ended the merriment.

"Lowry, Sister's on her way back from her coffee break."

Lowry walked across to Leif's bedside and plumped up his pillows that didn't actually need plumping. She smiled sweetly as Sister entered the ward. Always good to look busy!

"You are so full of fun, Lowry," Leif said.

"Well what's the point of being miserable?" she responded. "Life's already full of people who seem to be happiest when they're at their most miserable. I used to go to a Methodist Church Youth Club which meant I had to show my face in church every so often. For some reason, the vicar there thought the more miserable you were the closer to God you got. He used to thump the tub in a voice of doom about the evils of alcohol and the sins of the flesh. Yet he was as pissed as a rat on a Saturday night and had six kids and there was talk that the child of the woman who did the church flowers was his."

Ben's Austin A40 cruised around the corner into Brownlow Hill. Lowry waved and the car drew to a stop. She slung her small weekend case onto the back seat and then climbed into the front seat, noticing that Ben was wearing a suit.

"This isn't the usual way to your flat," she announced.

"No, we're going through the Mersey Tunnel to Heswall to have dinner with my parents," he replied.

Lowry's heart sank. The last thing she wanted was to have to sit at a table with Ben's parents talking politely and remembering her manners. Ben's father was a cardiac surgeon, his mother probably mingled with polite society and used doilies.

"Why didn't you tell me we were going to your parents for dinner? I'm hardly dressed for swanky scran, in jeans, white boots and a white polo neck sweater."

"You look gorgeous, Lowry, you always do and anyway they're very nice people. Mum can be a bit of a pain, but they're not going to eat you," Ben explained.

"I should bloody well hope they're not cannibals, but I just wish you had given me some warning," she petulantly responded.

Ben's family home stood detached and aloof in its own grounds. The driveway formed a circle around a large flower bed. The car pulled up outside the steps leading to a highly polished oak front door that opened as the young couple emerged from the car.

"At last, Ben you have seen fit to honour us with a visit," his father called. "How long is it now, since your mother last saw you?"

"Hi, Dad," Ben said, as he climbed the steps with Lowry close behind him. "This is Lowry, the young lady I told you I was bringing. Lowry, this is my father, John."

Lowry shook hands with John. She had seen him in on the ward. He was Dai's consultant, and as a heart surgeon was one of the suited Gods and known as Mr Novak. No way could she call him, John.

"Hello," she coyly said.

Ben had inherited his father's dark good looks and boyish smile. They entered the hall as a tall elegant woman emerged from the kitchen. Ben's mother wore a silk creation that must have cost a fortune from Henderson's, the shop that was seldom frequented by the hoi polloi. Her immaculate blonde hair looked like a wig.

"Please go into the dining room," said the woman who had been introduced as Penelope. "Dinner is ready. Benjamin, show Lowry where she is to sit and pour the wine please. And when are you going to get your hair cut?"

"When I think it's too long," Ben replied, with an emphasis on the word I.

This is going to be a fun night, Lowry thought.

The dining room looked like a smaller version of a baronial hall. A large oval, highly polished table stood in the centre of the room with two candelabras dancing their flickering lights onto the walls and the crystal chandelier that hung from the centre of room. Lowry wished she were somewhere else. Preferably in the flat with Busty Bonaparte, eating fish and chips smothered in tommy ketch, out of the Liverpool Echo, with her fingers.

"Please help yourself to the vegetables, Lowry," her hostess prompted.

Lowry had lost her appetite, but spooned a small amount of peas and carrots onto her plate. Three peas fell off the serving spoon and onto the polished table. Shit, shit, shit, she silently groaned. Should she leave them there or pick them up one by one and pop them into her mouth? There had to be some etiquette attached to peaing on the table, she thought. The three peas remained motionless. They were provoking her to flick them across the table at Ben. Instead she politely and delicately picked them up and put them on the side of her plate. That's what a well brought up young lady would do, she surmised.

Her vegetables were joined by the beef that had arrived on a plate the size of a dust bin lid. John had carved the meat with the precision of a man accustomed to wielding a knife. Lowry noticed his wonderful hands and delicate fingers. They were ideal tools for poking around the ventricles and auricles.

Ben winked at her. She glared at him.

"Pass me the horseradish sauce, please Benjamin," she facetiously asked. She had never called him Benjamin before.

"What does your father do, Lowry?" Penelope asked, leaning forward interestedly, whilst delicately dabbing the corners of her red lipsticked mouth with her napkin.

"I haven't got a father, Mrs Novak. I wouldn't know my father if I fell over him. But I have a pretty wonderful mother called, Lou."

Silence followed. Only the scraping of knives and forks on plates could be heard. Lowry took a large swig of red wine from a crystal glass, its stem so slender she was fearful of snapping it. She shuddered at the bitter taste.

"And how is your mother?" the woman enquired, in an artificial disinterested voice.

Lowry remembered her manners and finished what she had in her mouth before replying.

"She is well, thank you. I normally have my weekends off with her, but she's away at the moment in Wiltshire. She's gone...."

"Oh how nice! I hear that is a lovely county," Penelope interjected. "Is she on holiday?"

"No Mrs Novak. She's gone with a group of women and is demonstrating outside the Chemical Defence Experimental Establishment near Porton. The Government is allowing some horrendous experiments to take place in their laboratories. Lou was arrested last time she protested there."

Ben laughed loudly and food from his mouth spluttered onto the table.

"Benjamin, mind your manners!" his Mother angrily shouted.

He wiped the food from the table with his napkin, grinning as he did so.

"Sorry, but I just thought it was funny," he laughed.

"Well, I don't," his mother exploded. "Seems to me there is far too much demonstrating going on these days. As a Justice of the Peace I have to deal...."

Ben's father interrupted.

"Let's leave it there shall we, and if everyone has had enough we'll move on to that wonderful sherry trifle you have made, Penelope." He turned to look at Ben. "Help your mother clear the dinner plates, please son."

Lowry silently fumed. How dare that stuck up wig wearing cow, criticise Lou.

"How do you enjoy nursing, Lowry?" Ben's father asked, with a note of genuine interest in his voice.

"I love it, thank you. I love the patients and caring for them. I'm not best buddies with Matron or my Ward Sister, but I've got plenty of other buddies at the hospital."

"What ward are you on? I must know your Ward Sister," he asked.

"Male Medical."

The cardiac surgeon laughed like a conspiratorial school boy.

"I know the one you mean. She terrifies us all. We know her as 'the harridan' but that's between you and me," he chuckled. "She's quite formidable."

"What does harridan mean? I've never heard the word before," Lowry asked.

"It means a sharp tongued bad tempered woman," he explained. "I think it comes from a French word meaning an old worn out horse."

"Mr Novak, she is not remotely like a beautiful animal such as a horse. I reckon with that fog horn voice and her broad beam she's more like a Mersey Docks and Harbour Board tugboat."

Ben's dad roared with laughter.

"I'll have to tell that one to my colleagues. They'll love it."

The trifle arrived. Lowry hated trifle. It looked pretty enough in the presentation bowl with its glace cherries and angelica, but once in her dish it looked like vomit. She quickly swallowed the first mouthful without tasting it. She felt, uncomfortably, that she was under scrutiny from the Justice of the Peace. The cross examination began again.

"Where were you educated, Lowry?" Mrs Novak nosily enquired.

Lowry hesitated before answering. She had nothing to lose. This woman obviously needed impressing.

"I actually received my education at Cheltenham Ladies College, Mrs Novak, and was then finished off at a school in Switzerland. That's where they taught me to how to be a lady and sit with my legs elegantly crossed and walk with books on my head for my posture. I was also taught to curtsy, would you believe, just in case I bumped into the Queen in the local grocery shop."

Ben lowered his head and sniggered into his bowl of vomit.

His mother's face became seriously animated. She was definitely impressed.

"You must know my friend's daughter, Annabella Forster-Swalebury. She is the same age as you and went to Cheltenham Ladies," Mrs Novak said.

Lowry could have kicked herself for being so flippant. Why can't I learn to keep my gob shut, she admonished herself?

"I'm sorry but I was pulling your leg, Mrs Novak," she admitted. She felt her face going red with embarrassment. "I didn't actually go to Cheltenham Ladies." Ben giggled again. His mother shot him a withering glance. "I've had a number of schools. The first two threw me out, one of them was a convent which is actually where I learnt to curtsy, so I had private tutoring for a few years because no other school would take me. It wasn't because I was seriously delinquent or anything. One school teacher just bullied the children. The convent just terrified them. But I went to secondary school, then to college to do a pre-nursing course."

The woman did not directly speak to Lowry again.

Cheese arrived at the table on a board. The biscuits arrived on a plate with a doily.

Jeans and kinky boots were very much out of place in the Novak drawing room. Lowry sat on the edge of the plush cream leather sofa hoping her heels wouldn't make holes in the thick cream Axminster carpet. She surveyed her surroundings and noticed there was no colour or warmth in the room, Not even her host and hostess showed any warmth towards each other. She wondered if they even slept together anymore. She was relieved when at nine thirty, Ben announced it was time to leave.

"Benjamin, don't you ever, surprise me like that again," she firmly said, as they drove out of the wrought iron gates. "Your dad is a pussycat, but your mother is, to put it bluntly, bordering on bovine. Referring to her as a bit of a pain is an understatement. She's bloody agony."

He put his hand on Lowry's knee and squeezed gently.

"I'm so sorry she put you through the third degree. Being a magistrate has gone to her head. The little people have to know their place, according to her. It's all about standards you know!" he said, mimicking his mother's voice.

"Little people! Who the hell are the little people?"

"The lower classes. Mum thinks it's very snobbish to call them the lower classes. She believes that by calling them the little people she's being kinder and more liberal."

"The woman is unbelievable. So, according to your mother, I'm from the lower classes, am I?" Lowry hotly challenged.

"If you haven't been to public school or speak with a plum in your gob, or have wads in the bank and live in a detached house, then yes, according to her, you are one of the little people."

"Well I hope that damn plum in her gob chokes her," Lowry laughed. "I bet she shits and farts just like the little people do, or is that too vulgar for an upper class bum?"

Ben burst into laughter.

"Sorry, I should have warned you about Penelope, but I knew you'd say no to coming with me if I'd asked you first. I've done my duty now, for the next three months. I needed you to dilute my mother a bit, but I never expected you to send her into apoplexy. God, her face when you told her about your mother and never having had a father. Dear Penelope probably thinks I'm going out with the bastard daughter of a rampant anarchist."

Lowry could now see the funny side of it, as she and Ben laughed together.

"Is she ever called Penny, or does she get her full title like you do, Benjamin?"

"God help anybody who calls her Penny," he giggled.

"That's probably because it's one of the lowest forms of currency, Ben, and anyway, that's all it costs to use a public loo."

"You really are a class act, Lowry, telling my mother you went to Cheltenham Ladies."

"No, I'm not, I just say it as it is. She wanted to be sure I came from the same pedigree as you do. People like her shouldn't be magistrates where they sit in judgement on others. What the hell does your privileged mother know about people who are down on their uppers?"

He drummed his fingers on the steering wheel as he waited for the lights to turn green.

"I doubt if she knows what 'down on your uppers' means."

"She probably thinks it means a working class tart going down on an upper class punter and giving him a blow job," Lowry said.

They were laughing so heartily they hadn't noticed the lights had turned green. The car behind tooted loudly and impatiently.

"Okay, okay," Ben tetchily said. "Keep your hair on."

Lowry turned to look at the impatient driver.

"He'll have a job keeping his hair on, unless he uses glue, Ben. He's bald."

"Serves him right," Ben responded.

"Your dad is a lovely man. You are so lucky to have grown up with a father. I've always wanted one, but Lou who adopted me was a widow so there was no chance there. I sometimes think that if anything happened to Lou, I would be all alone in the world, because I have no family anywhere. D'you know, Benjamin, I don't know anything about me or where I come from, because I haven't got a past? Weird isn't it?"

"I think it's more sad than weird," he replied. "We all have to have a sense of where we came from. I know all about my grandparents in Holland and my grandparents in England on my mother's side, but my dad never talks about his family or the war. Something bad happened, but he doesn't speak about it. Anyway, dad liked you."

"I'm glad he liked me. I liked him too. I must admit I get on better with men than women. But I worry sometimes that some women don't like me and I don't know why. It's not that I mean to upset them, but I look back on the women in the orphanage, that fat teacher who hit me, Mother Superior, the home making teacher, Miss Evans, Matron, Ward Sister and now your mother and wonder what it is about me that makes them want to crush me."

"I don't think Mum, disliked you, sweetheart, she...."

"Yes she did, Ben. She thought I wasn't good enough for you. I know I'm gobby and like to turn everything into a joke, but Lou always taught me to ask questions and challenge what I believed was wrong. Anyway, apart from Lou and Staff Nurse, who like me, I couldn't give a fig for the rest of them. I like being on a male ward 'cos the men want to flirt. And that's fine by me so long as they keep their hands off the goods."

"Just be yourself, Lowry. Don't let people change you, 'cos I love you just the way you are. But please don't call me Benjamin. Penelope is the only person who gives me my full title and I hate it." He quickly changed the subject. "By the way, have you got any shillings in your purse?"

"No, I haven't. Why?"

"Bugger! I haven't got any either and we need some for the gas meter. It'll be freezing in the flat," he groaned.

"Come back to my place then, Ben. We can have a nice log fire," Lowry suggested. "Lou's not back until tomorrow, unless she's in a police cell somewhere. And guess what? Right in front of the log fire is a lovely Chinese silk rug."

"The Chinese silk rug sounds like fun and I went to the barber shop today."

"It doesn't look like you had your hair cut," Lowry chuckled.

"I didn't," he quipped back. "I bought a pack of three."

"Is that all you got, Ben? Three aren't going to last a weekend."

The car turned into Lou's driveway. Ben switched off the ignition and turned to face his passenger.

"It was all I could afford at the time, but dad gave me five pounds, so tomorrow I'll toddle to the barber's shop in Penny Lane and get a couple of dozen. How does that sound?"

"Sounds like we'll both have some difficulties walking the hospital corridors on Monday morning," she joked. "By the way, do you like cocoa? That red wine was ghastly."

"That was a classy Chateau de Nerf du Pap, I'll have you know," Ben pompously explained.

"Exactly what I thought," Lowry responded. "It was a classy load of plap."

"I said, Pap, not plap," he laughed. "But is it okay if this man flirts with you and handles the goods?"

"This guy is welcome to manhandle the goods, Mr Novak," she coquettishly said.

With the help of the gas poker, the fire roared to life and warmed the Chinese silk rug, and the two energetic naked bodies that rolled around on it.

"Whoever invented sex should be awarded a Nobel Prize for services to debauchery," Lowry said. But Ben had fallen asleep.

BORIS

The trolley forced the ward doors open. Two porters struggled to control an elderly man who protested angrily at finding himself being rolled into a ward against his will.

"Come on Pops, we're only trying to help you," the older porter kindly said.

The elderly man looked blankly at him. According to the ambulance crew the patient's home help had arrived to care for the old man and found he had forgotten to flush his toilet. She panicked when she found the bowl splattered with blood. The Russian man's name was Boris Petrovich, aged eighty one. He spoke no English. Together, a third year nurse and Lowry undressed him and clothed him in a revealing backless hospital gown.

"The doctor will be with you shortly," the third year nurse, Susan, gently told him.

Half an hour later, Lowry and Staff prepared a trolley ready for the patient to receive a barium meal enema in readiness for an X ray of his lower bowel as recommended by the doctor.

"Have you ever done one of these before, Lowry?" Staff asked.

"No, but I gave a sapo molis enema, to Mr Bradley, if you remember, because he was so badly constipated. He kept going oops, oops, oops, the poor chap, but thankfully he wasn't constipated anymore."

Staff laughed. She rolled Boris onto his left side and held firmly onto him to stop him rolling onto his back.

"This is much the same," she explained. "Only we need a larger diameter catheter tube because the meal is obviously thicker than soapy water. Now, put some jelly on the rounded end of the catheter with the side opening and then attach the other end to the funnel. Remember not to pour it into the funnel too quickly, just keep pouring gently until all the meal has gone."

Lowry gently separated Boris' buttocks.

"Oh God, Staff, I can't find his anus" she urgently said.

"Don't be daft, Lowry, even Russians have anuses," she laughed.

"Well this one hasn't. Look!"

Staff leaned over the patient.

"It's somewhere under his haemorrhoids, so go gently. He's got a bunch of grapes here, but they're very shrivelled and not bleeding, so that's not the cause of his problem."

"I wouldn't call them a bunch of grapes," Lowry said. "They're more like sultanas."

Lowry eventually found the orifice and gently inserted the jellied end of the catheter into Boris' rectum. Holding the funnel high, she slowly poured the contents into his backside. Oops, oops, oops sounds much the same in any language.

"Don't worry Lowry," Staff encouragingly said. "You're doing fine. He doesn't understand what's happening, the poor old bugger." Eventually his ordeal was over. "I'll get Nurse Mason to take him to x-ray. You clear up here and put the steriliser on while you're at it. There's a lot of equipment that needs sterilising. You did a good job there, kiddo," Staff said.

The young nurse beamed.

Three quarters of an hour later Boris returned.

"Would you like me to make you a cup of tea?" Lowry asked him.

She realised he wouldn't understand. Putting her thumb and index fingers together, she held an imaginary cup to her lips. He understood and nodded.

"How many sugars?"

Daft me, she thought. Holding an imaginary spoon in her hand she pretended to stir it round and round. He held up three fingers. Suddenly, Lowry realised this patient might be nil by mouth until they had diagnosed his problem. She approached Staff.

"Can I give Boris a cup of tea, or is he nil by mouth?"

"No, give him a cuppa, he deserves one," she answered.

On leaving the kitchen with Boris' cup and saucer, Lowry was confronted by an agitated middle-aged man hovering by the ward door.

"Can I help you?" she asked.

"Yes," the man nervously said. "I at work and they say my father, Mr Boris Petrovitch, here. I see him, if you please? Is it bad for him? You tell me please."

"Hold on, I'll get Staff Nurse to see you. It's Sister's day off, so she's in charge." Lowry explained. "Please wait here. I'm just taking your father a cup of tea. Would you like one?"

The distraught man nodded.

"Tea, yes, if you please."

"Any sugar?"

"Three, if you please." he replied.

Lowry smiled.

"You Russians have a sweet tooth."

"Beg pardon, please."

"I'll go and get the Staff Nurse for you," she said, to avoid any complicated explanation. Staff escorted the man to his father's bedside. Father and son immediately began talking rapidly in Russian. The old man gesticulated wildly. A number of words appeared to have the letter K in them. Lowry wondered if he was swearing obscenely. Lowry silently giggled. Boris threw off his covers. He was becoming bolshie. He shouted at his son. Once again they conversed in Russian and the old man calmed down.

"Can you ask your father how long he has been suffering from rectal bleeding when he has a motion?" Staff asked the son.

Boris' son appeared confused.

"Excuse please?"

Staff tried again.

"Will you ask your father how often he has blood in the toilet when he sits down and uses toilet paper?"

The son understood. A lengthy conversation in Russian ensued. Staff and Lowry didn't dare look at each other. Laughter would have been inappropriate. The talking stopped.

"My father has not got blood when he is at the toilet. He likes the borscht. Sometime two time a day," the son slowly said. Boris pulled on his son's arm and they spoke rapid Russian again. The son nodded to his father. "There is big mistake, please. It is the borscht. My father has not got the teeth so the borscht is easy for him with the bread, yes. Sometime he has it hot sometime he has it cold."

"What on earth is borscht?" Staff curiously asked.

"He likes, what you say, the beetroot soup," the son replied. "My father has sometime the loose bottom and he forgets to pull the toilet string. The borscht has the shitting very red and the pissing, so too."

The two men sat together finishing their tea. Staff and Lowry fled to the kitchen and fell apart with laughter. An hour later and with the doctor's permission, Boris and son left for home.

"Poor old Boris," Lowry grinned. "He's gone home with a cup of tea and three sugars in his belly and a cartload of barium meal in his bowels which should turn his motions pale pink tomorrow."

"I wonder what the home help will make of that," Staff chuckled. "She'll probably have him re-admitted with pernicious anaemia."

ILL GOTTEN GAINS

Christmas drew near and gaudy decorations added some cheer to the normally drab green and cream of the hospital wards.

Lowry couldn't wait for her shift to end as she was off to a fancy dress party that night with the following day off.

The boring party had hardly any food apart from pickled onions and crisps. But Lowry's rum and cokes were going to her head without food.

"Ben, it's Christmas. Shall we hit the town and go and see the tree in Clayton Square?"

"Okay. Let's see if anyone else wants to come," he replied.

There was only one take up on his offer. Ben the policeman, Obi, a white rabbit with a black face and Lowry the nun climbed into Ben's car and went off to hit the town.

Liverpool City centre sparkled with Christmas lights. Ben parked the car and they walked the short distance to Lewis's Store, aware of the strange looks they received from passers-by. Why a nun and a big white rabbit with a black face were being escorted by a policeman, was obviously a conundrum they couldn't work out?

Obadiah hailed from Nigeria. Lowry loved his giggling, his sense of fun and his dazzling white toothed smile. He was studying at the Liverpool School of Tropical Medicine after which he intended to return to his homeland and put his skills into practice.

The three stood on the steps of the Adelphi Hotel opposite Lewis' store. High above the door to the store the enormous

Epstein bronze statue of a full frontal naked man, with his arms in the air, towered above them like a naked policeman directing traffic.

"See that fellow there," Lowry said, pointing to the statue. "We girls used to dare each other to strip off in front of him to see if he'd get an erection 'cos none of us had ever seen a real one, only a cross section diagram."

"You're pissed, Lowry Stuart," Ben retorted.

"No I'm not you handsome hunk. I'm hungry for food and a man in a uniform. But I'll concentrate on my belly for now and move on to the uniform later."

The first objective was to find something to eat, but between them they had only one shilling and sixpence halfpenny.

"I've got a brilliant idea," Lowry told her companions. "When I'm shopping in Allerton Road, I see loads of nuns brazenly walking into the shops and asking for charity money and they get it, so I'm going to have a go. What d'you think, Ben?"

"You can't do that, woman," he stated in horror. "It's against the law. It's called obtaining money under false whatsits or something."

"Look Benjamin, if you want to arrest me then go ahead. You've got the uniform, so where are the hand-cuffs?"

"Don't involve me in this," Obi moaned. "I'll be deported."

The three of them were still standing on the steps of the Adelphi Hotel where throngs of people were making their way to the Empire Theatre for the night's performance.

"Obi, stop whingeing," Lowry told him. "A six foot white rabbit with a black face is a darned sight more conspicuous on the streets of Liverpool, than the likes of a sweet virginal nun. So you and Ben go and hide behind those cars." She pointed to a line of swanky motors parked against the curb. "And don't come out 'til I tell you," she bossily shouted.

She approached a small group of well dressed, middle aged, middle class theatre-goers who, from the satisfied expressions on their faces, had obviously just eaten well in the

Adelphi Restaurant. It was now Ben's, Obi's and her turn to eat well.

"Excuse me," she said, as she approached the group, "but have you seen my Mother Superior? She can't have gone far. We are collecting for the starving peoples of Africa."

This was in fact, the truth. Obi was from Africa and he was starving.

"No, I'm sorry Sister, but we haven't seen her," the kindly gentleman replied.

Lowry gave him her most saintly smile.

"Never mind, Sir," she simpered. "She's bound to turn up. Meanwhile I'll go on collecting and may the Christmas blessings of Jesus Christ our beloved Saviour, be with you all."

She couldn't believe her luck. Not only was the kindly gentleman reaching into his top inside pocket, but so was his friend. Wallets appeared. Her heart raced with excitement. Wallets meant paper money not small change. Each man gave her a one pound note. An absolute fortune!

Sister Lowry thanked them profusely and calculated in her head that they now had two pounds one shilling and sixpence halfpenny which was as much as she earned in a week as a nurse after laundry and living costs had been deducted. The generous group made their way to the theatre as the ecstatic nun sauntered to the line of cars.

Obi had tears of laughter running down his cheeks.

"What a performance, Lowry," he chuckled. "When you said, 'you were collecting for the starving peoples of Africa,' that nearly finished me."

"That, sweet Obi, was the truth. You are a starving African, so I wasn't doing anything dishonest," Lowry laughed back. "However, Ben and I will share your good fortune. I've got two pounds. Those guys must be rich. Shall I see if I can get any more?"

"Not on your life! Let's get out of here before our luck runs out," Ben urgently advised.

The new Chinese restaurant on the corner of Dale Street, supplied them with a takeaway fit for the Emperor of China and Lowry still had enough change to buy some cigarettes and a couple of pairs of black stockings with some change left over.

They devoured their banquet sitting on a pile of rubble in the roofless bombed out church of Saint Luke. The three happy people then marched back to the car with their arms linked together.

The slightly tipsy nun in the middle irreverently sang.

"I'm Mary the nun, never been done, Queen of all the virgins. I'm just a cripple with only one nipple, Doing amazing things with some gherkins."

They were half way home when they all realised they had forgotten to see the tree in Clayton Square.

"Never mind," Ben said. "Bedecked Christmas trees all look the same to me."

"Like us black folk," Obi laughed.

Life was such fun.

THE PAIN IN THE NECK

Lowry loved her every third weekend off with her mum. The woman was so much fun. Lou had managed to stay within the law at the research establishment. Her next show of strength and solidarity was to march with the Campaign for Nuclear Disarmament. That should please the wig wearing magistrate! Her teaching career had ended when she reached sixty years of age. She missed the children and the classroom and resented being classified as too doddery to teach when she knew she had so much to offer.

Mr Hargreaves was sounding off again as Lowry approached the ward on Monday morning. He had arrived five days earlier with a huge carbuncle on the back of his neck. Once the infected matter had been removed it left a crater that almost touched his spine. Oxygen gauze was now packed into the cavity.

"You're just a bunch of useless women," he ranted at Sister. "I sat 'ere all night calling for a bottle and did any of the night staff come? Did they 'eck as like. So I pissed me bed. Are you 'appy now?"

Sister endeavoured to calm him down

"There's no need to shout, Mr Hargreaves. I am not responsible for the night staff, but Nurse Stuart will change your bedding and give you a blanket bath to freshen you up. She will also bring you a bottle."

"I don't need a damn bottle now, you useless woman. Didn't you 'ear me. I've already done it in me bed."

Sister walked off, offended at being called a useless woman.

Lowry drew the curtains round the bed and helped the unhappy man into the chair, determined to ignore his continued ranting. She stripped the soaking bed. It was a good job he hadn't soiled the sheets or she would be tempted to rub his nose in them.

"When I've finished washing you I may as well do your pressure points to stop you being disturbed again," she suggested.

"No you don't," he roared. "I can 'ear 'em giving out breakfasts. Just get a move on or that miserable orderly woman will miss me out. Are you trying to starve me now, girl?"

Lowry snapped.

"Don't you ever call me girl. My name is Nurse Stuart to you. Next time Staff packs the oxygen gauze into your neck I'll ask her to pack some into your mouth as well, 'cos you're ranting is getting on my nerves. I'll also ask the orderly to do you an extra piece of toast so you don't starve. How's that?"

"Well I suppose that's some compensation for the treatment I'm getting 'ere."

As Lowry gathered the washing equipment onto the trolley she wondered if perhaps Mr Hargreaves had an enlarged prostate. She knew it was a problem for men his age. The little smiley Methodist Minister had been a constant dribbler.

"Mr Hargreaves, when I go off duty tonight, I'll smuggle a bottle to you, but don't crack on, it's not allowed. Keep it hidden under your sheets. Okay!"

"I won't say anything, me dear. But what's wrong with me walking to the toilet. There's nowt wrong with me legs? They said to bring slippers with yer, but I've never worn the bloody things since I got 'ere."

Lowry laughed.

"You lot are under control when you're sitting in a bed with sheets that are tucked in too tightly. Anyway, you'd only make Sister's ward look untidy if you were wandering around.

Those are the rules, Mr Hargreaves. Anyway I'll put these wet pyjamas in a bag for your wife to collect when she visits. Don't forget to tell her that they are in your locker."

Lowry bent down to open the locker door.

"Don't you go nosing in there," he aggressively said. "Leave them on the chair."

"Why, what have you got hidden in your locker that you don't want me to see?"

"Mind your bloody business," he rudely retorted.

"Mr Hargreaves! I'm shocked. You've got naughty magazines hidden in there, haven't you?" Lowry chuckled.

"No I haven't, I've got some Guinness me wife brings in."

"Is that all? Well keep them hidden from Sister. I think she's temperance."

"I know she's got a temper, you don't 'ave to tell me," he earnestly said.

THE TAPEWORM

Without alcohol for three weeks, Leif's liver mended itself remarkably quickly. The doctor had been pleased with his recovery and arranged for him to be discharged, with a warning that any further drinking would be seriously detrimental. The liver was now repairing itself and would continue to do so unless Leif took to drinking again. Lowry helped him clear his locker.

"I don't want to see you in here again," she said. "Not because I don't like you, because I do, but it will mean you are drinking again and there's only so much your liver can take."

"Yes, Nurse Lowry, but I've already had a lecture from the doctor," he said,

"Well, have you taken heed of his words?" she asked. "I know I'm sounding bossy, but they say that drinking excessively is usually a substitute for something that's missing in your life."

Leif shut his small suitcase and put on his jacket.

"I'll show you something, young Lowry," he sadly said, digging into his inside pocket. He produced a black and white photograph. "This is what's missing from my life. My beautiful wife, Inger and my lovely little daughter, Lori. I've lost them both. The war may be over, but the dreadful consequences remain."

Lowry felt shocked. She remembered Lou's words. 'Never judge anyone, until you understand why they do what they do.' She studied the picture for a while before handing it back to Leif .

"Your wife really was beautiful. Her hair was so blonde and your little girl was absolutely gorgeous and she was dark haired like you."

"Yes, I was the happiest man on earth at the time."

The face of Marcus Marriot appeared at the ward door. He waved and smiled his beautifully ugly smile. He approached the bed.

"I've come to fetch my Viking friend," he announced.

She watched as Leif went from bed to bed, shaking hands and wishing the patients all the best.

"Look after him please, Marcus," she said. "He's a very sweet man, but so sad."

"I know," he replied. "I'll do my best, but he's a man who has a mind of his own. He's going to have to be strong. I'll help him as much as I can."

The men walked towards the door. Leif turned and smiled.

"Look in the drawer of the locker, Lowry," he said.

The ward doors closed behind him. Lowry opened the drawer and found six pairs of black stockings, a box of Black Magic chocolates and a banana. Bananas were not part of his diet, but Leif not wanting to offend his friend Marcus, distributed them to the other patients. This one he had saved for Lowry. Drawn on the top of the firm yellow skin was a face with a big smile. A double breasted jacket, in black ink, had been carefully drawn with anchors in the centre of the buttons. Lowry smiled. She knew this was Leif, the banana man. Are well, there goes the captain, she thought. I really had a soft spot for him. We're like ships that pass in the night. She pulled the sheets from the bed.

Another patient was due for discharge on that day. Mr Hargreaves' carbuncle had improved sufficiently for him to be sent home. The District Nurse would have to listen to his grumbling from now on. His long suffering wife arrived to fetch him, with the wrong pair of trousers, black shoes instead of brown and 'where was his bloody cap?' Lowry watched in amusement at the farce that ensued as the bedside curtains billowed and flapped, with two hidden bodies bumping into each other.

"Get out of my way, woman. You're more 'indrance than 'elp," the old grump shouted. "And did you bring them things I asked you to?"

Eventually the performers appeared from behind the curtains. It surprised Lowry to see how different the patients looked without their pyjamas. Mr Hargreaves unceremoniously thrust a package into Lowry's hand.

"This is for you," he said.

"You shouldn't have," she answered, feeling embarrassed. The parcel contained a woolly hat, woolly scarf and woolly gloves. "Thank-you, you're very kind."

"No, I ain't," he gruffly said. "She knits 'em, not me."

Lowry watched as the couple left the ward. Amazing what an illicit urine bottle and an extra round of toast will do, she thought.

Mr Pritchard died. He had been on the ward since Lowry first started there. She had grown fond of the gentle man whilst chatting to him about his family and grandchildren when she changed his colostomy bag. His bronchitis had developed into pneumonia and he was in heart failure. For three days he had been shrouded by the bedside curtains and surrounded by his family and a Roman Catholic Hospital Chaplain who cited Latin prayers that Mr Pritchard couldn't hear, nor, probably, understand. The ward atmosphere was respectfully sombre, each patient being aware of a pending death behind permanently drawn curtains, even though Mr Pritchard's deteriorating condition was never discussed.

As a new student, undergoing training, she had been taught to lay out a dead body, but it had been a large rubber dummy. The lesson had been a giggle, especially when Helen had poked the cotton wool so hard up the anal orifice with the slim metal probe, it punctured the dummy's abdomen giving it two belly buttons instead of one. This almost reduced the tutor to tears as she heard the air slowly hiss out of the new orifice Helen had created. The tutor seemed to have developed a great fondness for her rubber dummies and skeletons over the years. However a bicycle tyre repair outfit and a pump sorted the problem.

But Mr Pritchard was a human being, not a latex model.

Lowry and Susan, the third year nurse, washed the corpse and filled every bodily orifice with cotton wool using the long slim metal probe. His ostomy pouching system on the left hand side of his abdomen was removed and put into the hazardous waste bin leaving the stoma that had been produced from part of his intestine exposed. More cotton wool was then packed into the opening. A bandage was looped under the chin with the tails running up the cheeks and then tied in a bow on top of the head. It may have stopped the jaw gaping, but to stick a bow in the thinning hair of an elderly dead man made him look ridiculous. Two small weights were finally placed over the closed eyes to keep them from opening. The mortuary trolley removed the body covered in a white sheet.

Susan had laid out many bodies and seemed to take it in her stride. Lowry found the whole procedure uncomfortably macabre. Facing death was bad enough, but having to stuff every hole with cotton wool was something a taxidermist should be doing not a young nurse, she believed.

No sooner had Mr Pritchard died, than a Mr Withers occupied the bed, with his exceedingly large body and difficulties breathing, caused by fluid in the chest cavity. He was scheduled to undergo the procedure called thoracentesis to remove the fluid from the space between the lungs and the chest wall. Lowry gave him extra pillows to prop himself against, to relieve his shortness of breath and also gave him an empty sputum mug. He could fill it to the top for all she cared. The steriliser could have the pleasure of dealing with it.

Withers seemed a most inappropriate name for such an obese man and it was going to take her twice as long to blanket bath so enormous an expanse of flesh, she decided. He was also going to need a hell of a lot of talcum powder under the spare tractor tyre he had round his middle. Indeed, his spare tyre hung so low it covered his genitals, making access to his toileting equipment something of a fumble for him.

The following morning another patient arrived. He was thin and pale with a shock of red hair. Mr Cowley's vomiting and diarrhoea had been diagnosed as caused by an intestinal tape worm. It was reported in his notes that he liked to eat raw bacon. Lowry remembered the lecture on parasites. Pigs snuffled around in the soil took in a bladder worm which then attached itself to the pig's muscle. Once in the human intestine it became a tapeworm. A toxic dose of Niclocide killed the parasite and the scolex suckers released their hold on his gut. Now it was time for him to pass the foreign body. Lowry was assigned to deal with the problem.

"Why do I get all the shitty jobs?" she moaned. She trundled the commode to his bedside

"Okay, Mr Cowley, this commode is going to be a bit uncomfortable, because you are likely to be sitting on it for many hours to come. I'll get you a rubber ring to sit on, but please make sure you aim through the hole in the middle."

The poor fellow nodded. Lowry drew the curtains around him and once her patient was comfortably posed she withdrew to the kitchen to make him a cup of tea. Staff Nurse had made herself a cup of coffee and leaned on the sink.

"Lowry, my sweet," she said. "Med School has asked for the tape worm to be collected in a jar of formaldehyde for teaching purposes."

"Good God, Staff! The man can't sit for hours on a jar of formaldehyde," Lowry exploded.

"You chump," she laughed, "he'll pass it in the commode and you'll have to get it out very carefully with some tweezers making sure you don't break it and gently pop it in the formaldehyde."

Lowry's mouth gaped open for an instant.

"You've got to be kidding me, Staff. As far as I'm concerned this goes above and beyond the call of duty. Is this some sort of joke?" she implored.

"No, Lowry. I'm on the level."

"Shit! Shit! Shit!"

"Exactly," Staff retorted. "Lots of it."

Lowry left the kitchen.

"Sorry the tea took so long, Mr Cowley, but I got side tracked," she said as she gave the patient his tea. She had six hours of duty left. "Mr Cowley, it's strongly advisable that you don't push the tape worm out too quickly. If you bear down too much, you'll get haemorrhoids and strain your bowels. So just let it happen naturally and don't force it out. Do you understand?" The patient nodded. "Are you sure you understand? Whatever you do, don't bear down. Are you sitting comfortably?"

"Yes thank you, Nurse," Mr Cowley replied.

With any luck, the revolting thing will emerge when the night shift arrive for duty and they can pickle it, Lowry prayed.

For some reason the hours dragged slowly. The last half an hour of duty seemed like an eternity.

"Staff, it will be just my bloody luck for the thing to appear now," Lowry bleated.

"Don't worry, honey, I've left a note in the book for night staff to deal with the thing if he hasn't passed it before we leave."

"Thanks, I'll go and tell Mr Cowley that he can start bearing down now. I told him not to in case he got haemorrhoids, in the hope that it would slow things up."

"You crafty little mare," she laughed.

On the stroke of seven o'clock, Lowry bolted through the ward doors and skipped light heartedly to join the attic gang.

Much to her delight, next morning, the offensive thin white segmented worm, measuring about thirty inches, floated as dead as a dodo in its jar of formaldehyde on the sluice room window sill. The medical students were welcome to it!

After being seen by the doctor, the patient was discharged home with a large box of nutritious but tasteless Glaxo Complan to build him up again.

Lowry pulled the sheets from the bed and remade it with fresh linen for the next occupant. She may not yet be a professional nurse, but she sure was a professional maker of beds with knife edged hospital corners!

THE SEAMAN'S HOME

Marcus Marriot had not seen or heard from his friend, Captain Svenerson, for three days. Leif had been very depressed the last time they had met. Marcus was worried. He called into the Adelphi Hotel.

"Can you ring Captain Svenerson for me please, and tell him I'm in the foyer?" he asked the attractive blonde receptionist who stood with a permanent smile on her face behind the desk.

"I'm sorry, Sir," she said, "but the captain booked out of the hotel two days ago."

"Good God!" Alarm bells began to ring. "Where the hell has he gone? Did he leave a forwarding address?" Marcus urgently asked.

The receptionist shook her head with the permanent smile still fixed.

"Sorry, no he didn't. He settled his bill and left in one of the taxis from the rank outside the hotel."

"What time was this?" he asked.

"Ten o'clock."

"Was that morning or evening?"

"It was the morning, Sir."

Marcus turned towards the door, shouting 'thanks' as he left. Two taxis waited to be hailed. He approached the first one.

"Did you pick up a chap from here two days ago at ten in the morning? He's tall, dark haired with…,"

"No mate. I was taking a passenger to Speke Airport at that time," the taxi driver explained.

Marcus approached the second taxi, but got the same negative response.

"How many of you normally stand here?" he asked.

"Five mostly. We're in and out all the time. What's this guy done?" the driver nosily asked.

"Nothing, but I need to find him as soon as possible. His mother is seriously ill."

"I thought you was the fuzz," the man said. "Leave it with me and I'll ask around."

Marcus took a card from his inside pocket.

"Here," he said. "It's my card, I'm only round the corner in Dale Street. There's five bob in it for you, if you can trace the cabbie for me by noon."

Marcus returned to his office and pondered on the fate of his friend. Leif had seemed to be doing well and keeping off the booze, but Marcus was pretty sure it wouldn't take much for him to hit the bottle again. He concentrated on a case of embezzlement he was investigating for a local firm of solicitors. At twelve thirty a tap on the door interrupted his note taking.

"Come," he shouted.

The grinning face of the cab driver appeared as the door opened.

"Your friend was taken to the Seaman's Home," he announced. "He was a bit the worse for wear. D'you know where the place is?"

"Of course, of course," Marcus irritably replied.

"D'you want me to take you there?"

"No, I can walk from here." He gave the taxi driver the promised five shillings. "Thanks for your help." He impatiently waved the cabbie away.

"I hope his mother gets better, mate," the cabbie kindly said.

Marcus locked the office door and strolled towards the Pier Head. What the hell was Leif doing in the Seaman's Home, he wondered? It wasn't the place for an officer, least of all a Ship's Captain. As a police constable he had attended many a drunken brawl between the ratings who stayed there when on shore leave. The door of the home stood open. Marcus approached a pipe sucking, bearded old sea-dog whose weather beaten face implied many years at sea. He could have been anywhere between fifty and ninety years old.

"I'm looking for a seaman called, Svenerson. Is he here?" he demanded of the sea-dog.

"What d'you want him for?" the man asked.

"Just answer my bloody question. Is he here?" Marcus angrily shouted.

"Keep your hair on, mate. He's in room eleven. We don't normally get a Ship's Captain staying here, but he was in a bit of a bad way. He asked not to be disturbed. I haven't seen him for a couple of days. Anyhow, what's he done?"

"Mind your damn business. Where's room eleven?"

"Fifth one down on the left," the sea-dog said, pointing down the corridor.

Marcus knew something was wrong. His friend was in trouble.

"Give me the master key for the door," he sharply asked.

The man slowly and arrogantly tapped his empty pipe into a large ashtray that had been shaped to look like a ship's wheel.

"I can't do that. Can't give you the key it's...,"

Marcus's patience ran dry.

"If you don't give me the fucking key now, I'll haul you in for obstructing the police."

The sea-dog bad-temperedly handed over the key.

The bedside light gave off a dim glow as Marcus entered the seedy room. He shut the door behind him. The strong smell of whisky almost intoxicated him as he walked to the window and drew back the sun faded curtains. He turned from the window and saw Leif, fully clothed, lying motionless on a single bed. Two empty whisky bottles lay on the floor.

"Oh, my dear friend, what the hell have you done?" he wailed.

He sat beside Leif's body and touched the inert man's clammy face. Clutched in his friend's hand was a black and

white photograph of a pretty blonde woman holding her child
in her arms.

THE EMERGENCY ADMISSION

The sound of an ambulance in a rush was a familiar sound to the occupants of the hospital, so much so, it appeared as no more than background noise. Lowry paid little heed to the crisis. Staff called the student nurse from her duties.

"Lowry, get the intravenous drip equipment, the trolley and extra pillows and bring them to the private room," she urgently said. "We've got an emergency admission coming in and that's the only bed we've got. Then you go for your coffee break."

"Okay, Staff," she replied. "Are you sure you don't want me to stay and help?"

"No, you go for your coffee and get back as soon as you can, honey."

After delivering the laden trolley to Staff, Lowry left the ward and made her way to the canteen. She stopped in surprise to see Marcus Marriot walking towards her. He looked solemn.

"Nurse Lowry, I think Leif is unconscious and the porters are wheeling him to your ward. I came with him in the ambulance. It doesn't look good. I found him in the..,"

"Marcus, you look shocked. I'm just going for a coffee, I've only got twenty minutes," she responded, interrupting him mid-sentence. "Come with me and have a coffee. He must be the emergency admission that's coming into the private room."

They walked in silence to the canteen and joined the queue.

"I think he's given up," Marcus said. "What sent me into a state of shock is the way I found him. I think he's reached the stage when he doesn't care if he lives or dies. Why did he move to such a place as the Seaman's Home?" he continued, as he and Lowry walked to a free table with their insipid coffees. "To think such a brave and highly decorated man can end up like this."

Lowry place her hand on Marcus's arm and squeezed it gently.

"We'll look after him for you," she earnestly said.

"He's in a bad way. I don't think he'll see forty five. He can't give up drinking."

"But you drink, How come it doesn't have the same effect on you?" she asked.

"I've probably got a liver that looks like a large Swiss cheese by now, but I drink all the time. Leif spent weeks and often months at sea and never drank. But he carries with him so much guilt about his child and Liverpool has a morbid hold on him. It was when he got back here that he'd go on a bender. It's the most dangerous way to drink. The liver never has time to recover from the quantity drunk, before it's being hammered again."

Lowry looked at her watch.

"I'll have to go," she said.

The chair scraped on the floor as she got up. Marcus stood and put his hand in his jacket pocket.

"Nurse Lowry, I found this photograph in Leif's hand. It's of his wife and baby daughter. Would you take it and make sure he has it close to him?"

"Of course! He showed it to me once. I'll see you soon, Marcus."

Lowry studied the portrait again, as she walked the corridor to the ward. The poor man! Their deaths must have been such a devastating blow to him, she mused. She sat on a corridor bench staring at the photograph. The smiling Mother looked so proud staring down into the face of her little daughter. The baby's smile showed four little bottom milk teeth. Lowry was not normally sentimental, but she felt her eyes well up. How had these two beautiful people died? She stood up and sniffed and made her way back to the ward.

The door to the private room stood open. Staff bent over her patient with Sister standing by watching on.

"Is that you back from your break, Nurse Stuart?" Staff called.

"Yes, Staff Nurse," Nurse Stuart formally replied.

"Come in, because I want you to sit with Captain Svernerson when I've finished with the drip."

Lowry saw that Leif had a bluish tinge. His breathing was shallow. His eyes were closed. The office telephone rang.

"I'll leave you to it now, Staff Nurse," Sister said, and left to answer the call.

"How is he, Staff?" Lowry asked.

"It's hard to say, honey. If he survives the next twenty four hours then he'll make it. So I want you to make sure he is propped up and doesn't go onto his back. Watch him closely even though the doctor has inserted a tube into his windpipe to assist his breathing. Keep him warm, his temperature is low. If he shows signs of wanting to vomit called me immediately. We must not let vomit get into his lungs. I've catheterised him. Also we have to stabilize him. The intravenous fluids will replace the electrolytes and re-hydrate him."

"What are electrolytes?" Lowry asked.

"The body's minerals, Lowry, like sodium, potassium, calcium, and magnesium. They carry electrical impulses to the cells for the body's healthy functioning. The word electrolytes means, salts. I think it's a Greek word, but I'm not certain. The captain will have a low blood sugar level. So everything in that drip, including vitamins will hopefully re-dress the imbalances in his system. According to the ambulance crew, it seems he had drunk two bottles of whisky that they are aware of, and that's a hell of a lot of toxic poisoning."

"Is he unconscious, Staff?"

"No. I think he's in a stupor. He's not responding to anything, but he did register discomfort when the endotracheal tube was inserted, so keep a watch on him and if anything worries you, fetch me immediately." Staff left with the equipment trolley.

Lowry took the photograph from her apron pocket and propped it against the water jug. She became mesmerised by the droplets of life saving fluids that dripped slowly into the bulb and into the tube and then into the vein of the patient's arm. The white of the hospital gown accentuated the bluish tinge of his skin.

She noticed Leif's uniform in a heap on the chair. She picked up the jacket with the wonderful gold buttons and ran her finger over the burnished surface. Her finger then traced the pattern of gold braid round the sleeve. She picked up the cap, took off her white hat and plonked the cap on her head and walked to the mirror above the washbasin. Suddenly from deep within the cubbyhole of her mind an image appeared of Mr King with Mrs Queen. She heard the sound of a child's voice calling, 'No, no, don't go away.' She removed the captain's cap from her head and replaced it with her nurses hat.

"Fancy remembering that," Lowry whispered as she carefully folded the uniform.

She detected a strong smell of alcohol, yet the shirt had a slight hint of Old Spice aftershave. The patient groaned. She hurried to the bed. He was shivering. She fetched an extra blanket from the chair and tucked it under his chin and round his shoulders. He groaned again. Lowry sat next to the bed and held his hand. She studied his fingers. They were long with immaculate nails, something one didn't expect to see on a drunk. She noticed his breathing was becoming less shallow.

"I know you can't hear me," she quietly said, "but you're taking the coward's way out by trying to kill yourself. What will your death do to Marcus? He cares a lot about you. And anyway, you were our patient and you did so well, but you've reached rock bottom now. I guess you'll have a thumping head when you come round and you need a blanket bath 'cos your pores are sweating alcohol and you stink."

Lowry realised she was prattling aimlessly into a pair of whisky sodden ears. She took a large piece of lint from the table in the corner and walked to the washbasin and ran it under the cold tap.

"I'm just going to sponge your face …..no, no, don't move your arm," she quickly ordered as he tried to raise his hand from the covers. "You've got a drip in your vein, so keep still."

Lowry gently smoothed the refreshing lint over her patient's face.

"You need a shave, Captain Svenerson. If you went on the bridge with this stubble they'd stick you in the brig." She hadn't really noticed his long dark eyelashes until now. "You don't deserve to have long dark eyelashes, Leif. Most women have to put thick mascara on and would die to have lashes like yours and what are you doing? Dying from alcohol poisoning instead of appreciating those eyelashes of yours."

The young nurse remained at the patient's bedside for a further hour, with Staff popping in occasionally. Leif opened his eyes. They closed again almost immediately. He groaned and his eyes opened again and remained that way.

"Are you coming round, Captain?" she asked, "because it's about time. I need to go for my lunch break and have a sneaky fag, so I'll go and get Staff. Now don't go anywhere. Okay!"

"Yes, he's waking up," Staff said. "My God, this man's got some constitution. Make sure he has plenty of fluids, Lowry."

"Shall I make him a cup of tea, Staff?"

"No. No tea or coffee, just water to re-hydrate him," she replied. "I'll get the doctor to give him another once over, and we'll remove the breathing support but I think he's going to be okay until the next time. You know, Lowry, we will do all we can to help him, but we're just wasting our time if he refuses to help himself and what a waste of a handsome guy that would be." She bent over the patient's bed and peered into his face. "Are you listening to me Captain?" she asked. He gave a slight nod. "You go off for your lunch break now, honey, and I'll stay and wash him down. I'll see you in half an hour."

Three days later, Leif requested to be transferred onto the ward. He had hated the isolation in the private room. Being alone, with feelings of disgust for himself had left him so despondent that Sister considered calling the psychiatrist to see him. Marcus visited his friend, bringing with him, pyjamas and toiletries.

"What the hell were you doing in the Seaman's Home, Leif?" he asked. "It's no place for a Ship's Cap...,"

"I know, I know," he answered impatiently. "I don't remember much about what was going on in my head at the time. I was sitting in the lounge reading the paper and having a coffee when a resident started chatting. He ordered himself a whisky and offered me one. I first said no. But, as I watched him downing it, I lost my resolve never to touch the stuff again. My whole being craved a drink. I said to the guy, 'I think I will join you in that drink.' I didn't think there would be any harm having just one. You can guess the rest. I ended up buying a bottle and going to my room. It was like the nectar of the Gods, yet with every mouthful I was filled with self-loathing. The more I drank the worse it got. I told myself I wasn't fit to be a father and perhaps it was best that I'd never found Lori. I wasn't even fit to be a Ship's Master. I bought two bottles of Scotch from the barman. The next morning I booked out of the hotel. The Seaman's Home was the only place that seemed suitable for me. When I got there, all I wanted was a drink to shut out the pain. You see, Marcus when I read the paper in the hotel lounge, I saw the date at the top and it hit me like a ton of bricks. It was Inger's birthday and all I could think about was how angry she would be with me if she had known that I had lost the child we both loved so much. Then I felt angry with her for putting her life in danger and leaving me and Lori without her. I know I'm not going to live long because whisky is the only means I have to blot out the self-reproach I cope with every day. I just don't want to go on living like this. So I told the caretaker I wasn't to be disturbed." Leif gave a long slow sigh. "There, Marcus, you have it. I have no reason to live."

Marcus sat silently, chewing on the grapes he had brought in for Leif. He was at a loss as to how help his friend. Visiting time came to an end. Marcus downheartedly left the ward.

THE REVELATION

"I never drank when on the bridge," Leif explained, as he and Lowry chatted while she washed him. "It was during shore leave that I really hit the drink, sometimes a bottle or more of whisky a day."

"I know, Marcus told me. No wonder your poor liver is protesting," she replied.

"But I never classed myself as an alcoholic because I only drank when off duty. I thought I had it under control but unfortunately it began to control me. The Ship's Surgeon recognised that I had a problem and recommended extended shore leave. Mind you, he wasn't one to talk. He prescribed himself pink gins like his life depended on them."

Lowry rummaged in the locker and found Leif's toothbrush and toothpaste.

"Here Leif, clean your teeth and I'll comb your hair. What style would you like today? You can have a fringe, a duck's arse or swept to one side like that German madman."

"I certainly don't want the latter, Lowry. I find anything remotely German quite repugnant to me."

"You were a ship's captain during the war, weren't you?" he nodded. "So you've always had gold buttons on your jacket and gold round your sleeves and hat." He smiled and nodded again. "I love gold buttons, always have done. I got into trouble at the convent because I cut all the gold buttons off my Nana' navy blue cardigan and cut the black buttons off my blazer and sewed the gold buttons on to it. It looked wonderful. As a punishment for my vanity I had to sweep the leaves off the long driveway of the convent. It was a windy day and Mother Superior kept making me do it again and again." Lowry stood back to admire her hair dressing skills. "I've given you a duck's arse," she proudly announced. "Have you got family in Norway, Leif? There's nothing in your notes to say who your next of kin are. Marcus Marriot is the only person you've named."

"No, not any more, I'm sorry to say. I have no family anywhere. The Nazi's saw to that. I understand that you put the photo of my wife and daughter on the locker. Thank you. It's very precious to me."

"Marcus gave it to me. You had it in your hand when he found you," she explained. "Your wife was lovely and your daughter looked so cute. Was it the Germans who killed them?"

"No, no, my daughter is still alive but my wife was killed. She worked with the Resistance."

"I'm sorry, I just assumed," the nurse said, with embarrassment. "I know I'm a chatterbox and if I'm asking too many nosey questions, then tell me to shut up."

"No, my dear, you're not asking too many questions. I like to talk about them. I think that's part of my problem. I bottle it up and sometimes find it too painful to think about them. I also carry this weight of guilt inside me which drags me down."

"What is it, Leif, that weighs you down? Can you tell me?"

"Not really, no."

"Okay, but when did you last see your daughter?" Lowry asked. "Is she living in Norway?"

"No, I put her in temporary care and came back for her after the war but sadly because of a serious oversight on my part she was lost and so she was adopted. She is actually living here, in Liverpool. That's why I remain here. I feel somehow closer to her. I don't know what she looks like, but I search the faces of all the young girls I pass in the street and wonder if one of them is my daughter. I couldn't leave her in Norway. You may find this hard to believe, but the Germans saw the Norwegians as good Aryan stock. My worry was, that a little motherless Norwegian baby would be whisked off to some German family who were looking for a child. I couldn't let the Fascist bastards get their hands on my daughter. She is of pure Nordic descent. It wasn't safe in Norway. I haven't seen my daughter for eighteen years." He loudly sighed. "Do you know, Lowry? I think about her every day. What does she look like? Is she as pretty as her mother? What is she doing, but most importantly is she happy."

"What a sad story, Leif. Is this the weight you told me about that pulls you down?" He stared forlornly at the ceiling and nodded his head. "Well I just hope your little girl was as lucky as me and found a wonderful mum, like I did," Lowry said, as she cleared away the washing equipment. "I was adopted, when I was seven, by a teacher called Louise Stuart. She was a widow which unfortunately meant I never had a dad. I used to be known as Lowry Stephenson and lived in a Liverpool orphanage, but my name was changed to Stuart on the day I was adopted. I don't know anything about my real parents."

Lowry noticed her patient's hands were shaking. He was staring at her in a strange way.

"Oh heck, Leif, you've got the shakes. I thought that was under control," she sympathetically told him.

"Oh, my God! Oh, my God!" he desperately repeated.

Lowry grabbed his hands to help quell the shaking.

"What's the matter with you, Leif? You're in withdrawal aren't you? You're shaking like a jelly. I guess your body is craving a drink, but not anymore, please. Try to be strong. I'll get some iced water for you."

She dashed to the kitchen fridge and filled his water jug with ice cubes and water. On her return to his bedside she noticed tears rolling uncontrollably down his cheeks. She poured a glass of iced water and held it to his lips. He cupped his hands around hers. She felt his hands trembling. Poor Leif, the young nurse thought. How could the desperate need for a drink reduce a brave man to tears when he had faced so many horrors of war? Leif lay back against the pillow and slowly shook his head from side to side.

"I can't believe it," he murmured. "It's not possible. I can't believe it."

"Well you have to believe it," Lowry seriously told him. "Your body is craving alcohol. It must be dreadful for you, but please don't rub your head on the pillow," she pleaded, in an attempt to lighten the moment, "you'll ruin the duck's arse hair style I've just given you."

The overwrought man gave a limp smile.

"My beautiful little daughter," he muttered. "My beautiful funny little Lori."

"I'm sure she is happy, somewhere, Leif," Lowry gently said. "Nobody adopts a little girl unless they want to love her."

A loud fog horn voice shouted from across the ward.

"Nurse Stuart, you cannot spend so much time with one patient. Would you please hurry along? It will be morning drinks time before you've finished the washes," Sister bellowed. "And when you've finished morning drinks I want you in the cupboard to tidy the bed linen on the shelves."

'Every despot seems to have a punishment cupboard,' Lowry mumbled.

LEIF'S DILEMMA

Sunday visiting time was exactly one hour from three o'clock to four. On the stroke of three, the ward doors opened and the stampede began again.

Lowry noticed Marcus carried a big brown bag of fruit for Leif. Her suspicions were immediately aroused. She approached him before he arrived at Leif's bed.

"Marcus, have you any alcohol in that bag, because if you have I must take it from you? I hope you don't mind."

"No, Nurse Lowry, I haven't, I do assure you. The last thing I want to do, is provide Leif with alcohol," he explained. "Would you like to check?"

"No, of course not! I believe you, but Leif was so desperate for a drink yesterday that he was in tears and he seems in a strange mood today and a bit pre-occupied."

Marcus smiled his beautifully ugly smile.

"I'll go and cheer up my old Viking friend, then," he said, and walked off.

"So, my old mate, it's not that easy to fight those demons, but you're getting there," Marcus said, dumping his assortment of fruits on Leif's bed. "Lowry says you're a bit pre-occupied."

"Thanks for these," Leif said, putting his hand on the bag of fruits, knowing his neighbours would be appreciative since he was not allowed to eat any of them. "I am pre-occupied because I'm in one hell of a quandary and I don't know how to handle it. I'm feeling numb. Yet I'm unbelievably happy, and I suppose, in a state of emotional shock."

"You can start by telling me what's the matter is. It's Marcus Marriot Investigation Agency, to the rescue! It'll be Marcus Marriot Investigation Bureau soon. I've hired a part time secretary. Unfortunately, she's not the sort you invite to sit on your knee. She's older than me with peroxide hair, a large rump and titty-bottle legs, but she's a bloody good shorthand typist."

"No, Marcus, I'm serious. My life has just been turned upside down so just listen to me, please. Nurse Lowry Stuart was adopted when she was seven years old by a woman called Louise Stuart. Her name before that was Lowry Stephenson and she lived in a Liverpool orphanage. She knows nothing about her natural parents. I tell you, Marcus, this is no coincidence. Two little girls called Lowry Stephenson, both adopted aged seven, both eighteen years old now. Not possible! And anyway, your investigations revealed only one Lowry Stephenson in care at that time. She's my baby. I know she's my daughter. She is my little Lori Svenerson. Have you noticed her gorgeous green eyes? Inger's eyes were the same colour. She was petite. My daughter is more beautiful than I imagined. Something told me, ever since I met her, that Lowry was special. She…"

"Leif," Marcus cut in, "I must admit hearing the name Lowry again, surprised me. I'd not come across it before, but I discovered it's quite a common Welsh name but spelt LOWRI" He studied his friend, "You've obviously not said anything to her."

"No! How can I?" Leif irritably said. "I'd be in contempt of court. I can't do anything until she is twenty one. I can't settle. I can't look at her without wanting to shout out, 'I'm your father.' I want to take her in my arms. That little girl I've been searching for, is here. She's here. I know she will have a small birthmark, like a little star, on her left shoulder. Jesus Christ! She's doing things for me that no daughter should have to do for a drying out drunk of a father. Don't you understand, Marcus, it's unbearable. She's got a fifth year medical student who is her boyfriend. He came on ward rounds this morning and I could see the secret way they looked at each other. Can you believe it, I resent him? A cruel twist of fate separated us, and an even crueller one is denying me the right to explain to my daughter that I am her father and I love her and always have done. I think I will have to discharge myself. God, Marcus! I need a drink. Will this bloody craving ever leave me? Have you got your hip flask?"

Marcus felt the comfort of the flask resting on his left buttock.

"No my friend, I haven't," he lied. "But Leif, take some advice from EM and EM. Telling Lowry who you are, is out of the question and anyway you don't know how she will react. As far as she is concerned her father doesn't exist. Be happy that you have found her after all these years. Be proud of your strong and confident daughter. She is without doubt a beautiful young girl. Be grateful to the woman, Louise Stuart, who raised her, because she did a pretty good job. Lowry is full of mischievous fun. She is happy. Isn't that what all fathers want for their children, just for them to be happy?" Leif smiled at his wise old friend and nodded. "Just cherish every moment you have with her while you're in this ward. And whatever you do, don't discharge yourself from hospital. Love her from afar, but don't wallow, Leif, because that's when you'll turn to the bottle to get you through and I don't think young Nurse Lowry would be very pleased with you."

The two men sat quietly, each with their own thoughts.

"Marcus, according to the court I have just over two years before I can hold my child again," Leif eventually said. "The last time I held her she was ten months old. She initially bellowed her head off when we left Norway. I didn't know what the hell to do with her. Fortunately a member of the crew was a father and had a daughter. He suggested she was probably hungry. I handed her over to him because I was clueless about babies, and anyway I had to be on the helm in awful weather and I was terrified for my baby's safety. On the train from Scotland I had a first class carriage to myself at the SOE's expense. It took me three attempts to change her nappy. Every time I picked her up it fell down her little legs and came off and I'd have to start again. I don't think she liked me. She grizzled and gave me a look that said she thought I was a complete ninco something. What's that word you use to describe an idiot?"

"Nincompoop."

"That's the word! But eventually we got to know each other and she stood bouncing on my knee and trying to pull the gold buttons off my jacket. She got bored with that and began to pull my hair and then my nose and then my ears. She was such a vulnerable motherless little thing, but so pretty and full of dribbling chuckles. I cannot begin to tell you what it was like to hold my own child. The joy was overwhelming. And what did I do? Eighteen days, that's all it was, that separated me from my child" He gave a deep sigh. "What the bloody hell do I do now?"

THE DECISION

Marcus Marriot sat alone in the bar of the Exchange. A sordid case had kept him busy. He was going to have to tell the suspicious wife that her husband was not sleeping with his glamorous young secretary. He was actually sleeping with the spotty office boy. Jeez, he thought, what a bombshell to hit the poor cow with!

He studied the address he had written in his note book. There had been only one Louise Stuart in the telephone directory. Should he announce his visit by letter, or simply knock on the door and hope for the best? He decided on the latter.

The blue front door looked as if it had just had a new coat of paint. Marcus rang the bell and heard it summoning the person inside. The door opened onto a large hall with a parquet floor and an ornately carved camphor wood Chinese chest against the wall.

"Hello!" the woman said, with no hint of an accent. "Can I help you?"

Marcus studied the woman, who was such an important part of his friend's daughter's life. She was taller than Lowry, with bright blue eyes, shielded by her glasses. Her grey curls framed a pleasant, friendly, aging face.

"My name is Marcus Marriot," he explained. "Here is my card. I wonder if we could talk?"

Lou studied the card.

"What would a Private Investigator want with me?" she asked, with a charming smile.

Marcus Marriot smiled his beautifully ugly smile.

"I really would like to talk to you, Mrs Stuart, if it's convenient."

The woman opened the door wider.

"Please come in and I'll put some coffee on, or would you prefer tea?" she asked.

The man vigorously wiped his feet. He had to make a good impression, although his first impression of Mrs Stuart was that she presented as a very pleasant, well-spoken woman.

"Thank you, Mrs Stuart. Coffee. Black, please."

He sat alone in the comfortable lounge, waiting for his coffee. The mantelpiece and china cabinet were adorned with photographs of Lowry at different stages of her childhood. A big black Labrador posed with the child in some of the pictures, her arms wrapped tightly around his neck. Marcus studied them all and felt a moment of sadness for his friend. He had missed out on so much.

The woman returned, carrying a tray with coffees and biscuits.

"That's my daughter, Lowry," she said, as he returned the frame to the cabinet. "She's a Student Nurse."

"I know, Mrs Stuart. It is Lowry I have come to talk to you about."

"She's not in trouble is she?" the surprised woman asked.

"No, no Mrs Stuart, far from it! I'm possibly being seriously unethical talking to you, but I would ask you to hear me out before you decide if I am out of order and should you decide that I am, I will leave and we take this matter no further."

"This is all very mysterious, Mr Marriot, so will you please get to the point of your visit," Lou tartly replied.

"Lowry is your adopted daughter. That is correct, is it not?"

Lou frowned. "Yes, but what's…."

"Please, Mrs Stuart, let me explain," Marcus begged.

He was finding the situation difficult. Lou listened in silence as Marcus told the story of a little girl called Lori

Svenerson, whose name was wrongly entered into the register of the Welfare Department as Lowry Stephenson. He spoke of the Norwegian father, and his fruitless search for his child until she was finally traced and then the court's decision to deny him contact until Lowry was twenty one years old. Lou sat impassive. Marcus Marriot always prided himself on his ability to know what people were thinking from the expressions on their faces, but the woman before him showed no emotion.

"Mrs Stuart, a situation has arisen that complicates matters," he explained. "Captain Leif Svenerson, Lowry's Father, is now a patient on the very ward where Lowry is a nurse."

Lou reacted immediately.

"Does she know any of this?" she urgently asked.

"No, she knows nothing. That is why I am here. It is absolutely your decision, as to whether Lowry is party to this information. You know her better than anyone. You will know what her reaction is likely to be. The decision is yours."

Lou hesitated before answering.

"Before we go any further, Mr Marriot, what proof do you have that what you are saying is correct? I do not know you. You have walked into my house and seem to know more about my daughter than I do. No-one in the court on the day of her adoption knew anything of Lowry's background apart from the fact that the child's mother was dead, so I ask you again, why should I believe what you are saying?"

"I do assure you, Mrs Stuart, what I am telling you, is correct," Marcus answered. "I have managed to acquire documentation revealing the original inaccuracy in the register, also I have a copy of the court records, pertaining to Captain Svenerson's application for the return of his daughter. But may I ask a personal question? Does Lowry have a small birth mark on her left shoulder?" Lou nodded. "How would Captain Svenerson know that?" Marcus asked.

"I'm sorry to question you, but this is an amazing story you have brought to me. I need to see the documentation you talk of, because I have to be sure that there has not been a case of mistaken identity," Lou quietly replied. "I must, and will protect my daughter at all costs."

Marcus delved into his battered brief case and handed Lou a bunch of papers. Lou noticed that Marcus' fingers were nicotine stained.

"Please smoke if you wish to," she said, pointing to an ashtray.

"Thank you," he said, drawing a packet of Senior Service from his pocket.

The room remained silent as she thoroughly studied every page.

"Mr Marriot, there is a serious discrepancy here," Lou announced. "The date of birth given on this Norwegian Birth Certificate is not the date of birth of my daughter."

"It actually is Lowry's true date of birth, Mrs Stuart. Captain Svenerson told the Welfare Officer that his daughter was ten months old. He gave no date of birth. The officer simply counted back ten months and assumed rightly that she was born in February. However, the officer decided on the date because it was the same birth date as her mother's which of course made it virtually impossible to trace the child."

"I see," Lou said as she continued to scrutinize the papers.

Eventually she looked up and rose from her seat and walked to the mantelpiece and picked up the first photograph she had ever taken of Lowry, aged six and a half. The picture showed a small knock-kneed, pigeon toed person with two front milk teeth missing. The child squinted up into the sun that shone like a spotlight onto the face of an unsmiling, bewildered small girl.

"My heart goes out to the father who lost his daughter," she sadly said. "I must tell you, Mr Marriot, that she was a little wild thing when I first got her. I believe she had been brutalised by the orphanage. The tops of her little arms were covered in purple finger bruises. She used to cower if I raised my arm, as if she were expecting me to hit her. And she was very surprised that I didn't have a punishment cupboard under the stairs. I remember this tiny little girl telling me she could fight and offering to 'learn me to fight.' It was tragic, but it was her fighting spirit that I admired and I made sure no-one ever broke that spirit. Lowry is, and always will be, a mixture of tough and tender."

"She still has spirit, Mrs Stuart, and I believe she should be party to this information."

"Good," Lou said. "But the decision, as to whether Lowry is party to this information, is not mine to make. This is her life. How can anyone make such a momentous decision on somebody else's behalf? She is now almost nineteen years old. How can we keep it from her? Do you know my daughter?" Marcus nodded. "Well then, you will know that she is a strong willed young woman with a mind of her own. She would be furious if she were kept in the dark. The decision as to whether Lowry has contact with her father, must be hers whatever the court previously decided. Nobody owns Lowry, not even me and we have no secrets, although I think she is secretly smoking, the little monkey. So, Mr Marriot, I would ask you to leave this with me. I need to think about the best way to handle such a delicate matter. I am grateful to you for telling me. I shall be in touch with you soon."

Marcus stood up as Lou offered him her hand. They warmly shook hands.

"Thank you, Mrs Stuart," Marcus said. "I shall wait to hear from you. Have I your permission to relay our conversation to Captain Svenerson?"

"Yes of course, but tell me, Mr Marriot, what is Lowry's father like? I would just like to have a mental picture of the man who lost the child I am so privileged to call my daughter."

STUFFED TOMATO AND BEEF TEA

"She's a remarkable woman, Leif," Marcus said, as he repeated his conversation with Lou. "No hysterics, no possessiveness, no ordering me out of the house because I was telling her something she didn't want to hear. I'd half expected some sort of drama, but she was completely cool, calm and collected. I liked her. She's a direct, honest, no nonsense sort of woman. Lowry has her sense of humour. Mrs Stuart walked with me to the gate and said, 'It looks like Lowry will get her wish. She was always badgering me to get her a dad because her school friends had one. She didn't want a vicar or a priest." Marcus grinned. "Apparently Lowry went and knocked on a neighbours door because he was a widower. She was about seven or eight, and told the man that her mum was looking for a man. Mrs Stuart said she had never been so embarrassed in all her life."

Leif angrily banged his hand on the counterpane.

"Just how bloody stupid can judges be?" he shouted. "We have a situation where a little girl is wanting a dad, when all the time she has one who is desperate to be a part of her life. I wouldn't have taken the little girl away from her mother, for God's sake, but the bloody idiot judge denied me access because he thought it might be unsettling for Lowry. What right did he have to…."

"Leif, my friend," Marcus interjected. "That's in the past, painful as it is. We are dealing with the present and the matter is in the lap of the Gods and Mrs Stuart. She knows Lowry very well. It seems Mrs Stuart had some problems with her to start with. She described her as a wild child, brutalised by the orphanage, yet she was apparently a mixture of tough and tender. So don't worry, Leif. If anyone knows how to handle, Lowry, it's Mrs Louise Stuart."

"What the hell did those people do to my child? Brutalised, you say. They should be shot." Leif placed his hand on top of his friend's hand. "I don't know how to thank you, Marcus," he eventually said, "or the woman, Mrs Stuart, for bringing up my daughter. It's such a difficult situation, seeing her at work, having her attend to me with her cheeky banter. I feel I am being deceitful and the longer this goes on the worse it will get. I can only hope she is able to let me be a part of her life. At the moment she just thinks I'm another patient, who, for some reason, can be improved with a duck's arse hair style, whatever that is."

"At the moment that is exactly what you are. Just a patient," Marcus laughed. "And as for the duck's arse hairstyle, it leaves the back of your head looking like Jemima Puddleduck's backside."

"I haven't a clue what you're talking about," Leif laughed.

"I'll have to go, Skipper. I've got to go and see a client who thought her husband was screwing his secretary and tell her that he's actually buggering the office boy. Seems we all have our problems, so do as your little nurse says and eat all the fruit I've brought in. Let's see how it pans out."

Leif watched his friend leave the ward. He thought of Lowry's words when he had first met her. 'Remember, positive attitude.' He had to be positive. He felt buoyant and hopeful.

Marcus marched with some urgency down the corridor to the public telephone box. He inserted the coins into the machine and dialled the number of the Stuart household. The ringing tone began. He heard the receiver being lifted. "Hello," said the voice on the other end. He pressed button A and the money clinked into the coin box.

"Mrs Stuart, this is Marcus Marriot. I wonder if….."

"Oh hello there!" she said. "I've just spoken to your secretary and left a message for you. I shall see Lowry tonight and explain everything to her then."

"Thank you, Mrs Stuart. Captain Svenerson is finding it very difficult to keep up the pretence when he is party to information about Lowry that she is not privy to."

"I understand. Thank you for your call."

The young nurse had seen Marcus leave. She approached Leif's bed.

"Marcus has left early. What did you do to upset him?"

"He's got to go and tell a woman that his investigations have unearthed the unexpected," he said, smiling.

"You two seem to have so much to talk about. Some of the patients and their relatives just sit there not knowing what to talk about, but you and Marcus look as if you're conspiring to rob the Hospital Chapel of its communion wine. Anyway Leif, let's get serious. You will be discharged from here in about a week, you know. How are you going to cope when you socialise with Marcus, who's an obvious old soak?"

"Perhaps having something to live for would help," he replied.

"Just being alive! Isn't that enough to live for?" Lowry enthused.

"Not to people who find that life has lost its magic," he seriously said. "You are young. Life is just beginning for you, with so many new and exciting things ahead. Some people suffer just that bit too much and life then becomes a burden to them."

"You're right," Lowry conceded. "Poor Mr Donovan, a patient I cared about, had a malignant brain tumour. I used to hold his hand when the pain got too bad. He always talked to me about how he welcomed death as a release and I found it very harrowing because I knew a dose of morphine would ease his suffering. But he was rationed to every four hours for some bloody reason." Lowry looked at the watch that was pinned and hung upside down on her breast pocket. "I must go, or I'll have Sister on my back again."

"She seems to be on your back quite a bit, I've noticed," Leif said. "I don't think that is fair, you are a…."

Lowry held up her hand.

"Leif, you don't have to stand up for me. I was fighting orphanage bullies like her when I was four or five, especially one called Raymond Gubbins who was bigger than me. Now try and have a rest, you look tired."

"Yes Boss."

An authoritarian voice called across the ward.

"Nurse Stuart. To my office, please."

"Shittin' hell Leif! What the blazes have I done now?" Lowry grumbled.

Leif watch the young nurse leave the ward and an image of his little girl, fighting bullies, sent a pang of guilt through him.

Visitors shuffled from the ward as Lowry left the office. She'd have to get her skates on if the men were to get bread and butter and jam with their cup of tea by four thirty.

"Lowry, be a doll and give us some extra bread will you?" Iolo Williams begged. "My wife couldn't make it in today and it's only the food she brings in that's keeping me alive. That fish pie, we had for dinner, was disgusting. I couldn't even find a tiddler's cock in mine, let alone its balls."

Lowry laughed.

"You're only allowed two rounds of bread, but you can have the crusts off the end of the loaf as well. How's that?"

"Diolch yn fawr, Cariad Bach," he gleefully said. "Two sugars, doll."

Lowry poured his cup of tea, stirring in the two sugars and placed it on his over-table.

"Eichyd da. Twll tin pob Sais," she said, as Iolo Williams raised the cup to his lips.

He laughed and almost spilled his tea.

"Where the hell did you learn that?" he asked.

"One of your fellow countrymen taught me. It means something like, cheers or bottoms up," she explained.

"He was pulling your leg, Lowry," Iolo Williams said. "Eichyd da does mean cheers or good health," he explained, "But twll tin pob Sais means, arseholes to the English."

"That's it!" Lowry vociferously said. "I've had enough of you lot teaching me your bloody language. The next Welshman that comes on this ward and tries to teach me Welsh will have a box of dried marrowfat peas sprinkled all over his bottom sheet and his bed sores can go to hell and fester."

"What's on the menu for tonight, Doll?" he laughed.

She moved on to the next bed, answering the question as she did so.

"It's a stuffed tomato," she lied, in an attempt to get her own back on the Welsh.

"A stuffed tomato!" he exploded. "How big is the bloody tomato and what's it stuffed with?"

"I've no idea how big your bloody tomato will be, but it's stuffed with horse meat apparently," she laughed. "But don't worry, you've got some steak as well."

"Bloody hell! Well, I ain't eating anything that comes out of a knacker's yard. But steak! What's happened to the hospital kitchens?" he asked in amazement. "Steak! Well I hope they've got chips to go with it."

Lowry grinned. She was enjoying her revenge on the Welsh.

"Don't get over-excited, Iolo. You don't eat the steak you drink it. They boil it in water and chuck the meat away and give you the nutritious juice."

Lowry could hear Mr Williams protesting angrily about 'hospital swill' to his bedside neighbours. So stuffed tomatoes and beef tea had come in handy after all! She approached Leif's bed.

"I'll just have a cup of tea, please," he said. She placed his tea on his locker and moved to the next bed. Leif called her back.

"How did you get on with Sister before? Was she on the warpath?" he asked.

"No, it was my mum on the phone, which is most unusual," Lowry shouted over her shoulder. "She's sending a taxi for me when I go off duty. She's doing me a special meal and wants me to meet the new Irish rescue greyhound with a tattooed ear she's got, called Baloney."

THE BOMBSHELL

"You beautiful creature," Lowry enthused as she stroked the lanky dog. "Lou, just look at the length of his legs, he's like a miniature giraffe." She gently stroked the dog's silky, brindle coat. "You're going to love it here, boy. You'll be spoilt rotten."

"He already is," Lou shouted from the kitchen, "He's decided the settee is his and nothing will budge him from it. He's very timid. An ex- racer, I understand, so he'll need gentle handling. I'm also going to have to put a runner down in the hall because his huge feet and spindly legs skid all over the parquet floor."

Mother and daughter sat together at the dining room table.

"Lou, you know spag bol and a Reeces' rhum baba are amongst my favourite foods, so why both in one go?" Lowry asked. "What are you leading up to? You've never rung me at the hospital before. Are you ill? You would tell me if there was anything wrong?"

"No, I'm not ill, sweetheart, but I do need to talk to you about a visitor I had the other day, who knew everything about you. How you came to be in care. He knew of your adoption and your country of birth, but most importantly he knows your father."

Lowry felt her heart beating faster and faster.

"Knows my father! What are you saying? Are you saying my father is alive? So I have got a dad? This person who came to see you, was he from The Welfare?"

"No my dear, he wasn't from The Welfare," Lou gently said.

"Well who the hell was this man who knows so much about me?"

Lowry began drumming her fingers on the table. Lou leaned across and touched her daughter's hand.

"If you want to smoke a cigarette, then I don't mind. I know you smoke, sweetheart. I can smell it on your clothes. So please light up if you want to."

Lowry rummaged in her bag and selected a Strand from her array of brands.

"Can I have an ashtray, please?"

Lou disappeared to the lounge and returned with a souvenir of Llandudno ashtray.

"Who was this man, Lou?" Lowry quietly asked.

"His name is Marcus….."

"Marriot," Lowry quickly interjected. "I know him. He's a friend of a patient on my ward. How the hell does he know where I live?" Realisation dawned. "Oh, of course, he's a private investigator. What's he doing sneaking around and investigating me. Who asked him…?"

"Lowry, Lowry, let me explain everything to you, please," Lou begged. "It seems you were placed in care by your father during the war. He came back for you, after the war had ended, but a serious mix up with names and dates of birth made it impossible for him to trace you. With Mr Marriot's help he did eventually find you, but you had been adopted by me, by then, and the court refused his application to have access to you. He has no knowledge of where you live. He is prevented by the court to make any contact until you have reached the age of maturity at twenty one years old."

Lowry felt herself trembling, but she didn't know why. Was it excitement or nerves or even anger? Why did her dad put her in temporary care? What she was hearing sounded like a fairy story.

"So am I going to have to wait over two years before I know who my father is, because some wig wearing judge decided it for me? That's crap, sheer bloody crap." she shouted. "I've grown up believing I was completely alone in the world, apart from you, and all this time I have had a father out there who was looking for me, and when he finds me, the twat in a hat more or less tells him to bugger off. Did Marcus Marriot tell you who my father is? Anyway, how the hell does he know him?"

"Sweetheart, your father is his friend."

Lowry sat in stunned shock. She felt a kick in her stomach as the adrenalin rushed through her body causing her heart to pump wildly in her chest and the blood to drain from her face.

"Are you saying my father is Leif Svenerson?" she eventually said. Lou nodded. "I don't believe it. This isn't true. It's a ridiculous story. I happen to know that those two men are piss heads and they're making it up. It's their idea of a joke, but it's a sick one."

She drew heavily on the cigarette and noticed that her hands were shaking.

"Your father has your Norwegian birth certificate where your name is registered as Lori Svenerson," Lou quietly explained. "You were born in Oslo on the twenty first of February 1944. You are actually eighteen days younger than the birth date that is recorded in your adoption papers."

A long silence followed. Lowry aggressively stubbed out her cigarette and immediately lit another one. Lou broke the silence and spoke quietly.

"What are you thinking, sweetheart?"

"I don't know what I'm thinking, Lou," she angrily answered. "I don't even know whether to believe it. I'm all over the place. I should be jumping for joy because I've got a dad, so why don't I feel that way? For some reason I feel angry. Angry because if it's true, he dumped me in a bloody home. If I'm Norwegian, then what the hell was I doing in a Liverpool orphanage? My whole life has been a lie. I've even been celebrating my birthday on the wrong day. If I'm really Lori Svenerson then who the hell is Lowry Stephenson? Where did she come from? I've never been the real me, I've always been somebody else. So how the hell do you expect me to feel, Lou, when I'm suddenly told I'm not who I think I am?"

"It is true, sweetheart. I've seen the documentation and there is no mistake. But you are Lowry Stuart, my beloved daughter and nothing can change that," Lou gently said. "The name Lowry Stuart belongs to you. That is who you are. The fact that you have discovered you have a father makes no difference to who you are. It simply means you have someone else in your life who loves you."

"How the hell could he love me when he abandoned me? D'you know what it's like to grow up as a small child and never be special to anybody? To stare out of a playroom window for hours waiting for your mum and dad to fetch you? At school I was always the girl who was adopted. It made me different from the other kids, like I had a sign round my neck saying 'unwanted.' I'm really angry, Lou. If he is my father why didn't he tell me when I first met him. He had the cheek to show me a photograph of his wife and his baby. Can you believe it? I was looking at myself and didn't bloody know it. He hid behind his sheets, letting me wash him, comfort him when he was sick, act the goat and call him a banana because he was yellow and he never told me who he was. He was being dishonest with me, Lou. It was a violation of my trust. All this time he's known who I was and he's never let on. The bastard! The underhanded bastard. I've grown up believing I was British and now I find I'm a bloody Norwegian. I don't know anything about Norway except that they give us a Christmas tree every year."

Lowry exhaled her cigarette smoke like an angry dragon.

"Sweetheart, I understand your anger," Lou responded, "But if he had told you who he was he would have been in contempt of court. He actually didn't know until a few days ago that my Lowry Stuart, was once Lowry Stephenson. You apparently told him that yourself. He wasn't being underhanded. He has only just discovered that you are his daughter. Years ago, Mr Marriot did some investigating and discovered that the little girl called Lowry Stephenson was in fact Lori Svenerson. How was he to know that Nurse Lowry

Stuart was once Lowry Stephenson until you told him? It must be devastating for a parent to lose the child they loved. It cannot have been easy for your father, once he discovered who you were. He had to keep his silence and it takes a strong person to do that. Don't judge him too harshly, Lowry. Life hasn't been easy for him."

"I know Leif Svenerson has had a hard time. He told me about his wife....."

"Your birth mother," Lou said.

"Yes, I know, but you are my mother. I don't want any other. Anyway, I've already told you, this man is an alcoholic?"

"People turn to alcohol for many reasons, sweetheart. Your mother was dead. She must have been young so it's probable she died as a result of the War. Norway suffered dreadfully at the hands of the Nazis. She was one very brave little nation, so don't dismiss your Norwegian heritage. Be proud of your parentage, but most importantly don't sit in judgement on your father until you can understand why he did what he did."

"I know. I know I'm being hard on him and I don't mean to be, but I've just remembered something. When I told him the other day that my name was Stephenson before I was adopted, I found him crying. I thought it was because he was desperate for a drink, but it was because he had just discovered that I was his daughter." Silence fell on the room. Only the noise of Baloney scratching his neck could be heard. "Bloody hell, what a weird world this is," Lowry eventually said. "I had a vivid imagination when I was a kid, but what you've just told me goes beyond anything I could possibly imagine." Another ponderous silence fell on the room. Lowry watched a fluffy white cloud of smoke from her cigarette rise slowly upwards. "D'you know, Lou, this changes everything. How the hell do I face him tomorrow, when suddenly I'm not sponging my patient down, I'm sponging my father? It's weird."

"Lowry, it makes no difference that he is your father. He is still your patient and you are his nurse. But remember, he was silenced by the man you called, a twat in a hat. That is very disrespectful of our Judiciary, I'll have you know," she laughed. And anyway judges in the Family Division of the Court don't wear wigs. But try if you can, to understand what it must have been like to have lost your child. It must have been like a bereavement for him. You wonder why you ended up in a Liverpool orphanage. Only he can answer your questions. He must have had a good reason to bring you from Norway to here. And don't you want to know how your mother died? I agree with you this does change everything. You have a past, now, something we all need to have. It gives us a sense of belonging to be a branch of a family tree that is rooted to the past the present and the future. With no past we are like leaves that have blown off the tree and flutter aimlessly in the breeze."

"And most of those leaves end up in the gutter, I suppose," Lowry mumbled.

Lou drew her chair closer to her daughter.

"Sweetheart. Do you think I could have one of your cigarettes? I haven't smoked for years, but I really feel I would enjoy one with you."

Lowry grinned at her mother. Something almost conspiratorial had just taken place. Her mum was about to have a fag with her. They sat silently smiling at one another through a vapour of white smoke. Lou finished half the cigarette, coughed and stubbed it out in the ashtray.

"Lou, did the welfare tell you anything about me when you first got me?"

"No, they knew nothing of your past apart from your mother being dead."

"Why did you never tell me she was dead?" Lou sighed. She was finding it difficult to justify her reasons. "Come on Lou, why was I never told that she was dead?"

"Because, my love, rightly or wrongly I didn't want to shatter that lovely image you had in your head, of a beautiful young woman with long black hair and a white dress who was your mum who didn't wear glasses like me. When I first got you, you had nothing. No toys apart from a little rag doll and what you called Mr and Mrs Wooden People. No clothes except what you stood up, and I had to wash them and send them back, and no photographs. All you had was anger and a deep mistrust of grown-ups. So how could I take from you the one precious picture in your mind that was yours?"

"Lou, it was another bloody lie I was living, but I do understand why you thought that way."

"Maybe it was very wrong of me not to tell you and I'm sorry, Lowry. But do you care to know about who you are? About how your mother died. Do you want to know your father? To have him as part of your life."

"I think so. But he's going to have to stop drinking. He could have died from alcohol poisoning or choked to death last time he binged on whisky. I'm not going to discover that I have a father only to have him kill himself before I get a proper chance to know him."

"Perhaps now he has found you it will give him a reason to stop. You can help him, I'm sure. But the most important person in all of this is you. It's not about what your father wants. It's not about how your father feels either and it's certainly not about what I think. Although I do think your father must love you very much."

"Lou, I have been Lowry Stephenson, Lowry Stuart and as far as Nana was concerned I was Brigit, for some weird reason. Now I find I'm Lori Svenerson."

"Brigit was the name of my little sister who died of diphtheria when she was three.

Mother was confused, as you know," Lou explained.

"Oh bless her! I didn't mind being called Brigit indoors, but I hated her calling me Brigit outside. The local kids called me Brigit the midget because I was smaller than them. But you know, Lou, that precious picture you talk about of my real mother with long black hair wasn't real at all. My mother was blonde. And I always believed that one day she would fetch me out of there. Even that was a ridiculous belief. She was dead. One of the bitches in the home used to say the reason I was there was because my mother didn't want me or love me.

And I believed her. But my mother wasn't alive, so how could she love me?"

Lowry lay her arms across the table and buried her head into the crook of her elbows and sobbed. She heard Lou leave the room and start clattering the dishes in the kitchen and talking to Baloney who had followed her there. Lowry sniffed hard. She didn't usually cry and she wasn't going to cry anymore. She stood up.

"Lou, I've stopped blubbering and I don't really know why I was, but I'm going to the bathroom to tart my face up again."

"Okay. Would you like a little glass of wine when you come down?" Lou asked.

"Yes please, Lou, so long as it's not a classy plap from a chateau. I'm going to have to catch the bus soon, or I'll be late back."

"Don't worry, I've arranged a taxi for ten thirty," she chuckled.

"That's too late, I'll be on the bluebottle's carpet at nine tomorrow. That's Matron if you're wondering who I'm talking about."

"Don't worry, I got an extension for you until eleven," she giggled. "I rang Home Sister and told her my arthritis was playing up and I needed you to help me to bed, so she said okay."

"Lou, you bloomin' liar! You haven't got arthritis."

"I know that, but she doesn't. Now Lowry, let's talk about how you are going to handle this when you see your father tomorrow. Do you want me there? I feel I should be there, if you want me."

Lowry looked across at her mum and realised just how lucky she had been when the fates smiled on her and brought a woman in dark green shoes to the orphanage doorstep.

"Lou, understand one thing. I am who I am, because of you. I don't need you to hold my hand anymore, like you used to. I'm a big girl now. You gave me self-confidence and a belief that I could take on the world, if I wanted to. If I think positively about what happened to me then I should be grateful to my father for putting me in care because I would never have met you, and you really are the most wonderful mum in the world. And I don't want you to be worried that I'll love my father more than you, because that will never happen."

Lou smiled, a gentle emotional smile that spoke only of love.

"How empty my life would have been without you, but I mean what I say. If you would like me to be there when you talk...."

"It's okay, Lou. I would like to talk to my father on my own. I honestly don't know what I'm going to say to him, but I'll think of something."

"You're not usually short of something to say," she laughed. "Anyway, here's the money for the taxi. And can I come and meet your Norwegian Sea Captain next visiting time?"

"Yes, I'd like you to meet him. He's actually a lovely man, so why shouldn't I have

Captain Leif Svenerson for a dad?"

"Because he is your dad, you clot," Lou chuckled.

"My dad! My dad!" Lowry quietly said. "I've never been able to say that before and d'you know what, Lou? It sounds good. Every kid should have a dad. I must tell Helen when I get back."

The sound of a taxi horn announced the arrival of Lowy's carriage.

"Lou," Lowry shouted as she ran down the path. "Visiting is three to half past on the dot and don't you dare bring any bloomin' flowers."

Sister unlocked the door of the Nurses Home and welcomed Lowry back.

"How is your Mother, Nurse Stuart?" she kindly asked.

"Poor Mum, she's bearing up, Sister, thank you," she grimly replied.

The attic was quiet. Lowry tapped gently on Helen's door.

"Are you awake, Helen? It's Lowry," she whispered loudly. Mumblings from within told her Helen was awake.

"Open the door, I need to talk to you, it's important." Lowry persisted.

The door opened and sleepy Helen, wearing baggy pyjamas, beckoned Lowry in.

"You've not got yourself pregnant, have you?" she asked, with a concerned look crossing her face.

"No, nothing like that, but I've got some very strange news and I had to tell you."

The girls sat side by side on the bed. "Here, have a ciggie, Hel, and I'll tell you all about it."

Half an hour later and with four cigarette ends in the saucer Lowry finished her story. Helen remained silent, only interrupting with expressions of gosh, bloody hell and 'cor blimey.

"Please don't repeat a word of what I've just told you to anyone, Hel."

"I won't, I promise, but gosh, it's so sad," Helen said. "I feel like I want to cry."

"It isn't sad, you sentimental pillock," Lowry laughed. "It's exciting. Now that I've got used to the idea I'm feeling happy. You see, I've always wanted a dad. I've never told anyone this before, but I used to cut pictures out of the Radio Times of men I saw on the telly and keep them in a pink box. I had Eamonn Andrews and Richard Dimbleby. He used to do 'What's my Line', and I even had Robin Day and Malcolm Muggeridge, because Lou liked them."

Helen roared with laughter.

"Malcolm Muggeridge? What was wrong with Dickie Valentine? I loved him, but Malcolm Muggeridge! For God's sake, Lowry."

"What's wrong with Malcolm Muggeridge? He's a very clever man. Anyway, I had loads of them and each week I'd decide which one was going to be my dad for that week and use the picture as a book mark and say 'Hi Dad' each time I opened the book. Don't laugh at me. Looking back on it I must have been as crackers as my Nana but I enjoyed pretending."

"Sorry, but I can't help thinking it's funny. You've always been a bit of an odd bod," Helen laughed.

"D'you know, Hel, for some reason I think I'm going to feel shy when I see Leif in the morning."

"You shy!" Helen exploded. "Talk about deluding yourself, Lowry Stuart."

Helen yawned.

"I'll go now, Hel, and thanks for listening." Lowry stood up to leave. "By the way, did you know my ancestors were raping and pillaging you lot hundreds of years ago?"

"Yes, Lowry, I've heard all about the barbaric Vikings," she countered.

DRITT! DRITT! DRITT!

It seemed no sooner had Lowry fallen asleep than the morning bell clattered her awake. She had tossed and turned with so much on her mind and her adrenalin pumping madly. Helen was, perhaps, right. Lowry wasn't feeling shy, she was on an emotional rollercoaster. She couldn't believe she had a dad. And how did a daughter behave with a father? She didn't know. She'd never had one. She was too old to sit on his knee. She was too old to hold his hand when crossing the road. Would she ever be able to kiss him without wondering if she was flirting with him? Nah! Girls don't flirt with their dads. Blooming heck it was all very complicated. Anyway, what should her first words be when she sees him in the morning? 'Hello Daddy.' You daft cow,' she murmured to herself before finally falling asleep.

"Why is my heart beating so fast?" Lowry asked herself, as she approached her ward. She pushed open the ward door and immediately focused on her father. Their eyes met and for an instant they stared, expressionless at each other, before simultaneously breaking into broad smiles. She walked across to his bedside.

"Hello!" she coyly said. "I don't really know what to say except, hello."

"Hello, will do just fine, elskling," Leif emotionally answered.

He took her small hand in his and squeezed it gently. Tears slowly trickled from his eyes. He wiped them away with the back of his hand.

"Don't cry, Leif, please," the young nurse begged, feeling uneasy. "You'll have me in tears next."

"They are tears of joy my elskling," he said. "I have waited all these years for this moment and here standing before me is my precious, beautiful, funny little daughter with eyelashes most women would die for."

His joke had eased the awkwardness of the situation.

"So you could hear me when I was sitting with you in the private room?"

"Yes, you gave me a sound ticking off which I deserved, you admired my eyelashes and told me I stink. I could hear you in the distance, but I couldn't respond, I was too stupefied. But Lowry, I want you to know that I let you down once, but I shall never do it again. I have no excuse for my actions when I first took you to The Welfare. I can honestly say that when I was on shore leave I visited every orphanage in Liverpool and Lancashire with a Welfare Officer, just to check their records. It was a heartbreaking, futile search."

Lowry's heart missed a beat. So here was the man with gold buttons. The man who waved his hat. The man she thought was Mr King. The banging on the window. The shouting, 'no, don't go away.' The pictures flooded back in a wave of sadness at the thought of just how close her father had been. Little Beth and Tommy standing excitedly next to her and Miss Bum's words. 'It's only a man looking for his kid.'

"Are you alright, Lowry?" Leif asked. "You've gone all white. You look as if you've just seen a ghost."

"I have, but I can't tell you now. I'll have to get on with my chores. Please don't tell anybody who you are because they'll move me to another ward."

He held his index finger to his lips, smiled and nodded slowly.

Sister emerged from her office brandishing her battle-axe.

"Nurse Stuart to the kitchen now, and help the Ward Orderly sort out breakfasts."

"Shit, shit, shit, Leif. That woman….,"

"You sound like your mother," he laughed. "Those were the words she used when she was frustrated."

"You what! She said, shit, shit, shit?"

"No! She said, 'Dritt! Dritt! Dritt!' which is the same thing in my language. We have so much to talk about."

The voice boomed again.

"Did you not hear me, Nurse Stuart? I said to the kitchen, now."

"Dritt! Dritt! Dritt!" Lowry said, grinning at her father before making off to the kitchen to help that other miserable cow.

She busied herself helping the Ward Orderly to serve breakfasts. She had an uncomfortable feeling that her father was following her around the ward with his eyes. Why should she be feeling uncomfortable, she asked herself? The circumstances had changed. She was no longer just his nurse, she was his daughter. He was no longer just her patient, he was her father.

True to her word, Lou met Captain Leif Svenerson at three o'clock on the dot. Lowry smartened up her father with clean blue pyjamas, a tidy hair style and a liberal smattering of Old Spice after shave.

"That's enough, Lowry," he pleaded, as she poured the stringent lotion into his hands. It trickled through his fingers and onto the bed linen. "I'll be smelling like a Chinese brothel."

"Well it's better than smelling like a camel driver's jockstrap. Anyway, what do you know about Chinese brothels?"

"And what do you know about camel driver's jockstraps?" Leif retaliated. "I think this may be your mother," he said, looking over Lowry's head, as a woman approached the bed.

Lowry turned and smiled at her mum.

"Lou, this is Leif, but don't crack on to anybody who he is, or who you are, because they'll probably take me off the ward in case I show favouritism to this guy here." she said, pointing towards Leif.

"I understand." She turned to Leif. "I am delighted to meet the father of my little girl and even more pleased that after all this time you have eventually found each other." They shook hands warmly.

"Mrs Stuart, I...."

"Please, it's Lou," she explained.

"Lou, I am so happy to meet the woman who has mothered my child all these years...."

"I haven't just mothered her, Leif, I have loved her," Lou said.

Lowry groaned and pulled a face.

"Oh, for crying out loud, both of you, this is all too slushy for me. I'm off to do my chores. I see there are loads more bloomin' flowers to deal with. Anyway Lou, what have you got in that brown parcel?"

Lou smiled impishly.

"Photograph albums. I thought Leif might like to see you when you were a little tyke."

Lowry curled her top lip and left to make another attempt at flower arranging. A hand gently touched her on the shoulder.

"Excuse me Nurse, but my father has had a little accident. He's very upset about it. Would you....?"

"Of course! Please don't worry. I'll be right with you," the Nurse said.

She collected a bowl of water, soap, talcum powder and clean bed linen and wheeled her laden trolley to poor distressed Mr Sidney Scott. As she closed the curtains she knew this was no little accident, it was a monumental explosion. She didn't know whether to laugh or cry. One moment she was a florist, now she was a sewage worker dealing with the result of a dysfunctional waste pipe.

"Okay, Sid, let's sort you out as soon as we can so your daughter can get back to you."

She did what she always did and put on a mask, stuffed with cotton wool and heavily soaked with lavender oil. It was the only way she could stop her stomach heaving.

"Don't get old, Lowry," Sid tearfully told her. "Your teeth go, your joints ache, your sight starts to fail, the bladder dribbles, the bowels loosen. Even your memory goes and finally your dignity. I was in the trenches, you know. Pretty God damn awful, it was, but getting old is just as bloody frightening. You appreciate your youth, lass, because it doesn't last forever."

Lowry listened as she quickly and efficiently cleaned up her patient and re-made the bed. Sid was one of the old school of gentlemen, always courteous and polite. She removed her mask.

"Sid, you may be losing all those things you mentioned, but as for your dignity, you will never lose that. That's yours to keep. No one can take that from you, not even an almost nineteen year old nurse, who's just sprinkled talcum powder all over your bare bum."

Sid roared with laughter. His bottom dentures flew from his mouth and landed on the counterpane. He picked them up and gave Lowry half a gummy grin.

"Theethe 'ave alwayth been looth ever thince the uthleth Dentitht made them."

He popped them back in his mouth with a clonk. Lowry and Sid laughed happily together. She drew the curtains back and beckoned Sid's daughter to join him.

"Thank you so much," the woman appreciatively said. "He was a very dignified old man and it upsets him…..,"

"Please don't thank me," Lowry interrupted, "and he still has his dignity. It's a pleasure to nurse such a lovely gentleman."

An agitated voice demanded Lowry's attention.

"Nurse, Nurse, what have you done with the scented bouquet I brought in for my brother?"

"They are in the sluice room awaiting my attention."

"Would you get them now so my brother can enjoy them?"

"Of course, but not until I have finished attending to my patient. I'll make sure your brother gets his scented bouquet, but I decided the patient was my priority at the time, not the scented bouquet."

"Well, as soon as you can then," the sharp voice demanded.

"As soon as I can," the busy nurse replied. 'She knows what she can do with her smelly posy,' Lowry muttered to herself.

After clearing the trolley into the sluice room, she gently tapped on Sister's door.

"Come," said the voice from within.

Lowry walked confidently to Sister's desk.

"Sister, can Mr Scott's daughter have an extra ten or fifteen minutes with him? She's only had about five minutes and visiting is nearly over. I had to clean him up, which took a while."

Sister frowned.

"No, Nurse. They will all want an extra ten or fifteen minutes and then what?"

"I only thought....."

"I said no, Nurse."

Lowry was dismissed. A furious nurse approached the door.

"Dip yer arse in lime," she quickly mumbled under her breath.

"Sorry I didn't catch what you said , Nurse Stuart?" Sister replied.

"I just looked at my watch and said, 'flip, what's the time,' Sister," Lowry fibbed. "I must get on with afternoon teas."

God, some people were impossible. She dashed to the sluice room and unceremoniously shoved the scented bouquet into a vase of water. She then dashed them to the bedside of the patient with a bossy sister.

"Oh for heaven's sake," the bossy woman snorted. "Don't you know anything about arranging flowers? I'll do them myself."

"No, I'm sorry, I don't," Lowry answered.

'But I can arrange your face for you if you want me to,' she muttered angrily under her breath as she rushed to the kitchen.

As she clattered the dishes onto the tea trolley, Lowry realised that the visitors were already leaving. She ran from the kitchen to see Lou walking down the corridor.

"Lou, Lou," she called.

Lou stopped and turned.

"I couldn't find you to say goodbye, but how are things going? I could hardly sleep last night for thinking about you."

"I'm finding it a very strange, Lou. To swing from being his nurse to being his daughter takes some getting used to."

"I'm sure it does, but your father is a very handsome and charming man."

"Lou, you're far too old to be contemplating romance. You can't be thinking of having my father for a toy boy" Lowry told her. "It would be so embarrassing."

"You cheeky little monkey. I'm not looking for a toy boy an old boy or a life buoy for that matter. I'm quite ...,"

"Nurse Stuart, what are you doing?" Sister's voice boomed from down the corridor. "You have abandoned the tea trolley in the kitchen and the patients are waiting."

"See you soon, Lou." Lowry quickly said, and returned to the ward. "Sorry Sister, she left her gloves behind, I was just returning them to her."

'Flipping hell! If this woman is teaching me anything, it's how to be an inveterate liar,' she silently groaned.

Two days later Nurse Stuart helped her father clear his belongings from the bedside locker. He had made good progress, but she worried that once with his friend Marcus, Leif could so easily make friends with a whisky bottle again.

"Please, please, please, Leif....."

"I know what you are going to say," he interjected. "I am going to make a solemn promise to my daughter. I won't be drinking again. I have too much to lose and I love you so much. I want to walk you down the aisle when you marry that young man of yours and bounce...."

"What on earth makes you think I'd marry Ben?" Lowry exploded. "You've never met his toffee–nosed mother."

"Is she that bad?" he grinned.

"Worse."

"Oh dear, but Lowry as I said before, I've made you a promise and it's my intention to keep it. I have the best reason in the world to live. When I first met you, my heart told me that you were special. Your mother had lovely green eyes and was petite just like you are. She was full of fun and she really loved you elskling. So you see why I shall never drink alcohol again."

Lowry took hold of her father's hand.

"I'll help you as much as I can, Leif. But look at it this way. You lost me once and it seems it broke your heart. Please don't break mine by killing yourself. Staff says you're on the road to a premature death unless you quit."

"I know, but you are the catalyst that will make me stop. I also want to get back to sea, but closer to home. I'm going to The Mersey Docks and Harbour Board to see if I can train as a Pilot to bring the big ships into Liverpool Bay. Having a Master's ticket should help. I'll be based for some of the time at Point Lynas."

"Leif, that's great, but where's Point Lynas? Is it far away?"

"It's on the north east coast of Anglesey, North Wales," he explained. "The big ships anchor in the shelter of Liverpool Bay but need a Pilot from one of the Cutters at Point Lynas to take them through the treacherous sandbanks of the Mersey. I'll never be far away from you, not now the fates and Marcus have brought us together again."

Father and daughter hugged warmly. Lowry felt emotionally flustered. Leif felt so strong. She could smell Old Spice aftershave.

"It's your weekend off isn't it?" he said. Lowry nodded. "I'll ring you then, when you're at home," he said. "And look what Lou kindly gave me." He produced four photographs of Lowry. "This is my favourite."

An image of a small girl in a gingham dress and wearing a Panama hat, with a satchel on her back and one of her knee length white socks rippled over her ankle, grinned cheekily at the camera.

"Oh happy days in the convent, curtseying in my navy blue knickers and white gloves," she facetiously responded.

THE XENOPHOBE

Leif's bed remained horribly empty and abandoned until twelve o'clock next day when Mr Manduku arrived to occupy it. He was suffering from cerebral malaria. Lowry approached his bedside. They needed a blood sample.

"Hello Mr Manduku, I'm Nurse Stuart. Can I have your arm so Staff Nurse can take a blood sample?" He obediently offered his arm and Lowry felt the cloying dampness of his pyjama sleeve. "Gosh, you're burning up, so I'll see what your temperature is."

It was one hundred and two point seven, Fahrenheit. Lowry entered it on his record chart. She watched Staff find the vein and slowly and carefully draw blood from his arm. Lowry labelled the sample for the lab and placed it in the kidney dish.

"Mr Manduku, I'll get you a jug of iced water. So please drink as much as you can because you'll become dehydrated." Mr Manduku nodded and winced as he did so. "Is the back of your neck very painful?"

"Yes, and I'm so hot," he complained.

"Don't worry, I'll be right back with your water and some cooling cloths and I'll sponge your face and arms. They reckon it helps. Your medication should kick in soon and that will help with the pain."

"Thank you Nurse," he said. "My name is Joshua Eli Samson Manduku, but you can call me Prince Joshua."

"Thank you, but not within earshot of Sister, and my name is Princess Lowry. I'll be back in a minute."

Mr Carmichael, Joshua's neighbour, beckoned Lowry to his bedside. He seemed agitated.

"I want to be moved," he whispered, indicating with his eyes towards Joshua.

Lowry knew instantly she was dealing with a prejudiced man.

"I'm sorry, I can't do anything about that, Mr Carmichael. Mr Manduku is a patient, just like you are, therefore you are all treated the same. I must go and tend to him."

"I'm not sleeping three foot from a nigger," he angrily stated. "I want to see Sister, now."

"I will discuss your xenophobia later, with Sister," Lowry tartly replied.

"My what?" Mr Carmichael shouted, in alarm.

"It's a rather nasty secondary condition you seem to be suffering from," she replied. "Hasn't anybody told you about it yet?"

"No they bloody haven't! So why haven't I been told about it before now?" he bellowed.

"Because, unfortunately, there's no medicine that will cure it," she answered.

She heard him complain to his neighbour that he needed to see the doctor immediately.

"Nurse, I asked you to get Sister," Mr Carmichael continued to shout.

"I'm busy at the moment, so why is it so important, Mr Carmichael, that you see Sister immediately?"

"Because I need to speak to the organ grinder not the monkey," he furiously yelled.

Lowry laughed.

"I shall summon the organ grinder for you as soon as I have finished with Mr Manduku," she retorted. "Meanwhile I suggest you calm down. It won't be doing your xenophobia any good by getting over-excited."

Mr Carmichael's nearest neighbours laughed, infuriating the man even more.

"I told you to get Sister," he yelled again. "I want the doctor here now."

"Mr Carmichael, please can I ask you to stop shouting. It's disturbing the other patients," Lowry gently requested.

A number of his fellow patients mumbled for him to 'belt up' and 'put a sock in it.' The skirmish was over.

The following morning Lowry found Mr Manduku had been moved to the empty private room. The xenophobe had got his own way. She tapped gently on the private patient's door and walked in.

"Good morning, Prince Joshua. So you've got the Royal Private Suite. How are you today?"

"I had a terrible night with the ague, but I am feeling a bit better this morning, thank you," he answered. "And I am honoured to be in the Royal Private Suite. Prince Joshua Eli Samson Manduku is the son of a Nigerian Tribal Chief. I have three wives back home and nine children, or is it ten?"

"If you don't know how many children you have, then how do you expect me to know?"

"I leave the women to get on with it," he replied. "But Nurse Lowry, you will make Prince Joshua Eli Samson Manduku a good wife."

"Not on your nelly, Prince Josh!" she chuckled. "One man one woman. That's my motto."

"That is a shame because you would be favourite wife number one. My father, the Biafran Chief of the Igbo tribe, arranged for me to come to this hospital because of your renowned Liverpool School of Tropical Medicine. I got this malaria when I was in Central Africa on a diplomacy mission on behalf of my father, the King."

"Gosh, are you really a Prince? Should I be curtseying to you, Your Highness?" Lowry cheekily asked.

"No," Joshua said, laughing loudly. "I was educated at an all boys English public school and nobody ever curtseyed to me there."

"Well Prince Joshua, I wasn't educated at an all boys public school and I was taught to curtsey by a nun, so in deference to your title, I shall curtsey to you."

She curtseyed obsequiously just as the door opened and the Ward Orderly entered with Joshua's breakfast.

"Is this where you're hiding?" the orderly rudely asked Lowry.

"I wasn't hiding," Lowry snapped. "I was simply checking on Prince Joshua Eli Samson Manduku."

The orderly disrespectfully banged the breakfast on the over table and turned to leave.

"Excuse me," Lowry said to the orderly, "but you obviously haven't been informed. We have all been told that we must courtesy to the Prince when we enter and leave the room. It's to do with Anglo-Nigerian relations or something."

The Ward Orderly respectfully curtsied and left the room.

Joshua guffawed and clapped his hands delightedly. Lowry nearly wet herself with laughter. She'd finally got her own back on the miserable cow!

Sister waited in the corridor as Lowry left the room.

"To my office, Nurse."

Lowry entered the office and stood before the desk. Sister eased her buxom stern into the chair. She picked up a pen and twirled it in her fingers as if she were rolling a fag. This doesn't look good, the nurse thought.

"Are you aware of the distress you caused to Mr Carmichael yesterday, Nurse Stuart?" Sister eventually said. "It took myself and the Registrar some considerable time to convince him that he was not suffering from an incurable illness as you apparently suggested he was."

"But Sister...."

"Be quiet, I haven't finished," she boomed. "In all my years of nursing, I have never come across a nurse who implies to a patient that he is dying. It is not a nurse's place to discuss such things. It is the doctor's responsibility. And to tell the man he was suffering from a made up disease is beyond belief. What were you thinking?"

"Sister, please can I explain what happened? Mr Carmichael said he wasn't going to sleep three foot from a nigger and he demanded to see you. So I told him I would speak to you about his xenophobia. If he doesn't know what xenophobia means then that's not my fault. He's just a racist bigot."

"He is first and foremost a patient," she sternly explained. "It is not your place to sit in judgement. Fortunately, he has calmed down, but when you leave this office you will immediately go and apologise to him. Is that clear?"

"Yes Sister, but Prince Joshua Manduku is also a pa…"

"Leave. And go and do as I say," the voice ordered.

Lowry approached Mr Carmichael's bed. He was scooping the last of his porridge from the bowl, intent on getting the last little oat into his mouth.

"Mr Carmichael," she firmly said, "Sister has told me to say that I'm sorry you called Prince Joshua Manduku a nigger, yesterday."

"That's all right, Nurse. Is there any more porridge, d'you think?" he asked.

"Sorry it's all gone, Mr Carmichael," she lied.

She had no intention of feeding his xenophobia.

TOMMY OLLERENSHAWE

Leif joined Lowry for one of Lou's superb Sunday roasts.

"I must go and clear up in the kitchen," Lou said. "You and Leif stay here and chat."

"No, you stay here and relax 'cos Leif and I will chat while we do the clearing up," Lowry insisted

As Lowry scraped the left-overs onto the Liverpool Daily Post, for the bin, a name she knew leapt up at her from the front page. 'Thomas Ollerenshawe aged nineteen, of no fixed abode had been sentenced to six years imprisonment in Walton Jail.'

It had to be little Tommy, she thought. She remembered his surname was Ollerenshawe. She read on. 'He had been disturbed whilst burgling a woman's house. She had confronted him, he had attacked her and she had required hospital treatment. He had shown no remorse.'

"Leif, I know this boy," she said. "He was in the orphanage with me, but he was a timid little chap, always crying and always with a runny nose. He used to wet his pants all the time. It's hard to believe he could do something like this."

Leif read the article.

"A lot of water has gone under the bridge since then," he said. "It says, of no fixed abode. He obviously had no one of his own and nowhere to live. He must have been a desperate young man."

"Jesus, Leif! Poor little Tommy! Why are some of us so fortunate when others have no chance at all? It's like we all roll round on a roulette wheel and your destiny is decided by which hole you fall into. I could have ended up like Tommy, if Lou hadn't found me."

"No, no, don't think like that. I would have found you eventually," Leif responded, as he vigorously scrubbed the roasting tin.

"If Tommy's got no-one, then he won't have any visitors. Do you think I should visit him? I always liked him because he was so sad and gentle and he had big brown eyes."

Leif pondered the question before responding.

"Perhaps you should write to him. You won't know each other anymore and you have both changed so much since then."

"What difference does that make?" she hotly responded. Leif took his time answering. He absorbed himself in the washing up. "I can't see the problem, just because we've both changed."

"It's up to you, but I ask you to think about it." he eventually replied. "Life changed for the better for you. You have a mum and dad who love you. You have a lovely home. You will never find yourself homeless or short of food. Tommy lived in the same orphanage as you, but as you yourself said, he didn't fall into one of the fortunate holes in your roulette wheel. He fell off the roulette table and was swept aside by an uncaring society."

"Why shouldn't I show him that I care then?"

"Because no matter how much you care, little lady, the young man will see a beautiful and very advantaged young woman who was once just like him. He may see you as flaunting your privileges when he has never had any. For him to be in prison means he has reached the depths. Might he think someone who has reached the heights was patronising him?"

Lowry let out a long sigh.

"I never thought about it that way. I've just remembered that his dad was Henry and he was killed during the war and his mum was Doris and she was mentally ill. It must have been harder for Tommy being in the orphanage because he had experienced life with a mum and a dad and suddenly they were snatched away from him. No wonder he was so miserable. Perhaps I should do nothing, but then perhaps I should send him one letter and if I get a reply then I'd know he'd like to receive mail."

"That sounds a more sensible idea," Leif replied.

The strident ringing of the telephone interrupted the conversation.

"Hello Ben, yes, I'll go and get her," Lou said. "Lowry, it's Ben for you," she shouted from the hall.

Lowry took the receiver from Lou.

"Hi Ben," she said.

"Hi Lowry, what time will you be back at the Nurses' Home tonight? I need to see you."

He sounded serious.

"I can be back anytime between now and ten thirty. Why?"

"I want to talk to you."

"What about?"

"I don't want to talk about it on the 'phone."

"Okay mystery man. Where are you now?" Lowry asked.

"I'm at the flat at the moment, but I can...,"

"No, stay where you are, I'll ask Leif if he'll drive me to your place. I'll see you soon."

The call ended.

"That was an odd call from Ben," she said, as she returned to the kitchen. "He sounded very serious. Will you drive me to...?"

"Of course," Leif said, cutting Lowry short. "To where?"

"His flat, please."

Ben greeted Lowry warmly, but obviously something was wrong.

"Do you want a coffee?" he asked.

"Not yet," she answered. "Something is wrong, so let's sit down and you can tell me all about it. Do you want to finish with me or something, 'cos I know I can be a pain in the bum sometimes?"

"Don't be daft," he said. "You're the best thing in my life." They sat cuddled together on the shabby sofa. "I had a call to meet Dad at the hospital this morning," Ben began. "He told me my mother has breast cancer and it's knocked me for six. She's apparently had the lump for eighteen months and said nothing. Now it's spread into the lymph nodes and beyond. Apparently, she had an idea that it could be cancer and no way was she going to have a mastectomy."

Lowry pulled Ben's head onto her shoulder and stroked his hair.

"I'm so sorry, Ben. Surely she would have had a chance with a mastectomy and the removal of the nodes under the arm. It could have stopped it advancing any further?"

"It's too late. The prognosis is poor," he sadly answered. "Why the hell didn't she mention it sooner? I guess it was vanity. She was always very proud of her appearance, but Dad will make sure she gets the best palliative care. He's been worried about her for some time because she was always so tired, but she kept insisting it was the menopause."

"Are you saying she's going to die, Ben?"

"Yes, I give her no more than a few months and I think that's being generous. She has developed metastasis in her liver and is jaundiced and suffering from fluid retention."

"Jesus, your poor mum and your dad and you, Ben. I know I can't do anything to help, but if you need me, please just let me know."

"I need you now," he pleaded.

"You've got me," she earnestly told him.

"I know Lowry, but for some reason, I need you to love me right now. It's not that I'm wanting to forget about my mother, I just want to be close to you and anyway I changed the sheets a couple of days ago. They actually crawled off the bed all by themselves and said, 'please direct us to the nearest laundrette."

"How disgusting," she said, as she stood up and pulled Ben from the sofa by his hand. "Come on, let's christen the clean sheets then."

Lowry, with Ben's tuition, had gradually learnt the delights of sex. Staff had been right. Once the initiation was over, it was fun all the way. Sometimes, it could be almost reverently tender, leaving Lowry feeling cherished. Other times it could be wildly abandoned and almost brutal, leaving her feeling gloriously wanton. She knew that Ben was expressing his anguish through her, but didn't mind feeling gloriously wanton when they both collapsed with exhaustion. They lay together in each other's arms.

"Thank you, sweet nurse," Ben said. "That was wonderful and I know I've told you this many times, but I love you. I really do. I've never said that to anyone before."

She knew Ben's emotions were all over the place with the news of his mother. She wanted so much to believe him, but it was nice of him to say he loved her.

"You don't have to thank me for anything, Ben. I just wish I hadn't called your mum a cow."

"Cancer or no cancer, my mum is a cow, but I love her. I don't have to like her values or her snobbery. I've never revealed this to you, because it's too painful, but my elder brother was killed in a motor bike accident and for any parent to lose a child must be unbearable, but I can't live up to the idealised image she now has of him. My mother and I used to have so many rows, that I sometimes wondered if she would rather it were me that was killed not Simon." Lowry drew Ben closer. "What she doesn't seem to understand is that she caused my brother to become rebellious and wild. She wanted him to become a doctor. She drove the college mad, ringing his House Master and insisting he did chemistry, physics and biology at O level and then at A level. Simon had other ideas, he wanted to join the RAF. My dad's brother was a Polish airman. She gave him hell, because he refused to do medicine. He eventually had enough and left home and the next thing we knew he had been killed doing a ton on the Preston Bypass. It was dreadful. It was wet and he tried to stop but he skidded and went under the back of a lorry. He was decapitated. The family went to pieces then. I think my mother believed that my father blamed her for driving Simon away, although nothing was said. I also blamed myself because my Dutch grandmother had left Simon and me a small legacy and I lent Simon mine so he could buy the motorbike. My mother screamed at me and slapped me so many times across the face that my father had to restrain her. So much destructive blame flew around that my parents fell apart and never really got it together again after that. The love had gone, buried with Simon."

Lowry felt sickened to the stomach. Decapitation was the worst thing she could possibly imagine.

"Oh my God! What a tragic story. It's bad enough that he was killed, but to know your beautiful child has been ...., Oh Christ, it doesn't bear thinking about. Is that why you're studying medicine, Ben, to please your mother?"

"Good God, no," he emphatically answered. "At the age of eleven I wanted to be a vet, then at sixteen I decided on human medicine. It was my choice, not my mother's."

"How long ago was it, when your brother was killed?"

"Five years ago," he replied, "but I've talked enough about me. Tell me how your dad's getting on? I still think it's an incredible story the way you found each other."

"You must come for dinner with Lou and him, Ben. He's a lovely man and I feel so lucky. He told me how my mother died and although I didn't know her, I cried. She was part of the Resistance and was betrayed and caught, but she threw herself under the train she was going to de-rail rather than be interrogated. My mother was a heroine and I am so proud of her. She was only twenty three years old. I know I said to you that I didn't care about not knowing my past, but now that I find I've got a past, I want to know about my grandparents on my mother's side and on my dad's side. His parents were shot by Nazis, you know. Somewhere in the Bible it says love thine enemies. Well Ben, the holy Jo who said that, had obviously never heard of Hilter and his fascist bastards."

"Obviously not," Ben laughed. "But I know on my father's side, his family perished at the hands of the Nazis. They were Polish but Dad never talks about it. Perhaps one day he might open up."

"You have a right to know about how your family died. Painful though it might be for your dad to talk about them. If he doesn't then they might just as well have not existed. Leif loves telling to me about his beloved Inger. I can see it in his eyes. She's coming back to life as he talks about her." Ben lay quietly on his back with his arms folded behind his head. "Am I talking too much, Ben? You've gone all quiet."

"I wouldn't exactly say you talk too much, you just seem to have a lot to say."

"That's just another way of saying I talk too much, you pig!"

The couple lay in silence watching a large spider walk upside down on the ceiling. From the size of its round body it seemed to find plenty to eat in Ben's bedroom. Three dusty cobwebs hung from the corners like filthy net curtains.

"Why don't you get a brush and knock those cobwebs down?" Lowry suggested.

"Because I am quite happy for Insy Wincy to use by bedroom as a pantry," he replied. "But to more important issues, Miss Stuart. I told you before, that I loved you and you didn't respond. You never do. Why?"

"I don't know. I sometimes find it hard to believe it, when people tell me they love me," she quietly answered. "In the orphanage when that red haired bitch was angry, she'd say, 'no wonder you're in this place. It's because nobody could ever love you. And when it's said often enough to you as a child, you believe it."

"Lowry Stuart, why the hell would I still be with a balm pot if I didn't love her?" he earnestly said. "I've had many flings with girls, mostly nurses, and I've never loved any of them until I met you. You make me laugh, you're totally unpredictable, you're the most beautiful creature I've ever set eyes on and best of all you're a good shag and I love you to bits. Just accept the fact that you are loveable. You may not have had any of the stuff when you were younger, but there's a hell of a lot of it around you now. So I shall ask you a direct question. Is it possible that you might love me?"

"Yes."

"Yes what? It's possible you might, or yes, you love me. Which one is it?"

"Yes, I love you, Ben. I honestly do. And if I'm such a good shag, then let's do it again."

He laughed and then pressed his mouth onto hers.

"I've used my last rubber. It'll be risky. Where are you cycle wise?" he asked, after coming up for air.

"Well I don't need stabilisers anymore, if that's what you're asking," she giggled.

A short time later, Lowry felt cherished.

Not even the bleak décor of her attic bedroom could bring Lowry down from her euphoria when she returned to the Nurses' Home. Niggles at the back of her mind told her she didn't have the right to be so happy when Ben's mother was seriously ill and little Tommy was in prison, but she found it difficult to over-ride her exhilaration and replace it with despair. She was loved by the most wonderful mum, a gorgeous dad and an oversexed medical student. She may not have had any of that love stuff in her early life, but since then she had certainly fallen into the winning hole on her roulette wheel.

THE LETTERS

Dear Tommy,

I wonder if you remember me. I lived in the orphanage with you when we were both very young. I was Lowry Stephenson then, but I was lucky enough to be adopted, so my name is now Lowry Stuart. I remember you very well. We were the two left-handers in the class and we used to take it in turn to sit in the dunce's chair. But neither of us was a dunce, we just had wobbly pencils so our writing was a mixture of scribbles and back to front letters. Just how cruel things were in those days.

I'm sorry to read that you've ended up in Walton. You must have been desperate, because I remember you as a gentle little boy. A long time has passed since then and maybe your teenage life has not been easy for you. I hope you can get all the help you need while you are in that place. Do you remember the bully boy called Raymond Gubbins? He was bigger than most of us. And then there was my friend Beth Hutchinson. But especially, do you remember the red haired Miss with a big mouth and a vicious temper? Her temper was so bad, we would wet ourselves with fright which made her temper even worse. Then came the slaps. I wouldn't mind meeting her again and giving her a slap or two.

I am a Student Nurse now and I'm scribbling this during my lunch break. It's nearly over so I'll have to go. Don't worry if you don't want to reply to this letter. I just wanted you to know that I was thinking of you.

Take care. Lowry.

The letter plopped into the hospital post box for the four thirty collection. Lowry doubted very much that she would hear anything.

Two weeks later she discovered that her doubts had been unfounded. A letter arrived written on Prison note paper in very childish scrawl. It had obviously been censored by a Prison Officer. Tommy's bad language had been obliterated with a thick blue pen.

'Lowry got yer leter I rember all of of yous I wer in Ray gubbins gang we lif in aemty warhows at the albut docks We dun robin and theevin and niger bashin The ome we was in shut coz all them bichis was theevin off off the kids We was sent to a uffer ome I ran away Yer nigger frend Beff uchinson was a xxxxxxx-hooer she ad a pach by the albut docks and gift yer a blow job for a bob but Ray gorrit for nuthin

Rays a ard man no buger crossis im It wer uchinsons biffday and er uvver niger hooers givd er eerings Ray gorrum off off er I seed im belt er 'ard and put the boot in It wer reel bad she wer screemin We aint seed er sins The womin I bashd ad red air an a red gob like that bich in the ome so I bashd er ard I ates this xxxxxxx xxxxxxxx

the screws are xxxxxxx xxxxxxx. rite to me if yer want Tom

Lowry had to read the letter twice before it made any sense. What had turned a timid little boy into a monster? Lowry knew Tommy wasn't really a monster. He had created the persona in order to survive. The picture she held in her memory was of Tommy when she last saw him. He hadn't grown in her mind. He was still scrawny, with big eyes, a runny nose and a wet patch darkening the front of his trousers whenever the red head had yelled at him. But what of little Beth? She had been afraid of bully boy Gubbins and now she had to suck his dick and get belted. How had she ended up on the streets? Lowry suddenly remembered, with a jolt of horror, a conversation between two little orphanage girls.

They were both sitting in the yard on the bottom step that led up to the back kitchen door. How come she had forgotten all about it?

"I wish I were back at home and not in here," Beth had said. "I likes my granddad, but they taked me away for doing naughty things with him."

"What naughty things?" Lowry had asked.

"He let me to play with his pinkie and kiss it to make it get big," Beth had innocently replied. "They said I were a bad girl, but my granddad liked it. That's why I is here."

The conversation had left Lowry somewhat confused, but she wasn't five years old anymore and she now knew that sweet little Beth had been abused from an early age. She felt the tears silently falling down her cheeks. Beth's smile was the loveliest smile she had ever seen, and now the mouth that had smiled so beautifully was once again being abused for a shilling. Leif had been right. Too much time had passed. Tommy and Beth were the products of a system that had failed them and they were strangers to her. Lowry preferred to remember them as the sweet little innocents who had shared their early years with her. She wouldn't be writing to Tommy again. What could they possibly write about?

Eight days later, much to Lowry's surprise another letter arrived for her on Prison notepaper.

Dear Miss Stuart,

I am a Prison Probation Officer and was assigned to Thomas Ollerenshawe. I am taking the liberty of writing to you because I am aware that you wrote to him because he asked me to read the letter to him. He was very pleased to hear from you. Unfortunately, I have to tell you that Tom hanged himself in his cell last Saturday night. He suffered from claustrophobia and the confines of prison life and a small cell was more than he could cope with. I'm sorry to give you such sad news. Should you wish to talk to me, please ring the telephone number which is at the top of the page and ask for ext. 38. I am available between 9am and 5pm Monday to Friday.

Yours Sincerely,
Jim Fairweather.

The news left Lowry feeling numb. She could not conceive of anyone being so desperate as to hang themselves. She knew why he suffered from claustrophobia. He had spent time in the punishment cupboard just like she had. She never developed the condition, but always slept with the curtains open and panicked when a power cut plunged her into complete darkness. Should she ring Jim Fairweather? If she did nothing it would look as if she didn't care. And she did. Leif would know what she should do. He'd got it right so far.

After coming off duty that same evening Lowry rang the Adelphi Hotel. Leif was not there. He was probably in the bar of The Exchange with Marcus Marriot, she assumed.

As Lowry walked the short distance from the hospital to Lime Street she prayed that Leif was not drinking. Hesitating at the bar door, she realised she had never entered a pub on her own before. It felt intimidating. Plucking up courage she pushed open the door and the smell of rank cigarette smoke, stale beer and sweat made her feel nauseous. The murmur of voices instantly stopped as the drinkers stared at a single female who had brazenly entered the usually exclusive domain of the male. A lecherous drunk with protruding teeth, stood up and thrust his hips backwards and forwards causing his mates to laugh at his lewd gesture.

"Are yer up for it, darlin'?" he asked, with a sniggering leer on his face.

He moved closer to Lowry. She was out of her depth, but an uncontrollable fury boiled inside her.

"Take one more move towards me and I'll punch your buck teeth straight into your scrotum," she viciously told him.

His mates cheered loudly. Where were Marcus and Leif? She walked to the bar, conscious of being stared at and aware that some of the men purposely stood too close to her. She could feel their beery breath on her neck.

"Yes love," the barmaid asked. Her huge cleavage would have put the Grand Canyon to shame.

"I'm looking for Captain Svenerson," Lowry explained.

"He's in the room, over there," the barmaid said, pointing to a door to the left of the bar.

The lecherous drunk laughed.

"She likes the sailor boys, lads," he quipped. "Show us yer bell-bottomed bloomers darlin'."

Lowry was incensed.

"Sod off, you ignorant waste of space," she fumed, her hands instinctively knotting into fists. "He's my father and he's quite capable of knocking the likes of you straight back into your cave."

His mates laughed again. Lowry felt invincible. Her father was only next door and having a big protective dad was something she had craved since her childhood. She walked towards the door.

"Yer can't go in there," the drunken lech shouted. "Women ain't allowed in there. It's men only."

Lowry bristled.

"I've already told you to sod off," she told the surprised man. "Why don't you listen?"

"Leave 'er alone," the barmaid said. "Go on, luvvie, yer can go in there. It's only yer dad and Marcus who's in there any'ow."

"Thank you very much," Lowry said.

She heard the lech referring to her as a 'posh bint.' She opened the 'Men Only' door wondering if the drinkers ever confused it with the Gents. The two men were deep in conversation and her entrance went unnoticed. Leif had an orange juice in his hand.

"Hello, you two," she said, approaching the engrossed men. They looked up in surprise.

"Elskling, what on earth are you doing here?" Leif asked.

She pulled up a stool and joined the men at the table. Lowry smiled at Marcus and kissed her father's cheek.

"I didn't realise how difficult it would be for a woman to walk into a pub on her own," she explained. "What bloody century are we living in when in the early nineteen sixties a woman can't enter a pub without being treated like a bitch on heat? I've had a hell of a time with a buck toothed piece of shit, who for some reason, thought I might like to have sex with him."

Leif flew out of his chair and made for the door.

"Show me who it was," he shouted.

"No, Leif, I've sorted him. I don't need a champion and I don't want a fight," she pleaded. He sat down again. "I am here because I needed to talk to you."

He looked concerned.

"Are you in trouble, elskling?"

"It's about Tommy, the boy I spoke to you about, who's in prison and it's about something I remember that happened at the orphanage. I need to share it with you because I think it's so sad. Well, I wrote to Tommy and got a reply and it was a bitter angry letter. You were right. Too much water has gone under the bridge since we last knew each other. Well, I got a letter from the prison today to say Tommy had hanged himself in his cell. It's too awful to think about."

Leif placed his hand on Lowry's and squeezed gently.

"Let me get you a drink and you can tell me all about it."

"Can I have an orange juice, please?" she asked.

Marcus jumped from his stool.

"I'll get it," he said and disappeared to the bar.

Leif slowly read the contents of Tommy's letter and sighed as Marcus returned with the orange juice.

"Thank you, Marcus," she said. "When I first read that letter, Leif, I thought Tommy had become a monster."

"Tommy wasn't a monster Lowry. The people who were supposed to care for him were the monsters. And to think I put my child into the hands of these people."

"Please don't blame yourself, Leif," she pleaded. "The past is in the past and I don't have any hang-ups about what happened to me. I've got you back and that's all that matters. You don't have to feel guilty. You're a wonderful dad and I love you, so please don't feel guilty about me, because I couldn't bear it. But I've been keeping something to myself," she quietly said. "Do you remember telling me you visited every orphanage in Liverpool and Lancashire?"

"Yes, I remember," he said.

"Well, you came to the orphanage I was in, because I saw you. I was six years old.

You looked so wonderful with all that gold round your jacket and hat and your gold buttons that I thought you were the King. I banged on the window and you waved your hat at us and smiled. I was shouting, 'no don't go away.' Do you remember asking me when I first knew you were my dad, if I'd just seen a ghost?" Leif nodded. "Well I had. I realised you were the man with gold buttons who came one day to the orphanage. I haven't mentioned it before because it made me feel so sad to think that wonderful man in the gold was my father and I didn't know it and he didn't even know it was his daughter banging on the window."

Leif sighed loudly. He rested his elbows on the table and raised his hands to his forehead. It was like the substance of what he had just heard required him to press his head into his finger tips to enable them to absorb some of the sadness.

"I remember one particular place I visited and seeing all those lovely little faces smiling and waving at me. God, how tragic," he eventually said.

"Leif," Lowry quietly said. "Shortly after I saw you, I was adopted. I had the most wonderful childhood after that. It was the best thing that could have happened to me apart from meeting up with you. You were at sea most of the time, so I wouldn't have seen much of you anyway. A fantastic woman stood in for you until I was able to look after myself." She smiled cheekily at him. "The worst part of not having a dad was I had no-one to run in the father's race at school."

He smiled affectionately.

"I would have won every race for you, elskling. I've missed you growing up and I regret that, but thanks to Marcus, I've got you back now."

Marcus smiled his beautifully ugly smile.

"Your gratitude is much appreciated, Captain, but a gin would be appreciated more."

Leif threw a ten shilling note across the table.

"Get it yourself and two more oranges, please."

"Leif, going back to Tommy, I feel guilty because I'm so lucky. What sort of a life did Tommy have? He didn't even have a life, he had nothing. Now he's dead and only nineteen years old. How many more people are there, Leif who are still suffering because of the Germans? His dad would still be alive if it hadn't been for the war and his dad must have loved him because he used to make him little wooden aeroplanes. And what about Beth? She was so sweet, with a beautiful smile that I remember used to show the whitest teeth. Now she'll be having all that sweetness knocked out of her by lecherous men who'll just use and abuse her. It makes me sick."

He lit a cigarette and handed it to Lowry. He then lit one for himself.

"You are not responsible for what has happened to Tommy or Beth, and Tommy certainly wasn't responsible for the way he turned out," he said. "The guilt is not yours. If he had been treated with love and kindness, he would still have been the gentle lad you told me he was. When you wrote to him you showed him that you cared. You didn't judge him. You treated him as a friend from the past and that's where it should be left now, Lowry, in the past. What has happened to those two young people is an appalling tragedy, but life isn't fair, it never will be."

"You're right. Perhaps I'm being indulgent by feeling guilty, because it makes me feel better about all the luck I've had. Does that make sense, Leif?" He nodded and stubbed his cigarette out into a glass Guinness ashtray. "But I can't get Beth out of my head, though. Why should I feel guilty about her and Tommy? It's possibly the wrong word. I suppose I just feel sad. I feel I need to find Beth. She's only nineteen years old. There must be something we can do to get her out of the hands of filthy men and according to Tommy it seems Gubbins beats her up."

"This Gubbins sounds a horrible character, but slow down Lowry. How are you going to find Beth? What can you do for her if you do?"

"Well she obviously had a patch at the docks. It surely can't be difficult to find a black girl at the docks."

"The docks are teaming with girls, black and white, who are protected by their pimps. Beth may not want to be rescued by you, have you thought about that?"

"Don't be stupid, Leif," she angrily replied. "How can any girl choose to be pawed by men they don't know, let alone have a dick in her mouth when it probably hasn't seen bathwater for weeks. It's revolting and demeaning. The least we can do is find her and ask her if she is happy doing what she's doing. If she says no then we get her out of there."

"And how do you do that and where do you take her?" he asked.

"We cross that bridge when we come to it," she flippantly replied.

Leif gave his daughter a ponderous look.

"I want you to listen to me, young lady," he seriously said. "You are not to go off half cocked and go looking for Beth at the docks. It's dangerous and no place for a woman on her own. Promise me you won't go near the docks."

Lowry nodded.

"I mean it. Promise me, now."

"I promise I won't go on my own."

"That's not good enough. Promise me you won't go at all. If it means so much to you to find Beth then I'll ask Marcus to do some sniffing around and see if he can find her and he can let you know how she is."

She smiled mischievously at her father.

"Brilliant! You must be that wise old Norse God called Odin."

"Less of the old, please," he laughed. "And I have two eyes. Odin only had one! But I want to ask you a question."

"Fire away," Lowry glibly said.

"Could you make me a proud man by calling me, Dad or Pappa with two pees?"

"Of course I could. I presume Pappa, with two pees, is Norwegian for Dad?" He nodded. "And d'you know that word elskling you use, sometimes? Does that mean daughter?"

"No, elskling means, darling."

"Oh, that's sweet, Pappa, with two pees," she chuckled. "Anyway, where's Marcus with the drinks?"

"I'll share a confidence with you," he said. "Marcus doesn't know that I am aware of the little game he plays. He goes to the bar to buy the drinks. He always buys himself two gins, knocks one back at the bar and then returns to the table with just the one drink for himself and one for me and always tells me there was a queue." He gave Lowry a side-long glance. "Did you wonder whether I might be drinking alcohol when you got here?"

"It crossed my mind."

"Well trust me, elskling. I have something to live for." He waved to Marcus who appeared with one gin and two orange juices.

"There was a long queue at the bar," he said.

Lowry and her dad smiled knowingly at each other.

"Marcus, was there a man at the bar with a blue check shirt and buck teeth?" Lowry asked.

"Didn't notice," Marcus replied. "Why?"

"Well I did tell him that my pappa, with two pees, would knock him straight back into his cave, because he was behaving like a Neanderthal."

"Well if I'd been there at the time, Lowry, I most certainly would have done. Anyway, when are you due back at the Nurses' Home?" Leif asked.

"In half an hour," she answered.

"Good, I'll drive you there before I take on a Neanderthal."

"Thanks, Dad." Lowry turned towards Marcus. "Marcus, my favourite uncle," she obsequiously said, "Dad has a big favour to ask you for me."

"I will not take on a Neanderthal with him, if that's what you're asking," he gruffly replied.

'BLOWED TO SARDINES'

Lowry's transfer to Female Surgical, to gain additional experience left her feeling homesick for the guys and her favourite Staff Nurse. The women were not so easy to please as the men, but their needs were virtually the same, apart from the application of face powder and lipstick at visiting time.

The ward gave off an air of fluffy pinkness with a touch of baby blue dotted here and there. Silk ribbons tied the pastel coloured bed jackets at the neck, making them look like baby matinee coats. Much to Lowry's horror almost every locker was adorned with a vase of flowers. She thought the room looked like the horticultural tent of the Liverpool Show rather than a hospital ward.

Ben had arrived on the ward at nine o'clock with an air of confidence as he sauntered to bed three. He had winked at Lowry, but she knew he was dreading the procedure he was about to perform. The self-assured air was nothing more than a front to assuage any fears the patient may have had, if she knew that Ben was about to carry out his first lumbar puncture without the usual supervision of his professor. He had carried out the procedure many times, but the security of having his mentor beside him had given him confidence. The last thing he wanted was to cause any suffering by hitting bone. He had to get the lengthy needle between lumbar vertebrae three and four and draw off cerebrospinal fluid to fill three sample bottles. Lowry had been his guinea pig the previous evening as she lay in the left lateral position while he meticulously measured from one iliac crest to the other and drew a line. She had giggled as he ran his fingers over her lower spine until he found lumbar three and four. He left an inked cross and a kiss on the spot for the needle's entry. The patient was in for a surprise if he kissed her inked spot. Sister and Ben were now closeted behind the curtains.

Ward Sister was approachable, bubbling with cheerfulness and engaged to be married to a Lab technician. The Sister on Female Surgical wasn't going to leave this mortal coil with 'returned un-opened' on her tombstone like the battleaxe on Male Medical. The patients loved her, so did Lowry.

Lowry also fell in love with an adorable Liverpudlian widow called Phyllis Postlethwaite, who sat in bed ten with her peroxide hair in rollers and minus her gall bladder. The rollers were quickly removed and the lipstick thickly applied ready for the doctor and medical student's ward round.

"Kiddo, that fella,' who's behind them curtains, with the black 'air, called Ben, 'as me creamin' me drawers when 'e touches me. Thems eyes are like limpit pools 'an' 'is smile..,"

"Phyllis, you are disgusting," Lowry laughed. "And his eyes are not remotely like marine molluscs, they're deep moody brown."

"That's exactly what I were sayin,' yer divvy."

"Anyway, Phyllis, Ben is spoken for. He's mine."

"Well yer berra' watch yer back, girl," she giggled, "'cos I could charm the stockin's off off them Yankee Airmen from Burton Wood, durin' the war."

"I didn't know Yankee Airmen wore stockings, Phyllis."

"They never wore 'em, yer daft wazzock, but do us a favour, Tilly mint," she begged. "Will yer ask that Ben, when 'es finished with Mrs Fletcher, if 'e'd 'ave a look at me scar where they took me gall bladder out? Me stitches is itchin' me, like crabs on a prozzie."

Lowry grinned and shook her head.

"No, Phyllis, you can show them to your surgeon when he comes round at eleven o'clock this morning. He's the one who did the sewing so he'll want to admire his own embroidery skills, not Ben."

Phyllis pushed out her bottom lip into a sulking pout.

"I never put yer down as bein' a stingy mingy."

"Now Phyllis, I've almost finished with your wash, but I can't find your tooth brush or toothpaste," Lowry explained as she rummaged through the patient's toilet bag.

"I ain't got none," she responded. "Me teeth cleans themselves at night in me glass with some steri powder. Watchin' them bubbles bouncin' off off me tomb stones 'elps me gets ter sleep."

Her stories of being a land girl, a munitions worker and her escapades with the Yanks from Burton Wood Airfield had Lowry in stitches. Phyllis's war sounded like fun. Chocolate, chewing gum and stockings replaced bouquets as enticements to the eagerly available young women.

"You sound like you enjoyed the war, Phyllis."

"Them friggin' German's blew 'alf me street off the bloomin' map, and me 'ouse was in the 'alf that got blowed up, kiddo," she explained. "We lived in Bootle near the docks. Yer know the place? Where the bugs wear clogs. We wasn't in the 'ouse at the time, but if we 'ad, we'd 'ave been blowed to sardines."

Lowry giggled. Phyllis had written her own dictionary. At night, when the lights were out, Phyllis secretly drank a bottle of stout her daughter had smuggled in. 'Lowry, kiddo, will yer get rid of this empty bottle I've got congealed in me bed?'

Phyllis's daughter had apparently been married twice and was now on her third man.

"Me girl 'as bin-bagged two 'usbands already. She's just a flibbertigiblet," she grumbled. "She giblets from one man to the other. Me 'usband were no better. I kicked 'im out for muckin' about with some Irish tart."

"Oh, I thought you were a widow, Phyllis," Lowry said as she gathered the washing equipment together onto the trolley.

"I am, 'e were a docker and got clobbered on the 'ead with a swingin' cargo of spuds." She chortled loudly. "He were Irish. Funny when yer think about it. A cargo of spuds finishin' 'im off. 'E's six foot under now, in the Anfield bone orchard."

"Postlethwaite isn't an Irish name," Lowry said.

"Nah, I reverberated back to me maiden name. Me married name were McGinty. He were known as Paddy, although 'is first name were Joseph, but I gorra lorra stick about bein' 'is old goat, so when I bin-bagged 'im I went back to callin' meself Postlethwaite. I used to put one of them things in the middle, yer know what I mean? A barrelled thing, and call meself, Mrs Phyllis Postle -Thwaite, like them posh folk, but no bugger ever took me serious, like."

Sister's voice summoned Lowry to duty.

"Nurse Stuart, would you make Mrs Fletcher comfortable and fetch her a cup of tea, please?" she asked, as she emerged from behind the curtains. "Would you make one for Mr Novak at the same time?"

"Yes, Sister," Lowry replied. "Would you like one?"

"No thank you," she replied. "I'm off for my coffee break in five minutes."

Sister disappeared into her office.

After Lowry had cleared the washing trolley into the sluice room she found Ben sitting on Mrs Fletcher's bed, smiling and chatting. Doctors and medical students were allowed to sit on patients beds, but for nurses to be found doing the same thing   was virtually a hanging offence.

"How did it go, Mrs Fletcher?" she asked.

"Well, my dear, you know I said to you I was dreading it, but it wasn't as bad as I'd expected. Mr Novak, here, was very nice. He's got a very gentle touch."

"I'm sure he has, Mrs Fletcher, and I understand Mr Novak would like a cup of tea."

Ben grinned cheekily.

"You understand correctly, Nurse Stuart. Two sugars please."

Mrs Fletcher began to fumble in her locker drawer.

"I've got some barley sugars I want you to have, Mr Novak," she said, as she rummaged about.

Ben stood up and whispered to Lowry.

"Meet me in the sluice room in fifteen minutes."

"Does gentle touchy Mr Novak need a bedpan?" she whispered back.

Fifteen minutes later the sluice room door opened and Ben entered. He did look handsome.

"I gather the procedure went well, Ben," Lowry said. "The poor darling was dreading it."

"I haven't come here to discuss my exceptional skills with a syringe," he grinned. "I've come to get my hands on that patch of bare skin between your suspenders and panties. What colour are they today?"

"You lech," she said, as his hand slid up her uniform dress. "They happen to be royal blue with white lace. But are you telling me the sight of sixty eight year old Mrs Fletcher's bare bum has made you randy?"

"Her bare bum was discretely covered," he retorted. "It's your bare thighs at the top of black stockings that make me randy."

Ben found the smooth bare flesh and Lowry groaned.

"Mr Touchy Novak, please stop," she begged. "There's no lock on the sluice room door and I'm quite likely to pin you to the floor if you carry on doing this."

His hand slid up the back of her knicker leg and he firmly squeezed her bare left buttock. He pushed his body into hers and she felt his hardness.

"I know why you lot wear white coats," she sighed. "It's to hide your…." Her sigh turned to a moan. "God, you've got me feeling as horny as you are."

"Sorry Nurse," he said, whilst dipping his free hand into his white coat pocket. "I can't oblige you at the moment because I'm due on gynae in ten minutes, but here's some barley sugar for you instead."

Nursing was such fun, but worries at the back of Lowry's mind told her it wouldn't be for much longer.

THE FAVOUR

The chains that held up the wide wooden gangway clattered as they slowly eased the gangplank down from the ferry and onto the jetty of the Pier Head.

Marcus watched as a surge of happy and boisterous passengers disembarked from the Royal Iris and tramped down the slope and back into Liverpool. He had always enjoyed watching the Mersey Ferries crossing back and forth to Birkenhead and New Brighton. As a young man he had often taken a pretty female to the beach at New Brighton and tucked into bloater paste sandwiches. He could never enjoy the picnic his mother had supplied. A young female in a bathing costume had his adolescent hormones running amok, but his inexperience and self-consciousness meant he spent most of his time sitting on the sand with his beach towel folded over his embarrassment. He gave a silent chuckle as he remembered those days when his dick had a mind of its own and popped up at the most inappropriate moments.

He watched the last of the stragglers leave the ferry and realised he couldn't remember the names of any of the girls he had taken to the beach apart from Norma. She had been something of a nymphomaniac and he lost his virginity to her. Norma had 'broken in' most of the boys in the sixth form. He laughed loudly as he thought of the number of cherries she had collected in her fruit bowl. She was now working in Africa as a nun.

He rose from the bench and turned up the collar of his jacket against the chill night air. Beth Hutchinson! She'd probably got herself a working name by now. Something that implied seductiveness or availability. He knew that most of the working girls cruised Lime Street or the lower half of Upper Parliament Street near the Anglican Cathedral, but Lowry had told Leif that Beth's patch was near the docks. He would start by searching the Dock Road where the now demolished overhead railway had once been. Apart from a gang of youths who were kicking a deflated leather football about, he saw no working girls.

He jumped out of his skin when a shadowy figure appeared in front of him from behind a solid concrete and steel pillar that still stood like a cenotaph to the amazing engineering that had once been the overhead railway.

"Lookin' for business?" the voice asked Marcus.

"Could be," he replied. She might be co-operative if she believed some business was coming her way, he thought.

"Well is yer or isn't yer?" she angrily asked.

The last thing Marcus wanted, was to do business leaning on a concrete pillar in the semi-darkness with some poor half dressed girl.

"Don't you have somewhere to go?" he asked her.

"Like where?" she replied. "I don't work in no brothel. I works on me own. Any'ow what's it to you?"

The street light from across the road enabled Marcus to study the young woman in front of him. She was white and no more than seventeen or eighteen years old. Her long, thin, naked legs, made even longer by her red high heeled shoes, hung from beneath a tight skirt, so short, it hardly covered her buttocks. She had done her best to reveal her small breasts by squeezing herself into a low cut, closely fitting top. But it was the heavily painted face that saddened the hardened private detective. It was the face of a child.

"I just thought being here with some punters must be dangerous for you," Marcus told her. She raised her short skirt and drew out a packet of Craven A cigarettes from her garter. "Here, have one of mine," he quickly said.

She stuffed her packet back behind her garter and helped herself to a Senior Service cigarette.

"Is you from the Sally Army?" she asked, drawing heavily on the strong cigarette. "Cos if yer is, then yer can bugger off." She coughed as the smoke hit the back of her throat.

Marcus laughed.

"I promise you I'm not Sally Army and I'm not the Old Bill either. Anyway, what's your name?"

"Gloria," she answered. "But lerrus get down ter business. Whats yer lookin' for? I don't do nothin' kinky like. I'll do yer a 'and job or blow…,"

"No thanks, Gloria, I'm not a punter, but there's money in it if you can give me any information about a working girl called Beth Hutchinson, who I understand had a patch near here. Can you help me?"

"Never 'eard of 'er," came the immediate reply. "Any'ows what d'yer wanna know for? What can she do for yer that I can't?"

"I've told you, I'm not a punter and she's not in trouble," Marcus reassuringly explained. "She's a black girl aged about the same as you. She may have changed her name. She's probably got a pimp."

"Stupid cow! What's she gorra pimp for when all 'e does is takes yer money and beats yer up. Thems bastards, them pimps, 'specially the nigger ones."

"So you do know her and her pimp then, Gloria?"

"Might do," she evasively replied. "What's it worth?"

Marcus was struggling to keep his patience. He was normally in control of information gathering, but this young whore was playing him for a nelly.

"Well do you or don't you know her?" he snapped.

"I said, 'ow much is it worth? And don't get shirty with me, Lar. Any'ow, I've gorra regular comin' soon, so yer goin' to 'ave to bugger off. So 'ow much?" she demanded.

"Depends on the information," Marcus replied.

"Yer pays me first, then yer gets the dope. Okay!"

Marcus reached into his pocket where he kept his loose change.

"I'll give you two shillings."

"Fuck off!" she viciously replied. "I'm a 'igh class working girl so I does nothin' for less than five bob."

Marcus's struggling patience finally snapped.

"Look here, Gloria, or whatever your name is. I can ring my old mates in the force and have you plucked off the streets before your regular has time to undo his flies. Now what d'you know about Beth Hutchinson?"

"Keep yer 'air on!" she angrily replied. "I don't knows 'er all that well and I ain't seed 'er for ages. She use to work the patch near the Albert but she must 'ave moved somewhere else. 'Er nigger pimp beats up on 'is girls if they don't earn enough. E's a right shittin' black bastard. Ask the girls at Vickie's Monument if they knows where she went. I works on me own so I don't have nothin' to do with that lot."

"Thanks, Gloria," Marcus said, "but can you tell me if she is working under another name?"

"Ye, she calls 'erself, Black Beauty. Yer know, like the 'orse."

He gave her a ten shilling note.

"Get yourself a decent meal," he said. "You look half starved and if you want to see middle age get yourself off the streets."

She pulled off her high heeled shoe and carefully placed the note under an insole inside the shoe.

He left and heard her shouting 'fuck off, yer wanker.' He grinned. He'd been called far worse in his time as a cop.

As he walked from the cover of the pillar a well dressed middle aged man appeared from the gloom. Must be 'the regular,' Marcus concluded.

"Does your wife know you're meeting up with young Gloria again?" he asked the astonished man.

THE CRYSTAL PYRAMID

Lowry was distraught that her nursing career would soon be coming to an end. Her morning sickness confirmed her condition. Only Helen shared the knowledge and her welcoming arms hugged some measure of warmth into Lowry's cold pit of despair.

"Listen woman, you are more than two months gone now. You've got to tell Ben and your mother," Helen pleaded. "It's not something you can hide for long."

The girls were sitting in the Kardomah Café, drinking coffee. Lowry sat in silence building a crystal pyramid with the sugar cubes from the glass bowl. No matter how carefully she placed the final cube on the top, her pyramid crashed onto the tablecloth.

"That's my life, Helen. It's crashing around me. I don't feel anything for the baby at the moment. I don't want to be pregnant and throwing up every morning and then going on duty. It's hell. I just don't want to get up in the morning 'cos I feel like shit. I stare at the bloody awful green wall and feel sick." Helen leaned across the table and squeezed her friend's hand. "Don't do that Hel," Lowry begged. "It makes me want to cry all the more when you're nice to me."

"That's your hormones, girl," Helen said, grinning at her friend.

"Well it's obvious somebody made this whore moan," Lowry bitterly responded. "Because that is how I'll be seen, as a whore, a tramp and a fallen woman. There are loads of expressions to describe the likes of me, but I'm not aware of any that are levelled at unmarried fathers. There never seems to be any shame attached to them. They have the right to sow their wild oats, but the only thing we girls are allowed to sew is a hole in a bloody hospital sheet."

Laura laughed.

"Lowry will you stop playing with the sugar and will you stop calling yourself names?" she pleaded. "You're none of those things. I'll never think any the worse of you because you're going to be an unmarried mum."

"Bloody hell, Hel, don't say that," Lowry exploded. "I don't want to be an unmarried mum at nineteen years old."

Her anguished voice had travelled to the next table. The elderly women held their toasted teacakes halfway to their open mouths and stared. Lowry angrily stared back at them.

"If you don't close your mouths soon, your dentures will drop out," she rudely told the gawping women.

They flounced their shoulders and looked away. Helen giggled.

"Well, there's still a spark of the old Lowry left," she said. "But you're going to have to tell somebody, preferably Ben first, and...,"

"How can I tell Ben I'm pregnant, when his mother is dying of cancer? He's also got end of year exams. And they are very important ones. Don't you think he's got enough on his plate?"

"Well then, you'll have to tell Lou," she responded. "Knowing her the way I do, she'll take it in her stride like she does with everything."

"But I will have let her down. She was so thrilled when I got into the teaching hospital. She always proudly tells people I'm a nurse. What of my nursing career now? It's down the pan."

Exasperated Helen snatched the sugar bowl from the table and put it on the window sill.

"Will you leave that damn sugar alone?" she heatedly said. "I don't seem to be getting through to you. You're going to have to tell everybody soon. People aren't likely to see your lump and think it's a bad case of bloat. Your father adores you, why don't you tell him?"

"Because he thinks I'm his sweet innocent little girl and sweet innocent little girls don't go round shagging a fifth year medical student, do they? That's why."

Helen threw her hands in the air.

"I give up, there's no point talking to you. You keep blocking everything I say with some pathetic excuse to put off the inevitable."

"I know and I'm sorry, but will you pass me the sugar please?" Lowry asked.

"No," Helen sharply answered.

"Please. I need two lumps for my coffee."

Helen picked two lumps from the bowl with her fingers and plopped them, with a splash, into her friend's coffee.

"Lowry, you have never told me what sex is really like. I know the earth is supposed to move but that doesn't mean a thing to me. I'd really like to know."

Lowry smiled at her sweet friend and realised their conversation was still being eavesdropped upon by the women at the next table.

"Well, Helen," she announced loudly. "There are two sorts of bonking. One is called, having sex, the other is called, making love. Do you remember when I first did it, I told you the earth had spun off its axis?" Helen nodded. "Well I lied. I just lay back, not knowing what to do, and gritted my teeth and hoped it would be over quickly because it made me so sore. Well, Staff told me the worst was over and it would be fun all the way and she was right. It is," she enthusiastically explained. "You can't get enough of it. You get to the stage when as soon as you see each other you can't wait to rip each other's clothes off. Having sex is a sort of pantomime, with four arms and four legs and two naked bodies inelegantly rolling all over the place and grunting like pigs digging for truffles. It's a bit like mud wrestling only without the mud."

Lowry and Helen laughed as the two ear-wigging women rose from their table with coffee cups in hand and moved some distance away.

"I think those two women have gone into shock," Helen laughed. "Anyway carry on with what you were saying."

"They're the sort who lie back in the dark thinking of England and humming Rule Britannia. Anyway, where was I?"

"Mud wrestling, I believe," Helen chortled.

"Oh yes. Well, I don't suggest you have sex in a single bed because sometimes the pantomime gets even funnier when you roll about, lose your bearings, and then fall out onto the floor. That tends to brings you down to earth with a real bang."

"I'm not surprised," Helen chuckled. "What about the other sort? You know, the making love bit."

"Well I believe the earth does actually move to make room for more stars when you make love, because it's unbelievably beautiful when two people in love can actually fuse together into one person. You want to stay that way forever. You have to keep your eyes tightly closed when you finally and simultaneously detonate together, or they'll pop right out of their sockets. It's like thousands of stars bursting into the heavens all at once. If you look at the sky on a clear night, Hel, you'll see trillions of stars, which indicates that all of humanity are at it and have been since time began. It's the bonking billions that keep the astronomers in work, don't you know?"

"Well, I'm not one of the bonking billions, don't you know?" Helen sadly said.

"That's because you are a Saint, Helen, and saints are virgins."

"I'd rather be a sinner than a bloody Saint, you silly cow," she laughed.

THE BODY IN THE MERSEY

Marcus walked slowly to the Bar of The Exchange. He hadn't liked the sordid search for Beth Hutchinson. The sleazy world of prostitution had left him feeling disgusted by the men who sort to take advantage of desperate young women who were caught in the vice trap. As a young police officer he had hauled many a prostitute off the streets, but after being processed they'd be straight back turning tricks again. What a bloody waste of time! How many of these women will see fifty, he wondered. And, if they did, the ravages of the game will leave them looking like ninety year old hags. Beth Hutchinson hadn't even made it to twenty. Black Beauty was dead.

Leif sat at the table in the bar waiting for his friend with a gin and tonic to welcome Marcus and an orange and lemonade for himself. Lowry had been constantly on his back, desperate to know how Marcus was getting on.

"Evening, Captain," Marcus said as he bounced into the room. "I see you've got one set up for me. Thank you, I need it."

"So you've come to the end of the road, I understand, from the message you left for me with Lou. You've had no luck finding Beth Hutchinson, then," Leif said.

"Well, yes and no," Marcus replied. "I managed to trace the girl whose working name was Black Beauty, but unfortunately the kid is dead."

"Good God! Christ, she's was only the same age as Lowry. What did she die of?"

"Open verdict. She was found by a couple who were walking along Otterspool Prom in Aigburth. They spotted what they first thought was a lump of wood jammed against some rocks at low tide, then realised it was a body and called the police. No-one knows how the poor kid got into the Mersey. Post mortem put her as being in the water for at least three months so you can imagine the state of the body. It's believed she probably entered the water around the dock area and the tide carried her down to the prom." Marcus finished his drink and stood up to get a refill. "Same again, mate?"

Leif nodded. He was shocked to hear of the girl's death and wondered how Lowry would react to the news.

Marcus returned and took his seat opposite his friend.

"You know, Leif, this is one favour I have not enjoyed doing for you, but at least we can stop Lowry putting herself in jeopardy by looking for Beth herself, and knowing that strong willed daughter of yours, that's exactly what she would have done."

He lit a Senior Service cigarette with the German lighter that Leif loathed. The menacing swastika was nauseating to him.

"Did the girl commit suicide, do you think?" Leif asked.

Marcus took a large mouthful of drink as he gave a gesture of 'who knows' with his shoulders.

"No-one can say. I went to the station and my old mate showed me the file. They don't really take the death of a prostitute terribly seriously, you know, Leif. These girls put themselves in danger. I spoke to a kid aged about seventeen or eighteen on the Dock Road. She was half naked and it was bloody cold. Her name was Gloria, well that's what she told me her name was, and she was alone in a dark isolated place. Anything could have happened to her, but she was as hard as nails. Mind you, I reckon the heels on her shoes could be classed as lethal weapons if she needed to defend herself. One of her regulars appeared. Well dressed, middle aged and probably married with a teenage daughter of his own. Makes you sick."

"Lowry's going to be devastated," Leif said. "She talks very fondly of her little friend Beth, although they haven't seen each other for thirteen years. I know she's going to start feeling guilty again because she's now got everything and her orphanage friends had nothing."

"I know the syndrome," Marcus said. "It's a bit like feeling guilty for being alive when some of your mates copped it during the war. To be honest with you, I don't think Lowry should know all the details because they're so sordid. But from the pathologists report it seems she was alive when she entered the water. Although the corpse was in a pretty bad state it was obvious it was emaciated and had suffered a number of broken bones, mostly to the face. None of them recent, but at some stage in her working life she'd had a broken jaw, a broken nose and a broken cheek bone plus she had four front teeth missing. There were signs of more recent bodily injuries, but they could have been caused by being buffeted about against the quayside or the rocks. The fish had had a go at her too, so you can imagine the state of the body. The kid Gloria told me Beth's pimp was a black bastard who beat up on his girls if they didn't earn enough. I tell you Leif, if I was still in the force I'd get that piece of shit alone and break every bloody bone in his body."

"Jesus Christ, the poor child," Leif exclaimed. "Lowry must never know of this. She told me Beth had the most beautiful smile with the whitest teeth. Surly the girl's injuries where sufficient for the Police to investigate her death. Why didn't they?"

"Well firstly, as I told you, the death of a prostitute is not a high priority, particularly a black one. There's one hell of a lot of racism in the force. Secondly some of the obvious injuries were not sustained just prior to going into the water, they were old injuries and thirdly how do you build a case when you have nothing to go on? Her pimp was given a hard time. He claimed she was working at the Albert Dock and never came back. He reckoned she must have upset some punter who did her over. They did the bastard for living off immoral earnings, so some justice was done."

"Marcus, Beth was a source of income to this man. Why would he get rid of her?"

Marcus frowned and nodded.

"Yep, a good question. Perhaps he beat her up and went too far, but then the path report said the injuries to the face were old injuries. A slap or punch to the face is not life threatening so to a man like Beth's pimp it's a way of keeping his girls in line. The more recent injuries to the body though could have been the result of a severe beating. I see what your driving at Leif. You'd make a good copper."

"Not at all, I may be way off beam, but I read the letter Tommy sent to Lowry. Remember him, the lad who hanged himself in Walton Prison? Well in the letter, Tommy said Beth would perform a sexual act on a boy they all knew in the home. He was a bully and would knock her about apparently and refuse to pay her. Actually the word used was 'belt her.' It seems this bully gave her a belting and according to Tommy he never saw Beth again after that. It would seem she just disappeared. This boy lives in a disused warehouse at Albert Docks and you couldn't get closer to the Mersey than that. The letter said something about Beth's birthday, but it was difficult to read. This bully could do with looking at. What d'you think?"

"Nothing came up in the file about him," Marcus said. "What's his name?"

"I can't remember, but I could ask Lowry. If this child died as a result of violence then she deserves justice. She had no-one in the world to protect her, so the least we could do for Beth is try and get to the truth."

Marcus stared into the ash tray, picked up a dog-end and drew squiggles in the ash with it.

"They traced the kid through a bracelet she was wearing. It had the words, 'To Beth from Granddad,' engraved on it. She had been reported missing by some of her working sisters and Missing Persons did the rest. The fact that there was water in her lungs means she was alive when she went into the water so with nothing else to work on the verdict was presumed suicide. Although I agree with you she could have jumped in herself or been thrown in. If Lowry still has that letter see if you can get it off her and see if you can confirm the scumbags name."

THE ADMIRAL'S DAUGHTER

Ben's Mother died.

Lowry accompanied Ben to the funeral. The church burst at the seams. It was only when seeing his mother's coffin carried to the open grave that Ben wept. Lowry held tightly to his hand. Dust to dust, ashes to ashes, the vicar said. What horrible words we use when saying goodbye to a fellow human being, she thought.

The mourners hovered outside the church offering their condolences to Ben and his father. Lowry stayed in the background. She felt the baby flutter within her and a feeling of tenderness stirred. But then it could have been wind. She had to tell somebody, other than Helen, about the baby. The stress was wearing her down. She had also given a month's notice two weeks previously and with holidays owing she only had six days left in the profession she loved. It had been an awful decision for her to make and a typical response from the Bluebottle.

"Well, I'm not surprised you have found yourself unable to complete your training, Nurse Stuart. You have never shown a sense of vocation or devotion to your profession. Your appraisals have improved, but...."

Lowry wasn't listening. Her brain wasn't registering the words. Matron might just as well be saying, blah, blah, blah.

"Your notice is accepted. Now leave my office," the Bluebottle buzzed.

Blah, blah, blah.

"Did you hear what I said?" the Bluebottle shouted. "Your notice is accepted."

Blah, blah, blah.

Lowry had wanted to cry when she left Matron's office. She knew it was her fault that she was pregnant. She had flippantly told Ben, that cycle wise, she didn't need stabilisers. Well, she had certainly needed some sort of protection because she now felt she had no stability at all.

The mourners were slowly moving away to the local hotel for buffet and drinks. A tomb stone beckoned her to sit. She hoped Jeremiah Jenkins, beloved husband and Father, born 1844 died 1906 would excuse her for sitting on him. She felt weak and tired. Ben and his father approached her.

"Thank you for coming and supporting Ben," Mr Novak said, with genuine sincerity.

Lowry stood to greet them both and the world span. She felt dizzy and lightheaded. Her knees gave way. Lowry fainted. She recovered to find Ben and his father squatting beside her.

"I'm so sorry," she pathetically said. "I don't know why I did that. I've never fainted before."

Ben helped her to stand.

"What happened, sweetheart?" he asked.

"I think it must have been the emotion of it all," she answered. "I feel fine now, so don't worry."

John Novak stared quizzically at Lowry before he set off to the hotel.

It struck Lowry, as they entered the buffet room, that the mourners were not so much lamenting, they were partying. The buzz of noise and laughter ricocheted round the room.

"Come and sit down, sweetheart," Ben coaxed. "I'll get you some food and a drink."

"I don't want a drink or food, Ben, thank you."

"Why not?" he asked. "Are you feeling okay?"

"Yes, of course I am," she irritably answered. "I'm not hungry. I'll just sit here and watch the revellers. You go and get yourself something."

She watched Ben wend his way to the tables of food and being accosted by everybody as he passed by. He looked so handsome in his dark suit and white shirt. She loved the way he tossed his dark hair from his forehead, only to have it fall back to its original position. His beguiling smile charmed all those he welcomed. Lowry loved him. There was no doubt about it, she decided. Eventually Ben extricated himself and returned with a plate of food. He offered her a stuffed egg with an anchovy garnish. She shuddered. The only foods she enjoyed these days were porridge, roll mop herrings and a raw rhubarb stick dipped into oodles of ice cream.

"How are you feeling, Ben?" Lowry asked.

"I'm okay," he muffled, as the last of the anchovy egg disappeared into his mouth. "My concern is for you. I have less than one year left at medical school and I have been trained to observe. I see a young woman who is tired all the time and one who, for no apparent reason, faints. I would pre-suppose anaemia, but coupled with the finicky appetite you've recently developed and the fact that you have put on a little bit of weight, I would recommend a pregnancy test." Ben stared at the dumbstruck girl. "Will the result be positive, my love?"

She slowly nodded. He placed his hand across his mouth as if not knowing what to say next. Lowry found the silence unsettling. What was he thinking? Eventually Ben spoke.

"How far on are you?" Lowry held up three fingers. "Jesus," he exploded, "and you haven't told me? Were you ever going to tell me?" she nodded. "For goodness sake, Lowry, speak to me. I'm not into communicating about this, in sign language. Have you told Lou and Leif?"

"The only person who knows about this is Helen and she's been wonderfully supportive."

Ben closed his eyes, shaking his head in bewilderment.

"God, you're so full of surprises. Did you not think I would be wonderfully supportive?"

"Yes, but your mum was dying and you had end of year exams. I thought…"

"Well don't think anymore, Lowry," he chided. "Life might be simpler that way. Have you been to any anti-natal clinics yet, or seen a doctor?"

Before Lowry could answer, two chubby revellers descended upon the serious couple. Ben courteously stood up.

"Benjamin, we will have to leave soon," the woman explained. "It's my turn to hold the whist drive, so I will have to go and organize the event and re-arrange my drawing room. I've just had it re-decorated with expensive flock wallpaper which will turn Mrs Leopold green with envy. Now remember, my dear, if you need a mother figure to talk to, just call on me."

"Thank you for coming," Ben said. "May I introduce you to Lowry? Lowry, this is Mr and Mrs Butterfield." With pleasantries exchanged the couple were about to leave.

"Is your father a doctor?" Mrs Butterfield asked, as she turned back to face Lowry.

Stuff it! What is it with these people, Lowry thought, when all that matters is what your father's occupation is?

"No, Mrs Butterfield, he's not a doctor. I am a Norwegian and my mother was a heroine of the Resistance and Winston Churchill actually mentioned her in dispatches and my father is the First Admiral of the Royal Norwegian Fleet," she glibly lied.

"Well I never!" the woman said. She appeared genuinely impressed. She put her arm round Ben's shoulder. "Now remember, Benjamin, you just have to call on me if you need to talk." The couple left.

"She can eff off!" Ben rudely said. "Now, let's see if we can slip away after I've seen Dad, and go to the flat, because we have plans to make." Ben grabbed Lowry's hands in his and held them tightly. "We'll get through this together. You do want me to be part of your plans, don't you? Because, I've always wanted to marry an admiral's daughter and I know some pretty disgusting rugby songs about the admiral's daughter. She was a real game girl, especially on the chart room table." He laughed like a naughty school boy. "Actually I've got that wrong. It was the captain's daughter who was a game girl on the chartroom table, which is even more appropriate."

Lowry felt cheered and laughed, suddenly feeling a weight had fallen from her shoulders now that she had shared her burden.

"You can sing them to me later," she said, "but if that was supposed to be a romantic proposal of marriage ....."

"Lowry, I'll show you romantic when we get back to the flat," Ben interjected. "Pregnancy tends to make some women very horny."

"They say all you medical students are over-sexed," Lowry quipped.

"Nurses aren't exactly renowned for their virtue, I'll have you know," he retaliated.

The couple left to drive back to the flat. Lowry had two more hurdles to overcome.

"Ben, will you come with me when I tell Lou and my dad about the baby, please?"

"Of course I will. But I'm not looking forward to facing your dad. Dad's don't like men who have their way with their favourite little girls. He'll probably throw me onto a burning pyre on a long boat and shove me out to sea. But, Lowry whatever we do, we do together. No more keeping me in the dark. Have you got that?"

"Yes, I've got that," she said. "And I'm sorry to put you in this position, but you don't have to marry me just because..."

"Listen, Fatty," he said. "I don't want to hear another..."

"I am not fat," Lowry shouted.

"Not yet, but you wait! I've done obs and gynae, so you can take my word for it. You will get fat," he laughed.

"It probably serves me right for having no morals," she answered. "But then, if I had remained a virgin, I would probably have ended up like Sister on Male Medical and Mother Superior at the convent, or even Matron. God forbid! So you actually did me a favour, Ben."

"I am always willing to oblige," he chuckled.

"What's Doctor–to-be Ben Novak's prescription for a happy marriage?" she asked, as they emerged from the Mersey Tunnel into Liverpool.

"Loads of sex, that's all," he laughed. "I'm not one for over prescribing. What's your prescription for a happy marriage, then?"

"Moderation in all things," she laughed back at him.

GOODBYE BETH

Once again Lowry found herself entering the Exchange Pub, but this time she walked in with confidence and woe betide any drunk who accosted her. It was lunch time and most of the drinkers were city slickers in suits. The barmaid and her cleavage smiled in recognition.

"Yer dad's in the there, love," she said, pointing towards the Men Only door.

"Thank you," Lowry replied.

The room resounded with hearty masculine laughter. She spotted Leif in the corner reading a newspaper. As she approached him, a pin stripe waved his index finger at her and announced that 'ladies are not allowed in here.'

"I am not a lady, never have been and never will be," Lowry sharply retorted.

"I can see that," he gruffly retaliated. "But as I said, women are…."

Leif dressed in his uniform appeared at Lowry's shoulder.

"Hello, George," he said to the pin stripe. "This young lady is my daughter and we are just leaving."

"Oh, I didn't realise, Captain," George gushed. "It's not a problem."

They left the pub and drove to the Pier Head.

"I wouldn't have felt comfortable in that pub with all those cardboard cut outs," Lowry said. "They're all dressed the same, in pin striped suits. They might just as well be wearing school uniform. D'you know Dad, I cannot believe we females are denied access to what you men believe is exclusive to the male. You lot must be very insecure if you feel the need to keep the more intelligent gender out. Anyway, I haven't got long before I've got to be back on duty. So I gather you've got news of Beth."

"Yes, I didn't want to tell you on the 'phone, but it's sad news I'm afraid, elskling. Beth died over a year ago."

"Holy shit!" Lowry said, feeling stunned by the news. "What did she die of?"

"It seems she had nothing to live for and ended her life in the Mersey. It will have been a very quick and painless death for her," he explained.

"Painless! You're saying her death was painless," Lowry shouted. "She must have been in a hell of a lot of pain before she jumped in to have ended her life that way, Dad."

"I know, elskling," he gently said. "But she will not be suffering now. If her life was so bad, that she had to end it, at least she is now at peace. I know it's a dreadful tragedy in one so young, but no-one and nothing can hurt your little friend ever again. Try and find some comfort in that."

Lowry was oblivious to the noise and bustle of the Pier Head. In her mind's eye was a picture of sweet little Beth aged six.

"We used to hold hands through the bars of our big cots, you know, Dad. Beth used to cry herself to sleep because she wanted to go home. She hated the orphanage. She was the only black kid there. I remember one horrible woman, with red hair, used to think it very funny to keep sending Beth back to the bathroom, because she hadn't washed her face properly because it was still black. The other bitches who worked there used to see it happening, but they never stopped it because they were as frightened of the red head as we kids were. D'you know, it was her granddad's fault that she was taken away. The filthy bastard abused her."

"It was a bracelet that enabled the police to identify her," Leif explained. "It was engraved 'To Beth from Granddad.'"

"The hypocritical pig," Lowry heatedly bellowed. "He must have known it was his sexual abuse of her that made the welfare take Beth away so why didn't they punish him and shut him away somewhere, rather than punishing Beth by dumping her in a shit hole of a place? She was the one who was blamed. They said she was a bad girl. The filthy bastard was probably quite happy at home and will no doubt have found some other little girl to play with his dick while his little granddaughter was so unhappy. And she was the innocent victim."

"I know you are angry, sweetheart," her father said. "But beating yourself up about it will not change anything."

"I know Dad. I am angry and I'm also heartbroken to think that Beth would probably still be alive now if some sick pervert had been punished instead of her. Like Tommy, she probably left care when she was fourteen. She maybe had no choice but to go on the streets to survive. The bloody welfare have a lot to answer for when two kids they were supposed to care about commit suicide. Lou said to me that without a family tree we are like leaves that flutter aimlessly in the breeze. Well Tommy and Beth were fluttering leaves that ended up in the gutter."

Lowry's anger suddenly turned to pain. Leif handed her a clean white folded handkerchief and waited quietly until her tears stopped.

"Why Dad? Why are things like this allowed to happen?" she sniffed, "When I think back to those days in the orphanage with Beth she was so vulnerable and being black didn't help. Even at such a young age I was big-headed enough to think I was tough, so I used to look after her so I could show the other kids how tough I was. She needed me and I wanted her to need me. That's not a very good basis for a friendship is it, but I really liked her?"

"We all want to be needed, elskling. She needed you to look after her and you needed her to give you a sense of purpose. It sounds like you and she had a very sweet friendship."

"We did, Dad."

Two rowdy seagulls landed on the concrete in front of the bench where Leif and Lowry sat. One had a piece of bread in its beak, but the other was determined to snatch it away. The

259

hopeful thief screeched loudly whilst viciously pecking at the feathers of the gull whose beak was too full to peck back.

"Look at that bloody bully," Lowry said. "There's always a bully somewhere, isn't there?"

He nodded.

The fight turned nasty. The grating noise of two screeching gulls was deafening. Large wings flapped loudly as small down feathers fluttered to the ground like weightless snowflakes. Finally, the gull with the bread dropped the tasty morsel and flew angrily at the assailant, pecking ferociously at its neck. They were too busy trying to maim each other to notice an opportunist gull fly down like a bird of prey, pick up the bread and jubilantly take off with it.

"Life's not fair is it?" Lowry sadly said.

"No it's not," he replied. "At sea we call seagulls, shite hawks. They have a nasty habit of shitting all over the decks."

The two fighting shite hawks surrendered when realising they had nothing to fight over. They flew off towards the River Mersey.

"Dad, will you ask Marcus if he could do me one more favour? Will you ask him if he could find out where Beth's buried? I remember once picking her a bunch of daisies from the field by the school and sticking them in her curly hair. She was so thrilled and said it was her fairy crown. We had a book at school with pictures of fairies dancing round a red toadstool and they had little flower crowns. She asked the teacher if there were any black fairies and the teacher said no. Beth was very disappointed. Well, I now want to give her a bunch of flowers that will bring on her biggest and most wonderful smile that will show her beautiful white teeth." Lowry studied her watch. "I must dash, Dad. I'll see you on Sunday and I'll have Ben with me."

"I look forward to that," he said. "I'll run you to the hospital, but before we go, elskling, can I ask you if you still have that letter you received from Tommy?"

"I'm not sure, I don't remember throwing it away. Why do you want to know?"

"Well you know what Super Sleuth Marcus is like. He doesn't like loose ends," her father explained. "And by the way, what was the name of that bully, Tommy mentioned?"

Lowry gave her Dad a slow sidelong look.

"You're bullshitting me and I don't like being bull shitted on. You're not telling me the truth about Beth. She didn't commit suicide, did she? You thought that piece of crap would be easier for me to swallow. I should have realised when you spun me that yarn that Beth would be too frightened to jump into the Mersey. You don't have the right to protect me from the truth, Dad. She was my friend and in my memories she always will be. So don't treat me like a child. Tell me why you want Tommy's letter and Raymond Gubbins name? I won't leave this bench until you explain to me what's happening and that means I will be late for duty and it will be your fault."

"You don't make things easy, do you?" he retorted.

"We've already agreed that life ain't easy or fair," she retaliated. "But you'd better tell me quickly or I will be late back."

"I'm sorry elskling. Lou once described you as a mixture of tough and tender. I was forgetting the tough bit, but there are a number of scenarios to explain Beth's death. One of them is the possibility that she did commit suicide, and injuries to her body could have been caused by hitting rocks or the quayside when she was in the water, or they could be the result of a beating she received before she was thrown in. There was something in Tommy's letter about that bully beating her up and Tommy never saw her again. You are right we must know the truth, whatever it is, about what happened to Beth. Your little friend deserves that."

"Thanks Dad. I'll find the letter for you and the bully's name is Raymond Gubbins. I bit him once when we were having a fight. I wish I'd given him rabies." She stood up and pulled her father up by his hand. "Come on Dad, you'll have to put your foot down and don't forget to ask Marcus if he would find Beth's grave for me."

THE TRIPLE F WOMEN

The car drew up outside the polished oak front door. The door opened. John Novak stood waiting. The suited god wore a T shirt and jeans. A cold lunch had already been prepared in the kitchen.

"Climb onto a bar stool, Lowry," he said. "I hope you like smoked salmon and egg salad."

Lowry hitched herself onto the stool.

"Yes I do, thank you."

"It's nice to see you and Ben again," he said. "Help yourselves and relax both of you. I think I know why you have come to see me with such serious faces, so I won't beat about the bush. Are you pregnant, Lowry?" The girl was so shocked she couldn't reply.

"Yes," Ben quickly answered. "Just over three months."

"Christ!" his father exploded. "Couldn't you have tied a knot in it, at least until your finals were over? How the bloody hell are you going to support a family on a student grant? Your mother would….,"

"Don't bring my mother into this," Ben shouted. "I'm sorry to hit you with such a bomb shell, but shouting isn't going to change things. We want your blessing. We want you at our wedding. Rant, if it makes you feel any better, but at least wait until Lowry and I have left. I don't want her going through any more stress than she's already coped with."

John Novak smiled at Lowry.

"I'm sorry, my dear. I had a strong inkling that you may have been pregnant when you fainted for no reason at Penelope's funeral. It sometimes happens in the first trimester, but I have the right to worry about you both. You are very young, Lowry. Ben has a lot on his plate, so please allow me to be angry, because I care about what happens to you and Ben. Now eat up both of you and let's talk about how I can help. Does your mother know?" he asked, directing his gaze at Lowry.

She nodded.

"Yes, we told my mum and dad a few days ago and I think they both initially felt like you do. Worried about how we would manage and disappointed that I had to give up my nursing career. But Lou's come round. My father is very supportive. He feels guilty about putting me in an orphanage and not being able to provide me with a home, although there's no need for him to feel that way, so he wants to buy us a small house."

The scratching sound of the pepper grinder scattered black grains over John Novak's smoked salmon. He appeared deep in thought as he twisted the mill round and round. He suddenly stopped.

"Good grief, what am I doing?" he said, as he surveyed the large amount of black dust smothering his lunch. "I was miles away."

"What were you thinking, Dad?" Ben asked.

"I was just thinking about Penelope and her untimely death and then the untimely arrival of this baby and wondering if it's all part of the great scheme of things. Her life is over, but her grandchild's life will soon begin. We can't put the clock back, so let us look forward."

The three serious people sat in silence concentrating on the meal in front of them.

"By the way, Ben," John eventually said. "Mrs Butterfield sent her love and asked if you were still courting the daughter of the First Admiral of the Royal Norwegian Fleet?"

Ben and Lowry laughed aloud.

"What was your answer, Dad?"

"Well, I wasn't sure what she was talking about at first, but I realised you must have spun the silly woman some yarn, so I said yes. I told her that I understood the First Admiral of the Royal Norwegian fleet was off somewhere, cruising his yacht with another sailor called Philip Mountbatten. She couldn't contain herself. Her adipose tissue wobbled obscenely as she quickly waddled off to tell all her triple F friends."

"What's triple F?" Lowry curiously asked, when the laughter had died down.

Ben answered with a grin.

"Triple F describes women who appear at the hospital with gall bladder problems," he explained. "They're usually fair, fat and forty."

"Like Phyllis Postlethwaite," Lowry said. "She was fair, fat, in her forties and had her gall bladder out. She had the hots for Ben."

"I remember her," Ben said. "When I first examined her, she asked me if I was a proper doctor. When I said no, not yet, she said, 'good, I like the improper ones."

"That's Phyllis," Lowry said.

The tantalising smell of coffee filled every corner of the kitchen.

"Ben," John said. "Do you remember when we had coffee at the hospital last week you asked if I would be able to share with you the story of my Polish family?"

"Yes, I remember," he replied.

"Well in the loft, I have a chest with a box in it that contains two letters I received from my mother and a photograph of her and my father on their wedding day. Next time you come I will show you both the letters and the photo. You need to know what happened, dreadful though it is."

"It will be my privilege to share them with you, Dad. Thank you," Ben gently said.

THE ALLEY CATS

The captain and Marcus poured over the contents of Tommy's letter.

"Have you noticed, Leif, that Tommy talks of Beth in the past tense. She was a whore. She had a patch. It's as if he knew more than he was letting on. He witnessed the beating and Gubbins putting the boot in. Unfortunately he can't now tell us what he saw, but it seems after that beating he never saw her again. Why?"

"Because she was dead. Is that what you're thinking?" Leif asked.

"Possibly. She was in the water for three months the pathologist report said. If I work back from the date she was pulled out I'll have a better idea of the date she went in and I might find it corresponds roughly with her birthday. All this happened some time ago, of course. I'll see if my old mate will let me have another look at the police file." He looked up and smiled his beautifully ugly smile. "Get me another gin my old friend. My brain needs a stimulant."

Leif returned with the gin and tonic.

"Marcus, Tommy mentioned nigger bashing, almost as if it were a sport. Beth was black," he said.

"Yes, poor kid. She stood no chance against those feral alley cats. It has crossed my mind that after she took that beating she may have had enough of the brutality of her life and decided to end it. On the other hand, she may have been…,"

"Killed by Gubbins. Is that what you're thinking?" Leif interjected.

"Ah ha," Marcus replied.

"If you find this Gubbins, how the hell are you going to get him to admit he even beat Beth up, let alone killed her, if he did?"

"I have my own way of dealing with scumbags. That's not your problem, Captain. Leave it with me."

"I can't leave it with you," Leif heatedly said. "I won't have you breaking the law, Marcus. Let's relay this information to the police, perhaps they'll re-open the case."

Marcus gave the captain a cynical smile.

"We're talking about the death of a black prostitute from over a year back. Don't be naïve, friend. I want to deal with this in my own way. This is what I call proper detective work. I'm sick of following straying husbands to seedy hotels and fingering people who've got their fingers in the till. You're back on duty tomorrow, so while you're away for the week in Port Lynas, I'll do some sniffing around and I might have some news for you when you get back."

"I'm beginning to regret asking for your help," Leif ruefully said. "I'm getting the impression your methods may not be exactly lawful."

"Sometimes, me old Viking, EM and EM's law gets results and if that means I have to beat the shit out of that Gubbins creature, then so be it."

The captain sighed heavily.

"For God's sake be careful. There is only one of you, there's a gang of them, all feral alley-cats, according to you."

"I'll get him on his own, don't you worry and when I do I'll give him a taste of what he gave Beth. That's the least I can do for Lowry's little friend, Black Beauty."

The friends left the public house and each went their own way. Marcus felt much like a bloodhound with the scent of alley cats in his strawberry nose. He first called into Hatton Garden Police Station and persuaded his old beat partner, Dave, to dig out the file on Beth Hutchinson.

"What is it about this dead hooker, Gerry?" Dave asked.

"The name's Marcus, Dave, as you well know. Marcus Marriot. Gerry is a thing you shove under the bed and piss in."

"It's a daft poncy name, if you ask me," Dave said.

"Who's asking you?" Marcus retaliated. "And as for this dead hooker, it's got something to do with another case I'm working on and it's confidential. So if you don't mind I want to take some notes in private while you go and make me a cup of tea."

"You're still the arrogant bastard you always were," Dave commented, as he sauntered off to get the tea.

Half an hour later Marcus left and returned to his office. He sat in his chair and opened the bottom drawer and took out a small tumbler and a bottle of Gordon's gin. He poured himself a large one. He imbibed his medicine with pleasure and opened his notebook. He tended to read aloud, believing that the sound of his own voice helped him think more clearly.

"So Beth went into the water towards the end of July, since her body was pulled out late October," he muttered. "She was alive on her nineteenth birthday which was the twenty sixth of July. I guess she died on that day. Now then, how could I have missed this the first time round?" he chided himself. "The pathologists report stated that Beth had pierced ears. But both her ear lobes were split in two," He turned to Tommy's letter. He read, 'it wer er bifday and er uvver niger hooers givd er sum eerings but Ray gorrum off off er.' Marcus poured himself another large gin. "No you didn't, you fucking piece of shit. You tore them out of her ears and split her ear lobes. Then you did her over." He took another slurp of gin and smiled. "But I'm coming for you 'ard man, 'cos I'm determined to discover what happened to little Black Beauty."

Marcus unlocked the bottom drawer of his metal filing cabinet. He took out a well worn duffle coat, a woollen hat and a pair of fingerless gloves. He opened the office window and smeared his hands over the Liverpool soot coated glass. Spitting in his palms he rubbed the dirt into his face and pulled the woollen hat over his forehead to his eyebrows. He inspected the results in the mirror. He had to admit it didn't take much effort to turn him into a model of a down and out drunk. From the desk drawer he took the obsolete bottle of whisky he had always kept for Leif and poured some of it down the front of the duffle coat. He put on the coat and the whisky fumes caught the back of his throat making him gasp. His hand went into the right hand pocket and he felt the cold hard steel of the knuckle duster. His rounds in the boxing ring during his army days made him a formidable opponent especially when wearing a steel glove. In his left hand pocket he felt the two pairs of handcuffs. From the desk drawer he produced a ball of thick cord. Marcus cut a number of lengths and on each one he looped a slip knot. He then slid his fingers into the rings of the knuckle duster and put on the fingerless gloves. He was ready.

Searching for a gang of feral alley cats in the vast expanse of red brick warehouses, would, Marcus concluded, be a complete waste of time. The bomb damage caused in 1941 was still evident, but the shortage of money in the coffers of the Mersey Docks and Harbour Board meant the magnificent buildings, that had once been part of Liverpool's fortunes, were becoming derelict. A sad sight, Marcus thought as he perched on a large capstan with his back to the Mersey. His wonderful City was losing its greatness. He looked at his watch. Ten twenty five.

Tom cats slink around at night in search of prey. Tonight he would be the quarry.

Marcus had never been a choir boy. He had hated singing at school especially when his voice was breaking. One moment he would be falsetto, next, almost baritone, but tonight he sang with gusto the song he had hated most. The words were hardly fitting for hormonal teenage boys.

"Where the bee sucks there suck I, in a cowslips bell I lie. There I couch when owls do fly."

Marcus' voice bounced off the buildings, echoing through broken windows. His eyes continually swept the scene in front of him. Nothing could approach him from behind with his back to the Mersey. It was then he saw a shadow.

"When owls do fly when owls do fly. On a bats back I do fly yi yi yi yi."

"Yous'll be on yer friggin back if yer don't belt up," a voice shouted. A gangly youth aged about twenty approached. "Yer stinkin' fuckin' drunk. I've gorra good mind to knock yer inter the water."

Marcus scanned the scene. This black haired youth appeared to be alone. The one he wanted had red hair.

"D'you want to try it, you scumbag?" Marcus viciously said.

He leapt up just as the youth produced a long bladed stiletto. With a fast, hard, right hook the knuckle duster made contact with the youth's jaw. The youth went down and the stiletto fell from his hand. Marcus kicked it into the Mersey. He placed his foot on the victim's chest.

"With or without a broken jaw, you're going to answer some questions and if you give me any crap my foot will move up to your throat and I'll break your bloody neck. Do I make myself understood?"

Blood covered the youth's mouth. He moaned and nodded.

"Are you part of Ray Gubbin's gang?"

The youth nodded.

"I said answer my questions. Are you part of Gubbin's gang?"

The youth winced as he moved his jaw to speak.

"Ye," he slowly said.

"Where is Gubbin's now?" The youth shook his head. Marcus moved his foot to the youth's throat. "I said where is Gubbin's now?" he pressed gently on the Adam's apple.

The terrified hoodlum groaned. "Thedral," he said, with difficulty.

"Where?" Marcus barked.

"The 'thedral."

"Are you talking about the Anglican Cathedral that's being built?"

"Ye."

"What's he doing there? The scumbag's not gone to say his prayers, so what's he doing at the Cathedral."

"Robbin' off off the builders. Me mouf 'urts. Lerrus go, yer friggin' old bastard."

"You call me old again and I'll crush your balls with my other foot," Marcus snapped.

"Lerrus go. Lerrus go," the youth pleaded.

Marcus removed his foot from the throat and from his pocket produced a pair of handcuffs and a length of tough cord. In one swift action the youth's wrists were manacled. The lad kicked out angrily, realising his ankles were to be tied. Marcus pinned the legs down with his hands and then knelt on them. The youth screamed. Tightly tying the ankles together, Marcus stood up and the screaming stopped. It was followed by a disjointed torrent of foul language and a detailed and sordid account of how Marcus was to die when the gang got their hands on him. He grinned and walked away.

His next destination - the Cathedral. He could see the outline of the impressive building in the background standing on St James Mount.

Marcus ignored the looks of disdain he received from passers-by. The smell of whisky reached them before he did. The fifteen minute walk brought him to the Cathedral. He was not a religious man, and even though the building was still incomplete he had to admit there was a certain holiness in the majesty of the structure. Decades of building work had gone into the creation and decades more possibly before its completion, making it the largest Cathedral in Great Britain. Heavy machinery and construction materials littered the incomplete section. Thick chain link fencing surrounded what resembled a bomb site. Marcus slowly walked the periphery of the fence, searching for a gap big enough for a large alley cat to squeeze through. He found it in a section of fencing closest to a completed wall. He squeezed his bulk through the gap, hoping and praying his quarry was somewhere on this vast location. "Cover your back," he murmured to himself. He sat on a neatly arranged pile of bricks and leaned against the wall of the completed section of the Cathedral. If Gubbins was there, now was the time to draw him out.

"Where the bee sucks...." Perhaps I should be singing a hymn, he thought, but he couldn't remember any. "There suck I."

Half an hour later he was sick of the sound of his own voice. Gubbins must have gone with his rich pickings of copper and lead, he decided. Marcus pulled his cigarettes from his pocket along with the lighter bearing the Nazi emblem. He flicked the lighter open and span the small wheel. Immediately a petrol smelling flame leapt into the air and ignited the cigarette. It was then that he felt a sharp point digging into the side of his neck just under the chin. It pierced the skin and a small trickle of blood ran onto his collar.

"'And over them fags and that lighter," a menacing voice demanded, "or I'll slit yer fuckin' throat."

Marcus inwardly fumed at himself. This alley cat was one smooth operator. He had crept up on him with the stealth of a panther.

"You can have the lighter, son. I've got plenty more where that came from," he said. "Take a look at the swastika on the front. I've got loads of stuff in my place to honour the Nazis. I reckon Hitler had the right idea about the Jews and the niggers. We ain't got no place for them here, especially the niggers. Look mate will you take that bloody thing off my neck," he pleaded.

Much to his relief the hand lowered the knife. He looked up into the face of a red haired young man.

"Here you are mate, catch it," Marcus said as he threw the lighter. The red head caught it and rubbed his fingers over the Nazi emblem. "Get yourself that wheelbarrow, turn it upside down and sit and have a fag with me," Marcus suggested. "I'm only here to sober up a bit before I go home to the battleaxe of a wife. She...."

"Belt up! Yer prattlin' on like a fuckin' woman," the red head shouted. "'Ow did yer get in 'ere?"

"I was staggering a bit and fell into the fencing over there," Marcus explained pointing to his right, "and it just

271

gave way. I hurt my bloody arm, I did. Anyway here's the fags. Why don't you get that barrow to sit on and have a smoke with me and I'll tell you what I do to niggers when I find them? Call your friends over, I've got plenty of fags."

"I'm on me own. Any'ow me and me gang knows what to do with niggers. Yer can't learn us nothin' about nigger bashin'," the red head boasted as he fetched the wheelbarrow. He decided not to turn it upside down. Instead he slithered his backside down the slope and sat with his long legs dangling over the front. "I've bashed more niggers than you've 'ad 'ot dinners," he continued to boast.

"Aah, but have you killed any? That's the only way Hitler dealt with the problem. By the way my name's Joseph King, but they call me Jo. What's your name?"

"What d' yer wanna know for?"

"No reason. It doesn't matter what your name is. You seem a nice lad."

"Me name's Ray. Ray Gubbins."

"Ray's a good manly name. If my memory serves me right, Raymond means, Leader of Warriors," Marcus lied. This cretin was too daft to know otherwise, he thought. " I bet nobody messes with you," he continued to flannel.

It was working. Ray smirked superciliously.

"No fucker messes with Raymond Gubbins, the Leader of Warriors, or they get this," he said pointing to his knife. "I slice 'em good."

"Even the niggers, Ray?"

"Specially the niggers. Mostly we just give 'em a good beltin' and a good kicking and nick their watches and money, but if they fight too 'ard we slice 'em."

"God, I wish I was young enough to join your gang. But give us another fag, Ray. Talking to you restores my faith in keeping Britain white."

Gubbins put the stiletto on the ground at the side of the barrow and lit a cigarette and then threw it at Marcus who didn't particularly want to put it in his mouth. This rat could be carrying the plague.

"Yer crazy man. We don't 'ave old fuckers in me gang."

Marcus was incensed. This was the second time tonight he had been called old. As far as he was concerned he was still youthful at the age of forty six.

"I was beating up niggers when you were in nappies son. I even beat up a nigger woman once. She was a whore and tried to steal my wallet, so I really let her have it."

"Did she snuff it, Jo?" Gubbins excitedly asked.

"Nah unfortunately."

"Well, the one I beat up on, she snuffed it. She were a whore. The way I look at it, is, that's one less nigger woman to 'ave lots of little nigger babies."

Ray roared with laughter. Marcus noticed he had yellow teeth. He felt revulsion for the creature in front of him, but he had to play the game.

"Wow, that took some guts, Ray. I bet her name was Topsy or something. They've all got names like that."

"No 'er name were 'utchinson. I knowed 'er when she were a kid. I never liked 'er, but she gived a good blow job 'specially when I knocked her front teeth out a few years back."

"You said she snuffed it, so did you slice her, Ray," Marcus said, rubbing his fingerless gloved hands excitedly.

"Why waste me blade on 'er? She were showin' off 'cos it were 'er birthday and she gorra lorra cards from 'er uvver nigger whores. I never gets any birthday cards. She 'ad these ear rings she said was gold. I didn't see why a nigger should 'ave 'em, and she got mouthy with me and no nigger gets mouthy with me, so I pulled them out of 'er ears and knocked the shit out of 'er."

"I don't blame you. There's nothing worse than a mouthy woman, let alone a mouthy nigger one. I'd have done the same thing, Ray. Did you kill her?"

"I suppose I did, if yer call chuckin' 'er in the Mersey killin' 'er." Ray laughed. It sounded like the cackle of a hyena. "Yer should have seed 'er, Man. She were splashin' about and yellin' 'cos she couldn't swim. Best laugh I'd 'ad fer years."

Marcus had heard enough.

"We'll have to meet up here again, Ray. I've enjoyed talking to you. You're saying all the things I want to hear."

"Ye, but bring some more of them Nazi lighters and some fags, will yer? Any'ows give us yer 'and and pull us out'a this barra'. Me arse 'as gone numb."

Marcus rose from the pile of bricks. He quickly put his hand in his left pocket and palmed the handcuffs.

"Okay, Ray, give me both your hands. If I pull you up by one hand the barrow will tip sideways."

Two hands reached towards Marcus. With the skill and speed of a practiced police officer he had the cuffs firmly clamped around Gubbins' wrists. Before the manacled youth could speak the wheelbarrow was kicked onto its side. He lay awkwardly with the barrow on top of him. Marcus looped the cord with its slipknot over the Dunlop pumps and tightened it around the ankles. His prey was going nowhere, but Gubbins' mouth was running away with him.

"Swear at me once more and I'll kick your nuts right up your numb arse," Marcus casually said.

"What yer playin'at, yer sick perv. Who the fuck are yer?"

"I told you. My name is Jo King you gullible idiot and I know all about you, Gubbins. You grew up in a home with Tom Ollerenshawe and Beth Huchinson and both those poor kids are dead. But you Mr 'ard man Gubbins is still alive." Marcus left a pregnant pause. "For the moment," he finally said.

"Yer can't do nothin' to me. Me gang'll slice yer inter strips and feed yer to the rats, yer fuckin' cu…"

Marcus' foot stamped down on Gubbins' groin. A howl of pain ricocheted into the night sounding like a Tom cat howling for a queen. The youth lay whimpering at Marcus' feet.

"Open your mouth once more and you'll get a taste of my foot in your crotch again."

Marcus paused, then pulled the upturned wheelbarrow towards himself and sat on the metal base.

"So 'ard man Gubbins is snivelling like a baby. Not so 'ard now are we, you piece of shit? Did it make you feel like a big man to beat up a little black girl who was only five foot one and chuck her body into the Mersey? She was a sweet kid. She may have been a whore, but she was earning her money, which is more than scum like you do."

"I were makin' it up to sound big," Gubbins pleaded. "I never touched 'er. I were just goin' along with yer when yer was sayin' about bashin' niggers."

A foot stamped on the youth's crotch. He yelled.

"That was for lying to me. And this one is for calling black people niggers," Marcus said as he stamped again.

"Oh God, man I feels sick," Gubbins wept. "Lerrus go, please."

"That's what one of your other sewer rats said, when I tied him up and left him with a busted jaw." Gubbins sobbed pitifully. "Did Beth cry for mercy when you were putting the boot in? Did she beg you to stop hurting her when you were beating her up? She was still alive when you threw her into the Mersey you revolting slime ball."

"Yer making…."

"If you open your mouth once more to lie to me, then I won't be stamping on your balls, I'll be grinding them into the ground," Marcus viciously said. "The pathologists report said she was alive when she went in the water, and Tom Ollerenshawe's letter said he saw you pull her ear rings off her then give her a good belting. He never saw her again."

"Yer lyin' 'cos Tom couldn't write proper."

Marcus pulled Tommy's letter from his inside jacket pocket.

"It's written on prison notepaper, so pin your ears back and I'll read it to you. 'It was Hutchinson's birthday and her other nigger whores gave her some ear rings. Ray got them off her and I saw him belt her hard and put the boot in. It was bad. She was screaming. We haven't seen her since."

"'e always were a pissin' lyin' rat. It were 'im that finished 'er off. Yer've gorra believe me."

"I haven't gorra believe anything that comes out of your foul mouth and I'm sick of the sight of your horrid little face. So, Gubbins, it's your turn to come to a sticky end. See that hole over there?" Marcus pointed to a deep trench with a mechanical digger standing close by. "I can't think of a better place for you than the foundations of a Cathedral. And see that cement mixer? Well 'ard man, they'll be filling the trench tomorrow and you'll be lying at the bottom and it's one hell of a deep trench. Now get onto your knees and lever yourself up."

"Oh Jesus fuckin' Christ, Mister. Please…"

"Shut up, you snivelling little rat. Save your voice. You're going to need it in the morning when you yell to the builders to get you out. You'll have to hope they hear you before they turn the noisy machinery on, and I'm not joking either?"

Fifteen minutes later Marcus left the building site and walked the short distance to his office. He immediately poured himself a large gin. He had one more job to do – find where Beth was buried. Gee, Lowry had caused him nothing but hassle from the moment he had first heard about her. But she's like a daughter to me, he sentimentally reflected. He topped up his tumbler and stared vacantly into the glass.

"I would have made a good dad if I'd had a little girl," he mumbled into his gin.

"Nobody would ever hurt my little girl with me to protect her." He lifted the tumbler to his lips. "You daft, inebriated, sentimental sod, Marcus Marriot. You ain't even married."

Three weeks later and lying on a mound of earth covered with weeds lay a large bunch of flowers. The card read, 'May your beautiful smile light up the heavens, sweet Beth. With special love from Lowry and two friends you didn't know you had, who made possible the justice you deserved. XXX

THE ARRIVAL

Ben and Lowry married quietly in a Register Office.

As Lowry got bigger her back constantly ached. Her abdomen stretched itself into a taut drum skin and her belly button popped out like the swollen head of a champagne cork. One of the baby's feet, or maybe it was a fist, seemed to have jammed itself under her right rib cage causing a permanent and painful stitch. Blue veins zig zagged across her hard painful breasts like tram lines laid down by a blind drunk. Her trips to the anti-natal clinic left her feeling like a fertile cow standing in line with other fertile bovines clutching a bottle of urine for testing rather than a bottle of milk. Ben brought her sample bottles from the hospital, but some women brought their samples in dandelion and burdock bottles, full to the top, all of which went down the plug hole, since only a drop was required. Lowry hated her pregnancy. She would have been quite happy to have sat on an egg and shared the experience with Ben. That was the least he could do.

The fat faced clock in the delivery room gave off a loud tick as each second passed by. She had arrived three hours earlier with Lou and her father, but they had been offhandedly banished from the Maternity Unit. It would have been good to have had someone to talk to and take her mind off the grumbling pains that were a caveat of what was to come. The groans and screams coming from the corridor said it all. Apart from an occasional nurse who popped her head into the room, smiled and popped out again, the fat clock was the only face she saw. With no one to talk to she chatted to the clock. Each time it said tick she said tock. But her silly game was simply a means of allaying her fear of childbirth. She knew nothing of what to expect, apart from intense pain and superhuman efforts to push out a bump a thousand times bigger than its exit point. Eventually the mechanical digger began working overtime as it gouge out Lowry's insides. The midwife bounced into the room.

"Yes, my dear," she cheerfully said. "Things are moving on nicely."

"I don't call any of this nice," Lowry moaned.

She was in no mood for hearty cheerfulness. The midwife proceeded to roll thick white woollen stockings up Lowry's legs.

"What the hell are they for?" Lowry belligerently asked.

"All our new mummies wear these when delivering," she exuberantly explained.

"Why, are we likely to get frost bite?" the miserable new mummy retorted.

Husbands were not allowed in the delivery room, but fortunately for Lowry Ben arrived and as a final year medical student talked his way to her trolley. She immediately felt less afraid and knew with Ben beside her she could do it.

Finally baby Anya Louise Novak arrived in a blaze of pain and a blue haze of strong language. Distant voices shouted, 'push Lowry, push.'

"I am bloody pushing," she argued, in exhaustion.

She held Ben's hand in a tortuous vice, unaware that he was wincing in pain. She didn't know until it was all over, that he too, was helping himself to the nitrous oxide whenever she took the gas and air mask off her face.

Much to Lowry's surprise, Anya was tiny. She only weighed six pounds two ounces. She hadn't been giving birth to a hippopotamus after all. The tiny girl with black hair was perfection. Ben cried with joy as her held her in his arms. He had hoped for a daughter, but Lowry was happy to have anything so long as it were a boy or a girl.

Thirty four new mums filled the Maternity Ward and twenty nine babies slept or howled in the cots swinging from the end of the beds. The unmarried mothers were segregated at the end of the ward. Some uncharitable person, had came up with that idea in the belief that the 'fallen women' might upset the virtuous Matrons, Lowry surmised. Five babies had been taken away from the unmarried mums for adoption. The grief stricken mothers just lay on their beds all day, crying or staring at the wall. One day those babies will ask 'where's my real mum,' Lowry believed.

Every morning the trolley clattered round the ward delivering small round metal bowls to the patients.

"Do you want to express yourself?" the nurse asked as she placed the bowls on the locker tops.

Lowry would love to have verbally expressed herself, but that was not what they meant.

"No thank you," she politely said.

Large engorged breasts were flopped out of nightdress tops and painfully squeezed. A syncopated pinging of milk jettisoned, at speed, out of dark red nipples, hitting the sides of the metal bowls and sounding like the tympani section of the Liverpool Philharmonic Orchestra.

No way could Lowry remain in the ward for ten days. She didn't feel ill. Yet she wasn't allowed out of bed. She was fine. The baby thrived, so why ten bloody days in the cattle shed?

The morning eleven o'clock ritual was the final straw.

The Maternity Sister entered the ward and clapped her hands loudly.

"Tummies mummies," she shouted.

Every mummy obediently removed the pillow from her bed and rolled face down onto her stomach. It was supposed to strengthen the abdominal muscles. Instead the pressure on the hard breasts caused them to leak and the warmth of the body soured the milk. The ward smelled like a gorgonzola cheese factory and Lowry worried that she smelled like Horace Hardcastle.

With stubborn determination, Lowry signed herself and Anya out of the hospital after seven days.

The newly-weds loved the nest they had made for themselves and Anya. Each item of second-hand furniture had been manufactured in every decade since the early nineteen hundreds, making the place seem like a pint sized museum dedicated to the cabinet making skills of the past. Nothing matched, the dining table was drop leaf oak, the pine dresser exhibited a kaleidoscope of coloured plates bought from Garston Market for twopence each.

Busty Bonaparte was consigned to the bathroom. Lowry wasn't happy having a human skeleton in the house. Ben assured her the bones were artificially made, but she didn't believe him. The sinuses in the nasal antrums were too perfect to have been man-made and the pubis symphysis of the pelvic girdle was definitely female. A compromise was reached. Busty stood erect with a bath towel over her head. It was the best way of drying it when wet. Her condom ear-rings no longer dangled either side of her skull. They had been commandeered for better use. The previous owners of the house had taken the towel rail with them and when money was short a towel rail was a luxury.

The new mum sometimes felt trapped by a little tyrant who bellowed her orders for instant attention and food. Breast feeding proved difficult. For two weeks Lowry had struggled to ensure her baby had enough nourishment. But eventually she had to supplement her own supply of milk with a bottle, until finally closing down her own dairy. She knew she wasn't an earth mother, yet felt slightly guilty every time she prepared a bottle feed. The Health Visitor seemed to enjoy reinforcing the feelings of guilt, but as an ageing spinster, Lowry doubted if the Health Visitor had ever had her nipples sucked by anybody.

The party line telephone, shared with her longwinded neighbour Mrs Barnabus, kept Lowry in touch with the outside world and her father at the Pilot Station.

The baby was asleep. A hot coffee filled the mug. It was time to chat to her dad. Lowry picked up the 'phone. The longwinded neighbour was talking to her sister again. She gently replaced the receiver.

Twenty minutes later she returned to the 'phone and confidently picked up the receiver. The jabbering women were still at it. 'Piss off, the pair of you,' she muttered to herself. Lowry was about to replace the receiver when she caught a snatch of the riveting conversation.

"Well, can you believe it? It were the size of a football," Mrs Barnabus said, in a voice that appeared to revel in the juicy gossip she was imparting.

"No way," replied her sister.

"God's honest truth, Vera. It were the size of a football. But she always did have a big belly on her."

Lowry felt uncomfortable eavesdropping on the conversation, but what the hell was this thing the size of a football?

"Makes you wonder, doesn't it. The size of a football you say," said Vera.

"Yes, that's right, the size of a football, so they took all her women's bits out and left a scar right down her belly. She's got to take it easy for six months, but she won't find that hard, she always was a lazy cow."

Lowry cringed as Anya let out a piercing wail. She quickly covered the mouthpiece with her hand.

"I'll have to go, Vera," Mrs Barnabus urgently said. "I've just heard the cat yowling at the back door. I didn't even know it was out."

At last the 'phone was free, thanks to Anya. Lowry chuckled to herself as she thought of the big bellied lazy cow with a scar right down her belly. The poor soul had obviously had a very large fibroid removed resulting in a hysterectomy.

She dialled the Pilot Station.

"Hello! Can I speak to Captain Svenerson?" she asked the voice on the other end.

"Hello again, Sarah, this is Idris," the voice replied. "He's out at the moment. Shall I get him to call you back?"

"This isn't Sarah. It's Lowry, his daughter."

"Oh, hello there, Lowry. I'm sorry. For a moment I thought you were Sarah," he apologetically said. "I'll get him to call you."

"Thanks Idris."

She stared hard at the hand piece before returning it to the rest. The name Sarah niggled at the back of her mind. Who was this woman who had her dad's 'phone number? She could be his girlfriend. Her dad wasn't into girlfriends. Was he? She didn't want to share her father with another woman. This Sarah could be a dolly bird, not much older than herself or she could be an ageing gold digger. Her dad was a wealthy man now that his father's fishing fleet had been sold after it was returned to his ownership after the war. This woman obviously rang the Pilot Station often, because Idris had said, 'Hello again, Sarah.' Why hadn't her dad mentioned her? Why had he kept her a secret? She had to accept that she was jealous. Jealous of a woman she had never met, who seemed to have captured her dad's attention. Lowry stomped into the kitchen.

"I'll see how long he keeps her a secret and like hell am I going to share my father with another woman," she loudly said "I've only just found him and I'm his girl and no interloper is going to come between us. This Sarah woman can piss off. So there!"

ANJA NOVAK 1903 –1942

Lowry heard the phone being picked up.

"Hi John, it's me," she said. "I bet you must be as proud as I am that Ben passed his finals."

"Hello me," he responded. "I am. He worked hard and he was a brilliant student. Don't tell him, but I really am so proud, that I've bought him a new family car. That other clapped out thing is not roadworthy enough for my son and two favourite girls."

"Wow, he'll be over the moon. He did talk about getting another second hand car now that he's earning seven pounds a week. He reckons it would be kinder to put the old one down rather than pay for repairs, 'cos all its problems are terminal. But John, do you remember saying you would tell us about your family in Poland? Well can we come to see you next Sunday? Ben has a day off at last."

"Yes, of course. Would you like to make it Sunday lunch?"

"Sounds good to me!"

"See you on Sunday, Lowry, and don't say anything about the car."

"I won't. Thanks again, John. See you soon."

Lowry replaced the receiver. Who'd have believed that one day she would be calling the suited God by his first name?

The young couple arrived and parked by the steps that led to the polished oak front door. A shiny red car had been parked by the garage.

"Dad's got a visitor," Ben said. "Smart car, looks new."

"Yes it's a really nice car," Lowry replied. "What sort is it?"

"It's a Ford Cortina Mark One. They've only just started making that model. God, I'd give my eye teeth for one of them," he enviously sighed.

Lowry grinned smugly.

"I can just image myself being chauffeured around in that and waving to the little people."

"Keep imagining, sweetie. It'll be years before we have one of them," he retorted.

John opened the door and walked down the steps to meet his guests.

"Hello, you two and how is my Princess Anya," he said, peering through the window at the baby strapped into her red car seat. She blew him a raspberry which implied she was well.

"Who's the visitor, Dad?" Ben asked.

"As far as I know it's only you three," he replied.

"Well who's is that Cortina?"

The young couple edged out of the battered heap and walked with John to the shiny red machine. Ben's father placed his arm round his son's shoulder.

"It's yours Ben," he gently said. "I'm very proud of you, Son. You have had to cope with the death of your brother, your mother and throw yourself into fatherhood and also cope with very demanding studies. You, Lowry and Anya are all the family I have left in the world and therefore very special to me."

Ben was speechless.

"Say something," Lowry persisted.

"I don't know what to say," he murmured. "Thanks Dad seems such a paltry thing to say in the face of such generosity."

"Say no more," John said. "But please remember to look after this one. Now I must go and look at my roast potatoes."

"I tell you what you could do for your dad, Ben," Lowry chipped in. "You can give him your eye teeth, 'cos that's what you said you'd give to have one of these."

The Sunday roast was good, apart from the lumpy gravy, for which John profusely apologised. He hadn't had much success with the custard, either.

At the end of the table sat a strong, cardboard, Palethorpe's sausage box, the lid firmly on in order to protect the history within.

At last the formality of eating was over. John held Anya on his knee before opening the box.

"Before we see what's in here, let me tell you something of my mother, Anja's, background," he said. "She was the third and last child of a non-practicing Jewish parents. They owned a tailor's shop in Warsaw where my mother became a seamstress when she was thirteen years old. They weren't wealthy, but they were not poor either, because most of their clientele came from the affluent side of Warsaw. Unfortunately I have no photographs of them. All of the family albums were lost during the upheavals. My mother married my father when she was seventeen years old. He was a Roman Catholic Polish Army Officer and ten years her senior. His name was Stefan Marek Novak. I was studying medicine at Warsaw University before Germany invaded Poland. My father had anticipated the war and the struggle that would exist between the Soviets and the Fascists for the acquisition of Poland. He arranged for my elder brother and me to come to England where we lived with my mother's eldest brother who was a diamond merchant in Hatton Garden in London. He never married. He died just after the war. My father was killed in battle in September 1939 when the Germans first invaded Poland. My grandparents were hounded out of their shop. Even their clientele turned against them because they were Jews. My mother chose to stay with her parents although she, too, could have escaped like we did." John took a photograph from the sausage box. "This is my mother and father on their wedding day," he said, handing the photograph to Ben. Lowry peered over his shoulder.

"I've never seen this before, Dad," Ben said.

"No, I've kept the horror of it all hidden away in a cardboard box and therefore out of my mind," John sadly answered.

"Perhaps I'm intruding," Lowry quietly said.

"No, not at all, my dear," he emphatically replied. "I think sharing it with you and Ben will be cathartic for me. And you are quite right, Lowry. This is Ben's and Anya's history and needs to be told. My mother would not want her memory to be shut away in a sausage box, now would she?" he said, grinning. "But last night I read her letters for the first time since I received them and I wept. It did me good."

"Look at the way they're standing?" Ben said, studying the picture and gently squeezing his father's hand. "They are at least eighteen inches apart, as if a man and a woman standing too close was perhaps unseemly in those days."

"They look very sweet and your mother looks so young, John. How come they were able to marry when one was a Jew and the other a Catholic?" Lowry asked.

"I understand it wasn't a religious ceremony," he explained.

The woman in the sepia picture smiled demurely at the camera like a shy child. Her black hair had been piled onto the top of her head with a crown of white flowers encircling the top-knot. Her long white shift dress allowed her slim ankles to be seen, but her arms were covered to her wrists. Lowry stared at the innocent face of the happy young woman, whose dreadful fate had already been pre-determined. The uniformed groom stood rigidly with his feet militarily apart and his hands behind his back.

"When my brother and I were younger, we used to play in the tailor shop until mother came to fetch us," John explained. "She had decided to train to be a school teacher. She loved to dance and sing and make all her own clothes, including ours. She was quite a strict woman. We boys received many a whack from her when we misbehaved. But she was very loving and full of life. I owe a lot to her. She more or less brought us up on her own because my father was away so much. Mother pushed and pushed my brother and me to study and work hard at school. I wouldn't be where I am today, if it hadn't been for her."

He fell silent, deep in thought. Even Anya stopped banging on the table as if she too felt the poignancy of the moment.

"Her letters are heartbreaking," he eventually said.

"Do you know what actually happened to my grandmother, Dad?" Ben asked. "Mum told me that she just disappeared."

John sadly nodded.

"I can only guess, Son. I have just two letters, that is all, that I received from my mother," he said, delving into the box. "I shall read them to you, because they are written in Polish. The first was written in early 1941, not long after the Germans set up the Warsaw Ghetto, and the second was written in August 1942. My brother had been shot down over the North Sea in 1940 during the Battle of Britain. He flew a spitfire from Duxford, as a pilot in a Polish Fighter Squadron, which was attached to the Royal Air Force. Rightly or wrongly, I never informed my mother of Marek's death. But Ben, let me read your grandmother's words."

John held the precious document in a hand with an almost imperceptible tremble.

"To my beloved sons, Marek and Janek," he read. He looked up from the letter.

"Marek is Mark in English and Janek is John," he explained. "Now I'll read on.

I write with much sadness in my heart. The world has become a cruel place. Mankind has turned on itself and we are being torn apart by young soldiers, some of them no older than my boys, because we are Jews. What would the mothers of these young soldiers think if they knew that their sons were committing such atrocities?

My dear friend, Rebekka, stole two potatoes to feed her children. The Judenrat reported her to the Germans. Stealing food is forbidden. She cried, and on her knees, she begged the soldier for mercy. I watched with such pain in my heart that I thought it would break, but I could do nothing. The German soldier laughed and shot her children so she would not have to steal to feed them anymore. I weep every day. Who can we trust? The Judenrat is a Council of Jews, but some of them spy on their own people and report them to the German authorities to gain favours, knowing that their own people will be punished.

I am looking after your grandparents but they are growing weak with hunger and despair. We live in a big house and have a room for the three of us. We have thirty eight others who live here and only one lavatory for us all. Some have to share a room with other families and they argue in loud voices. It is not good, but we are lucky to have our own room. The house we live in was once an elegant place for the wealthy people of Warsaw. Our window looks on the wide avenue that was once lined with trees, but no more.

The Germans have built a wall around the Ghetto to keep us all together, with barbed wire on the top and sentry posts with guns. There is much sickness. The typhus is killing many. The children are thin and hungry. We have less than two hundred calories to eat a day, so you see why Rebbeka stole the potatoes. They were not good potatoes. They were starting to go rotten. Her babies died for two rotten potatoes. Sometimes children just die of hunger and lie in the street. They climb in bins to search for food, but no-one throws food away even if it is going rotten. Rotting food is better than no food at all.

The Judenrat have asked the German Governor-General for permission for me to set up a small school for the little children. We have no schools. We have no work. We have nothing to do. We are powerless. We are defenceless. We are Polish Jews and despised. I do not understand why we Jews are hated so much and treated like animals when we are all part of the human race.

I give thanks that my sons are safe in England. Are you still flying with the British Air Force, Marek? Keep safe son. Are you still in the Medical Corps, Janek? You will be a good doctor one day. Do not write me. Not because I do not want to get your letters and to hear from you. I will have to pay the Judenrat for a letter and I do not have the money to waste on them. I have two stamps left so I can write to my sons if I can pay somebody to smuggle the letter out of the Ghetto.

Until we meet again I hold you both close to my heart. Matka."

A heartbreaking silence followed the tragic letter. No words in the vocabulary of human languages were fitting enough to justify the desolation felt, after hearing, first hand, the suffering of the Jews at the hands of the Germans.

Ben placed his hand on his father's arm.

"I had no idea, Dad," he gently said. "You've kept this to yourself all these years."

John nodded.

"Yes, I had to go on living, and I believe I have lived up to my mother's belief that I would be a good doctor one day. I am a good doctor. She would be proud, but let me read to you, her final letter. Are you okay, Lowry? You are very quiet."

"I'm just so sad, and I feel awful, because I have never heard of the Warsaw Ghetto."

"It's not there, anymore. The Nazis raised it to the ground, but not before deporting hundreds of thousands to the Treblinka gas chambers and killing those fifty or more thousands who got wind of what was happening and so began the uprising. I believe my family died in the gas chambers of Treblinka Concentration Camp. This final letter I received was written in August 1942."

John carefully removed, from a crumpled envelope, a loving mother's final words.

"My beloved Sons Marek and Janek,

It is with a sad heart that I tell you they have taken your grandparents away. It is now two months since I saw them last and I ask about them but no-one tells me where they have gone. Many thousands have been marched off with guns pointing at them, even little children who can barely walk. Why would anyone point a gun at a small harmless child? They were told they are going to a better life in the East and to take three days food with them. How do we get three days food all at once? Your Babcia is not strong. She has a weak heart now. I would have gone with them, but I was waiting in the queue for a small loaf. The Judenrat deliver six thousand Jews every day to the Germans and I now wait my turn. There are rumours that say they are killing all the Jews, even the children, in buildings full of gas. So many bad rumours are spreading round the Ghetto, but I do not believe such dreadful things. It is not possible, my dear sons, that people could do that. I know these Germans are cruel, but why have they lost their humanity? My old neighbour was a concert violinist. How I loved to hear him play. Even in these troubled times his music lifted my spirit and made me want to dance. But they came one night and ordered him to stop, but he kept on playing and refused to bend to the will of these young German bullies. They smashed his priceless violin and put his hands on the table and with the ends of their rifles they broke his fingers. The silence tells a tragic story and breaks my heart.

They closed my school ages ago. I argue with them and the Germans say it is a waste of time teaching Jewish pigs. Some of the younger men are talking about fighting back, but we are weak from lack of food. My friend Rebekka never recovered from the murder of her children. She did not eat anything. She lay down in the street and would not move. She died. Her body stayed there for over a week until the Germans got the Judenrat to throw petrol on her body and burn it. Will this suffering ever end? I do miss my parents and my boys. I worry for you all in this troubled world.

I have been away from my letter writing for half an hour because there has been a banging on the main door. It is a noise we dread when the night comes. They came and took away the teenage sons of my friend, Marta. They hit them with their guns and threw the boys into the back of a truck. I know the boys go out at night. I think they are part of the resistance but I do not ask questions. They are only fourteen and sixteen years old. Anybody who is taken away never comes back. Sometimes they don't bother to take people away, they shoot them in the street and make us watch. I have tried to comfort my friend, but she is a broken woman.

I have a young boy with me and he keeps me company. He is twelve and called Jakob. He is a very frozen boy. He steals from houses and dead bodies and smuggles himself out of the Ghetto and exchanges his stolen goods for food. He then sells some of the food back to the people he stole from. He tried to sell half a smoked sausage to a member of the Judenrat and they are looking for him. I fear for him if they catch him, so he hides in my room. Jakob does not know what happened to his family. I do not think he is bothered about them. He is without emotion, poor child, but I do have a bit more to eat now and I do feel bad about that, but what else can I do?

This war cannot go on much longer some people say. When it is over I will see my sons once again. I should be with your grandparents soon because the Judenrat have told me I am on the list for the next deportation to go to wherever the others have gone. I have one stamp left after this letter and I will tell you where I shall be when I am moved away. Jakob will smuggle this letter out for me so I will not have to pay. I try to persuade him to come to the East with me, but he wants to stay living here. He knows no other place.

I am sorry my news is always so bad, but I have nothing good to write about. My next letter shall be a better one, my dear sons, because I shall be out of this place.

Keep safe and well until we all meet again. I hold you both in my heart always.

Matka."

John carefully folded the letter and returned it to its envelope.

"There, my dears, you have the whole story," he sadly said, staring into his granddaughter's face. "My mother lives on in little Anya, here."

"You actually know that my grandmother died in Treblinka, Dad?" Ben asked.

"I am almost one hundred percent sure of it," he answered. "Remember, she had one stamp left. She would have written had she been alive."

"I wonder if that frozen little boy called Jakob survived," Lowry said. "I do hope he did."

Ben picked up the sepia wedding photograph and studied the picture of his grandparents.

"I think my grandmother sounds like a remarkable woman," he said. John nodded. "So why shut her away? Why don't we put this in a frame and....?"

John smiled.

"That's a good idea, Son. She can watch over me and make sure I don't misbehave."

WHO IS SARAH?

Lowry and her father sat together on the park bench. Anya lay contentedly in her pram. Baloney lay lengthily on the grass in the early spring sun. The park keeper came into view and Lowry inwardly smiled remembering sweet, nutty Nana and her quest to find her two-timing husband. The daffodils stood tall and proud in the flower beds as three early butterflies danced a minuet in the spring sun.

"It's a beautiful day," Leif said, turning his face up into the warming glow.

"Yes it is," Lowry replied. "And do you know, Dad, that I've been coming to this park since I was six and a half years old, so I love the place. Lou used to bring a gang of kids and we'd all play rounders or cricket."

"She's a wonderful woman, your mother, Lowry," he said. "She's so full of enthusiasm for life. She's a joy to know."

"I know, I lived with her for years and she never gave up on me, even though I didn't always make her life easy. My friends loved her, but they thought she was a bit crackers and not like their mums at all. She was older than the other mums and I didn't like that much when I was younger, yet she was more full of life than any of them. Lou is the only woman I really want in my life, you know, Dad."

"I'm sure she is," he replied.

"Would you say Inger was the only woman in your life?"

"Yes, she was."

"So who is, Sarah? I've known about her for ages, now," Lowry threw at him. She looked up to see him smile.

"She's a friend of mine," he said.

"What sort of a friend?" she challenged.

"A very nice friend, Lowry," he said, continuing to grin.

"Don't be flippant with me, Dad," Lowry rebuked him. "I need to know who she is and why you have kept her a secret. Is she your girlfriend?"

"I suppose you could say she is, although she's not a girl," he answered.

"So she's an old gold digger then."

"No she's not. Sarah is younger than I am," he explained.

"So she's a dolly bird then."

"I don't know what a dolly bird is, Lowry, but why are you putting me through the third degree? I wanted to be sure about how I felt for Sarah. So why don't you agree to come with me tomorrow, when I shall be having lunch with her."

"So you're sure of your feelings for this woman, then?" Lowry persisted.

"Yes, and I know she feels the same about me"

Lowry was not happy with the way the conversation was going. He'd been having an affair behind her back with some unknown woman.

"How long have you known her?" she asked sharply.

"Nearly two years, now," he glibly answered. "I'm sure you'll be pleased to meet her, elskling."

"No I won't," she childishly responded. "Are you sleeping with her?"

"That is not a question for you to be asking, Lowry," he sharply answered.

"Why not. I don't want you taken advantage of."

"I'm not a child young lady. And I'm not aware that I questioned you about your relationship with Ben or showed any anger or disappointment when you announced you were pregnant. Please be courteous enough to remember that you are my daughter, not my keeper."

Lowry was left smarting by her dad's words. Two strollers passed by, with a scruffy little mutt on a lead. It was obviously the result of generations of random mating. Baloney raised his aristocratic head, decided he couldn't be bothered with a scruffy mutt and the pedigree disdainfully lay back in the sun.

"Why don't you want to meet Sarah?" Leif asked, when the strollers were out of earshot.

"Because, if you want to know the truth, I don't want to share you with another woman," Lowry answered. "And don't laugh at me, either."

"I'm not laughing at you, but you have no reason to be jealous of Sarah."

"Who said I was jealous?" she snapped.

"Well, forgive me if I've got it wrong, but your attitude leads me to believe otherwise and I understand why you ….,"

"No you don't," she interrupted. "Anyway, I have to get back home for Anya's tea."

She stood up and released the brake from the pram. Her dad grabbed her arm.

"Lowry, sit down, please. Anya is asleep. Let's talk this through. You are angry with me and it is not my intention to make you angry or to hurt you. So will you just listen to me without interrupting or getting cross?"

"Okay, I'm listening and I'm not getting cross," she crossly replied.

Lowry watched two courting blue tits bobbing about on a branch of the beech tree.

"Have I got your attention?" her dad asked.

"Yes, I'm listening," she replied.

"Do you remember when I first discovered that you were my daughter?" he began. "I was so protective and possessive of you that I felt somewhat envious of Ben when he came onto the ward and I saw how you re-acted to each other. But I realised just how happy you were and how childish I was being. Having just found you, and being your father, I didn't want to share you with another man, just like you don't want to share me, with another woman. But, my dear daughter, nobody in the world can take the place of you in my heart. You see, Lowry, the love I have for you is a father's love. It's not the same sort of love that I have for Sarah. The love you have for Ben, is not the same sort of love you have for me or your mother, Lou." Leif took hold of Lowry's hand and played with her fingers. "A parent's love for their child is tender, protective and unconditional. But as I said before, love comes in many forms. I am so fortunate to be a part of yours, Ben's and Anya's lives. Ben is your husband, he makes you happy. I am your father and we both love you in our different ways. Sarah makes me happy. She makes me laugh. I have been a rootless man for too long. Now that I have found you, I know I will never drink again. I can't bear the thought of the stuff and I really feel the time has come for me to settle down."

"So you're going to get married. I can't believe it. This is ridiculous."

"I haven't asked Sarah, yet, so give me chance, will you, Lowry?"

"Don't you think you're rushing into things?"

The two little love birds had flown from the tree and a cheeky sparrow sat in their place singing his heart out. He probably had a Mrs Sparrow sitting on a nest of eggs in a nearby bush. Lowry hoped she could hear his heartfelt serenade.

"For God's sake, Lowry," her father impatiently said. "I'm nearly forty five years old. I've been a widower for twenty years and you ask me if I'm rushing into things. My whole life, after the end of the war, was swallowed up trying to find you. I had nothing else on my mind, least of all romance. The only thing I was having an affair with was a bottle of whisky, as you know. So please don't deny me the happiness I am finding with Sarah."

A long silence followed. Lowry felt angry, not with her father, but with herself. She had selfishly challenged his right to be happy when all he had ever cared about was his daughter's happiness.

"Dad, I'm so sorry I gave you a hard time before. You're right it was jealousy. I didn't want another woman making you happy, I wanted it to be just me doing that, but I realise now this woman and I can both make you happy in our different ways."

Leif smiled and kissed Lowry's fingers.

"I really would like you to welcome Sarah into our lives? Do you think you can do that?"

"Yes, Dad. If she makes you happy then she makes me happy. I was just being a selfish petulant teenager, even though I am twenty. When can I meet her?"

"Tomorrow at one o'clock at Reece's Restaurant in town. I'll pick you up at twelve thirty."

"Great!" Lowry enthused. "I think I'll leave Anya with Lou, so I'm not distracted when I give this Sarah woman the once over."

Leif laughed.

"I reckon Sarah could give you the once over, twice over, you cocky little madam."

Lowry laughed back at him.

"Don't worry, Dad. I shall be the essence of decorum, lady like, polite and obviously delighted at the prospect of having a bloomin' step-mother."

Lou was thrilled to have Anya to herself. She had never pushed a pram in her life before Anya was born, so parading the local streets and park with her granddaughter was the thrill of a lifetime for her. Baloney plodded slowly beside her on his lead. He had been trained, when racing, to walk on the right hand side of the body, virtually attaching himself to the thigh. Lou arranged to meet two of her retired school teacher friends in the park for a chat and an ice-cream.

"I'm not exactly swanking," she boastfully said. "I'm just showing off my ability to manoeuvre a basinet."

At twelve thirty a toot on the horn announced Lowry's chauffeur.

"You look lovely, elskling," her dad said.

"Thanks Dad. I want this woman to see how sophisticated your daughter is."

"She'll be overwhelmed by your effort," he laughed.

"Are you making fun of me?"

"As if!" he answered, grinning broadly.

Lowry and her father walked through the large food store to the wide staircase that led up to the restaurant. A wonderful smell of newly baked bread and fresh coffee gave a warm hug to each hungry and thirsty customer.

Reece's large restaurant had an air of gentility about it. Clean white cloths covered the tables. White linen napkins were rolled beside each place setting. A huge cooling cabinet had been stacked with the store's own fresh cream cakes and a coffee and walnut gateaux. Waitresses, efficiently buzzed about with trays of food. They were all dressed in white aprons and white hats, adding an air of refined sterility to the scene.

Leif surveyed the room.

"Sarah's not here yet, so let's choose a table near the window," he suggested.

Lowry made herself comfortable. She could see the top half of the stairs that swept in a curve into the room. People were moving up and climbing down. She spotted an elderly lady slowly ascending with the help of her walking stick.

"I think this must be Sarah," she said.

Leif leapt up and turned around. He grinned.

"Very funny," he said, and sat down again. He passed Lowry a maroon folder. "Have a look at the menu and decide what you want to eat."

Lowry took the menu from him.

"Thanks Dad. Your date's late. I hope she turns up. I won't put up with any woman letting you down."

"Oh, she'll turn up, elskling. She's never let me down, yet."

Lowry studied the available dishes. Should she go for the ham salad or…? A figure, standing beside the table, cast a shadow over the white tablecloth.

"Lowry, may I introduce you to Sarah," she heard her dad say.

Lowry looked up from the menu into the smiling face of her favourite Staff Nurse.

"Dritt! Dritt! Dritt!" she said, laughing joyfully.

The End